THE WAR PHOTOGRAPHERS

A catalogue record for this book is available from the National Library of New Zealand.

Soft cover ISBN 978-0-473-69643-6
Kindle ISBN 978-0-473-69645-0
epub ISBN 978-0-473-69644-3

Cover design by Amanda Sutcliffe

Design & layout www.yourbooks.co.nz

This book has been printed using sustainably managed stock.
Printed in New Zealand by www.yourbooks.co.nz

THE WAR PHOTOGRAPHERS

SHE WILL RISK EVERYTHING
TO EXPOSE THE TRUTH

SL BEAUMONT

For all the unsung heroes

"In wartime, truth is so precious that she should always be attended by a bodyguard of lies."

— Winston Churchill

PROLOGUE

Paris, France
November 23, 1944

Jack Knight had witnessed some horrific sights in four years as a war photographer, but nothing prepared him for the surreal scene he was about to encounter. After a day of capturing images of a newly liberated Paris, Jack was strolling back to his room at the Hotel Scribe when the hackles rose on the back of his neck. Following his instincts, he deviated from his path and turned down a side street. As always, his trusty Leica rested against his chest, secured by a worn leather strap wound across his body. A significant proportion of Jack's war had been viewed through this camera lens, and several of his award-winning images had featured in newspapers worldwide.

Jack found the source of his unease when he rounded the corner into a cobbled square overlooked by apartment buildings still displaying the vestiges of war; pockmarked, chipped brickwork, cracked windows and flaking paintwork. In the square's centre, a fountain stood empty, blackened and dirty from years of neglect. On the far side, chairs and small tables were clustered beneath a faded red awning, where an aproned waiter was serving small glasses of pastis to his handful of customers. The bodies of two men swung from a pair of lamp posts. Their mouths hung open as if in disbelief at the manner of their deaths, their tongues distended and black. Their distorted and swollen faces spoke of a sustained beating before their demise. A scrap of paper with the word '*collaborateur*' was pinned to each of their chests.

Nauseated, Jack dragged his gaze away. Wearing worn, patched clothing, a group of women stood to one side clutching shopping baskets and conversing in rapid French, seeming to ignore the grotesque sight. Small children ran around their mothers' legs, playing chase, giggling, and squealing, showing remarkable resilience to a childhood marred by the violence and fear of recent years. Jack raised his camera and captured the juxtaposition of the laughing children and the legs of the hanging men. Two older men sat at an outdoor table a few doors along, their chess game abandoned as they viewed the corpses, openly pointing and discussing some aspect. This, too, Jack photographed before hearing the whistle of an approaching *gendarmerie*. He slipped away unnoticed.

It might have seemed harsh, but the French people had their way of dealing with collaborators, those who'd profited from the war or had done nothing to stop the brutality of the Germans against their people. And retribution had been swift. Jack had heard stories of the French mistresses of German officers having their heads shaved, stripped naked, and marched through the streets.

Jack took several more turns before realising that he was a little lost. The sun was setting, and there was still a curfew, so he needed to hurry. He knew the general direction of his hotel and continued walking until he found, with some relief, that the paved street he was on led to the rear of the building. He was about to cross to the opposite side when he spotted two men in the shadows by the kitchen entrance. He recognised one of the men and went to call out, but something in their body language caused him to hesitate.

He watched as they shook hands and murmured a few words before checking their surroundings. Jack crept forward, keeping to the shadows of the shuttered shopfronts, and watched as his acquaintance pulled an envelope from the inside pocket of his overcoat and passed it to the other man. Jack raised his camera. *Click.* The man took the envelope and looked over his shoulder, a look of fear on his face. *Click.*

"*Do Svidaniya.*"

Jack lowered his camera in disbelief and watched the two men part. The man he knew, hands thrust in his pockets, strolled, whistling, down the side of the hotel towards the main entrance in forced nonchalance. The other man hurried in the opposite direction, swallowed by the shadows.

Jack leaned against the shop wall, a sick feeling in his gut, and wondered why someone he knew and trusted had just had a clandestine meeting with a Soviet.

CHAPTER 1

Oamaru, New Zealand
September 5, 1989

Rachel Talbot pulled the late model silver Toyota to a stop in the new section of Oamaru's rambling historic cemetery which sprawled across several undulating blocks on the town's South Hill. Long, straight rows of gravestones, some decorated with flowers, photos and personal memorabilia, were separated by strips of freshly mown grass.

She pushed her sunglasses into her long dark auburn hair and undid her seatbelt.

"Who's she talking to?" her friend Gemma asked, leaning forward and peering through the windscreen.

Rachel looked over to where her grandmother was seated, straight-backed, on a park bench beneath a tree. She wore her hair longer than most women her age, curling softly around the nape of her neck, the once rich chestnut now faded and streaked with grey. Her petite frame was clad in a floral dress topped with a thick pale blue cardigan. She wore a serene expression, and her lips moved as she spoke. Her eyes had a faraway gaze, and she didn't appear to have noticed the car's arrival. Rachel's mind framed the image; the drooping kowhai tree, a grieving widow, the memorial plaques; and her fingers itched to pick up her camera and capture the picture. She resisted.

"My grandfather, I expect," she said. "Or maybe Uncle Joe."

"I always forget that she was married to someone," Gemma said.

"Not someone, Jack, my grandfather."

"The one who was a spy or something during World War Two?"

Rachel shrugged. "He was a war photographer, although my mum said that Joe once told her that Jack was working in military intelligence too. Grandma doesn't talk about the war, I think it's too painful, and I never like to bring it up."

"You should," Gemma said. "Once she's gone, there'll be no one to remember."

"True." Rachel gazed across at her grandmother. She was very fond of her and couldn't imagine asking something that would cause her pain.

"How much longer are you staying, Rach?" Gemma said, flicking her bleach-blonde fringe out of her eyes.

"Why? Are you keen to get rid of me?"

"No," Gemma said. "You know that I've missed you. I only meant that you came home for Cole's wedding, but now that that's over, I expect you'll be keen to return to London."

"Yeah, I can't hide here forever," Rachel said. "Now that I've calmed down, I need to go back and rescue my career."

"Remember, 'girls can do anything'," Gemma said, quoting in the high-pitched voice of the headmistress of Waitaki Girls High School that both had attended as teenagers.

Rachel laughed. "Give me a break. You only need me to still be there with a place for you to crash when you eventually get off your arse and save up enough money to join me."

"God, am I that transparent?"

"No, you're completely opaque," Rachel said, still laughing

as she opened the driver's door and unfolded her long legs from the car. She walked along the grass verge past the beautifully maintained curving cremation garden to the war memorial section.

Mae looked up as Rachel approached, the crunch of boots on the gravel finally drawing her attention from the plaques at her feet. Rachel's heart tugged as Mae looked confused for a moment, then blinked, and a warm smile formed.

"Is it time to go?" she called.

"Yes, Grandma," Rachel said, climbing the slight rise and picking up the now-empty flower basket from the seat beside Mae. "Shall we?"

Mae rose to her feet with a sprightliness that defied her age. Rachel glanced at the plaque at the end of the row. A mass of fresh flowers tumbled across the inscription, but she could make out the surname Knight and an army service number. From what Rachel understood, Jack wasn't buried here; his remains, like so many other New Zealanders of his generation, were interred in a cemetery on the other side of the world.

Rachel took Mae's arm as they descended the gentle grassy slope to the parked car.

"Your hands are cold," she said.

"Are they?" Mae said. "I suppose they are. It was very pleasant when you dropped me off, but that wind has come up."

As they approached, Gemma alighted from the passenger seat and leaned against the car. "Hi, Granny Mae," she said, holding open the passenger door for her.

"Hello, Gemma dear," Mae said, smiling at the young woman. "I love what you've done with your hair."

Gemma ran her hand over the closely cropped back of her head before pushing her long fringe out of her eyes. A fleeting, surprised expression crossed her face. "Thanks."

They dropped Gemma at her flat, an ugly square grey-brick 1950s build with an unkempt front garden, before making their way down the long straight main road that ran through the north end of town. It was slow going as the single lane crawled with the end of the workday traffic. But when they left the town boundary, Rachel sped up past the racecourse and the Pukeuri freezing works, one of the district's major employers. She drove past the two-storey farmhouse where she'd grown up, to her grandmother's cottage on the family sheep farm in the tiny settlement of Hilderthorpe.

Mae's cottage was two paddocks over from the main homestead. It was a whitewashed, one-level wooden structure with a wrap-around veranda surrounded by an enormous well-maintained garden with undulating flowerbeds, fruit trees, and shrubs.

Twenty minutes later Rachel set the small wooden kitchen table as Mae stood at the stove, apron over her floral dress, scrambling the eggs she'd collected from her hens that morning. Mae's cat Whiskey was curled up asleep on a chair beneath the table and opened a lazy eye as Rachel sat beside him. She scratched between his ears and was rewarded with a loud purr.

"Are you sure you don't want to spend your last few nights at your mother's?" Mae asked. "Not that I don't love having you stay here," she added.

"Mum and I get on far better when we don't live in the same house, even for a few weeks," Rachel reminded her.

"True," Mae said with a smile. "But why don't we invite her over for a cup of tea after dinner?"

"Okay," Rachel said. She crossed the kitchen, picked up the telephone handset from its cradle on the wall, and dialled her family's home number from memory. She wound the curly telephone cord around her finger while waiting for her mother to answer. It rang eight times before the answerphone clicked on, and Rachel hung up without leaving a message.

"Not there?" Mae asked, spooning the bright yellow, fluffy eggs onto two plates and covering them with a layer of finely grated cheese.

"No, I'll try again after tea."

They sat opposite one another. Rachel grabbed a slice of toast from the toast rack and buttered it.

"Are you ready to go back to London?" Mae asked between mouthfuls.

Rachel nodded. "I suppose so."

Mae put down her knife and fork. "Now, I may be old, but I'm not blind. All you ever wanted to do was travel and take photos, and by all accounts, you have your dream job working for a London newspaper, so the only reason you're delaying your return and hiding here has to be a man."

Rachel looked down at her plate and shrugged.

"Is he the one who has called your parents' house a few times?" Rachel nodded. "I won't ask what he did to break your heart," Mae said. "But please, please don't let any man dictate the direction of your life. You are living your dream, don't allow him to ruin it for you."

Rachel felt a tear spill over and run down her cheek. Mae reached over and squeezed her hand. "Oh, my darling girl."

"He's a journalist," Rachel said. "We were supposed to fly to Hungary at the start of last month to report on their border reopening with Austria. The Hungarians have basically torn a hole in the Iron Curtain. They switched off the power to 165 miles of border fencing in May, and now there are photos of Horn and Mock, the foreign ministers of each country with bolt cutters, snipping a hole in the barbed wire fence that separates the two countries."

"I saw that on the television news," Mae said. "The Soviets must be livid."

Rachel nodded. "Especially as it seems that Hungary is softening its stance on East Germans trying to cross the border into Austria. It's a huge story. And that is what we were supposed to report on. But I found out the day before we were to leave that he'd requested another photographer accompany him, a male friend."

"Oh," Mae said. "And did he say why?"

"Apparently, it's too dangerous for a woman photojournalist to enter a Communist country, which is crap," Rachel said. "Sorry, Grandma."

Mae waved her hand, dismissing the apology. "Well, he may have a point. Remember the two women journalists whom the Stasi detained in East Germany last year and accused of being spies? They weren't treated at all well."

Rachel remembered the case. The two women had been assaulted and tortured before international outrage forced the GDR government to release them. "We weren't going anywhere near East Germany."

"But you were planning to go to Hungary, which is still a Communist country the last time I looked, even if they are thumbing their noses at Moscow."

Rachel sniffed.

"So, he was trying to protect you."

"By sabotaging my career," Rachel said, swiping at the tears that continued to fall despite her best efforts to rein them in. "I applied to go separately, but I was turned down. Daniel had reminded the editors about the two women, and by suggesting there was a serious potential security issue for any female journalist travelling to a Warsaw Pact country, the paper's lawyers said no. But, Grandma, it was one incident, not a pattern."

"Oh, Rachel."

"Anyway, I've worked out what I'm going to do. My flight back to London takes me via Vienna, and I'm going to make a day trip to the Austrian side of the Hungarian border. I won't be going to Hungary, and as far as work is concerned, I'm still on holiday, but they won't be unhappy if I get some good photos. It's a win-win."

Mae gave Rachel's hand a final squeeze. "Your grandfather would be very proud of you. You're brave like he was and following in his footsteps."

Rachel gave her a watery smile and wiped her face with the

backs of her hands. "Thanks, Grandma. Although he was an actual war correspondent, it's not quite the same."

"I'm not sure," Mae said. "You're a Cold War photojournalist at a time when the world is on a knife edge. We may not be at war, but there are lots of parallels. Now, let's do the dishes before the news."

Rachel leaned against the bench drying the dishes as Mae washed them in the sink of soapy water, pondering her grandmother's comments. She was right, the world was on the cusp of something, and she had the opportunity to be there and record history as it was happening. She'd been home too long; Saturday couldn't come soon enough. In fact, she would call the airline in the morning and see if she could bring her flight forward.

The opening credits of the six o'clock news blasted from the lounge TV. Rachel put the final handful of clean cutlery in the drawer, draped the wet tea towel over the oven handle, and joined her grandmother. The lounge wall was hung with black and white photos taken by her grandfather in the 1930s and 1940s depicting foreign lands. Rachel had spent hours analysing them over the years, the shadows and light, and the skill behind each composition, but was still awed every time she entered the room. She wished she could have learned from him. In pride of place on one wall was her grandparents' wedding photo. They were standing on the front steps of a building in London, her grandfather in his uniform, and Mae wearing a simple white dress with a matching jacket and jaunty little hat. They both looked young, happy, and very much in love as they were showered with petals.

Mae was seated in her usual armchair and had picked up her knitting. The needles tapped rhythmically against each other as though picking out a beat. Rachel plopped down on the blue velvet sofa, kicked off her Ugg boots, and tucked her bare feet under her. She turned her attention to the television on a small table in one corner.

The newsreader began with a report on New Zealand's first female deputy Prime Minister.

"She'll be Prime Minister before very long," Mae said. "Isn't it strange that New Zealand was the first country in the world to give women the vote, but one hundred years later, there still hasn't been a woman PM?"

The story changed to events in Europe. "History was made today in Leipzig in East Germany," the news anchor began.

Rachel reached for the remote control and increased the volume.

"Despite the country's policy of state atheism, a demonstration today was led by church pastor Christoph Wonneberger following a prayer service. Crowds gathered on the forecourt of the Evangelical Nikolai Church and unfurled banners reading 'For an open country with free people.' In town for the Leipzig Autumn Trade Fair, Western journalists filmed the event."

Video footage of the gathering began playing. A large crowd, men and women, young and old, milled around in front of the old stone church before moving in long rows out of the square and down the street. Some linked arms and others carried lit candles.

Rachel's feet hit the floor as she sat forward. "Oh my God," she said. "This is huge."

Mae's knitting needles stopped clicking as the camera panned from the crowd of protestors to a building overlooking the square and zoomed in on a first-floor balcony where a group of uniformed police officers were watching the public. Mae gasped and clapped a hand over her mouth.

"Grandma?"

Mae pointed at the screen. "It's him," she whispered, shaking her head from side to side. "It can't be."

The clip ended, and the news anchors came back on screen. "Tomorrow's Schools…" the news reporter began the next segment.

But neither Rachel nor Mae heard.

"Who did you see, Grandma?"

The colour had drained from Mae's face. "Replay it; I always tape the news in case I miss it. I must be mistaken."

Rachel grabbed the remote control for the VCR, which sat on a shelf below the television. She pointed the remote at the box, rewinding the tape before hitting the play button. The tape whirred in the machine, and the opening credits of the news sounded again. Rachel pressed the fast-forward button running through the programme until the East German segment played. She froze the image of the protesters on the screen.

"Further forward, on the balcony, the policeman," Mae said in a breathless whisper.

Rachel moved the recording forward frame by frame until the camera honed in on a dozen officers dressed in the black uniform of the feared East German military police, the Stasi. An older man in a black hat with grey hair showing at his temples was in the centre. When the camera closed in on the group, Rachel pressed the pause button on the remote control and turned to look at her grandmother.

Mae was sitting forward in her chair with her hands on her cheeks and her blue eyes wide with disbelief. "It's him."

"Who, Grandma?"

"The man who murdered your grandfather."

Rachel stared. "Murdered, Grandma? I thought he died in the war."

"It's a very long story."

"I'm not going anywhere." Rachel pointed the remote control at the television, and turned it off. She pulled her legs up under her on the sofa and turned to face her grandmother.

"I suppose it's time," Mae said with a deep sigh. "How much do you know about my life before I came to New Zealand?"

"You were born in England," Rachel said. "And thank you very much for that, it's given me my residency visa so I can work there. But now that you mention it, not much else. I'm sorry, Grandma, I should have taken more of an interest."

Mae waved the apology away with a flick of her hand. "Young people are not interested in the stories of old people."

"Well, I am. Please tell me about your childhood, your parents."

Mae's smile was tinged with sadness.

"My parents were minor aristocracy, but they both died when I was young, and I was brought up by my grandmother, Alice. According to her, my father returned from the Great War, the First World War, a changed man. In what we now know were appalling conditions, he'd served at the Somme. I suppose he had what we'd call Post-Traumatic Stress Disorder, but it was called shell shock in those days.

"I was born in 1923, and I can only recall him spending all day in his study, shouting at me if I made too much noise in the house. He died in 1929 in what was called an accident at the time. He was cleaning his shooting rifles, and one discharged. I learned later in life that he never went shooting, and in all probability, he took his own life."

"Oh no," Rachel murmured.

"My mother was about to remarry when she contracted tuberculous two years later. She succumbed before her thirty-second birthday, and just like that, I was an orphan. My father's mother, Alice, took care of me, and we got through our grief together. She'd lost her only son and a daughter-in-law she loved like her own."

"I'm sorry, Grandma, that must have been very hard," Rachel said, reaching over to squeeze her hand. Rachel's pale youthful hand, with manicured red nails, remnants of decoration from her brother's wedding, rested on Mae's wrinkled, weather-beaten one.

"Don't feel too sorry for me," Mae said. "I had a wonderful childhood. I missed my beautiful, funny mother, but Granny was kind, and I wanted for nothing. We lived in Chelsea in London, with three servants who doted on us. My Italian nanny moved in with me and taught me to speak Italian and to cook."

"That's why we ate homemade pasta growing up," Rachel said, her eyes bright as if that information answered a previously unformed question. "My friends' mothers never cooked anything exotic like that, they only ever had dried macaroni from a packet."

Mae smiled. "So many of my warmest memories revolve around making pasta, first with Isabella, my nanny, then with your mother, and later with you and your brother.

"Anyway, I was well educated. Granny was keen to ensure that I would have the knowledge to manage my affairs once she was gone. I would have gone to Cambridge, like my father, but the outbreak of the Second World War put paid to that dream."

"Why was that?" Rachel asked, sitting back.

"My life was sidetracked somewhat. First by the war, then by the Park, and then by your grandfather and what came after."

"The Park?" Rachel said, frowning.

Mae held her hand up. "First, the war," she said. "Granny refused to leave London. 'Those Nazis are not going to chase us away', she'd say. It was terrifying some nights. We'd go up on the roof and watch the planes winding their way along the Thames. We lived in a big house in Chelsea, one of the areas which bore the brunt of the Blitz in 1940 and 1941 because of its proximity to the river, but miraculously Granny's home survived the early onslaught. She was a stubborn old thing and refused to go to the public air raid shelters, so we converted the wine cellar and ended up sleeping there for many nights while the bombs rained down. By the end of 1940, half the street would join us when the air raid sirens sounded. It was almost like having regular house parties, except we were being bombed.

"I had to do something to help the war effort, so I volunteered to drive ambulances. Granny's driver had taught me to drive her big old Morris up and down our street, which meant driving an ambulance wasn't much of a leap. Navigating the bombed-out streets in the blackout was the most challenging thing.

"After the Blitz, life in London took on a different kind of excitement. There were dances and the cinema, lots of soldiers on leave..."

Mae pushed herself upright using the arms of the chair and walked over to the roll-top desk in the corner of the lounge. She opened the drawer, pulled out an old metal box, and carried it back to the sofa. With a deep breath, she opened the lid. Black and white photos of varying sizes were nestled inside along with old greeting cards, a strip of fabric, ribbons, and assorted buttons. Tears pricked at her eyes as she shuffled through several photos before extracting two and handing them to Rachel.

"My parents, your great-grandparents, on their wedding day, and Granny Alice."

"Your father was handsome," Rachel said of the man standing formally upright in military uniform. "And your mother looked so young." The young woman was dressed in a long straight lace gown from another era, with a faint smile on her pretty, petite features.

Mae leaned across to look at the photo again. "She would have only been eighteen." She glanced at Rachel. "You look like her."

Rachel turned her attention to the second photo. "Granny Alice looks formidable." The stern, unsmiling photo showed an elegant older woman wearing a long dark-coloured dress covering every inch of flesh, topped by a hat with a large feather plume.

"She wasn't as stern as she looked there. She spent years dressed in black, first mourning her husband, then her son, but she was kind and had a wicked sense of fun.

"I applied to Cambridge in 1942 to study languages, but after I was accepted and before I had matriculated, my mother's brother came to visit. He had some secretive role in the Foreign Office." Mae shuffled through the photos in the box for a moment before finding the one she was after, and handed it to Rachel. "Uncle Charles."

"Oh, he looks debonair," Rachel said with a grin. Charles Montague leaned against a tree in the photo, wearing a long winter coat, Trilby at a rakish angle, smoking a cigarette.

"That he was," Mae agreed. "And persuasive. Once Charles set his mind to something, there was no changing it. When he'd been contacted by someone at Cambridge and told that I was to study languages, he recalled that I was fluent in Italian, thanks to my nanny. I'd also studied German and had spent a few months in Germany during my schooling, which was to prove useful."

Mae hesitated and took a deep breath. "What I'm about to tell you has been a secret for over forty years. You see, I signed the Official Secrets Act, which forbade me from ever discussing my war work. But I have seen mention of it in the media recently, and of course, Gordon Welchman wrote that book about Hut Six a couple of years ago, so I suppose the cat is out of the bag."

Rachel looked puzzled. "I'm not following you, Grandma."

"Charles recruited me for the Park," she said.

"What Park?"

"Bletchley Park, Britain's top-secret code-breaking facility. The reason we won the war."

MAE

1943

CHAPTER 2

London, England
September 6, 1943

Syd Dean's band was in full swing when we arrived at The Astoria on Charing Cross Road around 8 p.m. Along with the piano, drums, and double bass, a brass section of trumpets, a trombone, and a saxophone completed the big sound. The popular entertainment venue provided a much needed morale boost for war-weary Londoners and had become a regular haunt for my friends when leave allowed.

"Now that's more like it." A mischievous grin spread across my friend Nancy's face as she shed her coat to reveal a clinging floor-length gown of red silk. With her hourglass figure and angelic face, she could have easily passed for a Hollywood starlet, not the crossword-puzzle-obsessed Londoner with whom I worked.

We left our outerwear with the coat check girl and descended the stairs to the ballroom. The dance floor was packed with soldiers in uniform and men in smart suits dancing with women dressed in pretty tea dresses or elegant evening gowns, their hair curled in the latest style and their cheeks rosy from exertion.

We helped ourselves to a glass of complimentary champagne, or what passed for champagne; there was a war on, after all. The tuxedo-clad waiter balancing a tray at the top of the stairs grinned at us as we passed.

"Look, there's Betsy and Arthur."

Nancy grabbed my hand and pulled me behind her as we made our way around the edge of the ballroom towards a table at the front of the mezzanine, where our friends sat, smoking and sipping from cut-glass crystal.

Betsy jumped up as we approached. Her dark curly hair was contained by hair clips above her ears and a dimple formed either side of her scarlet lips as her mouth broke into a delighted smile. "I thought you two were never coming," she said.

"The train was delayed, and then we had to get ready," I said.

"Yeah, looking this good takes time," Nancy agreed, popping one hip and resting her hand on it. Seconds later, a man in an American airman's uniform approached and held out his hand.

"May I have the next dance?" he said.

Nancy flashed him a sunny smile. "Lead the way." She tossed back her drink and handed me the empty glass.

Betsy took my arm. "I like your dress. Is it new?"

"No, it's pre-war and a bit like everything else, out of style, but I have a closet full of them at Granny's. I figured I might as well wear them."

"The midnight blue suits you, although it's a bit loose. Are they feeding you in the country?"

"Yes, although it's all a bit limited with rationing, right?"

"And you're not going to tell me what they have you doing out there?"

I shrugged. "There's nothing much to tell, Bets, it's just boring typing and stuff."

"But important typing for you to give up Cambridge?"

"I haven't given up, just postponed. As I told you, studying languages seems frivolous when we're at war. I've got to do my bit, however tedious it is."

Betsy nodded, seeming to accept my reasoning. "Come, I've someone I'd like you to meet."

Betsy's fiancé Arthur, resplendent in his RAF uniform with the double-winged patch above his breast pocket which identified him as a pilot, stood and leaned over to kiss my cheek. His green eyes sparkled with mischief and a silvery scar along his jawline served as a reminder of a dog-fight with a German *Messerschmitt* a year earlier. "Mae, it's good to see you," he said. "Where've you been hiding?"

"Just working," I said. "They've given you a night off flying? Who's protecting the London skies?"

"It's a good question."

I hadn't noticed the other man seated next to Arthur until that moment, but he stood when we reached the table. He was tall and handsome in what Nancy would have described as a rugged kind of way. His dark hair was cut short, military style, and he wore a black double-breasted suit with a fine pinstripe. Smoke curled from the cigarette resting between the fingers of his right hand, and his face held a pleasant smile.

"Mae, this is Jack Knight," Betsy interrupted. "Jack, this is my friend Mae Webster."

"G'day, Miss Webster, pleasure," he said, holding out his hand; his accent, possibly Australian, was one with which I wasn't familiar.

"Call me Mae," I said, reaching out to return his handshake. Our fingers touched, and a jolt of static passed between us. I glanced at him to see if he'd felt it, but his expression didn't betray whether he had. From the corner of my eye, I saw Betsy exchange a smile with Arthur as we all sat down.

I took a sip of my drink and recovered my composure. "Where are you from, Jack? You don't sound like a GI."

"New Zealand," he said.

"You're a long way from home."

"Yeah."

"Jack's been attached to my crew for the last three months," Arthur said, raising his voice to be heard above the chorus of brass coming from the stage.

"Oh, are you a pilot too?" I asked, intrigued.

"No, I'm a photographer," he said.

"Jack's photos have been splashed across the pages of newspapers worldwide," Arthur added. "He's that good."

Jack inclined his head at the compliment as though embarrassed.

"So, how did you end up with the RAF?"

"I originally came across with the New Zealand Army as a regular soldier stationed in North Africa, and I'd brought my camera with me. When our main war correspondent was injured, I stepped in, and it's snowballed from there."

Nancy returned to the table and flopped in an empty chair beside Jack. "Those American fly boys are all so handsy," she moaned before registering Jack's presence and straightening to look at him. "Hi, I'm Nancy, and you are?"

"Jack Knight, pleased to meet you." Jack's eyes flicked to Nancy, but his attention returned to me after a polite nod.

A sultry voice rose from the small raised stage. A willowy blonde with bright red lips in a shimmering gold gown leaned an arm on the microphone stand as she broke into song. Seconds later, the band joined in, and Jack held his hand out to me.

"Would you like to dance?"

"Me?" I was used to men flocking to Nancy's side, not mine.

Jack's eyes crinkled with amusement. "Yes."

"Oh," I said, standing and taking his outstretched hand. He led me away from the table and down five steps to the dance floor. I glanced over my shoulder back to the table. Nancy gave me an exaggerated thumbs-up gesture, something she had picked up from one of her American beaux. I shook my head at her and laughed.

We threaded our way through dancing couples to the centre of the dance floor, where Jack rested one hand on the small of my back and clasped my fingers with his other, and we began to move in time to the music. Jack was a good dancer, and I relaxed into his lead.

"Do you come here often?" he asked, his words a whisper against my cheek.

I nodded. "Either here or the Savoy whenever I'm on leave."

"Are you with the Women's Auxiliary Service?" he asked.

I shook my head. "No, I'm with a government department, secretarial."

"Oh?"

"It's fairly boring," I said.

"What would you do if we weren't fighting a war?"

"I would be studying at Cambridge."

Jack pulled back and looked at me anew. "Beauty and brains," he said. "What are you going to study?"

"Languages," I said. "I speak French and Italian, with a smattering of Spanish and German, although the latter isn't all that popular at the moment."

Jack laughed. "Well, I speak English," he said. "Did a bit of Latin and French at school but could never get it to stick."

"It's hard to become fluent in a language if you don't get to speak it often," I said as the song ended. We held on to one another for a beat longer before we sprang apart and clapped the band, who launched into a livelier jive number, popular on all the London dancefloors.

Jack grabbed my hand and swung me around. We jitterbugged for the next four songs before I was out of breath and thirsty. We returned to the table to find Arthur arguing with another man.

"We cannot trust a thing that the Soviets say," Arthur said.

"One minute, they've signed the Molotov-Ribbentrop Pact and have split Poland with the Germans; the next, they're our allies. They only do what suits Russia. We cannot and should not trust them."

"Are you trusting the word of the Nazis then?" the other man said, sitting back and taking a drag on his cigarette, appearing to be thoroughly enjoying the debate. "They conveniently just discovered the bodies of five thousand Polish officers and claimed it was the Soviets. Are you sure they aren't just shifting the blame for their mass murder?"

"When the Soviets agreed that Anders could set up a Polish army-in-exile in Russia, surely they would have expected him to request the transfer of 15,000 Polish prisoners of war to his command," Arthur said. "They wouldn't have done that if they'd already killed them all."

"Don't be so sure. Remember, Stalin put out the story about them all escaping to Manchuria. Strange that they escaped, never to be heard from again. Take my word, the Soviets killed them back at the start of the war, before we were on the same side; there is no other explanation," the other man said.

"Ladies." Arthur stood, a little unsteady on his feet, as I took my seat and Nancy returned from dancing with yet another American serviceman.

"Are you discussing the Katyn Massacre?" I asked.

I saw Jack's eyes register interest in my comment as he reached for his cigarettes, silently offering me one before leaning forward to light it. I inwardly cursed; I needed to think before I spoke about things that might not be widespread knowledge.

"We were, but it's not a discussion with ladies present," the man said. "I'm Bertrand de Haler, and you must be the famous Jack Knight that I've heard much about." He shook Jack's hand and ignored me.

I sighed and sat back. Women would never be allowed to

participate fully in politics or society, for that matter, if men such as Mr de Haler continued with antiquated views on what should be discussed in front of us. Hopefully, our participation in this war would change all of that.

Two British soldiers approached our table, and Nancy and I were whisked off to the dance floor again.

Bernard de Haler was gone when we returned to the table. Arthur's head rested on his hands, and he was sound asleep. Betsy was draped against him. Jack smiled as we approached.

The sultry-voiced singer spoke into the microphone again. "Grab your partners for the last dance."

Jack stubbed out his cigarette, stood, and held out his hand to me. "Come on, Mae, last dance."

It was, of course, a slow number. Jack pulled me close, and I relaxed into his embrace as we moved in time to the music.

"I'd like to see you again," he murmured, his breath tickling my ear.

"I don't have leave again for a few weeks," I said.

"When you do, can I call on you?" Jack asked.

I hesitated. Obviously, he couldn't call on me at work or at my billet, but the thought of seeing him again was an attractive proposition.

"Won't you be flying with Arthur?"

"I don't know," he said. "I just go where I'm told, although I will be in England again in the next few weeks if that's what you're asking."

"In that case, I'll give you my grandmother's London number. She can get a message to me."

CHAPTER 3

Bletchley, England
September 7, 1943

The train from London's Euston station was crowded. I was exhausted after spending what felt like most of my forty-eight hours of leave on the dance floors of the Astoria and the Grosvenor House Hotel. The carriage I entered was so full of soldiers dressed in khaki that one could be forgiven for mistaking it for a troop train rather than the passenger service of the Northwestern Railway.

I gave one group of soldiers my most charming smile, and sure enough, the youngest, who couldn't have been a day over sixteen, stood and offered me his seat next to the window. I dropped gratefully into it and leaned back, closing my eyes for a moment. I could feel the clouds of sleep descending and pulled myself back, sitting up and addressing the man beside me.

"Wake me at Bletchley?" I murmured.

"Yes, ma'am," he replied, a look of disappointment crossing his face that I wasn't about to engage him in conversation. "Late night?"

I let sleep take me.

I was shaken awake what felt like seconds later.

"We're pulling into Bletchley," the soldier said. "There are always young women getting off at this station. What do you do here? Do you think I could get a transfer?"

His mates laughed, but I was immediately awake and wary. I straightened my hat and picked up the bag at my feet. "Just boring typing," I said, easing past him and into the aisle. "Good day," I said before stepping onto the platform, grateful to breathe fresh air again, after the stuffy, odour-filled carriage.

Several boys leaned out of the windows and waved as the train pulled out again, leaving me alone in front of the old station house.

"If only you knew," I murmured.

What went on at Bletchley Park was Britain's best-kept war secret, one we hoped would remain undiscovered. In 1938, as war with Germany was increasingly likely, the Admiralty moved its code-breaking operation from Room 40 in the Broadway Building at St. James's Park in London to a little-known outpost in the village of Bletchley, purchased specifically for the purpose by Admiral Sinclair.

When war broke out, and parts of Western Europe and France had fallen, the British public was sure that it was only a matter of time before Britain was invaded too. But they didn't know that an enormous effort was already underway, not just on the battlefield but back home in Britain. The unlikeliest of warriors – academics, mathematicians, crossword puzzle enthusiasts, and debutantes, young unmarried women of good breeding, deemed loyal and security conscious, such as me – were set a near-impossible task; break the German Enigma code. Later, many young women from the Woman's Royal Naval Service, known colloquially as WRENS, joined Bletchley in an operation that ran day and night, breaking German (and more recently, Italian and Japanese) military codes. Britain and her allies had a secret back door into Hitler's plans, which needed to be protected at all costs.

I learned all this on the day my Uncle Charles sent me on the train to Bletchley Park, the ramshackle manor house around which my life would revolve for the rest of the war. I signed the Official Secrets Act that first day, forbidding me from revealing to anyone what my new job would entail.

What I now knew was that the British, with the help of a group of Polish codebreakers, had worked out how to break the coded messages sent by Germany's Enigma machines.

Uncle Charles had shown me an Enigma machine on one of his visits to Bletchley Park. It looked like a typewriter, but when the operator typed a letter onto the keyboard, an electronic current would send the letter through rotating wheels, and a different letter would be illuminated on the adjacent lampboard, thus encrypting the letter. This process would be repeated for the entire message, which would be sent using Morse code to its intended recipient. The encryption depended upon the position of the three rotating wheels, of which there was any combination of eight, which the Germans changed every twenty-four hours, resulting in 150 million possible combinations.

I couldn't begin to understand how the boffins were able to break the codes. All I knew was that in Hut 3, we received a constant stream of slips of paper from the machine room once the codes had been broken. They were around the size of a Post Office telegram with five-letter groups that resembled German words if everything was working as intended. If it didn't make sense, we would translate it as best we could.

I glanced at my watch – nine a.m. My shift didn't start until noon, time for a couple more precious hours of sleep. I headed for the manor house to see if I could borrow Mavis's bicycle to ride back to my billet.

•••

There was a tap on the glass behind me later that afternoon as I sat on a hard chair at a wooden desk with my back to the window. My friend Joan was jumping up and down, waving her arms.

"Mae, quick, the NAAFI is open."

I scribbled a star in the margin of the message I was attempting to translate to mark my place, jumped up, grabbed my handbag from beneath the desk, and weaved my way through the rows of desks, and into the long corridor leading to the door. Several other young women with whom I worked looked up as I passed, and I soon heard footsteps behind me. I hurried out to where Joan was waiting for me.

Across the lawn, several groups of women emerged from the other similar huts to mine and dashed across the driveway. We picked up our pace and raced towards the imposing mansion house to see that a queue of predominantly women was already snaking along the path from the little kiosk with its shutters raised beside the house. The two women manning the NAAFI, the armed services canteen, were working frantically to serve the growing line of customers.

I sighed. "It's worse each time they open. Look at all these people, they're like little children eagerly waiting by an ice cream van."

"Oh, ice cream." Joan's eyes looked dreamy. "But what I really need are chocolates and cigarettes."

"You need them?" I teased.

"You have no idea," she said. "Actually, the chocolate is for Dilly. All that man seems to survive on is tea and chocolate."

I smiled. I only knew Joan's boss Dilly by sight, but his reputation preceded him around Bletchley Park as one of the smartest codebreakers. Whenever I saw him hurrying about the place, he didn't look well; perhaps it was something to do with the amount of tea and chocolate he consumed.

"I put a ladder in my last pair of stockings. I'm hoping they have some left by the time we get to the front of this queue," I said.

"I wouldn't get your hopes up," Joan said as the queue inched forward.

Ten minutes later, we rounded the east end of the mansion, walking along the driveway towards the cottage where Joan worked, smoking our newly acquired cigarettes. Stockings were in short supply, and I'd missed out. I'd have to mend mine and try again next week. I was determined not to resort to drawing a line up the back of my bare calves to simulate wearing stockings, as I'd seen some of the women doing. We stepped aside when the roar of an engine signalled the arrival of a dispatch rider. The motorbike pulled to a stop in front of the garages behind the main house. The head of the dispatch riders, a robust, red-faced army man, Sergeant Harris, appeared from the garages to greet him, clipboard in hand.

"You made good time, lad," he said, leaning over and reading the machine's odometer and recording the result on his clipboard. The rider dismounted and removed his helmet and goggles. The black motorcycle had an uncomfortable-looking seat with a large spring beneath it and two canvas saddlebags attached to a frame across the rear wheel.

"Yeah, the roads were quiet," the rider said. "Who do I give these to?" He unlatched his satchel.

I did a double-take at the voice, the accent. My head was immediately filled with images of being spun around the dance floor at the Astoria by a man with intense blue eyes. I felt the colour rise in my cheeks.

"What is it?" Joan asked.

"That dispatch rider sounds exactly like a New Zealander I met in London at the weekend." I tried to sound nonchalant.

"This your first time here?" Harris asked the motorcyclist.

"Yeah, I'm filling in for Tommy Harkens, who has taken ill. He messaged ahead that I'd be coming in his place."

Harris nodded. "And what is it that you normally do?"

The motorcycle courier straightened. "I was with the New Zealand force in Egypt until I was seconded to the British Army as a photographer."

"Name?" Harris's tone had turned decidedly cool.

"Lieutenant Jack Knight."

"Come with me, Lieutenant. We can't allow photographers here."

"I'm not here to take photos, I'm just doing Tommy a favour," Jack said.

"That may well be, lad, but this is not normally the way things work around here," Harris said. "You need to come with me."

Jack hooked his helmet over the handlebars and removed his riding gloves. He glanced across the courtyard to where Joan and I were staring. He didn't seem surprised to see me and tapped his finger to an imaginary hat before following Harris into a hut at the far end of the courtyard.

"That's him," I said. "That's the guy I met at the Astoria. He's a friend of Betsy's."

"Maybe he has come to see you?" Joan teased.

I shook my head. "There's no way he would know that I worked here."

"In that case, someone is about to get in trouble for allowing him in here without the correct authorisation," Joan said, looking at her watch. "Anyway, I had better get back."

"Me too," I said, retracing my steps along the driveway. Halfway along, I glanced over my shoulder, hoping for another glimpse of the mysterious Jack Knight, but the courtyard was empty.

•••

I spent the next two hours in my uncomfortable chair trying to translate a series of messages based on a guessed crib. The room was quiet; the only sound from the twenty or so women and three men was the scratch of pencils on paper and the occasional cough. I gazed around at my co-workers, engrossed in trying to translate the decrypts in front of them.

The room was spartan, resembling a schoolroom, with groups of plain desks and chairs and several filing cabinets. The only decoration was a large map of the United Kingdom and Europe covering one wall. The small windows along one side of the room let in some light, but the green-shaded overhead bulbs provided most of the illumination. A throat cleared from the desk at the front of the room, and I glanced over to see the head of the hut, Mrs Winter, a stern woman in her late thirties, frowning at me and breaking me from my daydream. I turned my attention back to the paper in front of me. There was an error somewhere, as although some of the words that formed resembled German, enough letters were missing that the message made no sense; much depended upon the skill of the intercept operator. I had no real clue who they would be or where they would be based, but from the few murmurings I'd overheard, I figured they would be young women who'd been drafted into some branch or other of the military and stationed somewhere along the coast of England. I had put enough together to realise that the dispatch riders had to be bringing the messages from somewhere further afield than London.

I felt like I'd only just refocused my attention when I heard the chairs of my colleagues scrape back against the wooden floor – meal break. The other women in my section rushed for the door, keen to maximise their time outside in the sunshine of the late summer evening.

A shadow crossed my desk, and William Brown, a young Cambridge linguist who worked in my hut, waited for me to stop writing.

"Care to join me, Mae?" he asked.

I threw my pencil down, dropped the message in the basket on the desk and stood up.

"I would be delighted," I said, smiling at him. William was one of the more attractive "brains", as the girls called the group of dowdily dressed academics who provided the analytical power behind the code-breaking activities at the Park. He was tall and broad-shouldered. With his fair hair neatly parted, William closely resembled the actor Lawrence Olivier, which made him sought after and the subject of much gossip and speculation among many of the women who worked at the Park. As fond as I was of him, he had no romantic interest in me.

"I wonder what *gastronomic* delicacy awaits us today," William said as he stood aside to allow me to pass through the door ahead of him. William donned his hat, and we joined a stream of people crossing the lawn to the canteen.

"I hope there's meat," one young woman said. "Not just lumps of turnips swimming in watery gravy and claiming to be stew."

"Ooh, I hope it's pie," another voice said with excitement.

Food was a frequent topic of conversation among the Park inmates, as we called ourselves, for two reasons. One, it was a safe subject; we were forbidden from discussing our work with anyone outside of our immediate hut; and two, due to the shortages that the war had brought, after four years we were all more than a little obsessed with food.

We reached the canteen and joined the queue, which snaked almost to the door. The purpose-built facility was massive and could accommodate hundreds of people at meal times. The most surprising thing about the canteen was its egalitarian nature. It didn't matter your importance in the hierarchy, we all had to eat, and everyone from the newest Wren to a Cambridge professor or American colonel just mucked in together. I raised up on my toes to look over the heads of the women in front of me. I pulled a face at William. "It's pie alright, Woolton Pie."

A variety of groans from those in line accompanied my comment. Woolton Pie was a regular feature on the menu at Bletchley.

All of the meat that should have been in a pie was absent, replaced with chunks of root vegetables. Due to the butter shortage, the pastry was more like a heavy scone, but it was a filling, if flavourless, meal. I accepted my portion with a smile when my turn came.

"Mae, sorry, duty calls," William said, nodding across the room to where a group of scruffy academics were having a heated debate. One of the men was beckoning to him.

"No, problem," I said. "See you after." I picked up a cup of stewed tea and headed outside into the early evening sunshine.

"Don't encourage him if you're not interested," said a young woman called Lizzie from my hut, joining me as I walked towards the lake.

"He's just a friend," I assured her. "Nothing is going on there."

I had no interest in William, and I was confident he had no interest in me other than friendship.

I joined a group of friends at the edge of the small ornamental lake at the end of the front lawn and sank onto the grass, turning my face to the sun and letting its rays soak into my skin. I gazed across the lawn at the mansion house. I'd heard many comments from my fellow code breakers about the building, primarily that it was hideous, but I thought the better word was eccentric. The house boasted myriad architectural styles and, as a result, had varying roof lines, windows, and materials used in its construction. I'd read somewhere that the original owner of Bletchley Park, Sir Herbert Leon, liked to travel extensively, and each time he returned from abroad, he would summon his builders with plans for a new extension reflecting the style of the region he'd just visited. As a result, Bletchley manor exhibited Gothic, Greek, Arabic, and Victorian styling. As souvenirs went, it was an interesting concept. I wondered what Leon would think of all the people working in and around his house now, especially the more recent additions to the property.

My gaze moved from the mansion to the rows of long buildings lined up east of the house. They were ugly, utilitarian structures. I suspected he would be dismayed that his yew maze had been torn out to make room for another hut. A shadow passed across my line of sight, breaking my reverie.

"Good evening, Miss Webster, mind if I join you?"

I looked up to see Jack Knight standing in front of me, his head blocking the sun so that it appeared to have a halo around it. The conversation around me ceased for a moment as everyone observed the newcomer before starting up again.

"Jack? I thought you'd be on the road again?"

"I will be shortly," he said, folding his long legs beneath him as he settled on the grass beside me, taking my lack of denial as acceptance of his request. He somehow managed to not spill a drop from the teacup he was carrying.

"You are certainly making yourself useful to the war effort. You didn't tell me that you were also a dispatch driver?"

"I'm not normally, I'm just filling in for a mate who's ill," Jack said. He gazed around. "So, this is Station X."

"Mm," I agreed as my mind raced. Despite our obvious attraction, I was wary all of a sudden. What was an ex-soldier, now war photographer, doing moonlighting as a motorcycle courier and wandering around Bletchley Park unaccompanied? "Did you get a grilling from Sergeant Harris?"

"They were expecting me, the message just hadn't gotten through to the correct people."

I frowned. "I'm confused."

"Don't be." Jack drained his cup and stood. "I'd best be on my way. Will you be here again tomorrow?"

I shrugged. "I could be."

Jack grinned. I watched him saunter across the lawn toward the garages beyond the main house.

"He's rather dishy," Mavis called to me.

I smiled and watched as he strode out of sight. Was it a

coincidence that the stranger I met on Saturday turned up here? And it appeared that he knew all about Station X, which was what Bletchley Park was known as in military circles. There was more to Jack Knight than simply a soldier turned photographer. Before I agreed to go out with him, I needed to find out what he was up to.

CHAPTER 4

Bletchley, England
September 8, 1943

The garages in the courtyard behind the main house were a hive of activity the following afternoon. A group of dispatch riders, men and women, were seated around a long table in the stables drinking tea and eating toast. Several others leaned against the wall outside smoking. Something tugged at my subconscious. If all the motorcycle couriers were confined to the courtyard for the duration of their short visits to Bletchley Park, then why was Jack Knight wandering around the grounds? The door of a small office at one end of the stables was ajar, and I could see Sergeant Harris sitting at a desk, talking on the telephone. He glanced over at me and held up one finger, signalling that I should wait for him to finish his conversation. The buttons of his tunic strained across his midriff and his posture exuded self-importance. I waited outside the door until he finished his call. He gave me an impatient stare.

"Yes?"

"Sergeant Harris, Mae Webster."

"How can I help you, Miss?" Harris stood.

I entered his office and closed the door. "It's probably nothing, but the dispatch rider who was here yesterday, Jack Knight…."

Harris held up his hand, interrupting me. "Now listen here; I have no time for romantic intrigue."

I blushed. "It's not that; it's just that Lt Knight was down by the lake at dinnertime and didn't seem surprised by all the people here. I thought it unusual for someone who was filling in. Come to think of it, he didn't ask what we were all doing here, it was as if he already knew."

Harris nodded. "Ah, I see. Very observant of you, Miss." Harris looked down at this desk, gathering his thoughts before replying. "Let's just say there is more to Lt. Knight than meets the eye."

"Oh? So, I shouldn't be concerned then?"

"Let me put it another way. Our Lt. Knight's security clearance outstrips either yours or mine."

"Oh, I see. Thank you for your time." I left the office and hurried back out into the courtyard. I now had even more questions, such as why someone with high-security clearance was working as a fill-in dispatch rider and why he had pretended to have no knowledge of Bletchley Park, when he clearly did.

I glanced up at the courtyard clock – 5:30 p.m.

I didn't have time to go back to my digs before the concert at 7, instead, I decided to make the most of the lovely evening and walk into town.

A fortunate side effect of the diverse array of people gathered together at Bletchley Park was that some incredibly talented musicians and actors were among them. We all eagerly anticipated the autumn revue in a few weeks, which would be full of well-written and acted comedy sketches, if past performances were anything to go by. However, tonight we were being treated to a performance by the Bletchley Operatic Society run by James Robertson, with the choir being conducted by the famous Sergeant Herbert Murrill. I was pleased that my friend Christine had agreed to swap my early shift tomorrow, meaning I could attend and still get some sleep before I had to work again.

I left the Park through the main gate. It was a balmy evening, and I had a lightweight cardigan draped around my shoulders. On the short walk into the village, my mind turned over my meeting with Jack Knight the previous day and the implications of Sergeant Harris's comments. I liked nothing better than a puzzle, and Jack Knight was proving to be anything but the straightforward chap he'd presented himself as when we met in London.

Many of the shops on Bletchley's high street were closed. Not that I would have bought anything there. I hated to say it because it made me sound like a snob, but Bletchley was a bit of a dump. There were two cinemas and the usual shops, but they were tired, with a limited variety of stock which the war shortages seemed to have only made worse. Still, with a war on, we all had to make do. The rumble in my stomach reminded me I should find something to eat before the show. I passed by the Shoulder of Mutton with its pretty thatched roof, and rued the fact that I was alone. The landlady was a gifted cook, but it wasn't done for a young woman to frequent a public house on her own. Sadly, the only other eating establishment open was a British Restaurant, not known for its culinary prowess, but needs must. I girded my loins and entered the restaurant, where the smell of boiled cabbage assailed my senses. I took a tray and selected a bowl of cloudy water masquerading as soup and a spoonful of beans on toast before sitting at an empty table by the window.

"May I join you?"

I looked up to see William standing beside me, holding a tray.

"Of course," I said. "Are you going to the concert tonight?"

William settled himself at the table and nodded. "Aren't we spoilt to have such talent among us?"

"Gosh, yes," I replied. "You must know some of the musicians from your days at Cambridge?"

He nodded. "I hear you were due to go up to Cambridge before this ghastly business began."

"I was supposed to start in '42, but I have delayed it until after the war."

"You know, I've never asked how long you've been at BP?" he asked.

"Fifteen months. You?"

"Eight months," William said. "I was at the Foreign Office first until my skills were thought better suited here. To be honest, I never felt like I fitted in with all the upper-class types in Whitehall, and I was happy to do something more tangible to help fight the Nazi scourge."

"I know what you mean. I drove ambulances in London for a time, but at least here, I feel I'm doing something that will make a real difference. I hope so, anyway."

"How did you end up here?"

"My uncle, on my mother's side, recommended me when he heard I was going up to Cambridge to study languages."

"Quite right. A waste of your talents driving ambulances."

"I was pretty good at it, I'll have you know."

"I don't doubt that for one moment."

The concert, held in the Assembly Hall which the authorities had recently built outside the Park gates, was magnificent. Every seat was occupied, and there was standing room only for the latecomers, but the audience, a mixture of Park workers and locals, was most receptive. I had to pinch myself that I could attend a performance by such talented musicians, let alone during wartime.

"Mae, would you like to get a drink?" William asked as we left the hall.

"No, thank you, William, I need to get home. I have had such a long day."

He nodded. "Very well, another time then. I'm starting a week of night shifts, so we'll pass each other on the changeover, no doubt."

I smiled, and he tipped his hat before turning away and striding off toward his billet in the village. Meanwhile, I joined the queue for the bus back to my lodgings.

"Hello, Mae. Did you enjoy the concert?" an American voice at my shoulder asked.

I turned to see one of the more recent American arrivals who'd joined the codebreaking team at Bletchley, standing behind me in his smart navy blue uniform.

"Hi, Alan. I did, very much," I replied. "You?"

He nodded. "Magnificent. You don't live in town?"

"No, my uncle pulled some strings, and rather than be billeted with a family in Bletchley, I'm staying at Liscombe Park with several other girls with whom I attended school."

"Sounds like you lucked out," Alan said.

"I'm a little embarrassed, if I'm honest, but not embarrassed enough to complain."

The American laughed as the first bus pulled in and began to unload the midnight shift.

"Most of the servants have been called up, so they had plenty of spare rooms," I explained. "The couple who own it are darlings, and I think they love the company."

"Mae, we're having a dance at the base this Saturday. I was hoping that you and your friends would come," Alan said, following me up the steps into the empty bus and sitting opposite me.

Giggles announced the arrival of two of my housemates.

"Here come two of them now; why don't we ask them?"

Mavis and Nancy dropped down beside me.

Nancy closed her eyes and leaned against my shoulder. "Wake me when we get there. I'm exhausted."

"Before you sleep, Major Shaunwell has just invited us to a dance at the American base on Saturday night," I said.

Nancy's eyes flew open, and she registered Alan's presence. She straightened her posture and patted her hair. "Why, yes, Major, that would be wonderful."

"Great, I'll send a car to Liscombe Park, say 7 o'clock."

"Thanks, Alan, we'll be ready," I said.

The bus bumped and wound its way around the narrow lanes surrounding the farms outside Bletchley, occasionally pausing to drop someone off. When it came to our stop, I shook Nancy awake, and we bade farewell to Alan before climbing out into the darkness.

"Don't you love the informality of Bletchley?" Mavis said. "Where else would you get away with calling a major by his Christian name."

"I'm glad you're with me," I said, pulling out my torch with its blackout covering. "I hate walking along this driveway when it's this dark, I'm convinced something will jump out of the hedgerows at me."

Mavis linked arms with Nancy and me and marched down the centre of the long winding entrance to Liscombe Park.

"Did you see your Kiwi again?" Nancy asked.

"Actually, I did," I said. "He came via motorcycle yesterday and joined me by the lake at dinnertime."

"They don't usually let the Don-Rs wander around the grounds," Nancy said.

"Don-R?"

"Dispatch riders," Nancy clarified.

"Apparently, he was filling in for a friend who is ill," I said. "And according to Sgt Harris, Jack Knight's security clearance exceeds any of ours."

"Really?" Mavis stopped walking. "That's interesting. Be careful, Mae, you don't know who you're getting involved with."

"There's nothing to be careful of," I said. "I'm far too busy and tired to get involved with any man right now."

"That shouldn't stop you from having a bit of fun," Nancy said, nudging me with her elbow. "And from what I saw on Saturday night, your Kiwi looked like a bit of fun."

"He's not my...." I began to protest before I realised she was teasing me.

Liscombe Park manor was in darkness as we rounded the top of the driveway. The light from the moon picked out its turrets and towers, making it appear like something from a gothic horror novel. I was again glad that I had company, stopping my overactive imagination from getting the better of me. The massive double-front door was unlocked, and we slipped into a vast, dimly lit foyer with several doors leading off. Music sounded from the drawing room, and we entered to see our fellow billets, Margaret and Sarah, drinking tea and listening to the wireless.

Nancy dropped down onto the nearest sofa. "I'm so exhausted that I don't think I can make it up the stairs," she moaned.

"At least your next shift doesn't start in less than eight hours," Mavis said. "I'm off to bed, goodnight, everyone."

She closed the door behind her, and seconds later, we heard the creak of her footsteps on the stairs.

"All these shifts, it's getting more like the army every day," Sarah moaned.

"I think it's because there are more and more people in uniform at Bletchley now," I said. "All the Wrens have to wear the same attire."

"I think they all look rather smart," Margaret said.

Nancy shuddered. "You wouldn't catch me dead in a military uniform, they do nothing for one's figure."

"I think that is perhaps the point," Margaret said.

"I preferred it when there were just oddball Cambridge professors, eccentric mathematicians and a mixture of people like us with just a few in uniform," Sarah said.

"Ooh, I don't know, those Americans have been a welcome addition if you ask me," Nancy said, chuckling. "Did Mae tell you that we're invited to a dance at the American base on Saturday night? Major Shaunwell is sending a car for us."

"Fun," Sarah said.

"Joan reckons up to six thousand people are working shifts at the Park now," I said.

"What do they all do?" Nancy wondered aloud.

"We're not supposed to ask, remember," Margaret cautioned.

Nancy waved her hand. "I know, Official Secrets Act and all that. I wonder if one day we'll be able to tell people what we did during the war?"

I shrugged. "Who knows? I guess it depends if we win."

Margaret looked aghast. "Of course we'll win, and to think anything else is impossible. Now I must get some sleep. Coming, Sarah? Aren't we on the same shift tomorrow?"

Sarah followed her to the door. "See you tomorrow," she said, winking to Nancy and me.

"Could Margaret be any more uptight?" Nancy asked, swinging her legs off the sofa and helping herself to a cup of tea from the pot. She waved a cup at me, and I shook my head.

"I'm off to bed too."

Nancy drained the cup and hooked her arm through mine. "Good, you can carry me up those stairs." She paused by the door. "Mae, I know you brushed it off earlier, but Mavis is right; you need to be careful with Jack Knight. I believe that he is not who he purports to be."

•••

I arrived at the Park the next afternoon to find increased security at the main gate as I approached through the drizzle via the avenue of trees. The soldiers in the sentry post were carefully checking the papers of everyone arriving and searching the belongings of all those leaving.

"What's going on?" I asked as I handed over my papers to Private Morris, who had been assigned to Bletchley Park for as long as I'd worked there and whom I'd come to know well.

"I don't know," he said. "But we need to check everyone, even those we know."

I raced to my hut, arriving just as the shift was changing. Those leaving looked tired and drawn, whereas those of us coming in were red-cheeked from the cold.

"What's the fuss all about?" I asked Mary, the woman opposite me, as I sat down.

"Rumour has it that some decrypts are missing," she whispered.

"Missing?"

A grim expression crossed her face, and she nodded.

"Not from our hut?"

She shrugged. "I'm not sure. But there are fears that we may have a spy in our midst."

I removed my coat and was about to collect my first batch of decrypts to translate when Mrs Winter called me over to her desk at the front of the room.

"You are wanted over at the mansion."

"Why?"

She shrugged and went back to checking the rosters.

Tendrils of fear wound around my chest, making breathing hard as I pulled my coat back on. Surely, no one suspected me of any wrongdoing. Why else would I be summoned?

I hurried across to the mansion where Mavis was waiting for me in the entrance hall.

"What's this all about?" I asked her in a hushed whisper as she helped me remove my coat before showing me into Travis's office.

I caught her eye and mouthed his name, but she shook her head. What was going on here? Mavis retreated and closed the door with a quiet snick behind me.

I stood in front of the Commander's desk as he scribbled a

note in his trademark brown ink, known around the Park as 'the Director's blood.' His nickname Jumbo suited his imposing build.

"Ah, Miss Webster," he said, rising. "Take a seat."

I perched on the edge of a hard chair in front of his desk.

"Hello, Maisie."

I twisted around. I hadn't realised there was anyone else present. My uncle was leaning against the bookshelf on the far side of the room, lighting a cigarette. In his well-cut suit and hand-made leather shoes, he was a sophisticated, elegant figure.

"Hello," I said, both surprised and delighted to see him. I crossed the room and kissed his cheek. Charles was my mother's younger brother and only fourteen years my senior. I wasn't entirely sure what he did, but I knew it was something important for the Foreign Office.

"You must be wondering why I asked you here," Travis said, drawing my attention back to him.

I nodded.

"Miss Webster, we have concerns that there are missing decrypts. At best, it's a procedural error, but at worst we have a spy in our midst, and our whole operation could be in jeopardy if secrets are shared with the enemy. I need someone I can trust to keep an eye on things in your hut and, if necessary, set a trap."

"A trap, sir?"

"We may need to supply whoever is behind this with false information to determine how far this breach goes."

I felt my mouth forming a silent 'oh'.

"I need you to report anything suspicious that you witness or overhear to either myself or, in my absence, to Mavis."

"I understand."

"You mustn't discuss anything you uncover with anyone. For now, I want you to observe and report back. Questions?"

"Do you think it could be someone in my hut?" I asked.

"It could be anyone."

"How do you know it's not me?"

Travis laughed. "You're Charles' niece, besides, you've been thoroughly vetted."

"Oh."

"That's all." Travis picked up his glasses and turned his attention to the papers on his desk.

I glanced at Charles, who gave me a warm smile.

I mumbled goodbye and fled. Mavis jumped up from her desk and rushed to my side when I closed Travis's door behind me.

"Sorry, I didn't have time to warn you," she whispered, leading me away from the earshot of the other women seated in the outer office area to a small alcove further along the passageway.

"I'm still unsure what he wants me to do."

"Just keep your eyes and ears open."

CHAPTER 5

Bletchley, England
December 12, 1943

The next few weeks dragged, and before we knew it, autumn turned to winter and the trees were bare. I wasn't looking forward to another winter in the cold, draughty Hut 3 and had determined to wear trousers once the weather turned icy this year. I'd altered two pairs left behind by Granny's driver when he was conscripted. I thought they looked rather smart, although I was a little uncertain of the reaction I would receive at the Park. I was sure that none of the men would even notice, but some of the women were quite old-fashioned and would most likely complain. But, when a snowfall blanketed the region in early December, I decided to heck with them; the time had come.

I breakfasted alone in the dining room that morning, as I was on a different shift pattern to the other girls. I was looking forward to a two-day leave pass in a few days and planned to go home to check on Granny and celebrate Christmas early. I still hadn't persuaded her to leave Chelsea for the countryside's safety.

I walked out into the late afternoon drizzle with William Brown after a rather tedious shift where every decrypt I translated related to the weather, some German soldier's girlfriend, or the standard nothing-to-report type message. The fact that all ended with Heil Hitler must be helpful to the code breakers, I mused. William was headed for his billet in the village, and I was going to wait for the bus that would take me to Liscombe and hopefully a hot bath to help thaw out my frozen toes. Although the four inches of water allowance couldn't be called a bath, a puddle would be a better description. But there was a war, and we all had to do our bit, including lukewarm pretend baths. As we passed the lake, I recognised a familiar figure deep in conversation with Commander Travis on the other side of the lawn, in front of the mansion's main entrance. My heart gave a skip.

William rested his hand on my arm. "Hang on a minute, Mae. There's an old chum of mine."

Jack Knight shook hands with Travis and walked across the lawn towards us. He buttoned his heavy overcoat as he approached. He had a dark grey trilby tilted over one eye.

"Jack," William called.

"G'day."

William shook Jack's hand. "How are you, old chap?"

"Very well." He looked past William to me and nodded. "Mae."

"Jack."

William looked from Jack to me. "You two are acquainted? This calls for a drink."

"Not for me, I should get home," I said.

"Has your shift just finished?" Jack asked. I nodded. "Then you won't have eaten," he said. "Does the Shoulder of Mutton still do a good meal?"

"Splendid idea, old chap," William said, offering me his arm.

I acquiesced and allowed myself to be led to the Park's security gates, where our bags were searched. To my surprise, the sentry greeted Jack by name together with a salute. At Bletchley Park, with such a mix of civilians and military, acknowledgement of rank tended to be a bit hit-and-miss. We walked along the high street to the popular local pub.

Jack held the door open for me, and as I passed through, he murmured. "It's good to see you again, Mae."

William located a dining area table and went to the bar to order drinks.

Jack helped me remove my coat before shrugging out of his own and tossing his hat onto the table. I noticed that he hadn't even glanced at my attire, let alone commented on it. Smart man.

I studied him surreptitiously as he stretched to drape his jacket across an empty chair. I tried not to notice that he was in great shape. In fact, he looked fighting fit to me, and I wondered why the New Zealand Army had released him to take photos.

I swallowed and raised my eyes to meet his. He opened his mouth to speak as William returned, balancing three drinks; beer for him and Jack and a pink gin for me.

"So, how do you two know one another?" William asked.

"Through mutual friends," I said. "Jack knows Arthur, my friend Betsy's fiancé."

William nodded.

"And how are you two acquainted?" I asked.

The two men exchanged a glance. "We worked together at the Admiralty in London for a time."

I opened my mouth to ask another question.

"We all know we can't talk about what we do, so let's talk about other things," he said. "Have you been to the Astoria again recently?"

"No, but I'm well overdue a visit."

Jack smiled. "Well, next time you're on leave, we should take another turn around their dance floor."

"I'd like that," I said, holding his gaze.

William cleared his throat. "You've taken Mae to the Astoria?"

I tore my attention away from Jack. "That's where we met."

"I see," William said, patting his pockets and producing a packet of cigarettes which he offered first to me, then to Jack. "What's the latest from Europe?"

Jack shrugged as he lit up. "Nothing new, I'm afraid, although the Germans are still bogged down fighting the Soviets, which has to give us opportunities in Italy and France."

"We need to support our Soviet allies more," William said, glancing around to ensure we weren't being overheard. "I do hope some of the intelligence coming out of the Park is being shared with them."

"The risk is having to disguise the source of the intelligence," Jack murmured. "You know as well as I do that the fewer people who know about the Park, the better."

"But…" William began.

"If the Germans even suspect that we're reading their messages, they could change the cypher, and it would take a long time, if ever, to break into it again, and we could very well lose the war," Jack hissed.

"But our allies could use our help," William insisted.

"And they are getting it, but the big man is insistent that the Ultra secret must never be known."

"We are doing the Soviets a disservice."

"Old chap, I disagree, and you need to keep those opinions to yourself."

William sighed. "You're right, of course. It's just…."

Jack shook his head as our meal arrived, and William clamped his lips together.

The hotpot appeared devoid of meat but was served with a generous side of mashed vegetables. I took a tentative bite and was surprised to find it flavoursome and tasty. Jack was watching my reaction.

"Good?"

"Yes, surprisingly good."

"Could do with a bit more meat," William complained. "What I wouldn't do for a steak."

Jack laughed. "I hear you. Freshly baked bread is one of the things I miss."

"That and a real egg," I said. "One with a bright yellow yolk that bleeds across the plate when you pierce it."

"A rare thing these days," William agreed. "I will be happy if I never see another powdered egg in my lifetime."

After dinner, we bade William farewell outside the pub.

"Are you certain I can't escort you back to the Park?" William said. "I'm sure Jack has to be getting back to London."

"It's fine," Jack said. "I'm heading that way as my car is parked behind the mansion."

William shook Jack's hand and kissed my cheek.

"What I said earlier about the Soviets..." he began.

Jack slapped him on the arm. "I understand, mate, but it's not our decision to make."

William nodded. "Goodnight then."

We watched as he turned to walk in the direction of his billet two streets back from the pub, his hands deep in his overcoat pockets.

"Thank you again for dinner," I said as Jack and I set off in the opposite direction. Jack had insisted on paying.

"It was my pleasure," he said, hooking my hand between his arm and body. I was wearing my camel overcoat and a matching cloche hat. The coat had seen better days, and I'd mended the cuffs several times, but it was warm.

"So, you're much more than a war photographer and sometimes dispatch rider," I said.

"What makes you say that?"

"For a start, you wander around BP unchaperoned," I said. "And you seem to know an awful lot about what it is that we do here."

We walked in silence for a moment, our feet striking the ground in unison. "Mae, things are complicated, but you can trust me. I can't tell you what it is that I do, for your safety as well as others. But once this dreadful war is over..." he trailed off.

"It's hard to look ahead that far," I said. "And who knows what peace will actually look like."

"True, but please be careful who you trust around here," he said. "Not everyone is as they seem."

"Including you?"

"Yes, including me. But, as I said, you can trust me."

I absorbed that for a moment. "Which is exactly what someone untrustworthy would say, of course."

Jack laughed. "Yes, I suppose they would."

"So, who should I be on the lookout for?"

"That's the problem. We're not sure."

"Now you're frightening me."

"I don't mean to, I just want you to be safe."

"Safe?"

Jack shook his head. "I've said too much already."

The silence ran again for a few paces.

"What do your parents think about you working here?" Jack asked.

"It's just my grandmother, my parents are dead."

Jack's step faltered. "I'm sorry, Mae."

"It was a long time ago," I said. "I grew up in London with my grandmother."

"She must miss you," Jack said.

"I suppose. I was leaving for Cambridge but got diverted here on the way." I clamped my lips together for fear of revealing anything else.

Jack smiled. "Ah yes, I remember, brains and beauty."

I inclined my head at the compliment. "I also drove ambulances during the Blitz," I added.

"So, I need to add bravery to the list?"

"Not really, I just had to do something. Nothing worse than feeling helpless," I said, somewhat embarrassed that Jack had easily pulled my life story out of me. "What about you? Do you miss home?"

He didn't speak for a moment. "Yeah, I do."

"What part of New Zealand are you from?"

"The South Island. I grew up on a sheep farm near the sea."

"How idyllic," I said.

Jack nodded. "It is, although I wasn't cut out to be a farmer. That's my brother Joe's thing, and he'll take over the farm one day."

"And what will you do?"

"I had already moved away before the war. I was a cadet reporter for the *Otago Daily Times* in Dunedin."

"Will you go back to that after the war?"

Jack was silent for a moment. "I'm not sure I will be able to settle back into sleepy old New Zealand after everything, but when I dream, it is of the farm and my family, so perhaps my subconscious is telling me that it will be okay."

We turned into the entrance to the Park.

"Let me drive you to your billet," Jack said. "I must go back to London tonight, and it's on the way."

"Oh no, it's fine, really," I said.

"I insist."

Once again, the sentry on the gate saluted Jack and called him by name while rifling through my handbag. A second guard appeared and drew Jack to one side. A whispered conversation ensued, ending with a curt nod from Jack. The soldier handed back my papers and let us through the gate.

"Come on," Jack said. "I just have to make one stop."

We strolled in silence around the edge of the lake and up to the mansion. The only light was the waning moon. The huts and the mansion itself were in darkness, with blackout blinds drawn over every window. There was no evidence of the hundreds of people currently hard at work inside the grounds. A soldier opened the mansion's front door, and we were ushered inside.

"Do you mind waiting here for a moment," Jack said. Without waiting for a response, he disappeared into Commander Travis's office.

I perched on the edge of a chair in the draughty hallway and waited. The walls were wood-panelled, and rugs adorned the wooden floor. Voices drifted from open doorways along one side of the corridor, together with the occasional clatter of a typewriter. Bletchley was very much a twenty-four-hour operation. The door at the end of the hallway, which I knew from previous visits led to the ballroom, was ajar, and I wandered over to peer into the darkened room. Blackout blinds were drawn over the windows, but the light from the hallway illuminated the magnificent Art Deco glass-panelled ceiling. Chairs lined the walls around an ample central space, but the dance floor stood empty tonight.

I returned to the main hallway as Jack came out of Travis's office. Travis's gaze drifted to me as they shook hands, and he peered over his glasses.

"Good evening," he said. "Miss Webster, isn't it? Charles Montague's niece, if I recall correctly?"

"Yes, sir," I replied. "Good to meet you again."

"Shall we?" Jack said, holding his arm out to me. With his other hand, he donned his hat.

I hesitated; indecision and something else I couldn't name, fear perhaps, ran through me.

"It's okay, I'm going to drive you home now."

I followed Jack down the hallway to the mansion's rear and along a narrow passageway to a side door attended by another armed soldier.

"What's going on? Do you suspect me of some wrongdoing?" I asked as we were let out of the mansion and into the darkness.

Jack stopped walking and turned to look at me. "No, Mae, not at all. You are above reproach."

A black car pulled up, and a young private climbed out of the driver's seat and handed the keys to Jack. The headlights had blackout shields, and the interior light had been extinguished.

"There you are, sir," the soldier said.

"Thank you."

Jack held the passenger door open for me, and I turned to face him when he slid in behind the steering wheel.

"Jack, I know you have a higher security clearance than me and can't tell me what you're working on, but I'm frightened. Travis has asked me to be on the lookout for any suspicious behaviour in my hut. Do we have a traitor in our midst?"

Jack started the car, drove down the driveway, and out onto the country lane before answering.

"Honestly, I don't know," he said. "We thought we did in the summer, but there has been no activity since then. We've set traps that haven't triggered, so I can only conclude that we were mistaken."

"And you have probably said more than you should."

"Yes."

"I'm sorry," I said. "I shouldn't have put you in that position."

"It's fine, Mae, just don't mention this to anyone."

"I won't."

"I know," he said.

We drove in silence for a few moments before Jack spoke again.

"William isn't terribly discreet. You must be careful what conversations he draws you into outside the Park."

I nodded, then realised that he couldn't see me in the dark. "Yes, the secret nature of our work was drummed into me when I started. After all, we were made to sign the Official Secrets Act."

"All I'm saying is that you never know who is listening," Jack said. "And I meant what I said tonight; if the Germans found out that we've broken Enigma…."

"They won't hear it from me."

"Now, where is the entrance?"

"Just around this bend," I said. "Be careful turning in, it's pitch black, and you won't see anyone walking until you're upon them."

To my surprise, six other vehicles were parked in front of the manor house when we pulled up outside Liscombe Park.

"Nice digs," Jack said, peering through the front windscreen at the manor house looming above us.

I opened my door, and the sound of laughter and music reached us. The blackout blinds were firmly in place, but it was clear from the noise that there was quite a party going on.

"Oh, I completely forgot. We're entertaining some of the officers from the American base," I said. "Would you like to join in?"

"Well, I can't abandon you to a bunch of Americans now, can I?" Jack said. "Lead the way."

We stepped into the gloomy foyer. Two large column candles burned on either side of the massive staircase leading to the upper floors, throwing soft light across the space. I removed my overcoat and hung it on a coat stand by the door. I was reaching for Jack's coat when a door to the right burst open, and Nancy stepped out with a uniformed GI on her arm.

"Mae, you made it," she cried and lurched towards me. "And Lieutenant Knight, isn't it? How lovely that you could join us. The party is this way."

Jack hung his coat and hat, and we followed Nancy and her American into the drawing room, where the rugs had been rolled back and as many as twenty couples were jitterbugging to the music supplied by a small band of US army musicians. Others were seated in groups at the edges of the room. The air was thick with a heady mix of cigarette smoke and perfume.

"They brought the music and the booze," Nancy said in a loud whisper. "Help yourselves." She spun off into the arms of the soldier on the dance floor.

Jack grinned. "No more booze for me since I'm driving and the roads are treacherous enough, but let's dance."

"I really should go and change into something more suited to dancing," I said, looking down in dismay at the trousers that had seemed like such a good idea that morning.

"Nonsense, you look perfect, and I'm sure it doesn't matter what you wear when you dance." Jack took me in his arms and spun me around the dancefloor. I melted into his embrace, and all too soon the musicians announced they were taking a short break.

"And I must be going," Jack said.

I led him from the drawing room and back into the foyer towards the front door. The temperature was much cooler away from the dance floor, and I shivered. Jack reached for my jacket first and settled it around my shoulders.

"I enjoyed tonight," I said. Jack lifted his coat from the coat stand and draped it over his arm before reaching out to tuck a stray strand of hair behind my ear. He leaned in to kiss me with a gentle brush of his lips on my cheek.

"When do you next have leave, Mae? I meant what I said earlier; I would love to see you again. I finally have some flexibility in my schedule over the next couple of weeks."

I pulled back and studied him. Jack Knight was becoming a most intriguing acquaintance, and after what I'd learned tonight, I found myself eager to know more.

I smiled. "As it happens, I will be in London on Wednesday."

"In that case, will you meet me for dinner on Wednesday night?"

"I already have dinner plans," I said.

Jack's face fell.

"But perhaps you could join us, and we could go dancing afterwards?"

Jack frowned. "Us?"

"Granny and me."

Jack grinned. "I'd love to. Just tell me where and what time. I'll bring the wine."

•••

I smoothed my hands over the skirt of my dress and ran down the stairs, pausing to check my reflection in the hall mirror. The dress was several seasons out of style, but it flattered my figure. I'd curled my dark chestnut hair into victory rolls, which bounced against my shoulders as I walked.

"You look as beautiful as always, my dear," Granny said, leaning on her walking stick in the drawing room doorway. "Perhaps a little too thin, but aren't we all, with this blessed war rationing."

Granny was in her early seventies. She had soft white hair curling around her nape and a twinkle in her eye. She had cared for me since I was orphaned as a little girl, and I loved her dearly.

"Thank you, Granny," I said, joining her and kissing her cheek. "Are you sure that you're alright here? I worry about you, especially now that the Germans are again doing sporadic bombing raids on London. Promise me that you are going down to the cellar when the air raid siren goes." Like many similar properties nearby, the large three-storey house near the river in Chelsea, where I had grown up, had a deep basement.

"Of course, dear," she said, dismissing my concern with a wave of her hand. "Now, tell me about this young man of yours."

"He's not my young man."

She peered over her glasses at me. "Mmm, that may well be, but you haven't brought a man home to dinner before."

I blushed. "Jack is a New Zealander that I met through Betsy and Arthur. I thought he'd like a home-cooked meal."

"Of course, dear." I could tell Granny didn't believe me, but a knock sounded at the front door before I could respond further.

"That'll be Jack."

Jack wore the suit he was wearing when I first met him at the Astoria. He was carrying a bottle of wine and a small bunch of flowers. He handed me the wine as he crossed the threshold.

"Good evening," he said, removing his hat. I took it from him and sat it on a side table.

"Granny, I'd like to introduce Lieutenant Jack Knight. Jack, meet my grandmother, Lady Alice Webster."

"Lady Webster, it's a pleasure to meet you," Jack said, shaking Granny's outstretched hand and offering her the flowers. If the title surprised him, he didn't show it.

"And you," Granny said, accepting the flowers. "Thank you. It's not often we have someone from the colonies to dinner. Come through." She turned and led us into the dining room.

Jack removed his overcoat and hung it on a hook before catching my hand and leaning over to kiss my cheek.

"Hello, you."

I couldn't help but smile at him as a warm glow flowed through me.

Dinner was a convivial affair. We sat at one end of the long mahogany dining table with candles providing illumination. The blackout blinds were drawn, and a tall potted plant in one corner had been decorated for Christmas. Light from flickering candles clustered together on side tables shone on the makeshift Christmas tree, causing the tinsel and shiny baubles to twinkle. Granny was in fine form and peppered Jack with questions about New Zealand, his family and his army career. Jack, in return, was funny and charming. He regaled us with anecdotes of growing up on a sheep farm, riding horses, swimming in the ocean and discovering his love of photography from an uncle.

"I'm working with the British Army now as a photographer," he said. "My fighting days are over, thanks to a leg injury in North Africa, but at least I can still participate and do my bit towards defeating the Nazis."

"Your leg injury doesn't seem to stop you from racing around the countryside on a motorcycle," I observed.

Jack laughed. "Or scrambling out of army trucks, but I'm only qualified to carry a camera, not a rifle now, according to those in charge."

Maggie, Granny's cook turned butler turned maid, returned to clear away our plates.

"Make sure you share any leftovers with the neighbours," Granny murmured.

Maggie nodded and left the room, returning a short time later with a steaming apple cobbler and a jug of cream.

My mouth fell open at the same time as Jack's.

"Is that real cream? How did you manage that?"

Granny tapped the side of her nose. "Maggie, please sit with us and have some," she said.

Maggie hesitated until I jumped up and got an extra bowl and wine glass from the sideboard.

"Thank you," she said, serving four generous portions of the pudding.

Jack groaned as he took his first bite. "My apologies, but this tastes just like my mother's."

We ate in silence, savouring every bite.

"Where are you two going dancing?" Granny asked, having cleared her plate.

"I think we should try the 400 Club," Jack said.

CHAPTER 6

London, England
December 17, 1943

I woke the following morning in my old bedroom at Granny's house. Outside, the squeak from the wheel of a passing bicycle, and birds chirping in the trees filled the quiet. For a fleeting moment, it was as though we weren't in the middle of war. A beam of sunlight sliced around the edge of the blackout blind, not the sumptuous lace curtains that usually framed the window. I sighed as reality flooded back, and I glanced at the clock – 8 a.m.

Granny was already sitting at the breakfast table reading the newspaper when I entered downstairs wrapped in my dressing gown. The small room adjacent to the kitchen was cosy, and more often than not where we ate our meals rather than the more formal dining room. Granny glanced up at me over the top of her glasses.

"And what time did you get in last night?"

"I believe it was more this morning than last night," I said, helping myself to coffee from the pot on the sideboard. I took a sip and grimaced.

"I know, dear. My supplier has run out."

I helped myself to a slice of toast cooling in the toast rack, and applied a thin scraping of jam.

"Lt Knight is an amiable fellow," Granny continued.

"Mm," I agreed, my full mouth saving me from having to elaborate.

"Is there anything I should know?"

"Granny, I told you, I've just met him."

"Mm."

After breakfast, I packed my small valise and bade farewell to Granny.

"I'll be back next month for a few days, as long as my leave doesn't get cancelled," I said, kissing her soft cheek and inhaling her perfume's familiar, comforting scent. "I'm sorry that I can't be here for Christmas."

She held me a little longer than usual before releasing me.

"I have the neighbours coming over. You know I won't be lonely," she assured me. "Maggie has tucked a little something into your bag, but you are not to open it until Christmas morning."

"Thank you, Granny," I said. I had left my gift for her under the tree in the dining room.

I walked to the end of the road and caught the bus to town, where I'd arranged to meet Jack.

He was waiting for me at the entrance to St. James's Park. I spied him as the bus trundled along Constitution Hill and paused outside Buckingham Palace. Evidence of the damage wrought on the Palace and its grounds in a German bombing raid in September 1940 had all but disappeared, apart from the plethora of sandbag walls dotted everywhere around the building and the presence of military vehicles every few yards. Queen Victoria, cast in Carrera marble, sat serenely on her throne in front of the palace gates with the Winged Victory soaring high above her. *We could do with the goddess of victory about now*, I thought as a group of soldiers marched past, rifles on their shoulders, their steps in unison.

Jack was leaning against the railings at the entrance to the Park, smoking a cigarette and watching passers-by. It was my first time seeing him in his uniform, and my heart skipped a beat. He cut a handsome figure.

He smiled when he saw me get off the bus, pushing off the wall and strolling in my direction as I crossed the Mall to join him. His camera was hanging around his neck by a leather strap. He took my valise from my hand and kissed my cheek, lingering for a brief moment.

"Good morning, Miss Webster."

"Good morning, Lt Knight."

He held out his free arm. "Shall we?"

I hooked my gloved hand through his arm's crook, and we began strolling through St. James's Park.

"No one would ever know that you were out dancing until 2 a.m. You look radiant," Jack said.

I inclined my head at the compliment. "You haven't scrubbed up too bad yourself."

Jack smiled at me, but his eyes were weary behind the smile.

"Why are you in uniform?"

"Because I'm leaving London today," he said.

"Oh? For how long?"

"I'm afraid I can't say, but you will be the first to know when I return."

I digested this as we strolled along the gravel paths to the Blue Bridge. I knew when I was being closed down, but I also knew better than to press the matter.

"Had you visited London before the war?" I asked, changing the subject.

Jack shook his head. "I hadn't been outside New Zealand. The war was a chance for me to see the world."

"This park was so peaceful before," I said, pausing halfway across the bridge. "Beautiful flowerbeds, swans and ducks on the lake...."

I trailed off and looked around the grounds. The flowerbeds had been dug over and planted with vegetables, and groups of older men were attending to them. One end of the park was closed off, and an anti-aircraft battery was established. The shouts of an army marching drill sounded from behind the trees.

Jack released my arm and stepped away from me, raising his camera.

Click.

I raised a self-conscious hand to my hat.

Click.

"There is still beauty here," Jack said. He brushed past me before stopping and turning back. He raised the camera again. "You see, from this angle, all I see is the lake, the trees, and a beautiful woman. No war."

Click.

Jack lowered the camera and held my gaze. My heart thumped, and at that moment, something shifted between us. Jack stepped towards me and reached for my hand at the exact moment as I moved towards him, oblivious to anything going on around me. As our fingertips touched, a scruffy dog, chased by a small boy, barrelled between us, followed by shouts and apologies from the child's mother. We sprang apart and watched the dog and the little boy race across the bridge.

Jack cleared his throat, and the moment passed. He retook my hand, and we continued walking.

"You are lucky to be going off doing something meaningful today," I said. "I'm going back to sit in a cold, damp room and do my 'secretarial work'."

"Mae, what you are doing is just as meaningful as what I do," he said.

I sighed. "Perhaps, but I never get to see that, to know whether what I've done has made any difference."

"You just have to trust that it does."

I nodded.

"Mae, would you like to see some of my photographs?"

"I'd love to."

"They're back in my rooms." Jack paused and shuffled his feet. "I promise this is not a plot to get you there alone. In fact, I'm sure my landlady will insist on the door remaining open," he said.

I laughed. "Oh, don't worry. Plot away."

Jack cocked an eyebrow at me and moved my hand, tucking it in the crook of his elbow. We strolled back through the park to his lodgings near Victoria station. The brass doorstep of the low-level red-brick terraced house shone, and the path to the door had been swept clear of leaves.

Sure enough his landlady, a robust middle-aged woman with short tight curls wearing an apron pulled across her ample bosom, stepped from the front room as soon as we entered the house.

"Ah, Mrs Panmore, may I introduce the honourable Mae Webster."

I held out my hand. "A pleasure, Mrs Panmore."

"Miss Webster." She looked me up and down before turning her attention back to Jack. "You'll be wanting tea?"

"Yes, please, but first, I'm going to show Miss Webster my photographs from Africa," Jack said in a tone that allowed no argument.

Mrs Panmore sniffed her disapproval as Jack led me up a flight of carpeted stairs to the first floor.

"Door, Lt. Knight," she called after us.

I giggled as we entered Jack's room, which consisted of a small cosy sitting room with an armchair on either side of a gas fireplace and a little round table in between. Through a second doorway, I could see a neatly made single bed. A wooden desk was scattered with black and white photographs, and two stacks of yellowing newspapers sat against the wall in one corner of the sitting room. But my attention was drawn to the photos propped up along the mantelpiece.

"Where were these taken?" I asked, studying each in turn. They depicted a vast and foreign landscape full of undulating sand dunes, the images all shadows and light.

"North Africa. It's a stunning place, breathtakingly beautiful," he said.

"Jack, these are amazing. It's like another world." I turned to the table. "What's in the newspapers?"

"Clippings to send to my mother whenever I have a photograph published." He dipped his head, looking a little bashful.

"She must be very proud of you."

"I suppose, although they are probably prouder of Joe, who is actually out there fighting, not just taking photos of the war."

"You've done more than your fair share of fighting, and you are probably placing yourself in more danger now if what I suspect you're doing is true."

Jack shrugged. "Of course, we can never really say, can we?"

"No," I agreed. "But inside, we know we are doing our bit to defeat Hitler."

"Hear, hear." Mrs Panmore pushed the door open with her foot and entered, carrying a tea tray she placed on the small table by the fire. "You're in luck, I baked this morning." The tray held two oaty biscuits, a teapot, and two cups.

"Thank you, Mrs Panmore."

"This is what I wanted to show you," Jack said as his landlady left the room. "It's from before the battle of Alamein." Jack spread out a series of images on the table. I leaned in to get a closer look.

"They don't really look like soldiers," I commented, studying the photograph's rag-tag band of men and women of varying ages.

"That's because they're not, for the most part," Jack said.

"They're artists who had been costume and set designers, painters, and sculptors before the war. They worked in the North African desert to design a fake army unit. Between them, they created a whole film set, complete with phoney tanks, food stores and bogus ammunition silos, all from boxes and palm fronds covered with tarps. Look at this. They even constructed a fake water pipe."

"Why?"

"To confuse the German spotter planes. They disguised the real army's location and created this fake one in another area, so Rommel received false intelligence. When the Allied attack came, it was from a completely different direction than he was expecting.

"That's genius."

"Yeah, look at this. The real army tanks were fitted with wooden shields bolted to their tops to make them look like regular trucks, and artillery was concealed similarly. The German reconnaissance planes were fooled.

"So, it's not just soldiers doing their bit for the war effort; it's people like these coming up with ingenious ideas to defeat the enemy. Much the same as you and the mathematicians and linguists you work alongside. No one sees what you or any of these people are doing, but they make such a huge difference. You are making a huge difference."

My eyes filled with tears.

"Oh no, I didn't mean to make you cry. I was only trying to show you how important what you are doing is," Jack said, shocked.

"Thank you." I blinked away the unwanted tears.

"Tea?"

I nodded.

Jack poured the tea and handed me a cup. "Where would you like to go when I get back?"

"I don't have any leave, but if you could come to Bletchley, we could always go to the cinema," I suggested.

"Let's plan to do that, then." Jack looked at his watch. "We should go to the station so that you don't miss your train," he said, holding out his hand.

I put my cup down and stood, allowing him to pull me close. He smoothed his hands down either side of my face, cupping my cheeks and staring at me.

"I'm trying to memorise every inch of your face," he said before kissing me. The gentle brush of his lips on mine soon deepened, and I opened my mouth to his. The creak of a floorboard outside the room caused us to spring apart.

"We will continue this next time we meet," he whispered.

I nodded, words stuck in my throat, and my heart thumped wildly, exhilarated. I finally found my voice. "And when will that be?"

"I don't know, Mae, but I will leave a message for you with your grandmother when I return."

CHAPTER 7

Bletchley, England
December 24, 1943

Christmas and New Year at Bletchley were somewhat subdued affairs. Everyone was a little blue that we were entering the fifth year of the war with no end in sight, and we were all still somewhat alarmed that the apparent spy among us hadn't been discovered. That meant everyone was under a cloud of suspicion, although no one knew what was missing or how it had been discovered that the decrypts were gone. But the rumour mill had suddenly gone into overdrive. Whispered lunchtime conversations tried to work out who the traitor could be and who would do such a thing and betray England at such a difficult time. Unspoken was the concern that if the Germans discovered what we did at Bletchley, they would be sure to bomb us in their next raid. One thing was certain from the increased security and sudden insistence that all protocols be followed; something was going on. Frustratingly, I had kept my ears and eyes open but had nothing to report.

"I thought last year's Christmas card from Travis announced 'the beginning of the end'," Nancy moaned as we rode the bus back to Liscombe through the grey, wintry countryside, after our afternoon shift on Christmas Eve. "And the end is nowhere in sight."

"Cheer up," I said. "At least we're still fighting. Are you going to the revue on Boxing Day?"

"I suppose," Nancy said. "I could do with a laugh."

Bletchley Park Drama Group's Christmas revue was full of satirical sketches and songs. It almost always included someone standing on a chair with a toothbrush beneath their nose, aping the Führer.

"John has organised a treasure hunt tomorrow morning after church," I said. "We have to attend that."

The bus pulled to a stop, and we descended the steps, wishing the driver and the other passengers a merry Christmas.

Nancy hooked her arm through mine. "Right, time for a stiff gin. Shake me out of this mood."

I slumped down onto one corner of the sofa closest to the fireplace in the drawing room. Sarah, Nancy and I were all on the same daytime shift as Mavis, and they joined me, bringing extra blankets to drape over our legs.

"I'm tired of feeling cold," Nancy moaned. "I swear it was colder in my hut than outside today." She made a nest out of the blankets on the floor before the fire and leaned back against the sofa's edge.

"They're still double-checking everyone going in and out of the Park," Sarah said.

"How do you think they know that decrypts were missing?" Nancy mused. "I mean, the amount of paper that passes through the huts is staggering, and more often than not, after a busy shift, the floor of my hut is littered with discarded teleprinter strips and pages from scribble pads. Perhaps the missing decrypts were simply swept up in the day's rubbish and incinerated?"

"Perhaps, but I think that information that could only have come from the Park must have been discovered by our enemies, meaning that someone is leaking intelligence," Sarah said.

"If the Germans discover that we've cracked Enigma, they will change the settings, and we will be locked out," Nancy said.

"Like we were back in '41," Mavis agreed with a shudder.

"We need to be vigilant. It could be any one of our colleagues." Sarah kicked her feet up on the low coffee table.

"Like one of us?" I teased.

"God, no, we would never betray our country."

"Did you see the two black cars from the Admiralty at the Park today?" Mavis asked, pulling her knitting from a bag.

"No," I said.

"I can tell you now that it's over, but Churchill was here meeting with Travis," Mavis said.

"Goodness, did you speak to him?" Nancy said.

"Only when he thanked me for his tea." Mavis laughed.

"There have been a few intelligence service types here over the last few days," Sarah said with a sidelong glance at me.

"What?" I was puzzled.

When she raised her eyebrows, her insinuation dawned.

"Have you seen Jack?" I asked.

The other girls exchanged glances.

"What?"

"Mae, he was here yesterday," Mavis said.

"Did you talk to him?" I asked, stung that he hadn't sought me out.

Mavis shook her head. "I didn't see him arrive, and he didn't want to be seen because he pulled his hat down low and turned away when he saw me."

"Was he on a motorcycle?"

"No, he arrived by motorcar but was acting strangely."

"Strangely, in what way?"

"He was lurking like he was waiting to meet someone. The telephone rang, and I was momentarily distracted, and when I looked again, he was gone. I glanced outside, and he was hurrying to a black car carrying something, and he climbed in and drove away."

I was speechless. This didn't sound like the Jack that I knew. And why hadn't he come to visit me?

"Are you sure it was him?"

Mavis nodded.

"Did you tell anyone?" Sarah asked.

"I mentioned it to Travis."

"You don't think Jack could have something to do with the missing decrypts?" Nancy asked. "Has he asked you anything, Mae?"

"Like what?" I said, sitting up. All eyes were on me, and no one said anything. The silence dragged on. "No, you can't think that Jack has anything to do with this."

"You have to admit it does look a little suspicious. He never seems to have a reason to be here."

I stood up, gathering my shawl around me. I shook my head. "No, you're wrong. He's not a spy. Sgt Harris told me his security clearance was higher than ours, so I'd say he's here trying to find the traitor." I started towards the door.

"Mae," Nancy called. "You might be right, but just be careful, that's all."

"You could just ask him, I suppose?" Sarah said.

I turned with my hand resting on the doorknob. "Maybe I will."

•••

A few days into the New Year, we had a sudden influx of decrypts to translate, and we were rostered onto double shifts. A group of us who had just finished our first shift of the day before starting the four-to-midnight shift raced to the canteen for a quick bite of dinner only to find that the boiler had broken down and there was no heat and no hot water. I excused myself to return to the hut for my hat, scarf, and gloves.

The blackout blinds were pulled down tightly over the windows, and the only light in the hut was from several desk lamps. The room was empty, although I could hear voices from another room down the hall. I hurried to my desk and found my hat, when I felt a tingling on the back of my neck. I spun around, but there was no one there.

"Hello?"

The only answer was silence, but a malevolent presence was in the room. I shook my head, dismissing the thought as fanciful. That would teach me to see *The Phantom of the Opera* at the cinema with Nancy a few days earlier. Nonetheless, I looped my scarf around my neck, scooped up my gloves, and rushed for the door. My hand touched the handle as I heard a noise behind me. Taking a shaky breath, I looked around again. The corners of the room were shadowy, but no one was there. I bolted out through the door and across the lawn to the canteen.

I joined the back of the dinner queue and calmed my breathing. A hand on my shoulder made me jump, and I emitted a small yelp.

"Sorry, Mae, I didn't mean to startle you," William said.

I pressed my hand to my chest.

He peered at me, concerned. "Are you alright?"

"I'm just being silly."

"That doesn't sound like you," he said. "What's happened?"

I moved forward with the queue and picked up a tray from the stack at the end of the servery. "I just went back to the hut to get my hat and gloves since it's freezing in here, and I swear someone was hiding in the room."

William frowned. "That doesn't sound right. Where would they hide?"

"See, I am being silly. I just had that sensation of being watched and thought I heard something."

"It was probably a mouse or the wind."

With a grim smile, I nodded and accepted the plate of mashed vegetables and gravy.

CHAPTER 8

Bletchley, England
February 14, 1944

The weather worsened over the following weeks, and I sat shivering at my desk one morning despite being wrapped in several jumpers, wool trousers, and a scarf. The single heater in the far corner was next to useless, and I was grateful when the tea trolley rolled through the door at 10 a.m.

"The Germans bombed East Anglia and Kent last night," William said as we gathered.

"What about London?" I asked.

He shrugged. "Not much, minor damage, from what I've heard."

"Thank goodness."

I had returned to my desk and begun translating a new decrypt when the shift supervisor, a humourless woman in her late thirties, called me over.

"You are needed over in the main house," she said, frowning as she peered at me over her glasses.

I grabbed my handbag before rushing outside along the slippery path to the mansion. I wasn't sure what to tell Travis. I had no evidence that someone had been hiding in the hut that night, just an odd feeling, but I couldn't exactly mention that.

The temperature outdoors wasn't a lot different to that of the hut. I entered the front hallway of the mansion, where Mavis was waiting for me. She took my arm and led me into an office.

"I haven't got anything new to relay," I said.

"Mae, it's your grandmother. She's been rushed to hospital, and you have been granted special leave to go to London immediately."

My hand flew to my mouth. "Which hospital?"

"Westminster," Mavis said, reaching for her coat, hanging on a stand behind the door. "I'll walk to the station with you."

We were searched upon leaving the Park and had to hurry along the road to the station, where the next train to Euston had just pulled in. After a quick hug, I was on board.

•••

The hospital had an antiseptic smell that I shall forever associate with death after spending hours outside the room where my mother's body lay following her passing when I was a child. Then, Granny had been summoned from the country and took several hours to get to me, and I was left sitting on a chair that was too big for me, swinging my legs. The nurses were kind, but they were busy. When I peeked through the window into the room, all I could see was a gurney covered with a white sheet. One of my mother's red pumps lay on the floor at the end of the bed. Even in her illness, she insisted on dressing correctly to be taken to the hospital. Now, pushing that memory aside, I approached the stern-looking sister behind the front desk and asked for directions to my grandmother's hospital bed. The hospital was busy with uniformed nurses and doctors in white coats rushing about.

I hurried up the stairs to the first floor and was surprised to hear laughter coming from Granny's room. I slowed, paused outside the door, and immediately recognised the deep male voice.

"...and the horse was spooked and took off across the paddock with me clinging to her mane for dear life. She ran until we reached the beach, where the waves were crashing onto the sand. At which point she stopped suddenly, sending me flying into the shallows."

My grandmother laughed, then coughed and said something I couldn't catch.

"The worst thing was that my father and brother had followed and witnessed the whole thing. When I emerged from the ocean, soaked to the skin, they were sitting on their horses, holding the reins of my traitorous nag, howling with laughter. I have never lived that incident down."

I peered around the doorframe to see Jack perched on the side of Granny's bed, holding her hand. The tiny utilitarian room contained a single bed, a side cabinet with a vase of flowers, a visitor chair, and several pieces of medical equipment.

"It sounds like a beautiful place," Granny said.

"After this dreadful war, you must come and visit," Jack said.

"Wouldn't that be wonderful?" Granny wiped a tear from her cheek and looked past Jack to where I stood. An affectionate smile formed on her face. Jack turned his head.

"Hello," he said, releasing Granny's hand and standing. "You made good time."

"I came as quickly as I could," I said, frowning at him, wondering what on earth he was doing here. "Granny, are you alright?"

"Oh yes, a fuss about nothing," Granny said. "I told them not to bother you." She broke into another bout of coughing.

I quirked an eyebrow at her. "Shall I fetch the doctor?"

"No need," Granny said. "It's just my heart playing up again."

"Miss Webster?" A doctor in a white coat with a stethoscope draped around his neck joined me in the doorway.

I nodded.

Jack leaned over and patted Granny's hand. "I'll go and get a cup of tea for Mae. She looks like she needs one."

"Good idea," Granny said.

I gave him the ghost of a smile and stood aside to let him pass.

The doctor entered the room and checked the chart hanging on the metal frame at the end of Granny's bed.

"How is she?" I asked.

"She is right here," Granny said.

The corners of the doctor's mouth twitched.

"Your grandmother has had a heart attack, a rather major one, I'm afraid, despite the show she is putting on for you," he said.

"Granny," I admonished.

"Pfft," she said.

"There was another bombing raid early this morning, and your grandmother was in her cellar when she was taken ill. One of her neighbours called for an ambulance once the all-clear was given," the doctor said.

"How long will she need to be here?" I asked.

"A few days," he said, turning to leave the room. "She needs to rest." He closed the door.

I took the spot that Jack had vacated on the bed and held her hand.

"How long has Jack been here?" I asked.

"I don't know. He was waiting outside when I came around," Granny said. "And he's been sitting with me ever since. He's a good man, Mae. And I can tell that he cares for you."

"Slow down, Granny. I haven't known him for long."

"Yes, but there's a war on, and you must find happiness amongst the misery. I hate to think of you being alone if anything happens to me."

"Don't talk like that. Nothing is going to happen to you," I said, feeling my throat constrict.

"You can stop that secretarial job anytime, you know that," Granny said. "There is plenty of money, and everything I have goes to you."

I smiled at her. "Granny, I can't tell you about my job because I signed the Official Secrets Act, but just know that what I'm doing is making a difference to how the war will go. I can't give it up."

Granny patted her hand. "I thought as much. I knew the day your mother's brother turned up that he had something special in mind for you." Then she frowned. "You're not putting yourself in any danger, I hope."

"No, Granny, I'm safer than I was driving ambulances around London during the Blitz."

"I'm extremely proud of you, Mae, and your parents would be too."

I swallowed the lump that had taken residence in my throat and blinked the tears from my eyes. When my vision cleared, Granny was snoring softly. I extracted my fingers from hers and laid her hand on the covers, standing just as Jack returned, balancing two teacups. I motioned with my head that we should move into the hallway and closed Granny's door behind me.

"How is she?" Jack asked, handing one of the cups to me. We sat next to each other on a pair of chairs outside the door.

"Sleeping," I said, taking a sip. The tea was hot.

"You look pale, Mae," he said. "I suppose the news of Lady Alice's ill health had been a shock."

"Thank you, it was," I said. There was a moment of silence as I framed my question. "Jack, how is it that you are here? I thought you were abroad again?"

"I've only just returned, and after hearing that the Germans had dropped incendiaries in the Chelsea and Westminster area last night, I went to check on your grandmother this morning. They were loading her into an ambulance when I arrived. So, I followed her to the hospital, sent a message to BP, and waited for you to arrive."

"Thank you."

"Of course, Mae. It was quite a raid last night. I believe they're still putting out the fires at the Palace of Westminster." He reached into his jacket pocket and pulled out a photograph. "Here, this is a belated Christmas present." He handed me an image of the two of us taken by Nancy using Jack's camera at the Astoria on the night we met. Jack had his hand resting on my lower back, and my cheeks were flushed from dancing. We were looking at one another, laughing. My heart clenched; we seemed happy and carefree, but that was then. I didn't know what I knew now. I passed the photo back to him and saw the look of confusion cross his face.

"You were seen at Bletchley last week," I blurted out, hating how clingy I sounded.

Jack let out a heavy sigh. He placed his cup and saucer on the floor beneath his chair, angling his body towards mine. He looked up and down the hall to check that we weren't being overheard. "Mae, like yourself, I have signed a document forbidding me to reveal what I do aside from being a photographer."

My eyes widened.

"You know I'm aware of the concerns at BP over the past few months," he said in a sharp whisper.

My mouth went dry, and I suddenly felt slightly out of my depth. "Is that because you're the cause of them?"

Jack's expression shuttered. "How could you possibly think that?"

"I don't know what to think. You sneak around, turn up unexpectedly, and are only in uniform sometimes. And we have to suspect everyone, even you."

Jack smirked. "So, you like a man in uniform?"

I shook my head to dislodge the image of him that day in St. James's Park. "Stop changing the subject. I hope you don't expect to use me to get information?"

Disappointment flooded Jack's face.

I put my cup on the floor and stood. Jack did the same. I tilted my chin and pulled myself to my full height to look him in the eye. I held out my hand. "Thank you for everything you've done, but I'll take it from here."

"Mae," he began, his expression softening.

"No." I held up my hand to stop him. "I don't trust you. You insert yourself into my life and then turn up unexpectedly with no explanation right when it's revealed that there may be a traitor at the Park. Now, if you'll excuse me, good day."

"There could be another reason I keep finding excuses to see you, Mae," Jack said to my back.

I hesitated with my hand on the doorknob to Granny's room. I spun around. "And what could that be?"

"I'll leave you to work that out." He turned and walked away from me down the corridor.

CHAPTER 9

London, England
February 18, 1944

Under strict doctor's orders to rest and recover, Granny was allowed to return home four days later. Maggie assisted me in converting the ground-floor sitting room into a temporary bedroom, as I figured the stairs would be too much for Granny, for a while at least. And it was only a few steps from the door to the cellar, should there be another air raid.

"Is this all necessary?" Granny grumbled as we helped her into a nightgown and tucked her into bed. "I'm sure I'd be much more comfortable in my bedroom."

"I can bring everything down from your room to make this one look and feel the same," I said, surveying the cosy room. A sliver of wintery sunshine cut across the foot of the bed and a small fire burned in the grate, warming the room. A rack containing a selection of Granny's clothes stood behind the door, and a porcelain wash jug and bowl sat on a side table. The bedside tables and lamps from her room upstairs had been brought down, along with a selection of family photos.

Granny dismissed my suggestion with a wave of her hand.

"Cup of tea?" I suggested.

"Thank you, dear."

Maggie and I slipped from the room. I followed her to the kitchen at the back of the house.

"She's going to be hard work," I said.

Maggie gave me a knowing smile and prepared a tray. When I carried it back into the room, Granny's eyes were closed, and she was resting against the pillows. I set the tray down, poured myself a cup, and settled in an armchair by the large bay window, kicking off my shoes and curling my feet beneath me. The heart attack had aged her almost overnight. I realised with a jolt that the woman who had raised me and been there for me every day of my life was growing old, and one day I would have to do without her. The thought sickened and frightened me. Granny always had an air of invincibility about her. She'd refused to leave London during the Blitz, only to be laid low by her failing health. She'd given so much to many people over the years, me included, but her big heart was now letting her down. How unfair life was.

My thoughts turned to Jack Knight and the conversation in the hospital corridor, as they had done many times over the past few days. Perhaps I was wrong about him. He did seem to know a lot about Bletchley Park, and plenty of senior people knew he was there, Travis included. It wasn't as if just anyone was allowed to wander around; everyone coming and going from there was vetted. He'd as good as told me that he was more than a war photographer, and he'd never given me any reason not to trust him. My stomach knotted as I realised I had let my imagination run away with me and come to the wrong conclusion.

"When are you going back?"

I looked over at the bed. Granny was watching me with her sharp, intelligent eyes.

I jumped up, poured her a cup of tea, and carried it over to the bed, placing it on the bedside table while I put another pillow at her back.

"I'm not, Granny."

"Whyever not?"

"I'm staying here to look after you."

Granny gave an inelegant snort. "I don't think so," she said. "You will drive me mad with your fussing, and besides, there's a war on, and your skills are needed to help defeat the Nazis. My neighbours Elsie and Maeve have offered to look in on me during the day and the hospital gave me the telephone numbers of several private nurses. Bring me my handbag," she instructed.

Unsure if I was insulted or relieved, I retrieved Granny's handbag from a chair and passed it to her. She withdrew a sheet of paper with three women's names and their telephone numbers. "Will you telephone or shall I?" she said.

•••

One of the nurses could start the following day, and by 2 o'clock the next afternoon, I was hovering, feeling surplus to requirements.

"Come and sit with me, dear," Granny said after the nurse had bathed her and settled her back into bed wearing a fresh nightgown and a pink knitted bed jacket.

I perched on the edge of the bed and took her soft, pale hand in mine. She looked small and frail, almost like a child in bed. "I will be fine," she said. "And if I'm not, it won't matter whether you are here or not." She raised her hand to silence me as I started to interrupt.

"I have lived a good life. I want to stay around to see victory for Britain in this damn war, but if God doesn't will it, then who am I to argue. You, Mae, have been the light of my life at the darkest of times and have brought me untold joy, but it's time for you to stop worrying about me and live your life. Maybe even with that dashing New Zealander."

I wiped the tears that tumbled down my cheeks.

"Don't cry, Mae," she said. "Hopefully, I still have a few more years ahead of me. But know this, you will inherit; I have made certain of that. None of the primogeniture nonsense in our family. I want you to go and live your very best life."

I lay my head on her lap and cried like a baby while Granny stroked my hair as she'd done when I was a child.

"There, there," she said. "Now, don't you have packing to do? Take one of my old suitcases with some more warm clothes."

•••

I caught a bus to Euston station around 4 p.m. It was dark already, the air frigid and rain threatening. I hoped that I'd get back to Bletchley before it snowed. I did not fancy being stuck on a train while the workmen dug out the snow from the tracks. As the bus trundled along, the rising and falling wail of an air raid siren sounded. There was a collective audible groan from the passengers. The bus driver pulled over.

"Quickly now, everyone down into the underground," the conductor called, ushering the passengers from her bus.

I grabbed my small suitcase and hurried after my fellow passengers. London's streets were shrouded in darkness. The drone of approaching aircraft could be heard above the siren's wail. People began running towards the sandbagged station entrance. A man stumbled on the kerb and fell in the blacked-out street. Two others hauled him to his feet and helped him towards the shelter.

"This isn't a drill, folks," an air raid warden called with urgency as he welcomed people through the doors of Green Park station. "Quick now, down the stairs." He was a man in his sixties, with a steel helmet held in place by a strap beneath his chin. On the ground at his feet was a stirrup pump and hose, a ceiling pike and a gas rattle.

I hesitated in the doorway, causing the woman behind to stumble right into me.

"Sorry," I said, stepping to one side as the woman scowled and rushed past. I turned back towards the bus, but the driver was nowhere to be seen.

"Er, love, the shelter is this way," the air raid warden said, placing his hand at my elbow.

"I need to get back to my grandmother," I said. "I never should have left her. I don't know how they will get her into the cellar."

The warden, grey hair showing from beneath his helmet and dressed in freshly pressed overalls, ducked his head as the ground shook from the impact of the first incendiary to fall. "That's close. There's no time to go anywhere except down, love."

"I thought the Germans were done with bombing London," I said.

"Apparently not," the man said. "The papers are calling these latest raids the Little Blitz."

The crash of bricks and mortar sounded from the streets nearby and the smell of smoke engulfed us with the next gust of wind. A flare of light lit the darkness as fire took hold somewhere in the city.

I forced myself to turn and run with him into the station, even though all my instincts were screaming at me to go back to Chelsea. I raced down the stairs to the underground platform. A damp, musty smell was mixed with that of too many bodies in an enclosed space, and I gagged before pulling my scarf over my nose. The platform was packed, and people were laying blankets and setting camp for the night behind the thick white line painted along the platform, which allowed space for passengers using the underground. Trains still rumbled through the station, but no one got on or off.

I wasn't planning on staying any longer than necessary and found space against the wall by the stairs and sank onto my suitcase, pulling my coat tightly around me. The dampness seemed to seep from the bricks and into my bones like an evil spirit. Next to me, a young woman clutched her baby to her, rocking and soothing it. She gave me a nervous smile. Electric lights strung up along the platform and across the concave roof dimmed and flickered, casting shadows across the tunnel.

Somewhere further down the platform, a woman began to sing. One by one, voices joined her until it seemed that the whole shelter was singing the popular Vera Lynn song, 'We'll Meet Again.'

A loud boom sounded as a bomb fell nearby, and little pieces of plaster showered down like confetti covering us with grey-white dust. The singing stopped, and several children began to cry. The platform was strangely silent as those sheltering waited for the next bomb to fall. My mind drifted to the incident at Balham station earlier in the war, where a German bomb fell, ultimately killing sixty-eight people using the station as an air raid shelter.

"I pray they're not bombing Buckingham Palace," said an elderly woman near me.

I glanced at those around me; their faces were etched with a mix of fear and determination as they clung to one another, some whispering prayers for survival.

After a while, I realised that no more trains had come through the station, and I hoped it didn't mean the lines were damaged.

I cursed my stupidity that I'd let Granny persuade me to leave. Why hadn't I waited until the morning? Maggie and the nurse would have a devil of a job getting her down into the cellar, especially when there didn't seem to have been very long between the air raid siren starting and the first bombs falling. Why had the air defences not kicked in earlier? I felt a squeeze of dread clench my heart. What if the Nazis had developed an aircraft to avoid our defence systems?

My mind drifted to Jack, and I wondered where he was. Was he still in London, or had he left after I had been rude to him at the hospital? I supposed I'd never know. I'd been a fool and let my imagination run away with me. Of course, he wasn't a spy – what had I been thinking? He was too good, kind and generous to be anything like that. And I had sent him away and would never get the chance to apologise. Tears pricked at my eyes, and I closed them lest they overflowed.

I was jolted awake a while later when the head of the young mother bumped against my shoulder. People around me were dozing; some were managing to sleep rather well if the snoring from further along was any indication. I glanced at my watch. It was 10 p.m. Somehow, I too had dozed off. Outside, the air raid siren had fallen silent, yet no one appeared to have left the shelter. There was a low murmur of conversation from those not sleeping. I stood, careful not to disturb the young woman beside me, who was somehow asleep with her baby in her arms. As I stretched my legs and back, the air raid warden from earlier caught my eye from his seat at the bottom of the stairs and raised his tea mug in invitation. Leaving my suitcase, I stepped over a prone form wrapped in a blanket and joined him.

"If you don't mind sharing," he said, pouring a hot cup of tea from a thermos at his feet and handing the cup to me.

"Thank you," I said, wrapping my frozen hands around it. Despite wearing gloves, my fingertips were numb with the cold. I took a sip and felt the hot liquid spread from my throat to my stomach.

"Ah, that's good." I gave him a grateful smile.

"My missus says there's little that a good cuppa can't fix."

"She's probably right," I agreed. "Why is no one leaving? Hasn't the all-clear sounded?"

"It has, but we've been told to stay put as they're expecting a second wave later tonight."

I groaned.

"Somewhere you need to be?"

I nodded. "Two places. My job and back to my grandmother. She had a heart attack after last week's bombing raid, and I've just settled her back home with a nurse. I fear they won't have been able to get to the cellar in time."

"I'm sure she'll be fine. From what I hear, the bombs were dropped on targets near the river in Battersea, Clapham, and the Docks."

I felt bile rise. "Granny is in Chelsea, right by the river," I whispered.

The man reached out and squeezed my hand. "Where do you work?" he said.

I knew he was changing the subject, and I let him.

"I work for the War Office outside of London."

He nodded. "Good lass, we're all doing our bit."

"Yes."

"Do you have a sweetheart?"

My mind drifted to Jack's handsome face, how his deep blue eyes crinkled when he laughed, and I felt a small smile form on my lips.

"It's complicated."

"Love shouldn't be complicated," the old man said. "Love just is."

"Except I accused him of something awful after he'd been nothing but good to me."

"Ah, well, if he's worth his salt, he won't let that put him off."

I smiled. "I hope you're right." I handed him back the now empty cup. "Thank you. I needed that. The tea and the chat."

"You're welcome, lass." He stood and put his hat back on. "Time for my rounds."

I returned to sit on my bag and drifted in and out of sleep until the wail of the air raid siren pierced the night once more, slowly becoming louder and louder, a haunting soundtrack to the cacophony of airplanes and explosions above ground. I sat up straight and glanced at my watch – 3 a.m. The warden was right. They were back.

•••

At dawn, we emerged bleary-eyed and grimy into the Green Park station ticket hall. The air was heavy with the stench of burning. Men and women in uniform were hurrying by outside along with many civilians, mainly women, and children. Rubble and debris from buildings that had once stood proud littered the streets. People were already hard at work clearing the road to allow emergency vehicles to pass. Despite the weariness and trauma in the faces of those around me, there was an air of determination not be cowed by this latest attack. People greeted one another with tired smiles and slaps on the back. A mobile tea canteen had been set up outside the station. I watched astonished, as a dishevelled nurse was served tea by a well-dressed woman in hat and gloves. Everyone was doing their bit, no matter their class. I rushed to find a telephone booth and put a call through to Liscombe Park. Sarah answered.

"Sarah, it's me. I got caught up in an air raid in London and spent the night in the underground."

"Mae, are you okay?"

"Yeah, but I need to go back and check on Granny. Can you ask Mavis to let Mrs Winter know? All being well, I'll be back later today," I said.

"Be safe." Sarah rang off.

I took a deep breath and picked up my suitcase. A bus was leaving from in front of the station. I climbed aboard, paid the fare, and took a seat. Along the road the Ritz Hotel stood proud and majestic, thankfully unharmed in last night's incursion, but other buildings had not been so fortunate. A cloud of dust and debris hung in the windless sky as we wound our way among the debris through the streets. The nonstop wail of fire engines echoed throughout the city. When we reached the Kings Road, the bus diverted from its usual route, so I pulled the cord to stop. I began to walk the remaining three blocks to Granny's road, lugging my bag. The day was beginning as any other. Shopkeepers opened their shutters and swept the footpaths in front of their stores while calling greetings to one another, refusing to be defeated by the fear and devastation being wrought around them. A sense of relief flooded through me at the normality of it all, but when I turned the corner, I was greeted with a sight that turned my blood cold. The road was littered with emergency vehicles. A fire engine had a stream of water aimed at the smouldering remains of a detached house halfway along the block, and two ambulances were parked in front with their rear doors open. I crossed to the opposite side and picked my way among the debris scattered across the road. The stench of burning wood and fabric hung in the cold air.

Two more sizeable white stucco houses had also been reduced to rubble, and rescue workers were digging through the pile of brick and plaster, calling for survivors. The streetscape looked like a gaping mouth with several teeth missing. Many of the houses still standing had windows blown in, leaving curtains and blackout blinds flapping and catching against the jagged glass in the window frames.

As I got nearer the river end of the road, I broke into a run. Smoke rose and twisted into the morning sky from what remained of my childhood home. The front of the imposing white brick Georgian house had been torn away by the force of a bomb blast. The second and third floors had collapsed inwards and downwards on each other. The rear and side walls were still standing, with a chimney stack wobbling precariously on one side. Where the pretty front garden had once stood behind a stone wall was now a massive pile of brick, shattered glass, torn fabric, and broken furniture. A policeman caught my arm as I rushed forward.

"Hold on there, it's not safe," he said.

A guttural, anguished cry sounded, and it was a moment before I realised that the noise was coming from me. I looked up into the face of the policeman. "Is she, are they...?" I couldn't finish the sentence.

RACHEL

1989

CHAPTER 10

Vienna, Austria
September 10, 1989

Rachel collapsed onto the bed in her hotel room, closed her eyes, and stretched her arms above her head. It was bliss to stretch out fully after being confined to an economy-class airline seat for the better part of the past twenty-six hours. She felt as though the top of her head was detached from the rest of her body, and she caught herself just as she drifted off to sleep. Forcing herself upright, she consulted her watch. Almost midday; if she slept now, she wouldn't sleep tonight, and she needed to get into the correct time zone as soon as possible.

Her room in the tourist hotel was typically compact and bland, with a double bed, a small table and chair beneath the only window, and a tiny ensuite bathroom. But it was clean, comfortable, and centrally located. After a shower and change of clothes, she selected the smaller of her two cameras, a Leica. She threw the camera bag strap over her head and across her body, the camera resting against her right hip. After a glance in the mirror, she headed out into the sunshine.

Vienna had been shaped into an artistic, intellectual, and cultural centre over the years by its famous residents such as Mozart, Beethoven, Gustav Klimt and Freud. The skyline was dominated by the spire of St. Stephen's Cathedral, and the city was renowned for the unique and stunning architecture of its palaces, music venues, and elegant buildings covering many different eras and styles. In other words, the city was a photographer's dream.

Rachel wandered past the wide entrance to Belvedere Palace. The last time Rachel was in Vienna, she'd taken a tour of the massive baroque structure to view the world's most extensive Gustav Klimt collection, including the famous painting, *The Kiss*. But today, she was headed to the old town.

She made her way along the edge of the park into the heart of the historic quarter and towards the imposing Vienna State Opera building, with its massive copper dome and giant stone arches which housed large bronze statues. She shot two rolls of film, exploring the area's stunning architecture.

Returning to the hotel mid-afternoon, Rachel ordered a strong coffee, purchased a couple of English newspapers from the shop in the foyer, and settled down on the hotel's terrace to read and catch up with world events whilst she'd been travelling.

An article on page three caught her attention.

'Hungary Rumoured to Reopen Border'

'Officials in Hungary appear to have overcome concerns regarding the reaction of Moscow and are considering the permanent opening of its border with Austria, according to unofficial reports.'

The article described how events had escalated since the Pan-European Picnic of August 19, which was organised as a peaceful demonstration by Austrians and Hungarians gathering in friendship at the border between the two countries. The organisers, however, hadn't counted on the arrival of hundreds of East Germans. East Germans were allowed to apply for visas to holiday in Hungary but not to travel further west. However, several hundred had burst through the border gate at Sopron. Fortunately, the border guards decided not to shoot, and the Austrians openly welcomed the immigrants.

Rachel set the paper down and stared out of her hotel window. Perhaps things were changing in Europe. She hardly dared believe it. Her plan to get to the border was timely; she just needed to execute it. She drained her coffee and raced down to the hotel lobby.

"Do you have any maps of Austria?" she asked the man wearing a business suit seated behind the information counter.

The concierge handed her a folded brochure.

"*Danke.*"

Rachel returned to her room and spread the map out on her bed. Sopron, the site of the Pan-European Picnic crossing, was fifty kilometres from Vienna; she would need to hire a car, or maybe there was someone from the paper in Vienna with whom she could catch a lift. They were sure to be covering this. She shook her head; her presence would only get back to her boss that she was poking around. Rachel was still annoyed he'd sided with Daniel and forbade her from covering the rapidly changing events in Communist Eastern Europe. Then again, she was still on holiday. Who cared what he thought? She didn't know where she was going, and she spoke very little German, so a driver would be helpful. Grabbing her bag, she left her hotel room and skipped down the stairs and through the spacious foyer to the street.

The paper's foreign desk shared a small office with several other publications. It was three streets from Rachel's hotel, on the second floor of a six-storey office building.

Rachel climbed the stairs and knocked on a door displaying the name plaques of several media companies. The door swung open, and the waft of cigarette smoke and the clatter of keyboard keys greeted her. A wall-mounted television played in one corner, but only two of the eight desks were occupied.

A blond-haired man peered over his wire-rimmed glasses at her. "*Ja?*"

"Hi, I'm Rachel Talbot from the London office of *The London News*," she said. "Do you speak English?"

"Good afternoon, Rachel from the London office," he said, grinning at her.

A woman seated at a desk in the far corner beneath the window stubbed out her cigarette and blew out a plume of smoke. "Rachel, what brings you here?"

Rachel crossed the room. "Hi, Rosa, I'm on a stopover on my journey back from New Zealand." She perched on one corner of her desk.

Rosa fluffed her shoulder-length blond waves and looked Rachel up and down. "You'll want to go for a drink, I presume?"

"Sure," Rachel said. "But I was also wondering if anyone is covering the rumoured Hungary border opening? I'm looking to catch a ride to Sopron."

Rosa cocked her head to one side. "I thought you were on holiday."

Rachel shrugged.

"When is a photojournalist ever really on holiday?" a voice behind her said.

Rachel spun around as the door opened, and the one person she'd hoped to avoid walked in. Her mouth dropped open.

"Hello, Rachel," he said. "You haven't been returning my calls."

"What are you doing here, Daniel?" Rachel's heart sank and she glared at the man who she blamed for sabotaging her career.

"There's your ride to the border," Rosa said with a smirk.

Rachel closed her eyes for a moment and groaned inwardly. "Of course it is."

"Now, what was that I heard about a drink?" Daniel said, crossing the office with several long strides. "You can tell me all about New Zealand."

Rachel pushed herself off the desk. "Not for me. Jet lag – I've just flown for twenty-four hours."

Daniel ran a hand through thick dark hair and frowned. "Where are you staying?"

"The Nova."

"Pick you up at 8 a.m."

CHAPTER 11

Vienna, Austria
September 10, 1989

Rachel woke with a start at 3 a.m., discombobulated, before remembering that she was in a hotel in Vienna. While she had gotten used to waking up in different countries, those first few seconds before she was fully conscious always left her adrift and untethered. She glanced at the bedside clock and groaned before rolling over, willing herself back to sleep. Half an hour later, she gave up and headed for the shower.

Rachel was dressed and sitting on the window seat with the curtains open, staring out into the darkness by 4 a.m. Her rumbling stomach reminded her that it was hours since she'd eaten, so she grabbed the room service menu and spoke to a sleepy-sounding hotel employee. While waiting for her breakfast, she cleaned and sorted her camera equipment, ensuring plenty of film was packed for the day ahead.

Trust bloody Daniel to be in Vienna. Their unexpected meeting yesterday felt like a Band-Aid being ripped off; short, sharp pain, but she was surprised to find that any lingering hurt was gone, and she was feeling somewhat ambivalent about spending the day with him. Go figure; perhaps the month in New Zealand had done her some good after all?

Rachel devoured her breakfast of coffee and fruit. She watched the sun rise over the city, the buildings and other landmarks slowly coming into focus like a latent image revealing itself in the developer solution.

When Daniel pulled up in his rented Volkswagen just before 8 a.m., she was waiting on the hotel's front steps.

"I thought I might have to wake you," he said, easing out from behind the wheel and greeting her with a double-cheek kiss. He was slightly shorter than her, with messy shoulder-length brown hair and a smile that produced a deep dimple on his right cheek. The effect was charming, but Rachel steeled her resolve and refused to allow herself to fall under his spell again.

"I've been awake since three," she said. "The joys of crossing multiple time zones."

Daniel relieved her of her camera bag and placed it on the backseat before opening the front passenger door.

"No Gilbert?" Rachel said, peering into the car, looking for the man who'd replaced her on Daniel's assignment to Eastern Europe at the end of July.

Daniel shook his head. "We only need one photographer today."

"I'm not officially working, Daniel," Rachel said, slipping her small backpack off her shoulder and climbing into the car. The sweet, buttery aroma of warm pastries engulfed her, and she saw a thermos of coffee, two cups, and a paper bag on a tray between the seats. Rachel's idea of a perfect breakfast – you had to give it to him, he was good.

"I know," he said before closing her door. "Still only need one photographer."

Rachel waited for him to get back behind the wheel. "Why are you here?"

Daniel started the engine, and they pulled away from the hotel. "Things are changing behind the Iron Curtain," he said. "All these little events, the Tiananmen Square protests, the Polish government negotiating with Solidarity after all this time, the Pan-European Picnic, and the Leipzig protests, are all leading to something." His eyes shone with a passion that reminded Rachel of why she'd fallen for him in the first place. "We could be witnessing the beginning of the end of Communism."

"That's a big statement," Rachel said. "We could also be about to witness the biggest crackdown on the general population since Stalin's purges of the 1930s."

Daniel shrugged. "Perhaps, but at the very least, I believe the Soviet Union could be about to lose some of its satellite states."

"I'm not sure that the Soviets will let them go that easily when it comes to it," Rachel said.

"So, you think there will be a violent reaction from Moscow if Hungary opens its border? The fence already has a hole," Daniel reminded her. "And they've done nothing about it since May."

"Yes, but the last time the Hungarians went against the Soviet's wishes, they were invaded. It was a brutal, bloody put-down."

"That was over thirty years ago, Rach."

"The memory of it seems to have been a pretty good deterrent. That, and the spectre of nuclear war."

"Well, I, for one, feel the winds of change in the air," Daniel said.

"We will see," Rachel said. "Whatever the Hungarians have planned, you can be sure that Soviet Intelligence will already know."

Daniel nodded. "That, I agree with."

The drive took just over an hour via the A4 Autobahn. They chatted easily enough, Daniel having the sense to avoid anything too personal, and soon they were driving through the village of Nickelsdorf and followed the signs for the border crossing.

"This has been nice. I've missed you," Daniel said as they stopped.

"Daniel, cut the crap. You sabotaged my career by taking Gilbert instead of me to Hungary."

"You're being a bit dramatic. It wasn't safe, and you heard what happened to those two women reporters in East Berlin."

"That was different, and you know it."

"After Hungary, my assignment was to look into the accusations by opposition groups of blatant election rigging in the May elections in East Germany. Don't you think they would want that kept quiet? I couldn't put you in that kind of danger."

"Regardless, you convinced Jones that it wasn't safe anywhere behind the Iron Curtain for any of the female journalists. It's hard enough in a male-dominated industry without you making it worse."

"You're here now," Daniel said.

"No thanks to you."

"Actually, thanks to me for driving you," Daniel said.

Rachel scowled at the laughter in his tone.

"Rach, I'm sorry," he said as she jumped from the car. "I couldn't stand it if something happened to you and thought I was doing the right thing."

"Yeah, and I'm sure Gilbert does too, thanks to his potentially award-winning front-page images."

Rachel grabbed her camera from the backseat and stormed off.

"Right, still mad then," Daniel muttered as he followed at a safe distance.

Rachel noticed that Daniel kept out of her way for the rest of the morning, instead speaking with people milling around on the Austrian side of the border. There was a small trickle of people passing through the crossing, all with legitimate travel visas, according to those they spoke to. Rachel was asked not to photograph at the border gate. Instead, she walked several hundred metres along the edge of the tall barbed wire perimeter fence until she could see across no man's land to the first watch tower on the Hungarian side. She took several images of the building with the barbed wire sharp in the foreground before dropping onto her stomach and taking several more, looking up through the wire. It wasn't until she saw movement in the tower that she realised that a border guard was waving to her. She zoomed in and captured his smiling face before returning his wave.

As the day wore on, the crowd at the border grew. A sense of anticipation hung in the air.

"Hey, I just learned something interesting," Daniel said, jogging back to join Rachel at the car, where she was labelling the canister of film she'd taken. "There is a clause in a 1969 treaty between Hungary and East Germany that says that Hungary must force East German citizens back to their homeland. It's this clause that the Hungarians are rumoured to be considering suspending. Apparently, there are thousands of East Germans either in or on their way to Hungary."

"Oh," Rachel sat forward, wide-eyed.

"Are you hungry? Do you want something to eat? Breakfast was hours ago."

"Yeah," Rachel said, and her stomach growled on cue.

They drove the short distance back into the town, found a small hotel restaurant with wooden tables and chairs, and ordered schnitzel and beer. A mixture of tables of workers and groups of families were dining. MTV was playing at low volume on a small TV on the wall in one corner, but as they carried their drinks to a table beneath the window, the volume rose on the TV. Silence descended on the café as all eyes turned to the television. The announcer, speaking German, cut to an interview with a politician wearing a suit and tie. There were gasps before everyone started talking at once.

"What just happened?" Rachel said.

Daniel shrugged. "My German is not that good." He turned to a man at the neighbouring table. "What did he say?" he asked, pointing at the TV.

"That was Horn, the Hungarian Foreign Minister, just announcing his government's intention to open the border with Austria," the man said in accented English.

"When?"

The man shrugged and turned back to his food.

Rachel and Daniel ate quickly. As they were paying, Daniel flashed his charming smile at the barmaid and asked to use the telephone in the bar, where he put a call through to the paper's Vienna office.

"Do you realise that you use that smile to get people to do whatever you want?" Rachel asked when he hung up.

"I do not," Daniel said.

Rachel dismissed his protest with a wave of her hand. "What did they say?"

"They were watching too. Rosa wants us to stay and report on any movement," he said. "Apparently, Jones is delighted that we're on the case."

Rachel scoffed. "Jones will be delighted that you're on the case. Does he even know that I'm here?" Daniel didn't reply. "Thought so."

The restaurant owner, a robust woman in her fifties, overheard their conversation. "We have rooms," she said. "Do you want a double?"

"Two singles, please," Rachel replied before Daniel could.

The woman led them up a set of stairs at the back of the building, along a gloomy corridor, and handed over the keys to the two rooms at the end. "You share the bathroom," she said before returning downstairs.

Rachel unlocked her door to find a small room with a single bed made with crisp white sheets and a blue floral eiderdown folded across the foot. A wicker armchair by the window overlooked the car park at the rear of the building. A second door led to a tiny bathroom with a shower, toilet and basin. Rachel sat down on the bed and opened her camera bag, checking how much film she had left on the roll in her camera. There was a tap on the door, and Daniel eased it open.

"Just like mine," he said. "Have you got a change of clothes?"

"Of course, I've learned to have my passport, toothbrush, and fresh underwear with me at all times in this job." Her little backpack contained everything she needed for a night away.

"We could have shared a room, just like the old days." He leaned against the door frame, studying her.

Rachel looked away. "It's better this way," she said.

Daniel sighed. "So, are you ready to head back to the border?"

"Yeah, you don't think they will have opened it already?"

"No, but something will happen soon. How long are you in Austria?"

"My flight to London is tomorrow afternoon," Rachel said.

"This was a long stopover in a city where you know no one."

Rachel closed her camera bag.

"Ah, I see," Daniel said. "What were you planning to do?"

"I was going to go to Sopron, where the East Germans crossed the border last month."

"And?"

"I don't know. Get some photos. See what was so dangerous that I couldn't witness it first-hand."

"Rach…" Daniel began.

"Come on, let's go." She pushed past him into the hall and waited while he returned to his room to gather his belongings and lock the door.

This time, they had to park further away from the border crossing. The crowd had swelled, and they could see several television camera crews setting up. While Daniel spoke with other journalists, Rachel pulled out her camera and shot the border gate and buildings in the twilight. She wandered along the road away from the main gate and looked across the empty land between the two border posts at the queue of cars at the Hungarian border. It was strangely silent on that side. She changed the lens on her camera and took several long-distance shots.

The sun went down, and large spotlights on either side showed more people, cars, and buses arriving at the Hungarian border. The excitement in the air was palpable.

Just before midnight, a hush descended on the Austrian crowd as the headlights of a convoy of fast-moving vehicles cut through the queue and approached the gate on the Hungarian side. Rachel looked through her viewfinder to see uniformed men piling out of the cars and marching into the booth. The young border guards stood to attention. Rachel lowered her camera and turned as footsteps sounded, running towards her.

"There you are," Daniel said, taking her arm. "Come on, let's get a bit nearer to the car. Something's happening on the other side. If they start shooting, you need to get out of here."

Rachel stopped walking and shook her arm free. "And what will you be doing?"

They glared at each other as a shout went up, followed by cheering, whooping and the tooting of car horns. They looked to see the frontier barrier go up on the Hungarian side and the first in a fleet of battered East German cars and Hungarian taxis drive through. A group of people began walking across into Austria carrying their worldly belongings. As the immigrants got closer, a wave of noise approached the Austrian border gate. Rachel rushed forward and began photographing the spectacle. The cheering got even louder as the first cars reached the Austrian checkpoint. The barrier arm was raised and stayed up. Once on Austrian soil, many cars immediately pulled over, and people leapt out. Rachel captured images of families and old friends reuniting, couples embracing, unable to believe they were free, champagne bottles having their corks popped, and people dancing, crying and singing. Rachel photographed Daniel interviewing many of the new arrivals.

Over three hundred cars had crossed no man's land within fifteen minutes, and the road surrounding the Austrian border resembled a disorganised car park. At one end, the Red Cross set up a stand and ushered those on foot towards buses. Rachel photographed a young German woman leaning out of her car window crying and repeating *danke, danke* over and over to the aid worker handing out envelopes.

"Have you spoken to the aid workers? What's in the envelopes?" Rachel asked.

"Enough cash for petrol to get to West Germany if they wish," Daniel said.

"The Austrians must have waived any visa requirements," Rachel said. "No one is checking passports."

They watched as a young East German man dressed in faded denim leaned out of his rusted Trabant and waved his passport at border officials, who gave it a cursory glance before waving him on through.

"Do you notice anything?" Rachel said.

"What exactly?" Daniel asked.

"The vast majority of East Germans are young and male."

"Extraordinary," Daniel said. "Isn't it always the youth who force change? The people I've spoken to tonight were so disillusioned with their lives that they've walked away to start again."

"How brave."

"There you go, Rach. It's what you wanted. You've just witnessed history being made."

CHAPTER 12

London, England
September 11, 1989

Rachel's flight from Vienna to London took just over two and a half hours, and her thoughts drifted from the events she witnessed and photographed at the Austrian border to Daniel and finally to her grandmother. Rachel was still digesting Mae's story. Now with some distance, it did seem a fantastical tale. Her little old grandmother, linked with World War II's best kept secret. Yet, when she'd read her grandfather Jack's final letter, she believed her. She needed some help getting to the bottom of this, and she knew just the person to confide in. Her best friend Juliette, a television news reporter, was a public school, Oxford educated, well-connected woman who would help Rachel navigate what to do next. From her bag, she pulled open the copy of Gordon Welchman's book on Bletchley Park, that her grandmother had lent her, and continued reading.

Rachel caught the underground into Central London. It was a warm day, and the carriages were stuffy. By the time she'd dragged her suitcase along Lower Thames Street to the paper's headquarters, her hair was stuck to the back of her neck. The lift took her to a windowless basement, housing the photography lab. A man with a receding hairline and sharp pointy nose looked up as she pushed through the double doors.

"Rachel, how was New Zealand?" he said.

"Hi, Ernie," she said. "It was good, thanks."

She dumped her suitcase by the door and approached Ernie's desk, pulling the camera bag's strap off her shoulder.

"I was at the Austrian-Hungarian border last night," she said, setting the bag down and unzipping it.

"Were you now," Ernie said, holding up his hand. "Don't tell me, you need a rush on the proofs."

"You're a mind-reader," Rachel said, grinning at him. She lifted out six film canisters and sorted them. "Can you do these two first, please?"

Ernie nodded.

"I want to get them up to Jones for the late edition," Rachel said.

"You're confident," Ernie said. "He won't change the late edition for just anything."

"You'll see," Rachel said.

"Does he even know that you were in Austria?"

Rachel shook her head.

"These had better be good then, he's gonna be as mad as hell that you went against his instructions."

"He can't be mad; I was technically still on holiday."

Ernie raised his eyebrows. "Whatever, it's your funeral. Now shut up and let me work."

•••

"Ah, the traveller finally decides to return." Jones's voice boomed out across the newsroom from the doorway of his corner office, as Rachel strode across the floor clutching the contact sheets and enlargements of what she considered her four best photos from the night before. The open plan office contained around fifty workstations, with four glass-fronted management offices at the far end.

Jones's shirt buttons strained against his wide girth, and several days' growth covered his jowls. He peered over his glasses at her as she got closer.

"Wait until you see the gift I got you," she said, giving him her most charming smile.

"Better be good," he grumbled.

Rachel followed him back into his office. Jones rounded his desk, reached for a packet of cigarettes, popped one out, and lit it. He inhaled. "Wotcha got?"

Rachel laid the four images facing him on top of the paper-strewn desk. The first image was the close-up of the Hungarian border guard in the tower waving to her, and the second showed a young man leaning out of the passenger window of a battered taxi, his face alight with joy and his fist raised in the air. The third image captured the trail of vehicles and people crossing no man's land towards the Austrian gate. But she left what she considered her best photo until last. A family – the mother with a toddler on her hip and a carry-all on a long strap over her shoulder, followed by the father lugging a battered suitcase in one hand, dragging a small boy alongside him with the other. The mother's eyes shone with hope and expectation, whereas the man's face carried a look of terror as he turned to look back over his shoulder, as though he expected a bullet in his back at any moment. In the background, the watchtowers on either side of the Hungarian border gate framed the image like imposing grey sentinels. Jones put his cigarette down in an overflowing ashtray, blowing a plume of smoke as he reached for the photo. He carried it to the window to study it.

Rachel waited. After a few seconds, Jones rushed past her to the door and yelled, "Hold the front page." The tapping of keyboards ceased for a moment before starting up again. A tall, willowy woman with dark hair pulled into a severe bun hurried into the office. She stood with her hands on her hips.

"What is it?" she said.

"Felicity, we need to replace the photo alongside Daniel's article on the front page of the late edition," Jones said, turning back to the desk. "And we have a new image for the morning edition, and is there room on Sunday's page five for a photo montage? Actually, make room on page five. She's got a complete photo story here." He gesticulated to the photos on his desk before snatching the proof sheets from Rachel's hand.

Felicity leaned over the desk and looked at the photos. She nodded at Rachel. "These are good. But I thought Gilbert was with Daniel in Austria?"

Rachel shook her head. "No, I was. Right place, right time, and I wasn't in any danger." She couldn't help but add the last bit.

Jones grunted and lowered himself into his chair. He grabbed a magnifying glass and studied the images before peering at her again.

"Talbot, these are good. Especially that one of the family, it encapsulates everything, the fear and the hope these people have for a better future." He grabbed a pen and put crosses against eight images on the proof sheet. "Get me enlargements of these. Well done."

Rachel beamed. Compliments from Jones were scarce, so she allowed herself to bask in this one for a moment before realising that this was an opportunity.

"Does that mean you'll reconsider sending me to West Berlin?" she said. "Things are moving, and I think that's the place to be, especially ahead of the GDR's fortieth-anniversary celebrations. I hear that special visas are being arranged for Western journalists to cover the event in East Berlin, and there'll be safety in numbers."

Jones looked at her long and hard. "You don't take no for an answer, do you?"

Rachel shook her head and took her gaze back to her photos to remind Jones of what she could do.

He picked up his still-burning cigarette, took a puff, and stubbed it out.

He nodded once. "Now, get out of here before I change my mind."

Rachel managed to contain the whoop she felt building inside her and fled from his office.

"Oh, and work with Features on the layout of page five. Make your images tell the story of what went on last night," Jones called before reaching for his ringing phone.

"I don't know how you managed to be there, but well done," Felicity said, following her.

Rachel spent the rest of the afternoon between the photo lab and the features desk working out the best images to use. It wasn't her first full-page feature, but she wanted this one to be perfect. She hoped this would prove to Jones, and Daniel, that she wasn't just another girl with a camera, but a proper photojournalist.

CHAPTER 13

London, England
September 11, 1989

It was early evening when Rachel unlocked the door of her flat in Earls Court. Judging by the garlic and tomato aromas wafting from the kitchen, one of her flatmates was cooking spaghetti Bolognese, again. The flat was spread across the first and ground floors of a yellow-brick terraced house near the tube station.

"Hey, welcome back," Tony called from the kitchen as she passed on her way up the stairs.

"Hi," Rachel called. "Be down in a minute."

Surprisingly, her room was just as she'd left it, and it looked like no one had slept in her bed while she'd been away. Unusual, really, for a predominantly antipodean flat, where there were always extra people staying for a night or two here and there between trips into Europe and Africa. She dumped her suitcase and camera on the bed and kicked off her shoes. She skipped back downstairs just as the front door opened and a petite blonde woman entered, followed by a large man carrying several heavy bags.

"Arrgh," the woman cried. "You're back." She threw her arms around Rachel. "I've missed you."

"Hi, Juliette," Rachel said, returning the hug. "It's good to be back. You're later than usual."

"Yeah, we were editing a piece for the morning show in Sydney, and they wanted me to voiceover the footage. I'll be even later tomorrow night as they also want me to cross live."

"That's exciting."

Behind Juliette's pretty face was a sharp intellect and quick wit that often rendered her contemporaries speechless. She was the foreign correspondent for an Australian news channel, which to many seemed like a dream job, but as Rachel knew, they worked long hours on a shoestring budget, with Juliette doing more than just being a glamorous mouthpiece. She wrote copy, scripted all their segments, did her makeup and wardrobe, interviews, travel arrangements, and editing, together with the man behind her – cameraman Josh.

"Rach." Josh deposited the bags and high-fived Rachel.

Josh was the ideal colleague for Juliette as not only was he a talented cameraman, but his bulk had also gotten the pair out of several tricky situations when Juliette's words couldn't. Rachel, always thought they would make the perfect couple, apart from the fact that Josh, in her grandmother's outdated words, batted for the other team and preferred his partners to be male, preferably Spanish or Italian.

"Right, I'll leave you two to catch up," Josh said, his hand on the doorknob. "I'll pick you up bright and early, Jules."

"K."

Juliette hooked her arm through Rachel's, and they walked into the lounge together. The room contained two battered sofas, a mismatched armchair, a scratched wooden coffee table, and an old television set in one corner.

Juliette sniffed. "Tony's taken over the kitchen again," she said, wrinkling her nose. "Shall we go to the pub, and you can tell me all about your trip?"

Rachel nodded. "Great idea. Let me get my bag."

Ten minutes later, the two friends were seated at the Crown, the local pub on a busy corner near their flat, Juliette with a glass of white wine, Rachel with a half of cider.

"So, no one stayed in my room while I was away?" Rachel asked.

"Freddo's mum did, actually, for about a week," Juliette said. "She changed the sheets, remade the bed, and left you a box of chocolates, but I think the boys ate those." She laughed. "Anyway, how was NZ? How was the wedding? Are you jetlagged?"

"All good. It went well," Rachel said. "And no, I'm not jetlagged because I spent a few days in Vienna on the way back."

"Really?" Juliette said. "Did you…?"

"Yip," Rachel said, digging into her bag and pulling out the proof sheets. "I got a ride to the Hungarian border with none other than Daniel yesterday."

"*Whaaat?*"

Rachel held up her hand. "Look at these. I was there last night when the Hungarians opened the border, and there were hundreds of East Germans among those crossing. It was unreal."

Juliette studied the photos. "Rach, these are fantastic. Look at the expressions on people's faces, they can't believe they're free."

"And I got the front-page photo in the evening edition. Look." Rachel passed the newspaper, folded in half, across the table.

"Oh, Rach."

"And that's not all," Rachel said. "I've got tomorrow morning's lead photo and a feature page on Sunday."

Juliette squealed as she leapt out of her seat and rounded the table, pulling Rachel into a hug. Several older men seated at the bar turned on their stools to see what the racket was about. Realising it was just two excited women, they returned to their pints and football conversations.

"It's about time they realised how good you are. I'm so pleased for you."

"Thank you, now tell me what's been happening here," Rachel said, a little embarrassed by the scene they'd caused.

Juliette sat down again. "Just the usual. Josh and I've been to Paris, Edinburgh and Dublin while you've been gone. Oh, and to West Berlin a couple of times. I tell you, Rach, it's an odd feeling flying into a city surrounded by a Communist country on all sides."

"Were you there when the Leipzig protests happened?" Rachel said.

"No, we mistimed that one, unfortunately."

"Jones has said that I can go to West Berlin and try to get a visa into the East for the GDR fortieth anniversary," Rachel said.

"I thought he was dead set against female journalists going behind the Iron Curtain. What's suddenly changed?"

"I'd like to think my photos convinced him, but I think it's the fact that there will be hundreds of journalists covering the celebrations. Safety in numbers and all that."

"Do you know when you're planning to go? 'Cos Josh and I will be there next week. We're heading to Poland first to cover the election, and then we'll be in West Berlin. We should stay at the same hotel."

Rachel nodded. "Good idea."

"Now, tell me about Daniel. Have you forgiven him?"

"Yes, but I'm over him."

Juliette pulled a surprised face.

"Seriously, I am. I didn't realise it until Daniel turned out to be my ride to the Austrian border. I like him, but I could suddenly see through his charm. He could have screwed up my career. Although, I do think he genuinely thought he was doing me a favour and protecting me, rather than just being a chauvinist."

"Good for you."

Rachel took a sip of her drink. "There's something else I'd like to discuss with you."

Juliette frowned. "That sounds serious."

"It is," Rachel said. "Well, it's a bit strange. My grandmother, Mae, told me this crazy story while I was home. Actually, we were watching footage from the Leipzig demonstration on the TV news when she recognised a face in the crowd and told me that it was the man responsible for my grandfather's murder in 1944."

"Your grandfather was murdered?"

"I know; it was news to me too."

"Who is he, this guy in the crowd?"

"A Stasi officer."

"How could she tell after all that time?" Juliette asked.

"It's quite a story. My grandmother worked at a place called Bletchley Park during the war. Have you heard of it?"

Juliette nodded. "It was a top-secret code-breaking facility, and no one talked about it until recently. Everyone who worked there signed the Official Secrets Act, which they took very seriously. What did your grandmother do?"

"She was a translator. She was fluent in Italian and German, among other languages."

"So, how did she meet a Stasi officer at Bletchley Park?"

"Apparently, he worked for the Foreign Office in the 1940s and spent time at Bletchley Park working in the same building as her."

"How did a British civil servant become a Stasi officer?" Juliette asked.

"According to a letter my grandfather wrote before his death, this guy was a double agent. My grandfather, Jack, was a war photographer. He made a name for himself in North Africa, and when he was injured, instead of returning to New Zealand, he worked for the British government. He had photographic proof that this guy handed secrets to the Soviets, but he was killed before he could show anyone."

"That's quite a story," Juliette said.

Rachel nodded. "I was hoping you could help me find out what happened to the Stasi officer. I have no reason to doubt my grandmother. She's really sharp and has the photos and a letter from my grandfather that supports what she says. I have copies."

Juliette took a sip of her drink and looked thoughtful. "We need to look into the war records. You know there were several high-profile double agents discovered after the war. Have you ever heard of the Cambridge Five?"

Rachel shook her head.

"They were a group who'd been at Cambridge together and were members of the Communist Party when they were students before the war. They held various high-profile positions in Britain during the war, and several defected after. Did your grandmother give you his name?"

"William Brown," Rachel said.

"You should start at the Public Records Office and go from there. Many of the government's World War II archives are at Kew, but we'd need to know what to request to go there."

Rachel nodded. "I'll go to the Records Office tomorrow."

"I was at Oxford with a guy who joined MI6. He owes me a favour. I could arrange for you to talk to him," Juliette said.

"That would be great, thanks," Rachel said.

"Of course, I love a good mystery, and this one has all the feels. Love, spies and murder."

CHAPTER 14

London, England
September 12, 1989

Rachel was still smiling when she pushed through the revolving doors of the newspaper office with the morning's edition in her hands, her photo of the East German family front and centre. She hadn't realised it at the time, but Daniel had pounced and interviewed them, getting some great backstory and soundbites alongside her image. There was no denying that they did make a good team.

She made a coffee in the small kitchenette on her floor and sat at her desk. Another copy of the newspaper was resting on the blotter with a note congratulating her. She put it to one side and picked up the roster of events that needed photographers to cover that day, and felt her heart sink. As a rookie her work assignments were still determined by her superiors. One day she hoped to have greater control over the stories she chased, but for now, she was tied to the whims of others. She ran her eye down the list of what was left to cover and tried not to sigh too despondently. It was always a comedown returning from a foreign trip. Her eyes rested on the fourth item. A minor royal was opening an exhibition at the British Museum, which wasn't far from the Public Records Office in Chancery Lane. She could photograph the exhibition opening and visit the records on her way back to the office.

•••

The British Museum is a vast monolith taking up a whole city block. At 10:45 a.m. Rachel used her press pass at the entrance to gain access to the exhibition, and joined several other journalists and photographers waiting just outside the exhibit space to catch a glimpse of the royal when she arrived. A short time later, there was a flurry of activity at a side door as plainclothes police officers cleared the foyer and kept an eagle eye on the press contingent.

"Shame it ain't Lady Di," one of the veteran journalists muttered.

"I don't think the princess would waste her time on something as mundane as a fossil," a magazine photographer said.

"Especially as she's married to one," another joked.

When the elderly duchess arrived a short time later, she hurried by clad in a pastel blue suit, ignoring the journalists' questions and the photographers' calls to look in their direction. All Rachel got was a side shot of her head. Many of the photographers left, moving on to their subsequent assignments, but Rachel decided to wait until the duchess left again to try for a more publishable photo.

She studied the list of the museum's greatest hits on a billboard by the door. The Rosetta Stone jumped out. 'In a metaphorical sense, the Rosetta Stone has become the calling card for the science of codebreaking,' the description announced.

Codebreaking hadn't been far from Rachel's mind since her grandmother had shared the story of her clandestine work during World War II. Learning about the poster child for codebreaking seemed like an excellent way to kill time until the duchess left.

She consulted the museum floorplan and followed the directions to Room 4, where the Rosetta Stone and the bust of Ramesses II were displayed.

The Rosetta Stone, housed in a secure glass case in the centre of the gallery, was just a broken piece from what must have been a much larger slab. Somewhat underwhelmed, Rachel read the information card and finally understood its significance. The stone was covered in writing in three different styles; Egyptian hieroglyphs, Demotic, and Ancient Greek. The ability to read and write the first two had been lost long ago, but scholars could still read Ancient Greek, which was used to crack the other two passages and enable academics to decipher other hieroglyphs.

Rachel imagined the excitement of the French scholar who cracked the code and realised her grandmother must have encountered similar euphoria.

Deep in thought, Rachel wandered further into the galleries and was soon lost.

She glanced at her watch; forty-five minutes had passed. Surely the duchess would be ready to leave soon, so she started making her way out following the exit signs when she came to a roped-off doorway. The sounds of convivial chatter reached her ears, and she peered through. The duchess was standing sipping tea from a pretty china cup and talking to two equally pastel-clad ladies, completely ignoring the priceless object from the exhibit she'd just opened. Rachel raised her camera and snapped two quick photos before a security guard spotted her and hurried over, his hand raised. Rachel rushed towards the front entrance, slipping into the crowds in the Great Court and out onto the street.

Safely away, she walked twenty minutes through the busy streets of Holborn to the Public Records Office on Chancery Lane, housed in a beautiful, sandstone listed building. A woman at the counter greeted her with polite efficiency.

Rachel showed her press credentials. "I'm researching a man

who worked with my grandmother during World War II, possibly at Bletchley Park," she said.

The woman nodded and directed her down the corridor to a second desk, where she repeated her request to a middle-aged man in a sombre grey suit.

"The Government Code and Cipher School records are still sealed for the most part," he said.

"The what?"

"The institution that worked out of Bletchley Park, which later became GCHQ, the Government Communications Headquarters," he explained.

"I don't need any information on what he did there, just when he was there and what became of him," she said.

The man nodded and stood. "Follow me."

Rachel walked down several flights of stairs and along a long corridor before the man turned into a room filled with floor-to-ceiling shelving racks. Each rack had a reference number on one end, and the shelves were filled with file boxes and books.

"What was your man's name?"

"William Brown," she said.

After several minutes of checking a card index file, he led her further into the archive, pulling on dangling light cords to illuminate their way. The ceiling was low, and there was little air movement. Rachel fought down the first tendrils of claustrophobia. The man turned down one of the rows, stopping halfway along, and pulled out a file box. He carried it to a table at the end of the row.

Rachel held her breath as he opened it. It contained a single manila folder with the word 'Classified' stamped diagonally across it in red ink. He turned the cover of the cardboard file, but it was empty. Rachel let out her breath.

"How disappointing," she said. "I thought all documents were publicly available after thirty years."

"Most, not all."

"How do I get access to a classified file?"

"You don't," the man said, closing the box and brushing past her to return it to its space.

"Surely that can't be it?" she said.

"I suppose you could file an access request," he said as they walked back to the entrance. "But they rarely get approved."

"Can I at least try?"

"If you wish," he said with a sigh.

Rachel filled out the form before returning to her office, where a message was waiting for her from Juliette.

'Come to the Coal Hole on the Strand at 5:30 to meet the friend I told you about.'

•••

Juliette was seated at a table in the window giggling at something her companion said when Rachel entered the pub just after 5:30 p.m. The pub, situated on the site of the original coal cellar of the nearby Savoy Hotel, was dominated by a massive wooden bar. Rachel crossed the checkerboard floor tiles to join her friend.

"Rachel, this is Monty, a friend of mine from Oxford days," she said. "He's an expert on the Allied alliances during the Second World War."

Monty stood and offered Rachel his hand. He was in his twenties, with fair hair parted on one side and flopping across his forehead. "Good to meet you, Rachel."

"I got you a cider," Juliette said, indicating the third glass on the table.

"Thanks." Rachel slid onto the chair opposite Monty, and he sat down again.

"Juliette has just been telling me your grandmother's story," he said. "It sounds a little far-fetched."

Rachel bristled and shot a glance at Juliette. "Perhaps," she said, "but I have some evidence to back it up." She reached into her bag and withdrew a copy of the last letter her grandmother received from her grandfather, containing three photographs.

She laid the black and white photographs down in front of Monty. In the first photo, one man passed a document to the other. Neither man's face was visible, nor was either man in uniform, but their clothing and the vehicle in the shot indicated the time period. In the next photo, the first man was turning to walk away, his face still obscured, but the second was looking over his shoulder almost toward the camera, his expression fearful. The third photo showed the first man strolling along the street with his hat tilted low across his forehead and hands in his pockets. "These were taken in Paris in November of 1944. You can see the French writing on the awning of the building behind the men. The man on the left is William Brown, a British Civil Servant who worked for the War Office and at Bletchley Park during the war. According to my grandfather's letter, the second man is Yuri Montan, a Russian intelligence officer."

Monty's face revealed nothing as he studied the photos. "And what do you want me to do with these?"

"I'd like to know what happened to William Brown after the war."

Juliette went to add something but thought better of it.

"My grandmother explained that they broke the German Enigma code at Bletchley Park using various methods, including a Tunny machine. She was a linguist and translated the German cyphers that were broken."

"You do realise that your grandmother is in danger of being tried under the Official Secrets Act for revealing anything about Bletchley," Monty said.

Rachel glared at him. "Stop being a bully; you know that cat is long out of the bag. FW Winterbottom and Gordon Welchman's books saw to that. Everyone knows the British had a secret code-cracking facility during the war. But honestly, this is the first and only time my grandmother has ever mentioned this. She would have taken the secret to her grave if she hadn't seen this man on the TV news."

Monty inclined his head as he acknowledged her words.

"Does that mean we weren't openly sharing the intelligence gathered by Enigma with our allies during the war?" Juliette asked.

Monty looked surprised at the question. "Yes and no. Churchill didn't trust Stalin."

"Even when the Soviets joined our side to defeat Hitler?"

"You must remember the damage caused by the Molotov-Ribbentrop Pact that the Russians and Germans entered into in 1939. It almost cost Britain and Western Europe the war, so that wasn't pushed aside easily in the minds of the British."

"It's a wonder we became allies when you consider that."

"Yes, Stalin's long list of horrific acts was tactfully overlooked, but they were certainly not forgotten. Many historians believe that Churchill foresaw a time post-war that they might again not be our allies."

"And he was proven correct," Rachel said.

Monty nodded. "So, you can see why something as strategic as the Ultra secret would be kept from the Russians."

Rachel frowned. "The Ultra secret?"

"That's what the intelligence coming out of Bletchley Park was called. Once they broke the German's unbreakable Enigma, the Allies had access to the German troop movements, strategies, locations of U-boats, and all sorts of information that proved invaluable to the war effort. It's believed that the work at Bletchley Park reduced the war by at least two years."

"And saved countless lives," Juliette added.

Monty nodded.

"Strange that no one really knows about it," Rachel said.

"As I said, those who worked there took signing the Official Secrets Act very seriously," Monty said.

"So, this William Brown could have put all of that at risk if he was passing decrypted messages to the Soviets – they'd have to wonder where they were coming from," Juliette said.

"There were instances where intel was shared, but with a false indication of the source," Monty said.

"So that it wouldn't come back to the British having broken Enigma," Rachel said.

"That's right."

"Monty, all I'm asking is, can you at least find out what became of William Brown after the war? Did he defect? Is it even possible that it's him that my grandmother saw in East Germany?" Rachel said.

Monty glanced at Juliette, who gave him a winning smile.

"Okay, leave it with me. I do not promise anything, but I'll see what I can do," he said.

CHAPTER 15

West Berlin, Federal Republic of Germany (FRG)
September 18, 1989

"We've now left West German air space, and we're over the German Democratic Republic," Bernard said, glancing at his watch before peering out of the aeroplane window. Bernard Cowley was one of the paper's senior political editors, and Rachel's job was to provide the photos to go alongside his stories. He fitted the old-school reporter stereotype in more ways than one – mid-forties, heavy drinker, heavy smoker, divorced, with a physique that was beginning to show the signs of years of hard living. Bernard treated Rachel like an intern and was always surprised when she pushed back. He wouldn't have been her first choice to cover the anniversary with, but she knew that she had no further leeway with Jones, so she grabbed the opportunity. At least they weren't staying at the same hotel. Jones had been more than happy for her to stay at the cheaper three-star Berlin Hotel on Stauffenbergstrasse, where Juliette and Josh were based.

Rachel's excitement was tinged with nerves as she recalled

Juliette saying it was an odd feeling flying into a city surrounded by a Communist country on all sides.

"Is there ever an issue?"

"As long as our pilots stay in the designated air corridor, we're fine."

"I'm amazed that the Soviets haven't taken over the whole of Berlin, given that the city is surrounded by the GDR," Rachel said.

"It's a hangover from the Second World War. Berlin has become the front of the Cold War," Bernard said. "The Soviets know they will risk a nuclear war if they threaten that somewhat tenuous co-existence. There's been the odd skirmish over the years, but peace has managed to reign, so far, at least."

Rachel shuddered.

The traffic crawled through the centre of West Berlin as the taxi carried Rachel and Bernard from West Berlin's Tegel airport, recently renamed Otto Lilienthalto, in honour of a German aviation pioneer, to the office where Bernard based himself in Berlin.

Rachel stared out the window as they drove along the wide boulevards. Berlin was not dissimilar to many other old, elegant European capital cities that she'd visited, except it was divided in two. The closer to the centre they drove, the busier the streets of West Berlin became, the pavements thronged with shoppers. Bars and cafés were humming, with music pumping out and neon signs advertising all manner of items.

"Ooh, look, there's the TV Tower." Rachel pointed to the iconic city landmark rising high into the sky from the East of the city. Atop the shaft of the tower was a large steel sphere above which an enormous antenna pierced the grey sky.

"Yes, that was Walter Ulbricht's attempt in the late sixties to display the GDR's advancement and technological superiority," Bernard said. "Did you know that some call it the Pope's Revenge because, during the build, Ulbricht was enforcing the secular nature of the country and had the churches in East Germany remove their crosses, but when the sun shines on the TV Tower, the shadow it throws is in the shape of a cross?"

"How ironic."

When the traffic stopped at an intersection near Bernauerstrasse, Rachel's gaze was drawn left. She gasped as she had her first glimpse of the Wall. Across the end of the crossroad stretched a tall concrete block structure topped with a rolled concrete pipe. The Wall joined an apartment building with all its windows bricked up. A pair of soldiers patrolled from a tall watchtower behind the Wall. One was looking through the sights of a rifle, the other with binoculars held to his eyes.

"It cuts right through the middle of the city," she said, an uneasy sensation settling on her.

Bernard grunted. "Right along the border of the old Soviet section."

"I knew that but seeing it…."

"Makes it real."

Rachel nodded.

"As I said earlier, it's the front line of the Cold War, and it's not going away in our lifetime."

"I can't believe they'd build something that ugly to keep people out."

"Oh, missy, it wasn't built to keep people out. It was built to keep people in."

"What do you mean?"

"After the war, the city was divided into occupation zones. The Soviets, Americans, British and French all had a piece, the spoils of war, you see. The Allies were terrified of the spread of Communism and held firm to their parts of the city."

"Even though Communist Germany surrounds it?"

Bernard's jowls bounced as he nodded. "But by 1961, the differences in opportunities and lifestyle offered by the West proved irresistible to many in the East. The GDR was losing thousands of its most talented people, defecting for a better life in the West."

"So, the Wall was erected to keep them in rather than keep people out."

Bernard nodded. "It's well known that the wives of Western diplomats regularly cross into East Germany to shop for wooden toys or Dresden china and attend the opera. Anyone from the West can cross into East Berlin with a daily visa, as long as you haven't annoyed anyone. If you end up on one of the Stasi's infamous lists, you can't and wouldn't want to go East."

Rachel returned her gaze to the Wall. "I thought it would be topped with coils of barbed wire."

"It was when I first started coming to Berlin," Bernard said. "But they've replaced it with the cement tubing because that apparently makes it harder for escapees to obtain any grip, which gives the soldiers more time to catch or shoot them."

Rachel gulped.

Bernard paid the driver, and they climbed from the car in front of a drab mid-century office block.

Rachel followed Bernard along the street to the corner and stopped. In the centre of the intersection ahead of them stood a small white wooden hut fortified by a wall of sandbags. Armed soldiers wearing the uniform of the United States Army milled about.

"Welcome to Checkpoint Charlie," Bernard said.

Rachel looked past the hut to the empty road beyond. Several hundred metres away past a break in the Wall stood a low single-level building surrounded by empty lanes for cars.

"Checkpoint Charlie is the crossing in the American sector," Bernard said. "Many people think it's a nickname, but it's actually named from the military phonetic alphabet after the Alpha and Bravo border crossings in the British zone."

"Why are we here?" Rachel asked.

Bernard pointed to a building adjacent to Checkpoint Charlie. Rachel followed his outstretched arm. A sign in the first-floor window of the six-storey red-brick building read 'Press Point Berlin.'

"My home away from home," Bernard declared. "Because Checkpoint Charlie has become the crossing point between the West and the East designated for foreigners, all visiting dignitaries pass through here, so I base myself at the Press Point to catch the action. I've interviewed Reagan, Thatcher and Mitterrand here over the years."

With a nervous glance over her shoulder, Rachel followed him into the building and lugged her bags up the stairs. They entered into a noisy, smoke-filled, open-plan room strewn with a haphazard mixture of desks and chairs. Most desks were occupied, with reporters either talking on telephones, typing on the keyboards of IBM computers with large square screens and blinking cursors, or smoking and chatting with the person at the next desk. A noisy poker game was underway in one corner.

"This is our base in Berlin," Bernard explained, raising his voice above the din. "All the Western media drop in and out of here."

"Bernard," an American-accented voice called. "Over here."

They crossed the room to join an obese man of a similar age to Bernard, who stood and exchanged a back-slapping hug with him. He peered over Bernard's shoulder at Rachel.

"Who is this?"

"Rachel Talbot, meet Randy Taylor from the NYJ."

Randy released Bernard and took Rachel's hand, raising it to his lips. "*Enchanté.*"

"Hello." Rachel resisted the urge to snatch her hand back from the creepy American.

"I didn't know you were bringing your secretary," he said to Bernard.

"He didn't. I'm a photographer," Rachel said.

"Why don't you set us up on this desk?" Bernard instructed, pointing at an empty place next to Randy.

Rachel bristled. "You can. I'm going to sit over there. Away from the smoke."

She turned and stalked across the room to an empty chair near the entrance. She set her heavy bags down and slumped down.

"Is Randy being a chauvinist pig again?" a woman seated along from her asked. She too had an American accent, and her bouncy strawberry blonde blow wave formed a halo around her head.

"How did you guess?"

"I'm Shelley," she said, smiling at Rachel. "Welcome to the pig pen."

"Hi, I'm Rachel. Where are you from?"

"Chicago, and before you ask, freelance, so I don't have to suck up to any of these bozos." She drew a cigarette from a pack on the floor beside her chair and lit it. She sat back, crossing her long legs, and exhaled a curl of smoke before offering one to Rachel.

Rachel shook her head and laughed. "Unfortunately, I'm working with Bernard Cowley, so I don't have a choice."

"You always have a choice, my dear. Now tell me, what are you here to photograph?"

"We're doing some prep for the GDR celebrations next month."

Shelley nodded. "I think we all are." She gazed around the room. "Everyone hears stories, but no one will go on record. I'm worried. Things feel very tense right now."

"Agreed," Rachel said.

Raucous laughter filtered from across the room. Bernard had his feet up on the desk, a lit cigarette between his lips.

"I'm going to go check into my hotel and drop my gear off," Rachel said. "I don't think he'll notice that I've gone."

"Be back in an hour, and I'll take you for a drink so that you can meet some of the other journos. They're not all as bad as bozo one and bozo two, over there," Shelley said with a flick of her head in Bernard and Randy's direction.

•••

An hour later, having determined that her windowless hotel bathroom was the perfect place for her portable darkroom, Rachel returned to the Press Point to find Shelley waiting for her.

"Let's go."

Rachel pulled her gloves back on and followed Shelley to a Bavarian Beer Hall in the next street. Bernard and Randy were already seated at a table in the dimly lit bar. From the array of languages and accents, Rachel gleaned that this was a popular hangout for foreigners to the city.

Rachel and Shelley ordered a glass of wine each and joined their counterparts.

"Ah, there you are," Bernard said, peering along the table at Rachel. "I wondered where you'd got to."

"Just checked in and took some photos of the Wall."

Bernard nodded. "Randy was telling me about Kohl's recent pronouncements regarding the reunification of Germany. We won't see that in our lifetime."

"I wouldn't be so sure," Shelley said. "Things are changing."

"The British and French politicians or the public of those countries wouldn't welcome a strong unified Germany again," Randy argued. "Especially after it has already been the aggressor twice this century, resulting in countless unnecessary deaths."

"Yes, but I think you'll find that the Americans are all for it."

"The Americans are only for things that have advantages for the Americans; present company excepted," Bernard said. "A democratic Germany with a leadership they can control, and a weakened Soviet Union would most certainly be advantageous for America."

"I think that is a little simplistic," Shelley said. "When Reagan said 'tear down this Wall, Mr Gorbachev' during his visit two years ago, he was hoping to reduce the threat of nuclear war, and that's advantageous to us all."

"But you don't disagree that the Americans will still seek to retain control in Germany, economically, if not politically?"

Shelley shrugged. "I don't know about that. That may have been true a few years ago, but times are different; you only have to look at the outcome of the Polish election a few days ago to see that things are evolving."

"The Soviets will never allow the election of a non-Communist Party Prime Minister to stand," Randy said, lighting another cigarette and taking a heavy draw on it.

"It won't last," Bernard agreed with his usual air of authority and superior knowledge. "I still can't believe the election wasn't rigged as usual."

"Shelley is right. Times are changing. A year ago, the Solidarity Party would never have even been allowed to contest the election, let alone win," Rachel said.

Bernard shook his head. "Gorbachev is seen as weak by many party hardliners, and he will be out by the end of the year, and then we'll see a crackdown."

"It might be too late by then," Rachel said. "It's not just Poland, look at what's happening in Hungary and Czechoslovakia."

"Idealists." Bernard dismissed the idea with a wave of his hand.

"But what about the reports of the steady stream of East Germans turning up at the West German embassy in Prague and refusing to leave?"

"They will be sent back," Randy said. "Or worse."

"You must remember that the GDR has a leader like Honecker who is extremely resistant to change. He will no more allow Gorbachev's *perestroika* on his watch than fly to the moon," Bernard huffed, before waving his hand at a passing waitress and indicating that another round of drinks was in order.

"We'll see," Shelley said. "I feel that the winds of change are gathering force."

CHAPTER 16

East Berlin, German Democratic Republic (GDR)
September 22, 1989

Rachel stood surveying the imposing flat-topped section of the Berlin Wall which stretched in either direction, as she waited for Juliette and Josh to collect her. In this part of the city, it was a double wall with a wide strip of deserted land in between. In the centre, the Brandenburg Gate, the triumphal arch celebrating Germanic victories of a bygone era, was isolated in no man's land. The winged victory riding the Quadriga atop the structure was dulled and chipped from years of neglect. Bomb damage from the Allied attacks in the closing days of World War II, was still visible even from a distance. Cross-shaped, rusted metal tank traps littered no man's land, along with coils of barbed wire. Armed guards patrolled the wall, their steely gazes a constant reminder of the city's fractured existence. Rachel ignored their stares and shot a roll of film capturing the sequestered historic monument from various angles. Berlin was a city divided and nowhere was it more apparent to her than here where the contrast between the two halves was stark; the vibrant lights and bustling streets of

West Berlin stood in opposition to the grey, austere landscape of East Berlin beyond the formidable barrier of the Wall.

A light rain misted as Juliette's taxi pulled up. She leaned out the window. "Get some good photos?"

"Yeah," Rachel said. "I was just thinking how odd it is that Germany has the Winged Victory on one of its iconic monuments, as does London. It's on the Queen Victoria Memorial outside Buckingham Palace."

"So the goddess of victory smiles on both sides?"

"And she has throughout all the conflicts of the twentieth century," Rachel said.

"Don't ya just love irony?"

"Thank you for organising this," Rachel said, climbing in. "Bernard somehow "forgot" to include my name on his visa application."

"No problem," Juliette said. "Many bigger networks have both photographers and cameramen on their teams, so adding you didn't seem unusual. Besides, didn't he get turned down?"

"Yup." Rachel grinned. "He's got a pass for the fortieth-anniversary celebrations, but it seems he's annoyed someone, so they won't let him over beforehand to prepare. He's flying back to London today, instead."

The taxi deposited them at Checkpoint Charlie. Josh adjusted the strap of a heavy bag on his shoulder and pushed his sunglasses into his dark curly hair. In his right hand, he carried a collapsed camera tripod.

"All set, Rach?"

"I think so."

She was finally doing it; after all the months of trying to get assigned to a story behind the Iron Curtain, here she was. She took a long, steadying breath and tried to capture the moment, the feeling.

Her smile was wiped away by the tread of heavy boots marching along the 'death strip' inside no man's land, and Rachel suppressed the urge to shiver as they approached the barrier. Across on the East Berlin side, she noted the large number of armed soldiers patrolling the border. They looked imposing in their belted khaki uniforms, with black leather gloves and flat-top peaked caps with a green band.

"Did you know that there are 302 watchtowers along the Wall, which are manned continuously by armed guards with shoot-to-kill orders for anyone trying to cross illegally?" Josh said.

"Really?" Rachel said. "That must take a lot of personnel."

"Apparently, at least 10,000 men."

They approached the Allied checkpoint, watching as the single horizontal pole was regularly raised and lowered to allow vehicles to pass through. A large white sign next to the checkpoint announced, "You are leaving the American sector" in English, French, German and Russian Cyrillic.

The American soldier at the checkpoint gave their passports and press cards a cursory glance before opening the barrier with a cheery, 'you folks have a nice day'. Rachel followed Juliette and Josh across a fifty-metre strip of concrete and kept close to them as they approached the second checkpoint on the East German side. This barrier was more significant, with lanes for traffic and pedestrians. A serious young border guard held his hand out for their papers and inspected them, one after the other, glancing up to check their faces against the photos.

"Purpose of visit?"

"We're preparing for our coverage of the fortieth-anniversary celebrations," Juliette said, giving him a winning smile.

The guard didn't react and continued to study their papers.

"This way," he said, handing back the passports. "We inspect the cameras."

They entered a low, squat building in the centre of the checkpoint complex and opened their camera bags, removing the cameras and lenses and placing them on a long wooden table in the centre of the room.

"Step back," a new guard ordered.

They shuffled back from the table and watched while the equipment was inspected and set aside.

The guard clicked his heels and nodded. "Proceed," he said, waving his hand over the cameras.

Rachel and Josh repacked their cameras and followed the guard from the room.

Rachel resisted the urge to look over her shoulder as they walked away from the checkpoint and into the East Berlin.

Alongside the walkway, four lanes of cars waited to pass from East to West among a series of concrete barriers and chicanes. Soldiers patrolled a wide barren strip of land immediately behind the Wall with black dogs straining on their leads. Cross-shaped anti-vehicle obstacles littered the space, and a second wall, this one mesh, was topped with barbed wire. Tall streetlights loomed overhead as they exited the border area and joined an empty street. This time, Rachel shivered.

"Come on," Juliette took her arm. "Looks like our ride is here."

A man in a tan trench coat was leaning against a battered white car. "Welcome to the GDR," he said with a French accent. He shook Josh's hand and kissed Juliette on both cheeks.

"This is Rachel," Juliette said. "She's with a London newspaper. Rach, this is Pierre, who works for AP."

"*Bonjour,* Rachel," Pierre said with a smile. "Jump in. Let's get out of here."

Pierre drove them through the city streets to the AP Office several blocks away from the Wall. They passed utilitarian multi-storey apartment buildings, and Rachel couldn't help but notice that the cars parked along the roads were all the same boxy-shaped Trabants she'd photographed crossing the Hungarian border. What did surprise her was how they spanned every hue of the rainbow, adding a splash of colour to an otherwise drab grey palette. Rachel stared out the window as Juliette and Pierre chatted, noting the differences between the city's two sides. In the West, people were dressed in vibrant colours of many styles and moved about at a leisurely pace. But in the East, most pedestrians wore plain clothing and hurried along the footpaths with their heads down.

"It's very grey," she said. "West Berlin is so colourful and vibrant, by contrast." This part of the city reminded her of an old sepia photograph, its subject matter interesting, but its façade faded and tired.

"Is this your first time in East Berlin?" Pierre asked, glancing at her in the rear-view mirror.

Rachel nodded. "Yeah."

"Well, it's an interesting place," he said. "Life here is very disciplined and controlled by the State. But small cracks are appearing. The youth watch West German TV even though they are not supposed to. They see the consumer goods available in the West, and luxuries the likes of which they've never seen. But when they turn the television off, they're back to buying a limited range of goods and being plagued by shortages. They listen to RiAS, Radio in the American Sector, but they cannot buy Western music. Their choices of career and housing are limited, and they want more out of life than they're currently being offered. The Stasi seem to have ears everywhere, so there is no opportunity for debate. That situation can only exist for so long, and it feels like something is brewing."

They pulled up in front of a plain four-storey building and climbed from the car. An unmarked car pulled in behind them with two uniformed police officers in the front seat. They did not get out.

Pierre caught the look of alarm that crossed Rachel's face. He took her arm and led her towards the building's main entrance.

"Don't worry about them, they're our minders for the day. All Western press is followed to ensure they don't stray into areas not approved by the Party. And I suspect our apartments are bugged and telephone calls monitored."

"Wow," Rachel said. "I had heard that happened, but I didn't believe it. Do they have enough officers to babysit all visitors?"

"The Stasi are one of the biggest employers in the GDR," Josh said, following her through the door.

"Let's grab a coffee before we head out," Pierre said.

"I nearly forgot," Juliette said, reaching into an inside pocket on her jacket and pulling out a small packet. "Fresh beans for my favourite Frenchman."

"Oh," Pierre said, grasping the packet and her hands. "You are truly an angel – I ran out yesterday."

Following weak office coffee, they slipped out a back entrance and walked through a carpark to a side street where another Trabant was waiting, this one pale blue.

"I've arranged for you to interview several people, student activists, Juliette, but voice recording only, no cameras. They are understandably wary," Pierre explained as he drove east through the city and into the suburb of Marzahn-Hellersdorf. "They've been burned before."

Pierre drove them along a wide boulevard lined with what must have once been elegant mansions, but the stone was blackened and in desperate need of maintenance and repair. Rachel stared as it dawned on her that no one was smiling or laughing. Those who were walking, kept their eyes averted from the other pedestrians and hurried about their business. They turned into narrower streets before stopping outside a row of rundown shops. Rachel was itching to photograph everything she was seeing, but did as Pierre had asked and left her camera in its case. The whole area had a derelict, unkempt feel, as though the people who lived there didn't care or probably couldn't afford to care. Suspicion hung in the air, a palpable tension that made it seem that even the most mundane exchanges could be fraught with hidden meaning. Pierre led them through an unoccupied barber shop and into a dingy back room. Two well-worn acoustic guitars were propped up against one wall, along with an ancient-looking keyboard.

Three men in their early twenties, dressed in faded denim jeans and matching jackets, were seated around a table smoking. Their hair was longer and more stylish than most of the East Germans Rachel had observed while they'd been driving. They stopped talking and eyed the newcomers.

"*Guten tag.* These are the reporters I was telling you about," Pierre said, approaching and shaking hands with each of the men.

"No photos."

Rachel studied the good-looking guy who had spoken. His fair hair was cut short at the back but left in long layers on the top and sides. His English was accented, and his manner established himself as the spokesperson for the group as he unfolded himself from his chair to return Pierre's handshake. "You can call me Hans, and this is Walt and Micha." His eyes slid to Josh and Rachel, where he held Rachel's gaze for a moment, a half-smile playing around his lips. She blushed under the scrutiny.

"Okay, Hans," Juliette agreed. "I'm Juliette, and this is Josh, my cameraman and Rachel, a photojournalist."

He stepped out from the table and shook their hands. "Josh. Rachel. Please have a seat."

The other two men remained where they were and observed the reporters with suspicion.

"Will you report what I tell you, or will it be censored?" Hans said.

"It depends on what you tell me. I won't censor it, but I can't give you any guarantees that my bosses won't," Juliette said. "However, I will do my best to tell your stories."

A series of wordless but meaningful glances crossed between the men before it was clear that a silent agreement had been reached. Rachel and Josh sat down on a bench along one wall while Juliette and Pierre joined the men at the table. Juliette offered them a pack of English cigarettes each, which they pounced on with nodded thanks.

"Can I ask why you've agreed to talk to us?" Juliette began.

"We're fed up with being controlled by fear. We all watch West German TV, even though it's illegal, and we know that only a few miles away, other Germans are living much better lives than us. Some of our friends have escaped to the West through Hungary and Czechoslovakia. But if we all abandon this country, who will instigate change? The economy is stuffed and Honecker refuses to do anything about it or even admit there is a problem," he continued.

"And who is going to speak for the ones the Stasi has detained?" Walt spoke for the first time, in heavily accented English.

"The problem we face is that the regime spies on us all. They recruit our friends and neighbours, even family members, through fear and coercion to pass information about our activities," Hans said.

"I've heard the statistic that one in nine East Germans is a Stasi informant," Juliette said.

Hans shrugged. "That wouldn't surprise me. They seem to know if you make a comment construed as being politically at odds with the state. If you oppose them, then your study choices are blocked and career options limited," Hans added. "Walt, tell them about your brother."

Walt, whose thin face bore a long scar across his cheek from nose to ear, leaned forward.

"My brother was an electrician; he could get anything to work. We had radios and televisions tuned into West German stations before anyone else we knew. Our parents were nervous and forbade us from telling even our closest friends in case someone found out. But hearing the music from RiAS and watching West German television shows made my brother realise we were being denied. He became very disillusioned, eventually coming up with a plan to escape.

"First, he and some others dug a tunnel under the Wall. It took months of work in the evenings, but someone betrayed them. Two of his friends were arrested, but he was held up at work and was late getting to the tunnel that day and managed to avoid capture."

"What happened to his friends?"

Walt shook his head. "No one knows."

There was silence in the room for a long moment.

"Anyway, my brother was undeterred. His next scheme involved swimming across the Spree. He monitored the timing of the patrol boats and worked out the best time to cross the river after dark. The day he decided to go, I followed him and watched from a distance to relay his success to our parents. He was a powerful swimmer, so I did not doubt he'd make it. He cut through the fence leading to the riverbank and crawled through the long grass. He wasn't even in the water when the patrol boat arrived out of nowhere, shining a powerful spotlight on him. They knew he'd be there; someone had betrayed him. He was scrambling up the bank away from the river when they shot him in the back." Walt's voice caught, and he stopped speaking to compose himself.

"I'm so sorry," Juliette murmured, reaching her hand across the table and squeezing his.

"That wasn't the worst thing. They left his body out in the open as a warning to anyone thinking of taking that route. Finally, weeks later, after the wildlife had been at him, they allowed my parents to have his remains buried. Bastards." Walt spat the last word, hatred twisting his features.

"And that's just one such incident. There have been many more failed escape attempts that have resulted in people simply disappearing into prisons and re-education camps," Hans said, slapping his hand on his friend's shoulder.

"Are you not frightened?"

"That's how they try to control us, with fear. But we must get our stories out to the rest of Germany and the world. For example, in May this year, there were elections, the results of which, as usual, were dictated from SED headquarters. But a group of us, mostly students, had fanned out across the city collecting as much information as possible from public polling centre counts and discovered what we had long suspected. There were huge contradictions between the results we collected and the official numbers. We managed to get the proof smuggled to West German TV, which beamed the story back into many East German homes. The SED were furious."

"I remember that story," Rachel said. It was another story she should have covered with Daniel. "That was you?"

All heads swivelled in her direction. Hans nodded.

"That was brave. You would have been imprisoned if they'd worked out what you were doing."

Hans shrugged. "It was necessary. The more the East German public realise that the SED is lying to them, the more people will support calls for change."

"So, what are you going to do next?" Juliette asked.

"You mean, what are we doing?" Hans said. "We protest."

Walt and Micha nodded.

"Leipzig was just the beginning. Peaceful demonstrations. Every Monday, we protest in Leipzig. You watch; it will grow each week and spread to the rest of the GDR," Walt said.

"Rumour has it that Gorbachev is coming next week for the anniversary. He is our best chance for real change. We want his *perestroika*. Look at the reforms his *glasnost* policy is introducing in the Soviet Union; we need him to bring that change here." Hans thumped the table.

No one spoke for a moment. Rachel, Juliette, and Josh were mesmerised by Hans's passion and determination.

There was a knock on the door, and the atmosphere was broken. It opened to reveal a slim young woman with short wavy hair. She peered over the top of her round sunglasses.

"Am I interrupting?" she asked.

"No," Hans said. "Come in, Maria. These are the journalists I was telling you about."

The young woman smiled. "Have you asked them?"

"No, not yet," Hans said. "Maria has finally been granted a visa to take her little sister to West Berlin to live with their aunt. Their parents have died, but Maria must come back."

"I don't trust the border guards to let me through. I was hoping to cross at the same time as you so that if they don't, you can at least take my little sister and deliver her to my aunt, who will be waiting on the other side."

"Of course, we'll help if we can," Rachel said. "What do we need to do?"

Josh exchanged a nervous glance with Juliette.

"We must pretend that we've never met," Maria explained. "Or else they will think I'm trying to escape. But I'm not; I just need to get Annette to safety, then I'll return."

The door opened again, and another youth joined them. "Have you heard?" he said in a breathless rush.

"Heard what?" Hans sounded wary.

"That bastard Honecker has just halted visa-free travel to Czechoslovakia."

Micha gave a heavy sigh and hung his head.

"I'm not surprised after the Czechs let all of those people who'd been holed up at the West German embassy in Prague cross to the West last week," Pierre said. "Honecker had to respond, or he'd look weak."

Maria moved across the room to where Rachel and Josh were seated. She was a bundle of nervous energy, bouncing from one foot to the other. "What time are you leaving?"

"Around 4 p.m.?" Josh said with a glance at Pierre, who nodded.

"What's your name?" Maria turned to Rachel.

"Rachel."

Maria clasped her hands. "Thank you, Rachel. I don't know what I'd do if anything happened to Annette. I will see you later." She turned and hurried from the room.

Rachel felt Josh tense beside her. She glanced at him and registered his worried expression.

"Will you be protesting during the celebrations?" Rachel asked, turning her attention to the group of men at the table.

Hans grinned as he stood up, crossed the room, and reached behind a free-standing cupboard, pulling out a large piece of card. Painted in red letters were the words, 'Help us, Gorbi.'

Rachel gasped. "You're going to appeal directly to Gorbachev?"

Hans nodded. "We are making hundreds of these so that he will see at least some of them."

"Isn't that dangerous?"

"Yes, but we need change. We need the world to understand that Germany needs to be reunified. And there will be hundreds of Western journalists present at the anniversary. What better way to get our message out?"

"Safety while the world is watching," Josh said.

"Something like that."

Pierre looked at his watch and stood. Rachel, Juliette and Josh did the same.

"Thank you for your time," Juliette said.

"Please, help us get our message out to the world," Hans said, shaking her hand. "By doing that at least some of it will get back in via West German TV and radio to the people here."

"I will do my best," Juliette said.

Pierre opened the door leading back through the barbershop. Rachel lingered in the room.

"Are you musicians?" she asked, pointing to the guitars.

Hans laughed. "As a hobby."

"What sort of music?"

"Pop," Walt said. "Bowie, Springsteen, Bryan Adams, the Eurythmics – Western artists, although if we sing in public, it must be in German, not English."

"Can you get hold of British and American music here?" Rachel was surprised.

"With difficulty, but it can be done."

"I'll bring you some tapes next time I come across," she said.

"Good luck with that," Hans said.

Rachel was taken aback at his rudeness.

"You'll only be adding to the border guards' collection."

CHAPTER 17

East Berlin, GDR
September 22, 1989

"**H**oly crap," Josh said once they were back in Pierre's car. "Those poor guys."

Rachel nodded. "I can't get the image out of my mind of Walt's brother's body left lying there by the river to rot. It's inhumane."

"But a good deterrent, no?" Pierre said.

"I wonder what happened to the brother's friends?" Juliette said. "Were they imprisoned or killed?"

"If they ended up in the Hohenschonhausen, they would be better off dead," Pierre said. "The rumours of conditions in that prison are appalling."

Rachel shook her head. "We don't know the half of it, do we?"

"Rachel, you shouldn't have offered to help that girl and her sister," Josh said. "We can't help them. The Stasi will have a file this thick on Maria." He held his thumb and forefinger wide apart.

"I know," Rachel said. "But if they let the little girl across, we can at least make sure she gets to her aunt."

"You're a soft touch."

Rachel bristled at the criticism. "Or am I just human?"

Pierre drove back to the AP building and parked in a side street. They re-entered the building through the back doors and followed Pierre around a series of corridors to the front entrance and out to the car he'd used to pick them up from the checkpoint. The vehicle with the two police officers was still parked behind them.

Ignoring it, they climbed into the Trabant.

"Have they just been waiting for us to come out?" Rachel asked.

"It would appear so. I'm supposed to take you on a tour of the sites that were renovated for Berlin's 750th Anniversary in 1987. They did a great job of sprucing up the façades of the old buildings, but inside, many are crumbling and practically derelict. It's all about perception to Honecker and his lot."

They parked in the Mitte district, where Rachel photographed the beautiful Friedrichswerde Church and the French Cathedral on Gendarmenmarkt square before they moved on to the Nikolai Quarter and Sophienstrasse, a street filled with historic workshops.

"The old architecture is stunning," Rachel said, adjusting her lens to take a wide-angle shot. "If it wasn't for the Wall a few blocks away, this would be a typical European city."

"Apart from the fact the people look half scared to death," Josh said.

They crossed the Spree River, passing the shining dome of the Berliner Dom on Museuminsel, a small island in the river containing various once-grand museum buildings, to Alexanderplatz. Rachel pulled the camera strap over her head, leaving the case in the car. She crouched and took several shots of the TV Tower before turning her attention to the buildings.

"There will be a big military parade along Karl Marx Allee from Strausberger Platz on the 7th," Pierre said. "Western journalists will be allowed to film from one corner of this square looking along the road."

"And that's it?" Josh said.

Pierre nodded.

Josh shook his head. "Not going to get much on the day, Juliette. I imagine there will be crowds in this small area, all vying for the best vantage point to film from."

"You'll have to film me as the parade passes," Juliette said. She turned to Pierre. "Will Gorbachev inspect the parade? Will we get to see him?"

Pierre shrugged. "We don't even know that he's coming."

"Those guys back there seemed pretty certain," Rachel said.

"Or hopeful," Josh added.

"Let's record a couple of pieces now," Juliette said, pulling out her makeup compact and reapplying her lipstick using the little mirror to guide her. "We can always edit them in if we don't get enough decent footage on the day."

Josh unpacked his camera and set up a tripod. He did a long angle sweep of the square and the entrances of streets leading to it. Men on ladders were attaching flags to the plaza's streetlamps, and the scaffold for a stage was erected. Rachel took several photos of the workers and the buildings.

"Careful," Pierre murmured as the two officers climbed from their car and marched towards them.

Josh swivelled his camera towards Juliette and silently counted her in using his fingers.

"We are here at Alexanderplatz in East Berlin ahead of the fortieth-anniversary celebrations of the GDR," she said, looking straight into the camera. "As you can see, preparations are well underway. Cut."

One of the officers began to speak as Juliette started again.

"We are here at Alexanderplatz in East Berlin ahead of the fortieth-anniversary celebrations of the GDR. Rumour has it that Soviet leader Michel Gorbachev will be in town for the commemorations. Cut."

The officer started towards Josh with his hand outstretched.

Josh ignored him. Behind, Rachel noticed Pierre looking anxious.

"We are here at Alexanderplatz in East Berlin ahead of the fortieth-anniversary celebrations of the GDR," Juliette repeated. "Our visit has been heavily monitored by members of the East Berlin police force, the Volkspolizei, who have controlled where we can go and who we have been able to talk to."

Josh spun his camera atop the tripod towards the officer, who froze for a moment before putting his hand over the camera. Rachel took several images of the officer confronting Josh.

"Enough, you have finished."

Pierre nodded and stepped forward. "Yes, officer."

Josh quickly repacked his equipment and collapsed the tripod under the officer's stern gaze, before returning to the car.

"They are twitchy," Josh said, folding himself into the backseat and closing the door as Pierre pulled away, their tail behind them again.

Pierre glanced in the rear-view mirror. "No more than usual. But you shouldn't antagonise them, or you won't be allowed back."

Pierre dropped them back at the border at five minutes to four. They sat in the car for a few moments watching a small stream of people approaching the checkpoint with their papers in their hands.

"There she is," Rachel said, spotting Maria and a young girl who looked to be around ten years old. She was wearing a warm jacket and carrying a small bag. Her blonde hair was styled in two long plaits, which bounced as she skipped beside her sister.

"Come on, let's go," Juliette said.

They farewelled Pierre after arranging for him to pick them up on the 7th when they would cross the border again for the celebrations. Avoiding any eye contact with Maria or her sister, they followed them along the pedestrian route to the checkpoint. Two armed soldiers looked down from a watchtower at one side of the central building, and another two stood to attention on either side of the metal barrier arm.

Maria and her sister approached the booth on the right-hand side while Rachel, Juliette and Josh were directed to the left. Rachel glanced sideways as one guard checked their passports whilst another rifled through their camera bags. There were raised voices at Maria's booth.

"What are they saying?" she whispered to Juliette, who was trying to eavesdrop.

Juliette shook her head. "They say she is on a list and cannot travel."

The guard handed back their belongings and ushered them towards the barrier.

"What about the little girl?" Rachel whispered to Juliette.

Juliette shook her head. "Neither of them."

"But…" Rachel hesitated and looked back at Maria, who had tears streaming down her face and was pleading with the border guard, who wore an implacable expression.

Rachel took a step towards them, but Josh snagged her arm.

"Leave it," he whispered.

"But we could take Annette."

"Is there a problem, *Fraulein*?"

"No problem," Josh assured the soldier, pushing Rachel in front of him. They passed through the barrier and walked across the concrete strip to the West Berlin barricade. A smiling American soldier lifted it, allowing them to pass through.

"Welcome back to civilisation," he said in a southern drawl, dropping the barrier arm behind them.

Rachel glanced over her shoulder to see Maria leading Annette along the road away from the border crossing. Annette was no longer skipping, and her head hung low as Maria took her away. As they headed for an idling taxi, Rachel spied a middle-aged couple turning away from the checkpoint; disappointment etched into their features. She broke away from Juliette and Josh.

"Excuse me?" she called. The couple stopped. "Are you Maria and Annette's aunt and uncle?"

"Yes," the woman answered in English. "It doesn't seem that they were able to cross today."

"I'm sorry, we tried to help," Rachel said.

The woman put her hand on Rachel's arm. "It's not your fault. But thank you. We hope we may one day be reunited with my sister's children."

CHAPTER 18

West Berlin, FRG
September 23, 1989

After a restless sleep filled with secret police chasing little girls through deserted streets, Rachel met Juliette for breakfast in the hotel's café on the ground floor.

"You look like death warmed up," Juliette said.

Juliette looked like her usual glamorous self.

Rachel ran her hands through her hair, pulling it into a messy bun. "I was haunted all night about leaving Maria and Annette at the checkpoint," she said.

"Do you still want to go back for the anniversary?" Juliette asked.

Rachel nodded. "Of course."

"Then it wasn't the time to make a scene. Those guys could cancel your visa and any future ones on the spot."

Rachel groaned. "I know. I'm sorry."

Juliette squeezed her hand. "We'll try to see if we can think of an alternative."

Josh slumped down in the chair opposite Juliette. "Morning," he said. "Messages at reception." He handed Rachel and Juliette each a folded note on hotel letterhead.

Rachel read hers and pulled a face.

"Good news?" Juliette asked, taking a sip of her coffee. Josh attracted the attention of a waitress and ordered coffee for himself.

"Jones wants me back in London until the anniversary," Rachel said. "This will be Bernard's doing, he'll be jealous that I got across and he didn't."

"Well, this might cheer you up. Monty left me a message saying he has further information on your William Brown. He disappeared into the chaos that was Germany in 1945 and was presumed dead."

Rachel's face fell.

"However, the Stasi officer in the TV clip that your grandmother saw has been identified as Hauptmann Wilhelm Braun," Juliette continued.

Josh snorted. "You're kidding. That's not very original. Wilhelm as in William and Braun, German for Brown."

Rachel began laughing. "She was right. Grandma was right." Rachel reached for Juliette's note. "Does he say anything else?"

"Nah." Juliette handed her the note. "Just to call him when we're back in London."

Rachel sat back in her chair, thinking.

"What are you going to do?" Josh asked.

"Do you think there is a newspaper archive here in West Berlin where I could do some research?" she asked.

Josh nodded. "I know someone who works there. I can take you."

Rachel drained her coffee cup. "Okay, I'll meet you back in the lobby in an hour. I need to pack and phone the airline to move my flight."

•••

"Thanks for this," Rachel said as they passed through the hotel's front doors and into the bustling street. She had her small Leica slung over her shoulder.

"It's not a problem. I'm fascinated by your grandmother's story," Josh said. "The archive is not far, but I have something to show you on the way. Get your camera ready; you'll be surprised. Parts of the Wall have been turned into a giant canvas."

They strolled towards Potsdamerplatz. For the first block, the Wall was comprised of large concrete slabs topped with rolled concrete, utilitarian and ugly. Further away from the watchtower, the Wall was covered with scrawled graffiti. Then, following a bend in the Wall, they came upon a colourful fresco of fish, animals and even a crocodile. Further on, a row of giant faces peered back at them from beneath a slogan demanding "Freedom for all people." Rachel loaded a second roll of film into her camera.

"Can we get closer?" she asked.

Josh looked up at a watchtower, where a guard had binoculars trained on them. "I wouldn't," he said. "The Wall is part of the GDR, not the West. The artists who do this risk the ire of the East Germans."

Rachel nodded.

"Anyway, we're up this way to the archive," he said, leading the way around the next corner.

The Deutsche Archive was housed in an impressive six-storey building, which appeared to have suffered only minor bomb damage during the war and retained many of its original baroque features. Josh introduced himself at the reception desk. They were shown to a wood-panelled reading room where a man in his late twenties met them, and Josh shook his hand.

"Rachel, this is Wolfgang," Josh said. "Wolfgang, Rachel is a photojournalist, and she wants some recent information on a man called Wilhelm Braun, a Stasi officer who may have been a friend of her grandfather's during the war."

Wolfgang frowned. "We won't have anything very current, I'm afraid, unless he's made the newspaper for some reason. The government maintains the records on Stasi officials."

"I'm more interested in the period after the war when Germany was divided into the four occupation zones. The man I'm looking for could also have been known as William Brown."

Wolfgang nodded. "Follow me; the historical newspaper archive is this way. Can you read German?"

"No."

"That's okay, you will be able to read his name on any index cards, and I can come back and read any articles to you."

"Thank you," Rachel said. "I appreciate your help."

Josh and Rachel spent the next two hours scouring the index card catalogue and noting the location numbers of references to either William Brown or Wilhelm Braun.

Rachel closed the final card index drawer and sat back on her heels, looking despondent. "I can't believe there are only four mentions of the man, if indeed he is the same man. Two for a William Brown and two for a Wilhelm Braun."

"Come on, let's find Wolfgang and see what the articles say," Josh said, holding his hand out to pull her to her feet.

The first two mentions of William Brown were as part of the Nuremberg delegation in 1946, but the reference was clearly for a much older man of the same name. The two mentions of Wilhelm Braun were in 1963 and 1970 as part of a unit of the Volkspolizei involved in thwarting several escape attempts over the wall. Unfortunately, there were no photographs alongside any of the articles.

"Sorry that we couldn't find anything further," Wolfgang said.

"Thanks for your help, anyway," Rachel said, trying to keep the dejection out of her voice.

"I'll keep the two names on my list if anything comes in," Wolfgang said.

Josh shook Wolfgang's hand, and they walked back into the sunshine.

"Sorry to waste your time," Rachel said.

Josh stopped at the bottom of the steps and turned to her. "Not at all."

"Can I buy you lunch to say thanks?" Rachel asked.

Josh looked at this watch. "Another time. I promised Juliette I'd edit the footage from yesterday so we have something ready to go immediately after the celebrations."

Rachel nodded. "Of course."

When they returned, Juliette was curled in an armchair in a sunny corner of the hotel lobby. She jumped up as they approached.

"Any luck?"

"No," Rachel said. "Anyway, I need to grab my stuff and head to the airport. I'll see you back in London."

Rachel climbed the stairs to her first-floor room and unlocked the door. She removed the roll of colour film from her camera, slipped the camera into its case and labelled the film canister ready to have it developed when she was back in London. She was closing her suitcase when the telephone rang.

She grabbed the handset from its cradle on the desk. "Hello."

"Is this Rachel Talbot?" a German-accented voice asked.

"Yes."

"I understand you want information on Wilhelm Braun?"

Rachel's heartbeat sped up. "I do."

"West Berlin is full of Stasi spies, Miss Talbot. If you know what's good for you, you will catch the next flight out and not return."

MAE

1944

CHAPTER 19

London, England
February 19, 1944

I dropped my suitcase and clutched at the policeman's arm as I surveyed the remains of Granny's beautiful Chelsea home, now reduced to a smouldering pile of rubble. Torn fabric, broken furniture and shattered glass mixed with brick and plaster had been tossed into the road, as though a giant had picked up a doll's house and smashed it. A team of men were climbing over the debris, calling out for survivors.

"It's Granny's house," I spluttered. "They'll be in the cellar."

"I'll let the rescue team know," the policeman said, lifting my hand from his arm. "You must wait over there behind the cordon."

I took a few steps back, then started forward again.

"Mae."

Strong arms encircled me, and I looked up into Jack's face. It was streaked with dirt, his hair was dishevelled, his uniform was covered in streaks of white, and he smelled of wood smoke.

"Oh God, Jack. I should have been here." I pulled back and stared up into his face.

"Thank God you weren't," he said, his voice catching. "I've been tearing at that rubble thinking that you were in there." He pulled me against him. "I thought I'd lost you."

"I spent the night in the underground. I didn't get any further than Green Park before the siren sounded." I shuddered.

"Come and sit, you're shaking."

I pulled away from him. "No, I'm not leaving."

"I'm not asking you to leave. We will stay right here until they find her. But it would be best if you sat before you collapsed. When was the last time you had anything to eat?"

I shook my head. "I have no idea."

Jack held out his hand. "Let's get you something then." He picked up my suitcase with his other hand.

I hesitated. "Jack, I'm sorry." A furrow appeared between his eyes. "For what I said at the hospital. I was wrong."

"Mae, it's forgotten already." Jack led me to one of the ambulances. "Wait here."

I sat down on the back step of the vehicle and looked in disbelief at the wreckage across the road. It didn't seem possible that the sturdy house where I'd grown up was gone, reduced to a pile of rubble. Yet, I'd seen it happen many times to other people's homes when I'd been driving ambulances earlier in the war. I understood the power of the German bombs. I just never thought it would happen to us.

Jack returned moments later with a hot cup of tea and a scone. "It's the best I could do. There will be soup soon, I'm told." He sat beside me, slipping his arm around my shoulders and burying his face in my hair. "Oh, Mae, I thought you were under all that. I don't know what I would have done."

A shout rose from the bomb site, and Jack leapt from the ambulance. "Please, wait here. I'll find out what's happening."

I nodded, too tired and overcome to argue. Part of me didn't want to know what they might have found. I clung to the hope that the cellar would have protected them.

I watched as Jack spoke to members of the fire brigade and rescue team, many of whom bowed their heads. When Jack turned to look at me, I knew. I stood, and the cup and plate slipped from my hands, smashing into pieces as my world spun. Seconds later, Jack was at my side easing me down onto the back step of the ambulance and forcing my head down towards my knees. "Breathe, Mae, breathe."

I did as he suggested, and the world stopped spinning. I eased myself upright.

"Tell me."

"I'm so sorry, Mae. They have found Lady Alice's body, along with those of Maggie and a nurse."

The tears I'd held in until then released, pouring down my cheeks.

"It would have been quick, Mae. They wouldn't have suffered."

"Where were they? Did they make it into the cellar?"

Jack shook his head.

"The raid was so sudden; there wasn't much time between the siren and the first bombs falling," I said.

"Mae," a voice shouted.

I looked up to see my uncle Charles, pushing through the gathering crowd of neighbours and onlookers. His long coat flapped about his knees as he hurried along, his fedora clutched in one hand. I jumped up and fell into his arms.

"Thank you, soldier, I can take it from here," Charles said, over my head, addressing Jack.

"It's alright, Charles. Jack is a friend," I said, pulling back.

Charles looked Jack up and down.

"In that case, thank you."

Charles regarded my tear-stained face. "Lady Alice?"

I shook my head. He hugged me again. "Oh, Mae, I'm ever so sorry."

"What happens now?" I asked, looking over at the ruined property.

"Leave all that with me," Charles said. "The best thing you can do is go back to work. You are needed now, more than ever."

"Can I see her?"

Out of the corner of my eye, I saw Jack shake his head at Charles.

"No, best to remember Lady Alice the way she was, so vibrant and full of life," Charles said. "She loved you very much."

"And I love her. Loved her." A sob rose in my throat.

Charles reached into his coat and produced a keyring. He slid one key off it and handed it to me. "Go to my flat to freshen up before you catch your train."

"Thank you, Charles," I said, taking the key from him. "What about her funeral?"

"Her solicitor will have her wishes. I'll instruct him and send you word." Charles turned his attention to Jack. "What's your name, Lieutenant?"

"Jack Knight, sir."

A flash of recognition flashed across Charles's face, but I was too grief-stricken to take notice. "Will you see my niece safely to her train?"

"Of course."

"I'll remain here, attend to Lady Alice, and see what can be salvaged," Charles said, hugging me once more.

CHAPTER 20

Bletchley, England
February 26, 1944

The next few days passed in a daze. Everyone was very kind, offering condolences, and I threw myself into work. There was a sudden increase in traffic, and Charles had been right; I was very much needed and worked double shifts, then fell into an exhausted, dreamless sleep. The monotony of the work was somehow soothing, and I lost myself in the concentration required to translate the strings of letters into something meaningful. At least it meant that my brain didn't have the chance to dwell on Granny.

Jack had ended up driving me back to Bletchley in a car borrowed from the carpool at the Foreign Office. Where he got the petrol rations, I didn't inquire. He dropped me at Liscombe Park, and I hadn't seen or heard from him since. Maybe he hadn't forgiven me after all, but in all honesty, I was too sad and too tired to care.

Granny's funeral was set for the following Saturday in the village of Evesham, where the army requisitioned her second home early in the war. Not that Granny cared, she much preferred to live in London. I often wondered why she kept the place, but whenever I mentioned it, she always said that no one in their right mind would want to buy the cold, damp pile she had inherited.

It took two trains and a taxi to reach Evesham from Bletchley. The drizzle turned to steady rain when I stepped from the car and raised my umbrella outside the fifteenth-century church in the centre of the village. I adjusted the veil on my black pillbox hat and took a deep calming breath. A steady stream of people were making their way along the path which wound between the gravestones towards the massive wooden doors of the stone church. An empty hearse was parked to one side of the entrance. Granny must have been taken inside.

A minister in his long robes was greeting people at the door as they arrived. Sombre organ music flowed from inside as I introduced myself. "I can take over welcoming people if you have to get ready," I said.

"That would be most helpful, Miss Webster," he said. "My deepest condolences; Lady Alice was a wonderful woman."

"Thank you. Do you know if my uncle is here yet?"

The minister shook his head before entering the church.

I propped my wet umbrella up against the wall, plastered a smile on my face, and spent the next ten minutes greeting those who'd come to pay their respects to Granny, many of whom I hadn't seen since I was a child.

The organist stopped playing, signalling that the service was about to start. I turned to head inside when running footsteps sounded behind me, and Jack, followed closely by Charles, rushed into the vestibule.

"Not late, I hope?" Jack said, offering me his arm.

I smiled at him. "No, just in time."

Charles pulled the door to the nave open. "Shall we?"

We took our seats in the front pew of the church. Granny's

casket sat on a raised dais covered in winter lilies. It was cold inside the old church, but many pews were filled with mourners, which warmed my heart.

"We are here today to celebrate the life of the indomitable Lady Alice Webster," the minister began. A shard of sunlight cut through the massive stained glass rose window at the front of the church, throwing coloured beams across Granny's coffin.

Jack reached for my hand and tucked it into his, keeping his fingers wrapped around mine for the full service, filling me with strength.

•••

Afterwards, we filed out into the graveyard, where Granny's casket was lowered into the frozen earth next to her beloved husband, who'd died so many years earlier leaving her a young widow. The burial plot next to it held the remains of my parents. If I thought I'd shed all of my tears, I was wrong; once again, they flowed freely. Jack held an umbrella over me and kept his arm around me at the grave, and remained silently with me long after the other mourners had moved into the parish hall for afternoon tea laid on by the local church ladies. Charles followed to do the rounds, accepting our condolences from the many people who had known her.

"That's my parents," I said eventually, pointing to the tombstone beside Granny's grave. Fresh wildflowers and winter berries filled the vase at its base, per my instructions.

Jack didn't speak; he bowed his head and continued to hold me.

"Bye, Granny," I said finally and looked up at Jack. "Tea?"

"There's a pub across the road; I thought perhaps something stronger," he said.

"Good idea. Let's find Charles. I'm sure he'll want to join us."

An hour later, the three of us sat at a small table in the snug of the ancient village pub drinking pink gins in honour of Granny.

On any other occasion the odour of stale beer, the busy wallpaper and swirling patterned carpet would have given me a headache, but all my energy was focussed on not allowing grief, and the emotion of the day, to overwhelm me.

"These are actually not bad," Jack said, sounding surprised.

"Lady Alice did like her pink gin," Charles said.

"To Lady Alice." Jack raised his glass, with Charles and me following suit.

The air in the pub was thick with cigarette smoke and the low murmur of conversation. I felt my shoulders loosen and neck relax. I opened my mouth to speak, but instead hiccupped a sob.

"Sorry," I murmured.

"One for the road?" Charles stood and headed to the bar.

Jack reached across the table for my hand and interlaced his fingers with mine. I gave him a watery smile before sucking in a deep breath and pulling myself together. Granny wouldn't have appreciated a prolonged display of grief.

"Does this mean you're the next Lady Webster?" Jack asked.

I shook my head. "No, it's not an hereditary title. I'm still plain old Mae Webster."

"I don't think anything is plain about you, Mae."

I blushed as Charles returned with our drinks. "That's not quite true, Mae. You're still an Honourable," he said, placing a fresh glass in front of me.

I shrugged. As far as I was concerned, it didn't matter one way or the other.

"Right, once we're done here, we'll take you back to Bletchley. Jack and I both have business to attend to."

"Wonderful," I said.

Jack's smile was gentle. "I'll be around for a couple of days, so can I take you to the cinema as planned?"

"Depending upon my shift, that would be lovely," I said.

A little while later, Jack ran through the rain to bring the car around to the pub's entrance while Charles and I waited under the front awning.

"Next time you have leave, you need to make an appointment with Lady Alice's solicitor, Mae. You are a very wealthy young woman, she left everything to you."

"I'd rather have her here still," I said, tucking my hand through his arm.

"I know, my dear," he said, patting my gloved hand. "I know. I will miss the old girl too."

CHAPTER 21

Bletchley, England
April 5, 1944

All leave was cancelled through March and April amid rumours that something big was about to happen. The volume of intercepted traffic was increasing, and we deduced that the huge workload meant something was afoot, perhaps even the long-awaited invasion of Europe.

I slowly emerged from my fog of grief, but for several weeks, we all worked double shifts, and I hardly saw my friends, or if I did, they were eating dinner as I was eating breakfast or vice versa.

I didn't encounter any suspicious activity during my extra shifts in my hut. However, I was concentrating on working and not letting my sadness engulf me, so I probably wouldn't have noticed if Goering himself had walked in and asked to see what I was working on. But in all honesty, I was beginning to think that the brass must have imagined the security breach.

On the Wednesday before Easter, Nancy came bounding into the dining room at Liscombe Park as I finished my tea and toast.

"What we need is a party," she exclaimed. "Everyone has been working too hard, and we must let our hair down. What do you think?"

"Splendid idea; when were you thinking?" Sarah said.

"This weekend," Nancy said, pouring herself a cup of tea and flopping down in a chair across from me. "It's Easter, perhaps things will be a little quieter. Regardless, I've had Mavis check the rosters, and all of us at the house are on the 8 a.m. to 4 p.m. shift on Saturday and then not on again until 4 p.m. on Sunday. Well, not Margaret, but that hardly matters. All she does is frown at us for having fun. It's the perfect window."

"How did you manage that?" I was suspicious that the four of us would suddenly be rostered on the same shifts.

Nancy winked. "I have my ways."

I laughed. "So, what is the plan?"

"I'll speak to my friendly American captain today. I'm sure they can supply the booze. I'm still working on the food, but I can probably get a hamper from London, so that just leaves music."

"You have it all planned," I smiled. It was easy to get caught up in Nancy's enthusiasm.

"You should invite your New Zealander," she suggested with a wink. "He hasn't been spotted around these parts in a few weeks."

"I would if I knew how to get hold of him," I said.

"It might be worth leaving a message with his landlady," Sarah said. "I hear he arrived back in England yesterday."

My mouth dropped open. "How did you hear that?"

Sarah grinned. "I have my sources."

But I didn't call, and I figured if Jack were indeed back from wherever he'd been, he would let me know. Still, it didn't stop me from jumping whenever the telephone rang, or the front door opened. It was a relief to catch the bus to Bletchley in the afternoon to start my shift at 4 p.m.

I spotted him as we filed off the bus and had our passes checked before passing through the gates into the Park. He stood just inside the entrance, wearing his double-breasted suit with his hat tilted to one side, his eyes scanning the crowd as the shift changed. My heart flip-flopped, and I hoped it was me that he was searching for.

I knew when he found me because his face lit up with a wide smile. He touched a finger to the brim of his hat as I excused myself around people and made my way over. As I reached him, he stepped forward and swung me into his arms, spinning me around, causing a chorus of oohs from several of the Wrens who were leaving the Park.

I ignored them and reached up on tiptoes to kiss his cheek when he set me down.

"Hello, you," he said.

"And you." I couldn't seem to wipe the grin from my face.

Jack tucked my hand into the crook of his elbow and led me away from the crowds. "Do you have a moment?"

I glanced at my watch. "Not really, my shift starts in two minutes."

"That's a pity," he said. "But may I walk you to your hut?"

"That would be lovely. How long are you back for?"

"Just the weekend, I'm afraid."

"We're having a party at Liscombe tomorrow night. Would you like to come?"

Jack nodded. "Yes, but can I see you before then?"

I shook my head. "I finish here at midnight and start again at 8 a.m., so you will have to wait until tomorrow night. Come for 7 p.m.?"

"Until tomorrow night, then." He lifted my gloved hand to his lips.

●●●

The party got underway when the first guests arrived at 7 p.m. from the American base in a series of army trucks. Nancy clapped her hands together with glee as Major Shaunwell led a troupe of four musicians into the drawing room, where they set up in one corner. The room looked beautiful. The rugs had been rolled back, and couches moved to the room's edges to create a dancefloor. The centre chandelier and alternate wall lights were lit, and large vases of daffodils picked from the gardens filled the side tables. It was a balmy spring evening, and the garden doors were thrown open, with the scent of jasmine and honeysuckle lacing the air. The tinkle of glasses and the hum of conversation interspersed with bursts of laughter brought a much-needed levity.

"We will need to pull the blackout blinds shortly," Margaret, ever the rule-follower, advised, peering out into the approaching dusk.

"I hope there's space on your dance card for me?"

I spun around to see that Jack had arrived. He cut a handsome figure in his uniform, and I noticed several other women looking his way. I was pleased that I'd worn my favourite pale blue ballgown and had Nancy curl my hair.

"I should be able to squeeze you in."

The band started, and Jack spun me onto the makeshift dance floor. From the first notes, it was clear that the band was here for a good time, and when the singer, a handsome black American, stepped up to the microphone, the dance floor filled. I danced with several American officers, Major Shaunwell, William and a member of an RAF aircrew based nearby whom Sarah knew. But between each different dance partner, I found myself back in Jack's arms. Taking a break for refreshments, we found the noise in the room impossible for conversation, so I led Jack out into the darkened garden. From the rustling of the shrubbery, we weren't the only people who'd stepped outside for some privacy.

"Come on, this way." I took his hand, leading him to a side entrance and into the conservatory at one corner of the house. The room was filled with indoor plants and wooden furniture that we often lifted onto the lawn on a sunny day. Moonlight bathed the room in a soft ethereal glow as Jack pulled me close, trailing his fingers down the side of my face before kissing me long and tenderly. He pulled back and studied my face. My cheeks flushed and my breath hitched a little.

"Marry me," he said.

"Pardon me?"

Jack shook his head. "I didn't do that properly." He took my champagne flute from my hand and set it aside before stepping back and dropping to one knee. He fiddled in the pocket of his uniform, producing a small black velvet box.

"Mae Webster, will you do me the honour of agreeing to become my wife?"

CHAPTER 22

Bletchley, England
April 8, 1944

In the moonlight, Jack's eyes shone with hope and love. The tiny diamond nestled into the velvet cushion sparkled.

"Yes, yes," I said as tears poured down my face. Jack stood and gathered me into his arms.

"I hope those are happy tears," he said, wiping his thumb across my cheeks.

I nodded, overcome with emotion. Jack slid the ring on my finger. "I love you, Mae."

"I love you too. Did you plan this?"

Jack shook his head. "Not exactly, but I've been carrying the ring around, waiting for the right moment. I knew you were special from that very first night, Mae."

"Will we tell anyone?" I asked. "It seems very sudden."

"Mae, there is a war on. We don't know what tomorrow will hold. I say we get married as soon as possible."

"What about after the war? Where will we live?"

"I don't care. As long as you're there, it will be home for me."

"Oh, Jack."

"Knowing that you will be waiting for me whenever I go away, is all I ask."

"But I don't want to stop my work here, it's too important."

Jack nodded. "I know and I wouldn't want you to. Surely there are married women working here."

"Some."

"Good, you can be one of them. My brave, smart wife."

He kissed me again before the door opened, and Mavis and an American airman joined us.

"Oh, sorry," she said, giggling. "I didn't realise you were in here."

"We've just become engaged, Mavis," I said, holding my hand aloft and showing her the ring.

"Oh, Mae, that's wonderful," she squealed, enveloping me in a hug.

"Congratulations, pal." The American shook Jack's hand.

"Come on, let's tell the others. This is cause for celebration." Mavis dragged us back to the party.

•••

Whirlwind preparations were made for our wedding. It was bittersweet for me as I'd always imagined getting married in my mother's wedding dress, on Granny's arm and setting off from her house, but all of that was gone, destroyed. I spent the time, when I wasn't working or sleeping, altering a plain white summer dress into my wedding dress. Sarah had somehow gotten hold of some fabric from an old silk parachute and had made me two sets of beautiful underwear.

The only dark cloud was William's reaction when I told him our news over lunch.

"Mae, it seems so sudden," he said. "Have you thought this through?"

"What's there to think through?" I said.

"What do you actually know about him? Has he confided in you what he actually does for the war effort?"

"I know enough," I snapped, disappointed that he wasn't sharing my happiness as my other friends had. "We love one another and somehow amidst the chaos of war, we have found each other. I'm hanging on to that as hard as I can."

"Exactly," William said. "Are you sure you're not jumping into this trying to find some normality in middle of the very abnormal situation that we find ourselves in?"

I had to concede that he had a point, we weren't exactly waiting the usual length of time before becoming husband and wife, but with everything going on, who was?

"And if we are, these are uncertain times," I said. "Look at Granny. None of us knows how long we have, why not make the most of things now? Jack makes me happy and I'm going to grab on to that and hold on tight."

"Look, I get that, Mae, I'm just saying, think hard, marriage is a forever thing. What happens when the war ends and he wants to go back to New Zealand? Will you really want to move to another country?"

"We'll deal with that after the war."

William laid his hand on my arm. "I'm not trying to be mean, but you are still grieving and it's understandable that you are looking for love and security."

"That has to be the most condescending thing you have ever said to me, William. This conversation is over."

I shoved my chair back and walked away from the table, taking the long route around the lake back to the hut, fuming.

Later that week, Jack and I managed our long-awaited trip to the cinema. From the outside the building was in darkness due to the heavy blackout curtains hung over the front entrance, and it appeared to be closed. Once inside, however, we found the theatre itself was almost full. Navigating using the light from the screen, we excused ourselves past embracing couples to find two seats together in the centre of a row.

"Mae, I'm being called away again," Jack whispered as the opening credits of the pre-film news reel ran.

"Where?"

Jack shook his head. "I can't tell you."

"William thinks we're rushing into getting married," I said.

"He wouldn't be alone thinking that, it does seem sudden, but I have no doubts that we're doing the right thing. I would make you my wife tomorrow if I could."

"Sssh," a cross voice whispered in the darkness.

I giggled and cuddled into Jack.

We parted at the midnight bus leaving Bletchley. Me heading home to Liscombe Park and Jack catching the train back to London and then to goodness only knew where.

It seemed that the next time I would see him would be when I walked down the aisle.

•••

The door opened on the hut the next morning, and a messenger, a young girl from the local village, scurried in and handed Mrs Winter a note. She read it before pushing her chair back.

"If I can have your attention, please," she called. "I've just received word that all leave is cancelled until further notice."

There were groans around the room, and I felt my heart sink. It had been hard enough focussing my efforts on translating German decrypts and not daydreaming about the future, but now that future had been thrown into jeopardy.

Over lunch, I discussed my predicament with Mavis and Nancy.

"The best I can do is adjust the roster so that you work until 8 a.m. on Saturday and don't start again until 4 p.m. Sunday.

That way, you can get to London for your wedding at 4 p.m. on Saturday and spend your wedding night together," Mavis said, her brow furrowed. "At least, I think I can make that work. But we won't all be able to come. I'm sorry, Mae, but it's the best I can do."

"I know."

"Leave it with me."

Mavis came through, and after catching a couple of hours of sleep, Nancy and I caught a midday train to London on Saturday and hurried to Charles's Pimlico flat, to change into our wedding finery.

"How are you feeling?" Nancy asked as she curled my hair into victory rolls and secured it with diamante clips.

"Good, excited, nervous. I know it all seems rushed, but I have no doubts that Jack is the one for me. I've never felt like this about anyone before."

"Then that's all that matters," Betsy said, helping me to set my small white hat on my head at a jaunty angle.

"William thinks we're rushing things."

Nancy waved her hand. "He's only jealous."

"Not of me," I exclaimed.

"Perhaps not, but maybe of your situation. You've found the safety and security of love during all of this madness. We have to take happiness where we can find it, because it could all end tomorrow. You are absolutely doing the right thing, darling."

I reached up and gave her hand a grateful squeeze.

There was a knock at the bedroom door. "Are you decent?"

"Yes," we chorused, and Charles entered.

"Oh my," he said, his voice catching. "You are a beautiful bride, Mae. How I wish your mother and Lady Alice could see you."

"I'm sure they're watching," Betsy said, passing me a lace hanky to catch the tears that threatened to spill from my eyes.

•••

The wedding at the Chelsea Town Hall was a quick but delightful affair. Betsy and Nancy were my attendants, and Arthur and Jack's brother Joe were his groomsmen. There were three couples getting married before us, then it was our turn.

Uncle Charles, looking as dapper as always, offered me his arm. "Ready?"

"As I'll ever be."

The doors opened and he walked me down an aisle between three rows of chairs in the small room designated to hold small wartime weddings such as ours.

Jack, waiting at the front of the room, turned as I approached and his eyes shone with love. I released my nervous breath and focussed the whole of my attention on him.

The service was quick and we exchanged our vows followed by a long kiss that had the registrar clearing his throat, before we emerged into the sunlight on the steps of the Town Hall, where Nancy and Betsy showered us with rose petals. Charles, entrusted with Jack's camera, captured our happiness.

There had been no time before the ceremony to be introduced to Joe. Still, afterwards as the champagne from Charles's private cellar flowed and we retired to the Ritz for a simple wedding breakfast, I was able to chat with him and, to my delight, found him to be as full of fun as his younger brother.

I'd dined at the Ritz many times with Granny, and I could almost feel her presence as we were ushered to a long table in a quiet corner of the main dining room.

"Nice not be crammed into the underground restaurant-cum-bomb-shelter, any longer," I said.

"Ooh, I don't know, there was something romantic about dancing in La Popote during an air raid," Nancy said.

"Although we're not out of the woods yet, are we?" I said, glancing at the tape-crossed windows and the blackout blinds poking out from behind the plush curtains framing the windows.

"I will never get used to the front entrance being surrounded by sandbags."

Nancy moved in front of me, obscuring my view. "Don't think about that today."

I noticed Jack and Joe gazing around them at the opulence of the chandeliers, gilded mirrors, gold and salmon-pink-accented marble, and an abundance of fresh flowers and potted palms. Quite where they had managed to source them with a war on, I didn't know. The two brothers exchanged a glance, then laughed.

I sidled up to Jack and slid my arm around his waist.

"Something funny?"

"Just that we're not used to dining at places like this," Jack said.

"Jack's worried that he might use the wrong fork," Joe said.

"We're the paying guests; as far as I'm concerned, there isn't a wrong fork," I replied.

Joe grinned. "I like you already."

"I'm terribly pleased that you were able to get leave at short notice," I said.

"I think Jack here might have pulled a few strings," Joe said. "But I'm happy that I could make it."

"I couldn't get married without my brother by my side," Jack said, slapping Joe on the back.

A pop and a whoop came from our table as Charles opened a bottle of champagne and Nancy filled the flutes. Once we all had one, Charles proposed a toast.

"To my little niece, whom I have watched grow into a beautiful young woman and her handsome new husband, wishing you a long life together, full of happiness."

"And children," Joe added.

We laughed and touched glasses.

"I'm dying to hear more about Jack's childhood," I said to Joe, seated on my other side.

"Where to begin," Joe said with a glint in his eye.

Jack leaned across and punched him on the arm. "It's my wedding day, only the stories that make me look good."

Joe frowned. "Well, then, that's going to be tricky."

We all laughed again and didn't stop throughout the meal. I looked around at the small group and sighed with happiness. For a brief moment, I could almost forget there was a war raging.

"All good, Mrs Knight?" Jack whispered in my ear.

"Better than good."

We dined on Scottish salmon and vegetables, followed by wild berries drizzled with honey, all washed down with more wine from Charles's cellar.

At the end of the meal, Charles took Jack and me to one side, and he pressed a key into my hand. "I took the liberty of reserving a room upstairs."

Jack began to protest, but Charles silenced him.

"It is the least that I can do after everything that Mae has been through over the last few months and after everything that you are both doing to help us win this damn war."

I hugged him. "Thank you, Charles."

Jack shook his hand.

After hugging Nancy, Betsy and Arthur goodbye, we arranged to meet Joe for lunch the following day before I'd have to return to Bletchley.

Jack took my hand and led me up the stairs to our room. I was in his arms as soon as the door closed behind us. Jack kissed me, not holding anything back. To my surprise, my nerves disappeared, and I responded with equal enthusiasm.

"Alone at last," I murmured.

"Well then, Mrs Knight, shall I help you out of this dress? Did I tell you how beautiful you look?"

"Yes, several times," I said, stepping away from him and standing in front of a mirror to remove my hat. Jack came up behind me and slipped his arms around my waist for a moment before slowly unbuttoning the row of tiny buttons that ran up the front of my jacket. He slipped it off my shoulders, threw it on a side chair, and turned his attention to the button and zip of my skirt. Seconds later, it pooled at my feet. He spun me around and removed my blouse, so I was standing in my parachute-silk slip.

"I should get my nightgown," I said.

Jack shook his head. "You won't be needing your nightgown," he said in a voice that sent an exquisite shiver of pleasure down my spine.

Jack dropped to his knees and removed my shoes one by one before pushing my slip up, unhooking my stockings, and rolling them down my legs and off each foot. Only then did he stand and scoop me into his arms. I shrieked as he spun me around before kissing me and laying me down on the bed. I propped myself on my elbows and watched him remove his uniform; jacket, belt, shirt, vest, trousers, and underwear. He stood stark naked at the end of the bed.

My mouth dropped open at the beauty of him. I ran my eyes over his broad shoulders, muscular arms, and chest, down to his narrow waist and lower. I had never seen a man fully naked, and I was surprised, delighted, and a little concerned about what would happen next.

But Jack took his time. He lay beside me, stroking, kissing, and caressing me until I was crazy with desire. He whispered nonsensical little phrases in my ear and kissed me with such longing that I pulled him on top of me.

Afterwards, I lay in his arms, pleasantly sore but happy.

"That was my first time," I whispered.

"I know," Jack said. "Mine too."

I looked at him with surprise. "But how did you know...?"

"Know what to do? I grew up on a farm, Mae." He laughed.

"I didn't mean that. I meant you took your time and made it good for me too."

"Well, I certainly hope I did," Jack said. "Honestly, I just made it up as I went along, did what felt right."

"Do you think you could do it again?"

"Why, Mrs Knight, I thought you'd never ask."

•••

I was reluctant to leave my new husband and return to Bletchley the next day, but duty called for us both.

Following a pleasant lunch with Joe, we walked along the river where Jack photographed Joe by the Houses of Parliament. All too soon, it was time for me to return to Bletchley.

"Mae, I will be away for the next few weeks, but I will write and call whenever I can," Jack said.

I nodded. "Something big is coming, isn't it?" I whispered.

"You know I can't say," he replied into my hair as he held me.

"I know. Just promise me that you'll be safe."

The conductor blew his whistle and with great reluctance I let him go and climbed aboard.

"I promise, Mae," Jack called as the train began to pull out of the station. "I have everything to live for."

CHAPTER 23

Bletchley, England
June 7, 1944

Then, D-Day happened.

Although the precise details were unknown to us at the time, we all knew something was up. In the days leading up to June 6th, there was a sudden travel ban, and the occupants of several huts weren't allowed to eat at the canteen and instead had food delivered. The volume of intercepted messages from German intelligence tripled, and the tension in the air was palpable.

I had no idea where Jack was, but I knew he would be in the thick of it. If the long-awaited invasion of Europe was about to happen, I didn't doubt that he and his camera would be among the first waves to hit France's beaches.

It wasn't until the morning of June 7, when the *Daily Mail* landed on the breakfast table at Liscombe Park, that our suspicions were confirmed. "Our armies in Northern France," cried the headline. "4,000 invasion ships have crossed the channel."

Sarah and I hugged one another, speechless, as we both thought of our beaux who were undoubtedly in the thick of it, one with a gun and one with a camera.

The next few weeks dragged on. Jack called me twice at Liscombe Park, and I received several letters with lines blacked out by the censors. His letters spoke of his love for me and his desire to show me his country after the war. I wrote to him daily, but I wasn't sure whether he received any of them.

At the Park, we continued to be swamped by the volume of decrypts to translate, and I flopped into bed exhausted after each shift, praying that Jack was safe and not putting himself in danger. I didn't dare entertain the thought that he could be killed, and it would be days before I knew.

I returned early from lunch one day to get my cardigan and found William looking through a file in a wire basket on the desk of Mrs Winter, the head of our hut. We hadn't spoken much since our disagreement about my marriage, although he had sent a telegram with his best wishes.

"William, what are you doing?"

William leapt back from the desk, and I swore he looked momentarily guilty.

"I was looking for some new pencils," he said.

"Over there on the shelf, William." I pointed to the opposite side of the room where the stationery items were kept.

"Oh yes, of course." He crossed the room and selected two pencils from a box on the shelf.

I studied him, and he was walking stiffly. "William, are you okay?"

"Yes, fine."

"Have you hurt yourself? You're walking strangely."

"Ah, I may have tweaked my back playing tennis," he said. "Now, if you'll excuse me, I'll take a turn about the grounds before the afternoon shift."

He hurried from the hut. I watched through the window as

he headed straight for the ablutions block. When he exited a minute later, he was walking normally again. My senses tingled; something wasn't right.

I walked to the desk and looked in the top folder of the wire basket I'd last seen William going through. The translations were annotated with our initials, and the decrypt was attached to the back. The last three I'd translated that morning just before lunch were missing. From memory, one was concerning German reports of Allied troop build-up near Calais, and the other two were to do with the Eastern Front. I peeked in the other two folders, but they contained weather reports or 'situation normal' check-in messages. The file William was looking at contained the translations that would be passed to the intelligence analysts shortly. The information I'd translated was definitely of interest, but it appeared to be missing.

I caught up with Mavis at the end of our shift and told her of my suspicions. We sat on a wooden bench beside the lake, enjoying the last rays of sunshine. "I know I'm supposed to go straight to Travis with anything unusual, but it's William, so I wanted to discuss it with you first."

"Oh my God." Mavis stared at me. "I hope you're not suggesting what I think you are."

"I hope I'm not either, but it was odd. And the messages that I translated right before lunch were not there. Although I suppose they could have already been passed on."

Mavis sighed. "Do you understand what happens here at BP?"

I shook my head. "I thought I did, but I probably only know my part in the process."

Mavis nodded. "And that's how the authorities try to keep it."

"Why?"

"So that the source of the intelligence can be kept secret. Not every decrypt is passed for translation, and not every translation is deemed useful. But everything, and I mean everything, is filed."

"Oh."

"The messages are intercepted at various listening stations around the country and sent here via teleprinter or dispatch riders. The code breakers analyse the messages to try and break the codes or cyphers, which is where all the mathematicians here come into the picture. They are devising the approach and building the machines that the Wrens are working on, that can complete more computations than several humans in much less time.

"The problem is that most German messages are coded using Enigma, and the code changes every twenty-four hours, so if we break the code, we only have a small window to decode that day's messages."

"That makes sense, so even after the twenty-four-hour period ends, we have people who continue to decipher that day's code and translate the messages until they are all done?"

Mavis nodded. "Yeah, late intelligence is better than no intelligence."

"Is that what those noisy machines in Block A are doing?"

Mavis glanced around and nodded. "Once the messages are deciphered, and you translate them from German to English, they're passed to the military intelligence analysts if they're deemed of value."

"Most of what I translate ends up being weather reports, situation normal type reports, or the odd crude joke," I said.

"But there will be times that you get something else."

"Yeah, and they go into the folder where William was looking. It's supposed only to be seen by the head of our hut, who then decides what gets passed on and what gets filed."

"Something big is brewing, that much is clear from the amount of traffic passing through this place over the last few weeks and the strain everyone seems to be under."

I sat back and considered this. "William has definite views on our relationship with the Soviets and told me he thinks we should share our intelligence more."

"Well, he did work at the Admiralty, so perhaps he does? We need to take this to Travis now."

"Let me talk to him first," I said, glancing at my watch. "If I hurry, I could catch him, our shift has just finished."

I scooped up my coat and bag, and we rushed along the path, around the lake, and through the checkpoint.

"Did you happen to see which way William Brown went?" I asked Private Morris.

"Towards the station."

Mavis and I broke into a run.

Several people were milling about, but at the far end of the platform, William's tall, broad figure was pacing.

He looked up as we approached.

"William, I know you stole the decrypts that I translated this morning," I blurted out.

William looked around to ensure that we weren't being overheard. "You foolish woman. Don't you realise that the invasion isn't going as planned? Why do you think we've all been working around the clock?"

"And you are putting all of that at risk."

William shook his head. "I am helping."

"Helping? By stealing decrypts? You are putting it all at risk."

"No, you have it all wrong. I may think that if we share this with our Soviet allies, they can help keep the Germans busy elsewhere, but there's a huge difference between thinking and doing."

"You mean..."

William grasped my upper arms. "I'm not a traitor, Mae. You have to believe me."

"Then why did you take the decrypts, and where are you going?"

"I have an appointment with Churchill," William whispered, dropping his hands and removing his hat to wipe a hand over his brow. "I need to make him see that despite his distrust of Stalin and the tenuous alliance he has formed with him, we have to share this intel."

"How do we know that's where you are going?"

"Come with me," William said.

The chug of an approaching train sounded in the distance.

"We can't let you do this, William," I pleaded with him. "You must return to the Park and explain this to Travis."

He shook his head and took a step away from me. The train rounded the bend and began to slow as it eased into the station. Mavis reached for William's arm, and he pushed her away, but she held on to his sleeve. He jerked his arm again, dislodging her grip. Mavis stumbled, losing her balance, and tumbled towards the edge of the platform, her leg in the path of the approaching train.

CHAPTER 24

London, England
June 24, 1944

"**M**avis," I screamed as the panicked train driver applied the brakes, the metal screeching in protest. William and I reached out and pulled Mavis back from the edge just as the train passed.

William helped her to her feet. "I'm sorry Mavis, but I must go."

The train doors opened, and William climbed aboard.

"I'm fine, Mae. Go with him," Mavis urged. "See if he is telling the truth."

I jumped on board as the conductor's whistle sounded, and he marched along the platform closing the doors.

William and I sat opposite one another but didn't speak for the entire journey to London. When we arrived at Euston, we followed the crowds of uniformed men emerging from the train platforms into the station's Great Hall. A group of children with labels attached to their clothing, carrying small suitcases, were being corralled by a stern looking woman. Some sobbed and clung to tearful mothers while others chattered with excitement.

William and I exited the station beneath the magnificent Doric arch where William hailed a taxi.

"Whitehall," William instructed the driver.

Fifteen minutes later, we stood outside a building in the beating heart of government on King Charles Street. The ground floor of the magnificent nineteenth-century structure was partly obscured by sandbag walls running around the entire perimeter to absorb the impact of any bombs falling nearby. I shivered as I registered the presence of anti-aircraft guns at regular intervals around the building, manned by alert soldiers scanning the skies. I felt my neck twist as I too looked skyward.

"What is this place?" I asked.

"The Treasury."

"Oh?"

"What I'm about to show you is top secret, Mae. Consider this falling under your signing of the Official Secrets Act."

We climbed the front steps of the building and were greeted at the door by two armed Marines in full uniform. Wordlessly, William handed his identity papers to one of the soldiers, and I produced mine for the second sentry to check. Unsmiling, he looked from the documents to me and back again before nodding once. I slipped my papers back into my handbag.

We entered a vast foyer. Men and women in smart suits hurried about carrying armfuls of files, greeting one another as they passed. William strode toward the rear of the building and through an unmarked doorway. Another soldier, standing in front of a second door, checked our papers again before allowing us through. We descended a steep flight of stairs into a basement that must have stretched beneath the Treasury building. Two more Marines were stationed at the foot of the stairs.

"I have an appointment with Churchill," William said.

"Wait here," the Marine instructed before returning with an efficient-looking older woman carrying a clipboard. She found

William's name on a sheet and, after looking me up and down, indicated for us to follow her.

A musty, earthy smell surrounded us, and electric lights strung along the walls flickered. I knew I had just entered one of the most secretive locations in England, but it wasn't a calm, mysterious environment. Quite the contrary. The clickety-clack of typewriters echoed along the passageway, and the din of various conversations reverberated with the occasional voice rising above others to be heard. The air-conditioning units whirred and hummed, and a plume of smoke hung from the cigarettes burning in the small underground rooms. My stomach turned over at the stench.

We were led along the corridor, where I spied a weather report indicator panel on the wall. The wooden sliding panel stated Warm and Fine. We paused at the corner, and the woman noticed my interest.

"We are down here for hours on end, and you have no idea what it's like outside," she said. "This lets us know. Although if it says windy, then you need to stay put."

"Why's that?"

"Because that is code for frightening – it means bombs are dropping above."

I immediately thought of the night that I'd crouched in the Green Park underground station, the night that Granny perished – no doubt this would have read windy then.

"Are you alright?" She peered at me. "You've gone a strange colour."

I put my hand on the wall. "I'm feeling a little nauseous, that's all."

"Mr Brown, your meeting is in this room here," she said. "Now, why don't you come with me, love, and we'll get you a nice cup of tea."

"It's fine."

"You go, Mae. I will come and find you," William said.

The woman led me around the rabbit warren of corridors to a tiny kitchen. I sat on one of two chairs and gratefully accepted the cup of tea.

"Feeling any better?"

I nodded. "Thank you. I don't know what came over me."

The woman's smile was kind. "Your husband is still in France?"

"Yes, I believe so."

"You rest here, and I'll come back for you, Mrs Knight."

It wasn't until she had left that I realised that I hadn't told her my name or that Jack was in Europe. My stomach rolled again, and I pushed the thought from my mind. I was sure that most women's husbands were in France right now.

Twenty minutes later, William's head appeared around the door frame. "There you are. Time to go, but first, I'd like you to meet someone."

I placed my empty cup in the sink and followed him along the winding passageways. There was no sign of the woman. A hacking cough sounded as we passed a series of closed doors and one flew open, and none other than Churchill himself marched into the corridors, his head bare, and a cigar clamped between his lips. A secretary hurried after him, notepad in hand.

"Thanks again for seeing me, Prime Minister," William said.

Churchill peered up at William's lanky form. "I'm pleased we have an understanding, William."

"Yes, sir."

"And who is this?" Churchill's shrewd eyes moved to me.

"This is my colleague from BP, Mrs Mae Knight."

"Pleased to meet you," I stuttered, praying that the contents of my stomach would behave as a cloud of cigar smoke swept around me.

"Ah, Mrs Knight," Churchill boomed. "The pleasure is all mine. It is not often that I get to meet one of our secret weapons." He gave me an exaggerated wink. "Keep up your important work."

With that he was off, striding down the corridor issuing instructions, with his secretary running behind him.

I stood staring after him, and it was several seconds before I realised William had moved on. I hurried along the corridor and up the stairs in his wake. We passed through the door into the bustling foyer of the Treasury.

"You never told me that you knew Churchill," I said.

"There's a lot that I haven't told you, Mae," William said. "Now, do you believe me? I'm not a traitor; I'm just trying to make sure that we do everything in our power to defeat the Nazis, including encouraging the sharing of intelligence with our allies."

CHAPTER 25

London, England
August 10, 1944

I unlocked the front door of our flat after a hot, sticky train journey from Bletchley to London.

I'd received a message yesterday morning from Jack that he would be back in London tonight, and I'd managed to swap two shifts allowing me twenty-four hours' leave. The Allied invasion of Normandy in June had succeeded despite the horrific loss of life resulting from retaking the French beaches. Thanks to our round-the-clock codebreaking efforts at the Park, we'd informed the Admiralty that the Germans had indeed fallen for the elaborate bluff that the planned invasion would take place at Calais, the shortest crossing point. Hence, the invasion force knew a little of what to expect regarding the size of the German battalions in Normandy. However, the resistance was still fierce. But now, two months later, Paris had been liberated, and the war's end was surely in sight.

I dumped the bag of groceries on the table and threw open the windows of the one-bedroomed ground-level flat that Jack had moved into just before our wedding. I kicked off my shoes, arranged a vase of the flowers I'd gathered from the roadside border outside Bletchley station that morning, and placed them in the centre of the table. I unpacked a small food bag for dinner and slipped into the bathroom to freshen up.

I couldn't wait to see Jack and tell him our news.

The flat was clean and tidy but rather uninspiring. The kitchen was tiny with little bench space, and although the bathroom was more extensive it had no windows, meaning it was cold and damp most of the time. Our bedroom and the small sitting room were fine, but once the war was over, I was determined that we would move to something a little bigger and much nicer.

I set to work using the precious egg that had cost me several saved rations to prepare tagliatelle, just as my Italian nanny had taught me, with garlic, herbs and fresh tomatoes. It would be the first meal I'd had the chance to cook for my husband, so I wanted it to be special.

A key turning in the lock a short time later announced his arrival. I threw myself into his arms, peppering his face with kisses before he crossed the threshold. Laughing, he half carried me back inside, depositing his camera case before returning my kisses.

"That was quite a welcome, Mrs Knight," he said.

"I have missed you so much," I said.

"Good." Jack lifted his kit bag off his shoulder and dropped it to the floor before scooping me up and carrying me to the bedroom to continue our reunion.

Sometime later, as we lay in each other's arms, I leaned out of bed to retrieve a package from the bedside table. Jack reached for me. "Where do you think you're going?"

"I have something for you, a surprise," I said.

Jack rolled onto his side and propped himself up on one elbow. I placed the small parcel, carefully wrapped in brown paper, in the bed between us.

"You know it's not my birthday, right?" he said.

"Just open it."

Jack tore open the wrapping and looked puzzled at its contents, a tiny pair of baby's knitted booties. He lifted his eyes to mine as realisation set in.

"Mae, you're not, are you?"

I grinned and nodded. "A wedding night baby."

Jack whooped and gathered me to him before trailing his hand down my body to rest on my still-flat belly. "When?"

"February."

"Hopefully this damn war will be over by then," Jack said. "We're chasing the Germans back across Europe, and it's only a matter of time."

"Were you with the invasion force, Jack?"

He nodded.

"Did you get lots of photos? I've been watching the papers, but no photos have been published from Normandy."

A look of pain crossed Jack's face. "I took a couple of hundred photos, some that would have been amazing."

I frowned. "Would have been?"

"There was a processing incident in the lab back here in London, and nearly every negative was destroyed."

"Oh, Jack."

"Yeah, they were left to dry too long by a rushed darkroom technician, and the emulsion ran off the cellulose. Film destroyed. Mine, Capa's and several others."

"Oh no."

Jack continued to stroke my stomach. "Are you still working?"

"Of course, why wouldn't I? I'm pregnant; I haven't lost the use of my brain."

Jack laughed. "I wasn't suggesting anything like that. But you know what the brass is like."

"I haven't told anyone, and I won't until I'm showing. Now would you like some dinner?"

"Yes, and a bath."

Jack had just sat down at the tiny kitchen table after his bath, his wet hair curling around his ears, when the telephone rang. He crossed the room to answer it while I piled the pasta into two bowls.

"Jack Knight."

I watched his face as he listened to the voice on the other end.

"Right away, sir."

He looked pained as he hung up.

"I'm sorry, Mae, but I must go as soon as we've eaten."

"Oh no, why?"

Jack shook his head and pulled out his chair.

"You can't say." I put our bowls on the table and sat down opposite him.

"What's this?"

"Tagliatelle, it's Italian pasta. My nanny taught me how to make it. You wind it around your fork like this." I twirled my fork in the tangle of noodles to show him. Jack copied me and took a tentative bite.

"Oh my," he groaned after swallowing. "That is amazing."

I glowed with pleasure as he devoured the bowl.

"Would you like more?"

"Yes, please, but only if you've had enough. You're growing our baby, you need to eat."

"There's plenty," I assured him.

Our farewell was tearful, and I clung to him until the very last moment.

"I'll be back before you know it," he promised.

It wasn't until he'd gone that I remembered that I hadn't told him about William or meeting Churchill. Oh well, that would have to wait until next time. We had our whole lives ahead of us. I tidied the kitchen, curled up in bed and slept.

CHAPTER 26

Bletchley, England
September 30, 1944

Mavis closed the drawing-room door behind her and hurried towards the couches where Nancy, Sarah, and I were sprawled after an extra-long shift. I was exhausted and wasn't sure I could climb the two flights of stairs to my bedroom. The sofa was looking more comfortable by the minute.

"What's wrong?" My heart leapt into my throat as I feared from the anxious look on her face she was bearing bad news, and I was suddenly wide awake.

"Nothing like that." She waved away my concern for Jack. "But Travis has issued a warrant for William Brown's arrest," she whispered.

"How do you know?"

"I overheard Travis tonight," Mavis said, wringing her hands. "They're going to arrest him in the morning."

"Why?" I said. "He's working for Churchill."

"Apparently, one of our Soviet spies received information that can only have come from here regarding the numbers of German panzers and troops in Romania and Poland," Mavis said.

"And Travis is concerned that the intelligence was leaked from here?" I asked, sitting forward. "Does he think it's come from William?"

Mavis nodded. "It appears that way."

"He must have some evidence."

"I believe so," Mavis said.

I shook my head. "I can't believe, after everything, that William would do that. Mavis, you saw him that day on the platform. He said there was a big difference between thinking and doing. He's sympathetic to the Soviets but loyal to Britain."

"Maybe something changed his mind."

"What do we actually know about him?" Betsy asked.

"He's one of the Cambridge dons, isn't he?" Nancy said.

I shook my head. "No, he came to Bletchley from the Admiralty, but he was at Cambridge before that."

The door opened, and Margaret entered.

"That means he could be military intelligence," Mavis said.

"Not if he was working as a code breaker," Nancy said.

"Please tell me that you're not discussing anything from the Park," Margaret said, her tone disapproving and her voice dropping to a whisper. "They will throw us all in prison or worse."

"Stop being so dramatic, Margaret," Nancy said. "We're discussing the latest contingent of Americans to grace the Park." She turned her attention to Mavis. "And have you seen that dishy Major Henshaw?"

Margaret sniffed and perched on the end of the couch with her knitting.

I excused myself and went to bed, but sleep didn't come easily. What was William up to, and had we been duped? Was he a double agent after all? Before I fell asleep, I determined that I would ask William outright the following day before Travis came for him, and I hoped that he would provide some much-needed answers.

•••

William wasn't in the hut in the morning, and I sought Mavis out in the cafeteria at lunch.

"Do you know if William has been arrested? He never arrived for his shift."

Mavis looked around and took me by the arm to one side of the room. "He's disappeared," she whispered.

"What do you mean?"

"No one has seen him since yesterday morning."

I looked at my watch. "I've got time to pop around to his billet."

"I'm coming with you."

Mavis and I left the Park and walked to the modest two-level red-brick house where William had been billeted during his time at Bletchley. It stood mid-terrace, one road back from Bletchley's main street, in a row of similar homes.

We paused at the corner. A black car was pulling away from the front of the house, and William's landlady was standing on her doorstep, watching it depart with a stricken look. She looked over as we approached.

"'e's not 'ere," she said. "All his things are gone too." She returned inside, slamming the door behind her.

Mavis and I exchanged a glance.

"This doesn't look good," she said.

Fear and disbelief were at war inside me. "Oh, William, what have you done?"

RACHEL

1989

CHAPTER 27

East Berlin, GDR
October 7, 1989

This time, the crossing to East Berlin took longer. Hundreds of Western journalists were being allowed over the border to cover the GDR's fortieth-anniversary celebrations, and each individual's passport, press credentials, and belongings were checked carefully.

Rachel glanced behind her and saw Bernard waving to get her attention, and she ignored him. When she reached the front of the line with Juliette and Josh, she anxiously watched the officer unpack her camera, lenses, spare batteries and extra rolls of film from her bag and tip the bag upside down, giving it a good shake. Her small backpack was emptied along with the pockets of her jacket, and she stood arms and legs apart as she was patted down. Her passport was stamped, and she was left to repack her equipment.

Pierre was waiting in a long line of cars and waved them over.

"The traffic is horrendous, and many roads have been blocked off. I will get as close as we can, and then we will have to walk," he said.

"That's fine. Thanks for picking us up," Juliette said.

"The visiting press has been allocated an area to one side of the parade ground. You are not to stray from there to take photos, film, or interview anyone," Pierre said. "The authorities are jittery; they want this thing to go off perfectly, especially while the world is watching."

Pierre parked several blocks away, and they joined a long line of pedestrians heading for Alexanderplatz, the TV Tower an easy landmark to navigate towards. Many people carried flags, and everyone seemed upbeat. Rachel clicked off a few photos of the crowds until Pierre looked back and frowned at her. Instead, she tried to listen in on the conversations around her. They were speaking too fast for her basic German, but there was one word that she kept hearing. *Gorbachev.* She hurried to catch up to Pierre.

"Has it been confirmed whether Gorbachev will be here today?" she asked.

He nodded. "According to my sources, he arrived from Moscow early this morning and has been meeting with the full Politburo."

The press area in Alexanderplatz was packed and guarded by officers wearing the green uniform of the Volkspolizei, the people's police.

"I'm glad we got that footage the other day," Josh said. "There's no way to get clean video today."

"Let's meet at that corner after the parade if we get separated." Pierre pointed in the direction that they'd come.

Rachel removed her lens cap and squeezed to the edge of the press box. She raised the camera and took several shots of the intense security presence amidst the growing crowds who were waving small GDR flags. On the opposite side of the square she saw a disturbance as several police officers rushed into the crowd. She watched as two young men climbed up to the first-floor window of a building overlooking the square and unfurled a handmade banner which said 'Freedom'.

Rachel raised her camera and adjusted the aperture. *Click*. She altered her angle and aimed again, but her view was obscured. She lowered the camera to see a large green uniform blocking her view.

"Excuse me," she said.

He shook his head and remained where he was.

Rachel tried to step to one side, but he moved with her before reaching out to snatch her camera. Rachel clutched the camera to her chest and felt herself being pulled backwards, as the mass of journalists quickly swallowed her.

"What are you doing?" Bernard hissed.

"Photographing the protestors. Did you see them?" she said.

"We're here to report on the celebrations, not protestors," Bernard said.

Rachel looked at him as if he had two heads. "Surely, we're here to report on the day's events, including any protests."

Bernard shook his head. "Stick with me and stay out of trouble."

Rachel fumed as she followed him to the opposite side of the press area, mumbling her apologies as she squeezed past dozens of reporters. She found herself at the back of the group, where Bernard was holding court with some older male journalists. She checked her watch; there was still an hour until the parade was due to start, so she slipped under the barrier and sat down with her back against the wall of the nearest building. She checked her camera and saw that she had two shots left, which she used to photograph the press gallery, and loaded a new roll of film into the camera, labelling the used one with the time and date before slipping it into an inside pocket in her camera bag.

She leaned her head back and closed her eyes, only opening them when she felt someone sit beside her.

"I wondered where you'd got to," Josh said, resting his camera equipment in front of them. He handed her a cup of coffee. "Pierre managed to get coffee from a street vendor."

Rachel took a grateful sip and then grimaced. "Thank you, I think. Did you see the protestors?"

"Not until the police dragged them down and threw them in the back of a van," Josh said.

"Did you film it?"

Josh shook his head. "Not for want of trying."

"Don't tell me; your way was blocked."

"Something like that."

A young girl broke away from a group of passing flag-waving civilians and skipped towards them. Rachel did a double take.

"Isn't that?"

"Annette," Josh finished for her.

Annette skipped past, not making eye contact, and dropped a piece of paper at Rachel's feet. Rachel went to scoop it up, but Josh snagged her arm, stopping her. Instead, he hooked a long leg over hers and placed his large shoe over the note. Rachel glanced up to see that an officer at the crowd's edge was watching them. She looked into Josh's face and tried to force a smile.

"Is he still watching?" Josh said.

Rachel nodded.

Josh dipped his head, giving the impression that they were being intimate. "Just give him a couple of seconds to lose interest."

A moment later, Josh pulled back and slid his foot between them with the note beneath. Rachel placed her camera bag before their feet while Josh unfolded the paper.

Rachel, come to Leipzig for a couple of days. Meet after the parade at Bavarian Café on Bruderstrasse. Maria.

"Leipzig?"

"It will be the weekly protest Hans spoke of the other day. Remember, the first one was filmed by the Western media who were in Leipzig for a trade conference back in September."

"I'll come with you," Josh said. "Juliette can take the camera back."

"Aren't you supposed to be going to Czechoslovakia tomorrow?"

Josh cursed. "Yeah, I forgot about that."

Rachel thought for a moment. "There's something that I haven't told you."

Josh's eyebrows rose.

"After we visited the archives, I had a threatening call to warn me off looking into Wilhelm Braun."

"What?" The word exploded out of Josh, attracting the attention of several passers-by. "What did they say?" he added in a whisper.

"It was a little odd," she said. "He said West Berlin was full of Stasi spies."

"You're right. That does sound odd," Josh agreed. "And he knew you were looking into Braun?"

Rachel nodded. "Yeah."

"That's not good, Rach," Josh said. "The Stasi have informants in the West. Someone knew what we'd been looking for at the archive."

"How trustworthy is Wolfgang?"

"Very, I thought, but who knows?" Josh shrugged. "Why didn't you tell me?"

"I didn't see you or Juliette again before I left for London that day, and I've only just remembered."

Josh frowned and flicked his eyes back down at the note between them. "If someone knows you're looking into this Braun chap, this could be a trap."

Rachel shook her head. "Not Maria. You saw how she was with her sister. She wouldn't use her."

"Don't be so sure. It's different when people are desperate. They will betray their friends and colleagues if they get something out of it."

"That's very cynical," Rachel said.

"Juliette and I will come to the café with you. It's in the direction that we have to walk back to Checkpoint Charlie anyway," Josh said as a marching band sounded in the distance. "Address memorised?" Rachel nodded. Josh screwed up the paper and added it to the coffee cup's dregs, disintegrating the note's writing.

They scrambled to their feet and rejoined the press contingent, watching as dignitaries and VIPs filed into the seating area on the raised stage. Flags fluttered, and brass bands played a rousing tune. The officials were all dressed in sombre black and grey overcoats, almost at odds with the supposed celebratory event. Josh located Juliette and shouldered his camera, filming her as the members of the ruling SED party took their places on the rostrum. Rachel stayed with them and shot another two rolls of film as row upon row of uniformed soldiers marched by, and bands played in a massive show of military might.

"Look, there's Gorbachev next to Honecker," Rachel called to Juliette.

"I always think Honecker looks like an old teacher that I used to have at boarding school, not the leader of a nation," Josh said. Rachel laughed and turned her camera to the GDR's leader. She could see what Josh meant. Standing ramrod straight in his trilby and overcoat, with small, pinched features, he looked humourless and stern, like an old schoolmaster. Beside him, a bald Gorbachev wore a slight smile and appeared to sway in time to the music.

When the last notes died away, and soldiers filled the square in long straight rows, Honecker stepped forward and addressed the crowd. Rachel couldn't understand what he was saying, but she guessed from the polite applause that it was all political rhetoric. The voice of another British journalist in their midst translated parts of the speech into English.

"The GDR has risen to be among the top ten industrial nations in the world and is strengthening its economic potential by the introduction of modern technologies. Something about being at the forefront of the scientific-technological advances."

"You mean at the forefront of imitating and reverse engineering Western computing technology," another voice muttered from deep within the gathering of journalists.

The original speaker continued translating. "The GDR is a reliable guarantee against neo-Nazism...the GDR will remain firmly anchored in the Warsaw Pact."

The crowd cheered as if on cue, clapped and waved small handheld flags.

Bernard arrived at Rachel's side. "I'm told that Gorbachev is going to walk through the crowd. Come on, I will try to get a quote, and you should get a photo of me interviewing him."

"Okay, good idea. I already have some photos of him, close up next to Honecker, on the podium," Rachel said.

However they watched, dismayed, as Gorbachev was swamped by his security team and escorted away in the opposite direction to the Western media pack before they could get anywhere near him.

Bernard huffed as the journalists began to disperse around them, many followed by their minders as they started the long walk back to the checkpoint. "Missed opportunity," he grumbled. "I'll see you at the office, and I need your photos to go with my story."

"Okay."

Rachel waited as Josh filmed Juliette's wrap of the day's celebrations. Then they made their way out of the square and followed the crowds. Rachel was aware of the presence of several Volkspolizei behind them, so when she saw the sign for the Bavarian Café, she glanced at Josh and flicked her head.

He nodded. "I'm starving. Do you think we have time to stop?" he asked Juliette in a loud voice.

If Juliette was surprised at the change of plans, she didn't show it. "Sure," she said. "What about here?"

Rachel nodded, not trusting herself to speak, and followed Juliette through the door. The café was uninviting, with wooden chipboard walls and well-worn lino on the floor. The place was busy however, and in one corner, Rachel spied Maria and Hans sitting with a glass of beer each in front of them.

She slipped into a seat at an adjacent table with her back to them. Josh deposited his camera on the floor and dropped into a chair while Juliette approached the counter to order.

"Come to Leipzig," Maria spoke softly. "There's going to be a big protest march there on Monday night, the biggest one yet. We need to get the story out, and I can't leave as you saw. But you can, AND you can take your photos with you."

"Just me?" Rachel asked.

"Yeah, one of you will blend in," Hans said. "More would attract attention."

Juliette returned to the table carrying three small glasses of beer.

Josh smiled at her and took a large gulp before grimacing and coughing.

Hans chuckled.

"What will happen if I don't go back today?" Rachel toyed with her glass.

"I doubt they will notice with this many people crossing."

Rachel thought for a moment. This could be her chance to prove to Jones and Daniel, and all those who doubted her ability, that she was a photojournalist worthy of chasing the big stories. "Okay, then."

"Just like that?" Josh said, scowling at her. "Stop and think this through. What they are asking of you is dangerous, especially after what you told me earlier. If you get caught, you will get thrown in a Stasi jail, and we won't be able to get you out."

"I won't get caught," Rachel said, more confidently than she felt. "Besides," she lowered her voice and leaned forward, "this could be my chance to do some more digging on William Brown."

Josh shook his head. "No, Rach. It's all very well investigating from the relative safety of the West, but it's a different story here, and to be honest, I wouldn't trust these people. They will use you to their own ends."

Hans and Maria sat silently at the next table, sipping their drinks, watching the interaction with interest. A frown crossed Hans' handsome features at Josh's words. He went to speak, but Maria put a restraining hand on his arm.

"What do you think, Juliette?" Rachel turned to her friend.

"I like to think that I'm a fairly good judge of character, and I believe that you can trust these two. I'd do it in a heartbeat if we weren't due in Prague tomorrow."

Beside her, Josh tsked and shook his head, his lip curled.

"Rach, as long as you are careful and stay with Hans and Maria, you'll be fine. Don't go off on your own. Be patient; this won't be your only chance to come to East Berlin. Make contacts, build your network," Juliette said. "Don't do anything rash."

Rachel reached across the table and squeezed Juliette's arm before turning her head and speaking to Maria.

"Okay, let's do this."

"Slide over to our table, and your friends can go."

Rachel gave Juliette and Josh a smile full of more confidence than she felt as she moved between Maria and Hans.

"Here." Maria produced a beige jacket. "Yours is too conspicuous."

Rachel pulled her warm red coat off and passed it to Juliette, who draped it over her shoulders as Maria lifted Rachel's camera bag into a paper shopping sack at her feet.

As Juliette and Josh stood to leave, Josh leaned over to Hans.

"If anything happens to her, I swear I will find you, and the Stasi will be the least of your worries."

Hans leaned back in his chair and grinned at Josh. "Don't worry, we'll look after her."

"Josh, it's okay, but could you get my film from today to Bernard?" Rachel said, handing him several rolls of film. "He can take them back to London tonight and give them to the lab at the paper."

"Won't he wonder where you are?"

"Perhaps tell him that I'm ill," Rachel said. "I'll be back in a couple of days anyway."

Rachel watched as her friends left the bar and turned to the couple into whose hands she'd just entrusted her life. "Right, then, what happens now?"

CHAPTER 28

Leipzig, GDR
October 7, 1989

Rachel followed Maria and Hans from the bar a short time after Juliette and Josh left. They walked several blocks in the opposite direction, deeper into the city, away from the historic buildings and along streets of square, concrete apartment blocks. The roads became less populated and more rundown the further they walked. Finally, they stopped by a rusting blue Trabant.

Hans dug the keys from his jeans and unlocked the little two-door car.

"We need to pick up Annette and Dirk before heading to Leipzig," Maria said, tilting the front passenger seat forward to allow Rachel onto the backseat.

"Are we going straight there?" Rachel asked, climbing in.

"Yes, there are things to organise before Monday night," Hans said.

After collecting Annette from a friend's house nearby and stopping on a street corner on the outskirts of the city, where a fair-haired youth who introduced himself as Dirk joined them, they set off. Maria was in the front passenger seat, and Rachel shared the cramped backseat with Dirk and young Annette, who bombarded Rachel with questions in broken English until she eventually fell asleep, curled up between them with her head on Rachel's lap.

Rachel caught Hans glancing at her in the rear-view mirror on several occasions. There was an intensity to his gaze that was magnetic. She examined his side profile as they drove. Artfully messy fair hair framing a strong jaw, and long fingers gripping the steering wheel. When their eyes locked for the third time, his expression was amused. She looked away, embarrassed at being caught studying him.

Mostly they spoke English for her benefit, occasionally slipping into German, but she quickly noticed that the occupants used another name when referring to Hans.

"So, let me get this right, is your name not Hans?" Rachel asked.

His eyes flicked up to look at her in the mirror again, and he grinned. "Leo. Pleased to meet you."

"You don't trust anyone?" she said.

Leo shrugged.

"Don't worry about him, he's paranoid," Maria said, twisting in her seat to look at Rachel. "I'm Maria, and Dirk is definitely Dirk."

"And I'm definitely Annette," Annette said, snuggling into Rachel's side.

Rachel laughed. "Okay, how long is it to Leipzig?"

"Another couple of hours."

"What are we doing when we get there?"

"Leo has friends who live there, so if we get stopped, we're on our way to see them," Maria explained.

"If we get stopped?" Rachel felt a sudden sense of unease.

"The Vopos do spot checks," Hans said.

"Vopos?"

"Volkspolizei."

"Is that likely?" Rachel's eyes widened. "What do I say? I don't speak German."

Maria looked surprised. "Oh." She bit her lip. "I hadn't thought of that."

"Pretend you're asleep," Leo said.

"Or we could teach you a few phrases," Dirk offered.

"I know *Guten tag, danke*, and *ein Bier bitte*," Rachel said.

"All the important things, then?" Leo teased. "At least you could ask the Vopos for a beer."

"You can joke, but seriously, what if?"

"It's unlikely, don't worry," Leo said, holding her gaze.

"Are you from England?" Dirk asked.

Rachel shook her head. "New Zealand." Dirk looked blank. "It's in the South Pacific near Australia," she explained.

"You're a long way from home."

"Yeah, I work for a British newspaper. Many young New Zealanders spend a couple of years living and working in England and Europe."

"I've heard New Zealand is a beautiful country," Leo said.

"Yeah, it is. Very green. More sheep than people, so they say." Rachel laughed.

"I'd love to visit one day," Maria said. Her voice had turned wistful.

"I hope you can," Rachel said.

"Freedom to travel, that's just one of the many things that we're denied," Maria said.

They drove in silence, each deep in their own thoughts, while Annette, who'd fallen asleep again, snored softly. Rachel stroked her hair. The sun began to set in the sky, and Rachel noticed that Leo had switched on the car's headlights.

"What happens when we get to Leipzig?" Rachel asked.

"Once we drop Maria and Annette off at Maria's boyfriend's,

we're going to church," Leo said, glancing in the rear-view mirror at Rachel, a teasing glint in his eye.

Rachel considered the first piece of information with interest. Leo and Maria were not a couple as she'd first assumed, making the eye contact all the more interesting. She forced herself to focus on the second part of his comment. "Church?"

"Yeah. Pastor Christoph Wonneberger has been leading peace prayer meetings every Monday night at the Protestant Nicolaikirche, the St. Nicholas Church, for several years. The church has become a safe space for political dissidents."

"But surely the authorities don't allow that," Rachel said.

"The protests have outwardly been directed towards the build-up of the Soviet Union's nuclear weapons in the GDR, and for some reason, Honecker has tolerated a small peace movement."

"Surprising," Rachel said.

"It's not been without its dangers. The Stasi pretend to be congregation members, but because it's been peace prayers and not a protest movement, they've had little to report. There have been an increasing numbers of arrests, but to date, on the whole, it's been allowed. Of course, more has been happening behind the scenes than peace prayers."

"It sounds dangerous."

"It is," Maria said. "But since September 4th, when the peace prayers spilt out onto the streets, support has grown."

"I saw footage of that on television back in New Zealand," Rachel said. "Everyone saw the Stasi snatching away the freedom banners. What stood out was that the protestors didn't look like radicals; they looked like everyday people. It was powerful."

"So, it's working then." The excitement in Leo's voice was hard to miss. "Television is the way for the rest of the world to see what is happening and apply pressure to the SED to allow more freedom."

"They've been lying, saying that the people who oppose them

are counterrevolutionary criminals or fascists, for too long," Maria said. "It's what got my father killed."

"Maria, I'm sorry," Rachel said.

"The state controls everything, even what you are allowed to study," Maria said.

"What do you mean?"

"Tell her what happened to you, Leo."

"I applied to study law at a university in Berlin, but I was instead offered a more suitable engineering degree at a technical college."

"Why?"

"My political views weren't conducive to a law career."

"It was a punishment for questioning too many things," Dirk said. "They watch the smart ones like Leo here closely for signs of dissension."

"Do you even like studying engineering?" Rachel asked.

"Not particularly, but it allows me a little more freedom than the alternative, a full-time job. And at least it meant I didn't have to spend my compulsory military service on the inner German border with orders to shoot any civilians trying to escape. I worked on a construction project at a military base for eighteen months instead."

"I can't believe that you don't even have a choice in the career you pursue," Rachel said.

Maria twisted in her seat to look at Rachel. "People are fed up with living in fear of the lies and propaganda, the pollution, the poor housing, the shortages of things."

"No matter what happens, it feels like things are about to change," Dirk added.

"Yeah, the time for revolution has come."

Rachel gulped at the enormity of Leo's quiet, determined words and wondered what she'd gotten herself into.

•••

"Wake up, Annette, we're here." Maria leaned over and shook her little sister awake as they reached the outskirts of the city. Leo pulled over outside a small house with a pitched gable.

Rachel helped her to sit up.

"Oh, I think I fell asleep," Annette said with a wide yawn.

"And you snored like an elephant," Dirk teased.

Annette stuck her tongue out at him.

Rachel climbed out of the car to let Annette alight. She hugged the little girl goodbye. "See you later, Annette." Annette clung to her for a moment before slipping her hand into Maria's.

Maria reached out to grab Rachel's arm as she started to climb back into the car. "Stick with Leo and Dirk, they will look after you tonight. You're staying with my friend Gilda, and I'll see you tomorrow."

Rachel nodded.

"Jump in the front, Rachel," Leo called.

They drove deeper into Leipzig. Rachel noted that the city appeared greyer and less affluent than East Berlin; the Soviet architecture was stark and utilitarian. With the dark evening sky, the town seemed bleak and unwelcoming. Rachel shuddered as they pulled to a stop outside a boxy apartment building with blackened brick, cracked windows, and paint peeling from the window surrounds.

Their steps echoed in the concrete stairwell as they climbed to the third floor. Rachel wrinkled her nose at the stale cooking smells permeating the air from the flats on each floor. Leo and Dirk were welcomed with hugs and backslaps by the apartment's occupants, a young man and woman around their age. The man was dressed in pale blue denim and had short straight brown hair. The woman gave Rachel a shy, but wary smile.

"This is Rachel," Leo said, introducing her in English. "She's here to help with the march. Rachel, meet Martin and Gilda."

"Hi," she said to the young couple.

"English?" Martin asked as he shook her hand.

"New Zealander," Rachel said.

"Oh wow," Gilda said, stepping back and ushering them inside. "Come in."

They filed into the tiny, tidy flat furnished in orange and brown with old dark wood furniture. Leo handed Gilda a bag with a loaf of bread, apples, and cheese.

"Thank you, Leo. Would you like something to eat?"

He nodded, and Rachel realised that she hadn't considered how or what she would eat, simply assuming that they would go to a restaurant or café, but when she thought of their drive through the city, she grasped that she hadn't noticed many at all.

Gilda made tea and sandwiches for them all, refusing Rachel's offer of help. They squeezed together on the sofa to eat, with Martin sitting cross-legged on the floor by the battered coffee table.

"I thought we'd head over to the church tonight," Leo said.

Gilda shook her head. "No, they want us to stay away until tomorrow. They're being watched."

Leo looked deflated.

"What brings you to Leipzig?" Martin asked, turning his attention to Rachel.

"Rachel works for a British newspaper," Leo said.

Gilda's eyes widened. "You're going to help us get the word out that the people of the GDR are ready for a change? We want to talk, work out a way forward that involves everyone, not just the party elite."

"I'll do what I can. I'm a photojournalist, which means I use pictures to tell stories."

"Perfect."

Rachel nodded. "Can I use your bathroom?"

Gilda jumped up. "And let me show you where you'll be sleeping."

She led Rachel back towards the front door. "The bathroom is in there, and are you okay sleeping in here?" She opened the door to a small room with a bunk bed. "Or you could sleep on the sofa, and the boys could have this room."

"Rachel and I will be fine in here." Rachel jumped at Leo's voice behind her. "Dirk is going to stay with his grandmother." He slipped past Rachel and set her backpack and camera bag down on the bottom bunk.

"On top or underneath?"

"I'll take the bottom," Rachel said, ignoring the innuendo but catching Leo's cheeky grin as she slipped past him to use the bathroom.

"Will Paul and Kathryn be dropping by tonight?" Leo asked, throwing himself back down on the couch beside Rachel once they'd freshened up.

Gilda tossed her head. "They've gone too."

The fleeting surprised expression on Leo's face was replaced with frustration. "How will we change anything if everyone under thirty just leaves?"

"In their case, it wasn't safe. Paul had already been dragged in and subjected to an all-night interrogation twice, and next time, he would have been locked up for good."

Leo ran his hand through his hair, leaving it sticking up. "Any more bad news?"

An hour later, Rachel could feel herself flagging. It had been a long, unusual day and she needed to sleep. After saying goodnight, she got ready for bed, removing her jeans and sleeping in the t-shirt she'd worn that day. She had a fresh change of underwear and a clean t-shirt in her backpack, along with her toiletries. She'd almost not brought the bag that morning but was glad she had. There was a soft knock on the bedroom door once she crawled into her bunk before Leo entered.

"Tired?" he asked. "You've had a long day."

"Yeah, my body is tired, but my brain is busy trying to process everything."

Leo kicked off his boots, and the bed creaked as he climbed onto the top bunk.

"Do you travel a lot with your job?"

"Some," Rachel said. "I was at the Austrian Hungarian border when it opened last month. It was unbelievable timing on my part, and I got some amazing photos."

"So, people know what's happening?"

"Oh yes, like anything, it's very political. Any Communist country in the Soviet bloc is said to be behind the Iron Curtain. The West are very frightened of Communism, which is why we've had the Cold War underlying everything since the end of World War Two."

"We keep hearing about the aggressiveness of the West and the threat of them using nuclear weapons against us."

Rachel gave a soft laugh. "We are told the same, except the threat is from the Soviets."

"If they just let ordinary people have a say, then this could be resolved tomorrow," Leo said.

"I don't think it's that simple."

"I know, but wouldn't it be nice if it was."

"Yeah."

"What do you think is stopping more European countries from supporting the people of East Germany?"

Rachel hesitated.

"What? You can't offend me."

"The Americans are all for tearing down the Wall between East and West Germany, but the British and French not so much."

"They fear a united Germany." Leo was wise, despite his politically sheltered life.

"Yup, and history so far this century supports that."

"We're not really a nation of warmongers."

"You and I know that, but it's back to the politicians."

They lay in the dark, each wrapped in their own thoughts, until Leo's soft, rhythmic breathing broke the silence.

Rachel's thoughts drifted to her family on the farm back in Oamaru. They wouldn't believe that she was spending the night in East Germany. Another thought struck her; if things went wrong tomorrow, they might not find out where she was for a long time. She felt her heart squeeze painfully. Nothing would go wrong, she'd make sure of that.

CHAPTER 29

Leipzig, GDR
October 8, 1989

Rachel spent the following afternoon with Maria and Annette, who took her on a walking tour of the city. She kept her Leica tucked inside her jacket, only taking it out to take photographs when there was no one about. The city was a mixture of beautiful historic buildings and plain post-war Soviet-style architecture. They wandered through the grounds of the city's old university and stopped to photograph the monument to Bach near to St. Thomas' church where he'd been choirmaster.

But the highlight for Rachel was the Völkerschlachtdenkmal, or the Monument to the Battle of the Nations. The colossal granite and sandstone monument was reflected in a tranquil pond at its base, the interplay of reflections a photographer's dream. It was shaped like a temple and protected by an enormous sculpture of the Archangel Michael.

"This was erected to commemorate one of the bloodiest battles of the Napoleonic Wars," Maria explained. "The water is known as the lake of tears."

After Rachel had photographed the memorial from several vantage points and patiently explained how the camera worked to an attentive Annette, they walked closer to the monument. They weren't alone. A few people were strolling around, including several police. Rachel tucked her camera beneath her jacket.

"Shall we climb to the top?" Maria said. "The view of the city is amazing."

Rachel could feel the eyes of the officers on them as they approached the monument. Up close it was a little worse for wear, with broken and chipped stonework.

"Don't speak in English," Maria murmured.

Annette slipped her hand into Rachel's as they passed by and entered the vast crypt, climbing the stairs to the viewing platform which gave a panoramic view of the city and its surroundings. But the subtle menacing presence of the police tainted her enjoyment. By the time they climbed back down, Rachel was feeling more than a little nervous as though her every move was being watched. She was pleased when Maria and Annette walked her back to Gilda's flat, although her paranoia informed her that they'd taken a rather circuitous route. Maria left with the promise that she would see her again later that evening for some fun.

Leo was sprawled on the couch in the cramped living room when Rachel returned to the flat. He sat up and gave her a warm smile.

"How was your afternoon?"

"Great, Maria showed me around the city," Rachel said. "What did you do?"

"Just some preparation for the march tomorrow."

"We're heading out to the Unter Tage tonight," Martin said. "Join us?"

"Unter Tage is an underground music club," Leo explained to Rachel. "Its location changes weekly as the Stasi always try to close it down."

"Sounds great. Can I bring my camera?"

Leo and Martin exchanged a look, and Martin shrugged. "I don't see why not."

The club was in the basement of a building four blocks from Martin and Gilda's flat. Bouncers were posted inside the door of the old office block and looked over the newcomers with suspicion. But when Martin and Leo were recognised, the group was allowed inside. The beat of the drums grew louder as they skipped down the stairs and into a cavernous cellar.

Rachel was surprised to find the live band, a group of four musicians, looking very much like the bands whose gigs she attended in London. A drum kit was set up on a small stage in one corner, with the three guitarists crowded around two microphones. They were playing a cover version of a song by David Bowie. She looked up at Leo in surprise.

"What?"

The song changed to the opening chords of a popular song by Bryan Adams.

"I wasn't expecting to know the songs being played tonight."

"Would you believe that I've heard Bowie, Genesis, and the Eurythmics live, although I did end up spending a night in the cells for the privilege," Leo said.

"How?"

Martin returned, balancing four cups of beer.

"It was a couple of years ago, and there was a three-day music festival in front of the Reichstag on the Western side of the Wall. Word spread, and we climbed up on the rooftop of an apartment building near the Wall to listen. It was great for the first couple of nights. Several hundred of us gathered to hear David Bowie and the Eurythmics after dark."

"How did you know that the concert was going to happen?"

"There's a radio station called RiAS, Radio in the American Sector, which broadcasts across the city. It's tough for the authorities to stop people from tuning into it, but it meant we were well-informed. On the third night, Genesis was headlining, and we decided to get closer, but we found that the roads had all been blocked off about a quarter mile from the Wall, and the Vopos were everywhere."

"Why? What was different about that night?"

"The Party have long considered rock music, particularly punk, to be at odds with their views on social morality. They consider it a corrupting influence. I guess by the third night, they'd had enough. There were pitched battles between the kids and the police, and they completely overreacted and hit people with billy clubs. Hundreds of us were arrested and dragged away."

"Oh my God, did they hurt you?"

"Not really. We were released the next day, but it showed the party that they needed to do something for the younger people in the GDR, so they let its youth wing, the FDJ, book a concert on East German soil last year."

"Springsteen," Rachel breathed, recalling the news reports.

Leo nodded, his eyes shining. "They reckon 300,000 people turned up for the concert. He played for four hours – it was amazing."

"And he said, 'I'm not here for any government. I'm here to play rock and roll for you in the hope that one day all the barriers will be torn down'," Martin quoted.

"The authorities were furious. There won't be any more rock concerts for a long time," Gilda added.

"Yeah, but it's made things worse rather than pacifying us. We realised, even more, the freedoms we are missing," Leo said.

"Things I take for granted, like being able to go to a concert," Rachel said.

"I thought I'd find you here. All okay, Rachel?" Maria arrived at her side, smiling.

"Yeah, this is great," Rachel said. "The guys were telling me about the Genesis and Springsteen concerts."

"They were amazing, especially Springsteen. But I'm not sure we'll be allowed any more concerts after the success of that one."

"Doesn't seem fair, does it?"

Maria shook her head. "Are you okay at Gilda's?"

"Yes, thanks."

Rachel set her beer down on a nearby table, as it wasn't to her taste; too strong and bitter. She stepped away from the group and raised her camera, taking a roll of photos of the band, people dancing and drinking. Apart from the austere surroundings, she could have been in a club anywhere in the world.

"Dance with me?" Leo broke away from his friends as she lowered the camera.

Rachel hesitated. There was an energy between them. They'd been flirting since she'd gotten into his car, but something between them was impossible. Although a little voice in her head told her there was no reason not to enjoy his company while she was in East Berlin. She put her camera back in its case and slung it across her body before taking his hand and letting him lead her to the crowded dance area in front of the stage.

Rachel and Leo moved around each other in time to the music, and just as he went to rest his hands on her waist, a group of his friends joined them, forcing them apart so that they all danced in a group. After half a dozen songs, Leo snagged her hand and pulled her towards the bar.

"What would you like? You didn't like the beer?"

Rachel shook her head. "Not really."

"Try this. It's schnapps." Leo signalled to the bartender and handed her a small glass of golden liquid.

Rachel took a tentative sip. "It's okay, although I imagine it's fairly high in alcohol."

"What do you drink back in London?"

"Cider or red wine."

"Do you live on your own?"

They moved from the bar to the far side of the room and leaned against the wall facing one another.

"No, I share a flat with three others, including Juliette, whom you've met, and two Australian guys, Freddy and Tony. What about you?"

"I live in an apartment in Berlin similar to Martin and Gilda's."

Leo took a mouthful of beer and studied her. "Boyfriend?"

Rachel smiled. "No. Girlfriend?"

Leo shook his head, and the air between them crackled once more.

"Do you go back to New Zealand often?"

"No, I've just been back for the first time since moving to London. My older brother, Cole, just got married."

"Will you stay in London?"

Rachel shrugged. "For now."

"There you are," Maria called. "Come on, Leo. You can't monopolise our guest. Time to dance."

CHAPTER 30

Leipzig, GDR
October 9, 1989

Leo and Rachel collected Maria and her boyfriend Ali and drove to the St. Nicholas church to meet with the other protest leaders. There were several groups of people sitting in a back room. A long table was laid with bowls, plates and cups, and a tea urn was placed at one end. Opposite, six people, two older women, two men dressed in clerical robes and two younger men, sat having a quiet but intense discussion. Two young women were opening cartons of long white candles, sliding cardboard circles onto the ends of each candle and placing them into smaller boxes for later distribution.

They joined the long table, and soon Leo, Ali and Maria were deep in conversation with the others. Rachel couldn't understand their words, but sat absorbing the atmosphere. There was an underlying tension and apprehension among those present, an air of excitement, a calm before an approaching storm. Shards of colourful light flooded into the room, filtered through the high stained-glass windows of the church, showering the grey stone walls and floor with pastel hues. Rachel itched to photograph the resulting mosaic, but Leo had warned her not to produce her camera just yet.

People arrived and left at regular intervals. Leo kept glancing over at Rachel, and she gave him a reassuring smile each time.

All of a sudden, Maria gasped and pushed away from the table. *"Nein,"* she said.

Ali reached for her and pulled her into his arms, murmuring.

"What's happened?" Rachel asked Leo.

"There have been reports leaked about secret plans by Mielke's State Security Ministry to open concentration camps for up to two hundred thousand dissidents," he said, his expression grave. He dropped his voice. "Maria's father disappeared into one such re-education camp, never to return."

"Oh." Rachel couldn't comprehend the horror of what she was hearing.

"Come with me, and I'll show you where you'll be during tonight's peace prayers," Leo said.

Rachel followed Leo through a door at the rear of the vestry, up several flights of spiral stone stairs, and into a small attic room. The room was used for storage, containing stacks of chairs and piles of old hymn books covered in a layer of dust so thick that Rachel could have carved her name in it. Sash windows on three sides of the room overlooked a medieval square with a large fountain at the centre, surrounded by a mix of new and historic buildings.

"It's beautiful," Rachel said, peering through one window. "I didn't expect to see this many ancient buildings."

"It's one part of the city that escaped the bombing during the war."

"Can I get out on the roof to photograph the people in the street tonight?"

Leo nodded. "But you will need to be careful that you're not seen. The Stasi will have people watching in the opposite buildings and mingling with the crowds outside. They may even have snipers on some rooftops, so you'll need to be vigilant and keep behind the parapets. If they come up here, you need to hide. There are several small spaces on the walls. Here, I'll show you."

Leo led Rachel across the room to a wood-panelled wall. He slid one of the panels aside to reveal a hidden cupboard. "If you're at all concerned, you are to lock yourself in here, and if you hear anyone on the stairs that doesn't identify themselves as either me, Dirk, or Maria, you are to hide in here until one of us comes for you."

Rachel shuddered. "Leo, you're scaring me. Is it that dangerous?"

"Yeah, but don't worry, we will keep you safe. I will keep you safe," he added, reaching for her hand.

There it was again, that energy that snapped and fizzled between them. Leo leaned closer to her as the door opened, and Maria burst into the room.

"There you are…" She broke off and looked at their entwined fingers.

Rachel snatched her hand away as a grin spread across Maria's face. "Don't mind me," she said. "I just wanted to say that there's soup downstairs. Come and have some. We are going to need our energy for later. And Leo, you must run a message to the Reform Church about the route and start time for tonight, and they will coordinate a separate group to meet up with ours."

Leo nodded.

"Also, there's a rumour that tanks are being massed on the city's outskirts."

Rachel gasped. "Will the march tonight still go ahead?"

Leo nodded. "It will be the biggest yet."

"Won't the police crack down?"

Leo and Maria exchanged a glance.

"It's the risk we take for freedom."

CHAPTER 31

Leipzig, GDR
October 9, 1989

"Leo should have been back by now," Maria said, looking at her watch. "It's almost dark."

Rachel frowned. He had been gone a lot longer than expected.

The door burst open, and a teenage girl rushed through, her cheeks pink from exertion. "Quick, it's Leo," she said. "He's hurt."

Several people rushed to the door. Maria stopped Rachel.

"Wait here," she said. "You don't want to be caught outdoors."

Rachel waited by the door for what seemed like an age until it finally opened again. Martin and Dirk entered, supporting a limping Leo. His right eye was puffed up, and swollen, sticky blood caked his lips and chin. He held one arm across his ribs and groaned as Martin eased him onto a seat.

"Oh my God, Leo, what happened?" Rachel rushed to his side and crouched down.

"The Vopos were waiting on the corner after I left the Reform Church on my way back here, and I didn't see them until it was too late to change my route. They asked to see my papers and then questioned what I was doing this far from Berlin. They didn't like my reply, and before I knew it, I was on the ground, and they were laying into me."

Maria placed a bowl of warm water on the seat beside Leo and handed a cloth to Rachel. "Let's clean you up," she said.

"Why did they let you go?" Ali asked, giving the door a nervous glance. "Were you followed?"

Leo shook his head. "A group of men came along, I guess on their way home from work, and the officers stopped. They were outnumbered and just got in their car and drove off."

"You were lucky."

"I know."

Leo sat still while Rachel cleaned the cut on his lip but hissed when Maria bound his ankle.

"Sorry," she said. "It's not broken, just sprained. You must have twisted it when you fell."

"Or when they stomped on it."

Rachel's stomach rolled at the thought of the violence handed out by the Volkspolizei. It finally dawned on her the precarious position that she'd put herself in. All to prove herself. *Damn you, Daniel.* Although she hated to admit it, perhaps he'd been right. She glanced around at the groups of people gathered in the church's back room. Men and women, young and old, who didn't look afraid; they were determined to instigate change. Who was she to baulk at the first sign of trouble? She caught Leo's concerned expression as she drew in a shaky breath and forced what she hoped was a reassuring smile. He rested his hand on hers when she pressed the cloth to his split lip.

"Thanks, Rachel," he murmured. "Now, how are things here?"

Rachel supported him to the main table. A group were poring over maps, discussing the different routes for the march. It was clear to Rachel that alternative options had been planned if they found the streets blocked. Cups of weak coffee and tea were passed around, and gradually the group disbanded, emboldened with hugs and handshakes.

At dusk, the church filled with worshippers silently occupying the pews. Rachel and Leo peered through a crack in the vestry door into the vast church as Pastor Wonneberger began the prayer service.

"Can you photograph the protest without showing the faces of the organisers or the protesters?" Leo asked.

"Yeah, I haven't taken anything that could be used to identify anyone," she said, turning away. "I'm aware of the dangers."

Leo closed the door before reaching out and grabbing her arm. "I wasn't suggesting otherwise. I just want to keep everyone safe."

"I know. I'm sorry. I'm a little nervous about what might happen tonight."

"That's understandable; to be honest, we all are."

Rachel glanced down at his hand on her arm and then at his face. His features were shuttered, unreadable. She rested her hand on his and gave it a gentle squeeze, releasing it when he winced as she pressed on a bruised knuckle. "Sorry."

Leo opened his mouth to speak as Dirk entered through a side door and beckoned to those remaining to gather around. "I've just heard from a friend who's a doctor at Klinikum St. Georg., that the authorities have ordered additional blood supplies and requested that extra beds be prepared." He glanced at Rachel. "St. George Hospital."

There was silence in the room.

"They know."

One of the protest organisers, Angela, her short brown hair flecked with grey, spoke quietly. "Yes, it seems they do, but we can't stop this now."

A gust of cool air blasted into the room with the next arrivals, a young couple wrapped in jackets and scarves. They began speaking German to those gathered, and Maria translated for Rachel.

"There are more Vopos on the streets than usual. And they're heavily armed."

"Oh no, Maria," Rachel said.

"They wouldn't fire on their own people." Maria seemed certain.

"Wouldn't they? Look at what happened in Beijing," Rachel said.

"She's right. Remember how supportive Honecker was of the Chinese response back in June," a young woman said.

"This is not China," Leo said.

"Leo, it's time to take Rachel upstairs so she can get into position. Rachel, stay put until someone comes to get you, okay?" Angela said.

Rachel nodded and gathered her belongings, slipping her small pack onto her back.

A young woman approached and whispered to Angela.

"Leo, why don't you stay with her? You're not going to be able to walk far with your injuries, and she must get back across the border as soon as possible with the video recording that we will get to her," Angela said.

"Video recording?" Leo said.

"Aram and Siegbert have a great vantage point from which to film the march. We need Rachel to get the tape back to West German television so the people of the GDR can see what is happening when they turn on their televisions tomorrow."

"Hang on," Leo said. "If she's caught with it...."

"It's too good an opportunity not to try," Angela argued.

Leo shook his head. "You can't make that call, Angela."

"It's okay," Rachel said, sounding far braver than she felt. "I'll do it."

"Rachel, you don't understand," Leo began.

"Let's go upstairs to give me time to set up." She turned away, swallowing her fear.

Leo cursed and limped after her. In silence, Rachel helped him as he hobbled up the twisting stone staircase. Leo shuffled into the storage room, his bandaged ankle protesting at every step. He leaned heavily against the wall by the door. Rachel crossed to the window and peered down into the square, which was empty apart from a few pedestrians and some police officers lurking in the shadows. Streetlights illuminated the old buildings across the plaza. It was gloomy, the only light coming from the shadowy half-moon. Rachel lifted a couple of chairs into the shadows on the far side of the room.

"Here, you should elevate your foot while you can."

She set her bags down and unpacked her camera, laying out the lenses and canisters of film. She checked her focus and turned to Leo, still leaning against the wall, watching her. She raised the camera, desperate to capture his image but knew she couldn't. She turned her body and instead took a shot of the room.

Leo pushed off the wall and started towards her.

"You don't have to do this, you know," he said. "Take the video back, that is."

Click.

Rachel lowered the camera as he reached her, and he rested his hands on her shoulders, turning her to face him.

"I can't risk them taking you," he said.

"I don't think it's your choice to make."

"Rachel." He leaned his forehead against hers, their breath mingling. "I was wrong to bring you here. This isn't your fight."

"Maybe, but I'm here now." She reached out and ran her fingers down his cheek. "Your poor face."

"It will heal," he said. "My heart, though, now that's another matter."

Rachel pulled back and looked at him, frowning.

"Oh, come on, from the minute we laid eyes on one another, we've been dancing around this."

"Nothing can come of it," Rachel said. "You can't leave, and I can't stay."

"So, you admit that there is something between us?" he said with a sly grin.

Rachel leaned in and placed a gentle kiss on the side of his swollen mouth. Leo closed his eyes and groaned. "Oh, I wish I wasn't injured right now."

"Probably just as well," Rachel said with a soft laugh.

"You could have done that last night when I was in a position to respond."

"Again, probably just as well I didn't."

"Was I part of why you agreed to come with us?" he teased.

"You are so cocky."

Leo smirked.

Rachel's expression turned serious. "Actually, Leo, there's another reason that I'm here in East Germany. I'm looking for someone."

CHAPTER 32

Leipzig, GDR
October 9, 1989

"Let me get this straight; your grandmother spotted the man she thinks had your grandfather murdered, on a TV clip from here in Leipzig?"

"I know it sounds far-fetched, but I've done some digging and identified the man who could be him. He's a senior Stasi officer."

"I'm listening," Leo said. He led her to the chairs on the far side of the room and they sat facing one another.

"The man who betrayed my grandparents was William Brown, and the man in the TV clip is known as Wilhelm Braun."

"Wilhelm Braun," Leo repeated. "There's a Hauptmann Braun. I wonder if it's him. I'd do anything to get one over on those Stasi bastards. Imagine if it is him. What will you do?

"I don't know. Confront him, I suppose?"

Leo shook his head and interlaced his fingers with Rachel's. "That's exactly the opposite of what you will do. People who confront these guys, even about minor things, disappear."

"You're the second person to tell me that. After researching him at the Deutsche Archives, someone called me and warned me to stop looking for him. They said the West had Stasi spies too."

"I'm sure that's true."

"What should I do, then? Let the man who murdered my grandfather continue to get away with it?"

A smile formed on Leo's swollen lips. "No, you don't confront him. You expose him. You have the skills with the camera and the links to the media. If you can get a photo of him, then you can get your press contacts to start a campaign on him."

Rachel was speechless. "Why didn't I think of that?" She was quiet for a long moment as Leo ran his hand up and down her back. "I will need more proof than just a photo."

"You're not going to get a confession, even if you do speak to him."

"No, but I could get something with his fingerprints on it. The British government will have them on file from his days with the Foreign Office, and I know someone who could compare them."

"And I might just know someone on the inside who could grab a glass or something he uses at a meeting," Leo said. "But it will take time."

Rachel nodded. "It's been forty-four years; we have time."

Leo looked at his watch as they heard voices rising from the street below. "Okay, Rachel, it's showtime."

Rachel grabbed her camera and hurried towards the window. Leo pulled her down towards the floor. "Careful, you don't want to be seen. Look across the square, two floors down."

Rachel crouched beside Leo and peered into the darkened windows of the building opposite, and as her eyes adjusted to the dark, she spied movement, followed by the glowing tip of a cigarette.

"Come on," Leo said. "We'll climb out through the other window and lie flat behind the parapet, and you can aim your camera down the road."

"But I won't see the square that way."

"Trust me."

Rachel ducked, followed Leo through the open window, and crawled behind him for several metres. Rachel watched as Leo dropped to his knees with some difficulty. He spun and sat with his back to the brick of the parapet, his handsome face contorted with pain. He cursed under his breath.

Rachel crouched beside him. "Are you okay? Are you sure you don't need a doctor?"

"And miss this? No way. I'll be fine. Just give me a moment."

Low voices drifted through the still, cold night air. Rachel manoeuvred onto her stomach and peered over the edge. Hundreds of people were milling about, many carrying lighted candles. A shaft of light cut across the cobblestones as the doors to the church opened, and more people spilled out into the square. Rachel raised her camera, adjusted the focus and began taking photos, some wide angle, some close up.

The volume of the crowd increased.

"Look."

Rachel followed Leo's outstretched hand. People were pouring into the square from the nearby streets, some carrying white sheets stretched between two poles, and she could make out the word 'freedom' on one banner.

"Leo, there are thousands of people here."

"Isn't it fantastic?"

Softly at first and gradually gathering momentum, the voices rose as one.

"What are they saying?"

"*Wir sind das Volk* – we are the people."

Rachel heard the emotion in Leo's voice and glanced across at him. He was staring down at the crowd, tears rolling down his cheeks.

"So many people have come," he said.

Rachel kept taking photos, pausing only to change film. The crowd comprised people of all ages, from young to old, men and women, all dressed for warmth. Some held candles aloft, others linked arms, forming long human chains.

Sirens wailed in the distance, coming closer.

"Oh no, Leo, look."

Rachel pointed to a side street. Uniformed police marched in straight, regimented lines towards the protestors, wearing helmets and holding riot shields. Behind them cars and vans pulled up, blocking the streets. Rachel aimed her camera and zoomed in, taking in the scene through the viewfinder.

"They're armed." She held the camera in front of Leo's face so that he could see.

Together they watched as the people in the square merged with those in the surrounding streets and started moving as one down Karl Marx Platz towards the ring road. The chant changed.

"What are they saying now?"

"No violence."

"Oh dear God," Rachel muttered.

"Oh dear God is right," Leo said. "They're headed for the Round Corner."

"What's that?"

"The headquarters of the Stasi in the next block. This could get nasty."

The sirens of the police cars and vans were drowned out by the chants of the protestors. Rachel adjusted her shutter speed and leaned out, taking several long-angle shots down the road. Hundreds, no thousands of people were marching, and their ranks swelled as many others joined.

"This is amazing. Is this what's been happening every week, Leo?"

"No, this is different. This is much bigger." He rested his hands on her arms, his eyes shining with excitement. "Rachel, this is it;

this is the beginning. I can feel it. Things are about to change."

Later, she wasn't sure whether it was his passion for the cause or the emotion and adrenaline of the moment, but when she leaned in to kiss him, he met her halfway. Their mouths collided in a frenzy of desire and exhilaration, and Leo seemed oblivious to any pain.

A noise behind them broke them apart. Leo moved his body in front of hers. Maria's head poked through the open window.

"There you are," she said. "Isn't this amazing?"

Together they watched the crowds continuing to progress down the road. The Volkspolizei surrounding the square appeared to stand down. It was as though an order had come and without warning riot shields were stowed, and officers piled back into the vans, which started up, reversing, turning, and driving away.

Rachel captured the retreat in a series of rapid shutter-speed shots.

"Are they really just leaving?"

Leo stared down at the empty square, shaking his head. "I don't believe it."

"Perhaps they're going to regroup elsewhere?" Maria said.

"They're going in the opposite direction to the march," Leo said.

"What will happen to the protesters now?" Rachel asked, lowering her camera.

"They will go home and return again next Monday," Maria said.

"I can't believe what we just witnessed," Rachel said. "There was no violence, not a single shot fired."

"The power of the people," Leo said.

Maria looked at her watch. "We need to go now, as Aram and Siegbert should have the tape of the march ready."

They crawled back to the open window and slipped inside. Leo winced as he straightened up.

"Where were they filming from?" Rachel asked.

"They were hiding among the pigeon crap in the bell tower of a nearby church," Maria said.

Rachel packed her camera equipment and held her arm out for Leo to lean on as they followed Maria down the stairs and out a side door into the cold night.

"They're waiting in a bakery in the next street," Maria said. "The Stasi are focused on the marchers right now, so this is the best time for you to get away." She drew Rachel into a hug. "I will see you again soon."

Rachel held her for a moment, then pulled back and smiled. "Say goodbye to Annette."

Leo nodded once to Maria before she melted into the shadows.

Leo and Rachel kept close to the church wall, hurrying towards a doorway leading into the next building. Marching footsteps approached, and before they could reach the door, a group of soldiers rounded the corner. Leo pulled Rachel into a clinch, cupping her face and kissing her, using her hair to cover them both. He turned them, placing Rachel's back to the wall, obscuring her camera case, and Rachel trembled with terror.

But the footsteps didn't falter, and the soldiers continued past and into the next block.

"Come on." Leo glanced at the retreating soldiers before covering the last few steps to the door.

As planned, it was unlocked, and they slipped inside. Leo reached up and shot the top and bottom bolts.

"That was close," he said.

Rachel was still shaking as they hurried across an inner courtyard and into a narrow alleyway between two buildings. "Too close."

At the end of the passage, they turned right and stopped at a heavy wooden door. Leo knocked a tap-tap pattern. Within seconds the door swung open, and they were ushered inside.

They entered the bakery's kitchen, where two men and a woman were waiting.

"Man, what happened to you?" one of the men asked, peering at Leo's face.

"Vopos."

The man, slight build, mid-thirties with a goatee beard and small round glasses, turned to Rachel. "And you must be Rachel; we can't thank you enough for doing this."

Rachel nodded. "I will do my best. I captured some great shots tonight, which will cause me enough trouble if they're found, so what's one extra thing?"

They all laughed, except Leo.

"Just for the record," he said. "I don't like this at all. It's not her fight."

Rachel laid a hand on his arm. "It's okay, Leo."

The woman, young with long curling hair, stepped forward and handed Rachel a small package wrapped in plastic. "You'll need to hide it on your body, in your bra or something."

Rachel nodded.

"We should go," Leo said. "We must get out of the city while the Stasi is busy watching the crowds."

"Take these." The woman handed him a bag of warm rolls. "They'll keep you going on the road."

Leo and Rachel kept to the back streets to avoid the authorities, and within five minutes they were in Leo's Trabant heading in the opposite direction from the protest, and joined a ring road out of the city.

"There's an opening in the fabric at the side of your seat. Slide your films in there now, in case we're stopped," Leo said.

"Really?" Rachel glanced across at him. His jaw was clenched, whether with nerves or pain, she wasn't sure.

"Yeah, we have more chance of talking our way out of things if they don't find the films."

Cold fear clutched at Rachel's throat. She really hadn't thought this through. The potential for problems on the return journey hadn't even crossed her mind. She went to speak, but nothing came out. She cleared her throat and twisted to check the road behind them.

"It's okay, Rachel. I'm just being cautious."

Rachel unloaded the rolls of film she'd taken and slipped them deep into the seat. She clicked off the remaining photos on the film in her camera, removed that roll, and wound on a fresh one.

The streets became less busy the further they drove towards the outskirts, until finally they were speeding along dark country roads. Rachel breathed a sigh of relief.

"Do you want to pull over, and I'll drive for a bit, give your foot a rest?" Rachel offered.

"That would be great, thank you," Leo said. Ten minutes later, he pulled over. "We should be fine from here. Just keep to the speed limit."

"Which is?"

"100 kilometres, but if you drive that fast on these back roads, you'll kill us."

Leo sprawled in the passenger seat with his injured right foot balanced across his left knee with his hand resting on her thigh. Every so often, Rachel would drop her hand onto his.

"Where did you learn to drive?"

"You don't grow up on a farm and not know how to drive from a fairly young age."

"You grew up on a farm?"

"Yeah, a sheep farm outside a little town called Oamaru on the East Coast of the South Island."

As they drove, Rachel told him of her childhood in New Zealand and discovering her love of photography. Leo's upbringing was much less idyllic and marred by violence that he didn't share with her. They kept talking to keep each other awake, but still they reached the outskirts of Berlin sooner than either wanted, just as the first rays of sunlight began to break in the sky.

"I should drive from here," Leo said.

"When will I see you again?" Rachel asked as Leo navigated the back streets to avoid any police. She extracted the film from inside the seat as they drove and slipped it back into her camera bag.

Leo was silent. "I don't know," he said, finally. "Tomorrow, if I could."

"I'll come back."

"Only if it's safe and only if tonight goes without incident. Promise me if anything goes wrong, you won't come back. If your name gets on a list, it won't be safe, and I won't be able to protect you." Leo pulled his Trabi to a stop outside the back entrance to the AP office.

Rachel opened her mouth to protest, and Leo silenced her with a long, tender kiss.

"Promise me," he insisted, his voice cracking.

"I promise," Rachel said, tears springing into her eyes.

Leo leaned across her to open the passenger door. "Now go, *Schatz*. I'll find a way to get in touch."

"Can I write to you?"

"Yeah, I don't know if your letters will reach me, and be careful what you say," Leo said. "Do you have a pen?"

Rachel passed him a pen, and he scribbled his address inside an empty cigarette packet.

Rachel kissed him again and climbed from the car, clutching her camera case, backpack slung over one shoulder, and hurried to the back door of the AP office, punching in the key code Pierre had given her into the keypad recessed into the door. She turned to wave to Leo, but the car was gone.

CHAPTER 33

East Berlin, GDR
October 10, 1989

Pierre leapt up from where he was dozing behind the desk in his small office when Rachel entered.

"Thank God," he said. "I was very worried. You realise how dangerous going off like that was?"

Rachel sank into the chair opposite and allowed herself a moment. "I know, but it was too good an opportunity to turn down." She tensed and glanced around the office, her voice dropping to a whisper. "Are we okay to talk?"

Pierre nodded. "I swept it for bugs when I got here earlier. It's clean."

Rachel visibly relaxed. "Have I got a story," she blurted out.

Pierre smiled. "Spoken like a true journalist. Did you go to Leipzig? Juliette told me that's where you were headed."

"Yeah, I've just driven back with Le... I mean, Hans."

"Was there a march?"

"Was there a march?" Rachel repeated. "Pierre, it was amazing. There were thousands and thousands of people. Young and old, from all walks of life, protesting peacefully, and from what I saw the police allowed it, even though they were heavily armed."

"It's true, then. We've been hearing rumours since last night."

"There was a huge police presence, and apparently there were tanks on standby, although I didn't see them."

"Did you get photos?"

Rachel nodded. "When do I cross back?"

Pierre looked at his watch. "Soon, it's almost 7 a.m. I think the sooner you leave, the better."

"I agree."

"They will want to know why you didn't cross back with the other journalists," Pierre said. "I've spent the weekend since the fortieth celebrations holed up in my apartment, only leaving for food and alcohol so it would appear you stayed with me."

"Okay, thank you. I don't want to get you in trouble."

Pierre shrugged. "The Stasi keep an eye on me anyway. Now, you should put a new roll of film in your camera and take a few photos of me and of us together in case you are detained."

Rachel gulped. "Do you think they will detain me?

Pierre shook his head. "No, but it pays to be prepared. They may say that you should have arranged an extension and registered with the Volkspolizei when you decided to stay longer. Just apologise profusely and say you didn't realise that you had to do that."

Rachel thought of the videotape that she was carrying in her pocket. She would be in all sorts of trouble if she were caught with that. There would be no apologising. And the Stasi could use it to try to identify the protest leaders, and the crackdown would be severe. She gripped the back of the chair, the need to get it safely to West Berlin almost overwhelming her. She considered confiding in Pierre but decided not to. If he was questioned, the less he knew the better.

"Are you alright?" he asked, giving her an odd look.

"Yeah, just thinking."

She pulled her camera out, took a couple of close-ups of Pierre's face, and then stood beside him and held the camera, facing them at arm's length. Pierre snuggled his head down on her shoulder, and she took another shot. He turned his head and kissed her cheek. *Click.* She pulled a face. *Click.*

"Have you labelled all your used canisters?" he asked.

Rachel nodded.

Pierre reached into a drawer on his desk and pulled out a handful of empty, unlabelled film canisters. "Leave any from the anniversary labelled and put everything you took at Leipzig in unmarked canisters as though they are unused. It's only good as long as they don't check your film, but it will slow any suspicion that you've been to places they don't want Western journalists visiting."

Rachel's hands shook as she pulled the used film canisters from her bag and sorted them on the desk. Pierre reached over and took her hand. "It'll be okay, Rachel. I'm just being cautious, that's all. Try not to look nervous."

But his assurances sounded hollow.

Rachel quickly switched the Leipzig film into unmarked canisters, leaving Pierre to destroy the marked ones.

"I need to use the bathroom," she said when she'd repacked and closed her camera bag.

"Down the hall at the end."

Rachel locked herself in a cubicle and pulled the wrapped video tape from her coat pocket. After relieving herself, she slid the package into the front of her knickers and did up her jeans. The slight bulge was hidden when she dropped her t-shirt and jumper back over it. She washed her hands and lifted her top again to check in the mirror; the tape wasn't evident. She let out a long breath and stared at her reflection. *Here's to being brave, Rach,* she told herself. *Show Jones just how resourceful you can be.*

Back in Pierre's office, she picked up her bags.

"Ready?" he asked.

She nodded. "As I will ever be."

"Stick to the story. You stayed longer to spend the weekend with me."

"Okay. Where's your apartment?"

"On Jagerstrasse. It's number 14, 87 Jagerstrasse."

"Oh, and here's your coat. Juliette left it here for you," Pierre said, opening a cupboard and lifting out Rachel's red jacket.

"Can you get Maria's one back to her?" Rachel draped the beige parka over the back of a chair and pulled on her coat, its familiar snugness giving her some comfort.

"Of course."

Pierre opened his office door, peering into the hallway, and beckoned to her. "Start acting now."

They exited through the front of the building, arm in arm. Pierre made a show of helping her into his car to drive the few blocks to the border crossing. Rachel glanced in the side mirror as they pulled away from the building. A second car pulled out, and they were tailed. Pierre parked across the street from the checkpoint. They climbed from the car, and he embraced and kissed her goodbye before whispering good luck. Rachel clung to him for a moment, knowing she was on her own when she let go. He had risked enough already, getting her this far.

With a final squeeze of his hand, Rachel walked towards the border crossing, her backpack and camera bag slung over one shoulder, her press credentials hanging on a lanyard bouncing against her chest. She glanced behind her and saw Pierre leaning against the car, watching her depart. As he blew her a kiss, her eyes caught movement in the third-floor window of the building behind him, and she saw a brief flash of a face that looked like Leo's, watching too. But she couldn't be sure. She lowered her gaze and gave Pierre a small wave. Parked a few cars back, she noticed the men tailing them, watching the interaction intently.

The man in the passenger seat raised a small camera and took her photo.

Several others were lined up in the foot traffic queue, waiting to cross. When it was Rachel's turn, she approached the booth where an unsmiling border guard held his hand out for her papers. She passed them across, dismayed to see that her hands were shaking. The guard noticed, too, and studied her face for a moment before looking down at her passport and visa.

"You are late," he said in English. "You only had a day pass, which expired at midnight two nights ago."

"I spent the weekend with my boyfriend," Rachel said, looking back at the street behind her. Pierre and his car were gone. "I forgot to get my pass renewed."

"Bags," the guard instructed, pointing to the bench beside her. "And pockets."

Rachel swung her bags off her shoulder, dropped them onto the long table, and emptied her pockets of chewing gum and a London café bill. The guard rifled through her backpack before pushing it to one side and opening her camera bag. He lifted out Rachel's camera and set it aside when he spied the rolls of film in their canisters lying underneath. He picked up one. It was labelled '7 Oct 1989, Alexanderplatz'. The guard glanced up at her, his expression inscrutable, and put the film to one side before selecting another. This one was not annotated.

He raised an eyebrow and held it out to her. "You didn't use all of your films?"

"I was inside for much of the weekend," she said, trying to keep her tone light while fear twisted in her gut.

The guard returned the film in the bag and picked up her camera. His cold eyes appraised Rachel. "And you have only been in Berlin?"

A trickle of sweat ran down Rachel's back. "Yes."

The guard turned the camera over and gave her a long hard

stare. With a flick he opened the back of the camera, exposing the film inside to the light and ruining it.

"Don't…" Rachel began.

"Oops, sorry." His voice dripped with sarcasm as he handed the camera back to her, but for a moment, she swore he genuinely looked apologetic before the mask fell again. Rachel took the camera with shaking hands, snapped the back closed, and nestled it back into its bag.

Time stood still for a moment. The telephone in the guard's booth started ringing, giving a loud piercing jangle. Rachel startled and gathered her belongings, stuffing everything inside and fumbling with the zip.

The guard's eyes flicked up to Rachel and held her gaze. He leaned forward as he handed back her passport and spoke in a barely audible whisper. "Go now and walk quickly. Don't stop or run, and don't come back. Your name is on a detain list."

Rachel stared at him for a moment, uncomprehending, until another soldier pushed past, heading towards the booth and the ringing phone. Rachel's guard stopped him with a word, instead entering the booth himself. He looked back and gave Rachel a sharp jerk of his head as if to say 'get moving', as he picked up the receiver with a harsh, "*Ja.*"

Rachel snapped out of her stupor, scooped up her bags, slipped past the booth, and hurried along the road towards the West. Each step felt like walking through treacle as she waited for someone to stop her with a shout or, worse, a bullet. She could see two East German guards patrolling in her periphery with their vicious-looking dogs panting and pulling at their leashes. In front of her, several US border guards began to call out, but she couldn't hear their words due to the rushing sound in her ears.

Ten feet to go. The barrier arm in front of her started to rise.

"Stop," a voice behind her shouted.

A dog barked.

Rachel hurried forward.

Four feet.

The soldiers in front of her came to attention and called to her. "Quick now."

Rachel stumbled. *Two feet.*

She could hear footsteps behind her and more shouting.

Hands pulled her to safety as the barrier arm slammed back into place, and the soldiers formed a barricade between her and the East German border guards.

Rachel let her bags slide to the ground and leaned forward, hands on her knees, sucking in deep breaths.

"Are you okay? Can we see your papers?"

Rachel handed her passport to the soldier.

"Rach?" a voice shouted.

Rachel looked up to see Juliette running along the street towards her.

"Anything you need to tell us, Miss?" the border guard asked, handing her back her passport.

Rachel shook her head before Juliette enveloped her in a hug. "Thank God," she said. "We were very worried."

"How did you know I would be crossing?"

"Pierre sent word. Come on, let's get you out of here." She picked up the backpack and looped her arm around through Rachel's.

"I need to get to the state television broadcast centre immediately," Rachel whispered.

Juliette's eyes widened, and she gave a quick shake of her head, signalling to Rachel to say nothing further. Together they walked away from the checkpoint to where Josh was waiting with a car idling at the curb.

"Rach," he said as she slipped into the backseat.

"Straight to the Deutscher Fernsehfunk office, Josh," Rachel said. "You won't believe what I've just smuggled out from the protest."

Juliette and Josh exchanged an excited glance.

"So, the rumours are true. The protest went ahead," Juliette said.

Rachel nodded. "Estimates are that there were 70,000 protestors, and the streets were full of people as far as you could see."

Juliette was open-mouthed.

"And the Stasi didn't try and stop them?" Josh said.

"No, there were a few scuffles, but it was a peaceful protest. The people gathered in the square and marched on the local Stasi headquarters. I have never seen anything like it."

"I assume you have photos?"

Rachel nodded and slid down in the seat, wriggling and reaching into the waistband of her jeans. "Better still, I have this." She held out the videotape.

"I promised to get the video to the TV station, but once they've copied it, it's all yours."

CHAPTER 34

West Berlin, FRG
October 10, 1989

Rachel burst into the office of Deutscher Fernsehfunk, the state broadcaster, with Juliette and Josh on her heels. The studio was bustling as the crew prepared to film the early morning news programme, but fortunately one of the editors, a long-haired man in his late twenties, spotted them and rushed across the room to greet Juliette like a long-lost friend, grasping her by the shoulders and kissing her on each cheek. Rachel saw Juliette flinch as his moustache brushed her skin.

"Nix, you have to help me. You have to see this. My friend Rachel was in Leipzig last night and witnessed a peaceful protest march with thousands of people, the biggest yet, and she has smuggled out video footage. We have to get it on the TV news," she said.

"Whoa, slow down," Nix said, leading them into a small office with a single desk and chair and a TV on a stand in one corner with a video cassette recorder beneath it.

Rachel pulled the tape from her bag and unwound the plastic covering before handing it to him.

"Can you make a copy so I can give Juliette the original?"

Nix nodded. "Let's see what you've got first." He pushed the tape into a video player, picked up a remote control, and pointed it at a TV screen. Seconds later, the sounds of hundreds of voices chanting echoed around the studio, and the images of thousands of marching protesters, arms linked or carrying candles, filled the screen.

"This was last night? Where did you get it?"

"I was there," Rachel said. "Two guys shot it from a church's bell tower on the route. I drove back to Berlin with it overnight and crossed the border this morning." Rachel handed him her passport showing the border stamps.

Nix's eyes widened and he bolted from the room, returning seconds later with half a dozen other people; two older men in corporate attire, who appeared to be the decision makers, two women, one dressed casually in jeans, the other with a full face of TV makeup. Two men around Nix's age, wearing large, chunky headsets also squeezed into the room, and watched as Nix rewound and replayed the footage of the march. Juliette, Josh and Rachel leaned against the wall as an animated discussion took place in German between the group before the jeans-clad woman wrote some notes on a piece of paper and rushed from the room.

"What's happening?" Juliette asked when Nix looked in their direction.

"Come," he said. "We're going to broadcast it."

Ten minutes later, they stood to one side of a much larger studio, where two enormous cameras were recording a live show, and watched as the morning news anchors delivered the breaking news of the peaceful protest march by thousands of ordinary East Germans in Leipzig the previous evening, before cutting to the footage that Rachel had smuggled out.

A wave of exhaustion passed over Rachel as the adrenaline rush left her, and the enormity of what she had just done hit her.

Juliette squeezed her hand. "You did it, Rach."

"I hope Leo and Maria were able to see that," Rachel said.

"Come on, let's get out of here," Josh said, returning with the tape. "If you want any chance of going back, you can't be associated with that film footage."

"I'm exhausted," Rachel said. "I've been driving all night with Leo to get the tape back."

"You mentioned Leo before," Juliette said. "Who's Leo?"

"Hans."

"Ah," Josh said. "So, he kept his word and got you back safe. Although I don't think smuggling illegal film footage was part of the deal."

"It wasn't," Rachel said. "But two guys managed to record it, and someone had to bring it across. Remember when Pierre told us that many East German households have TVs which tune into West German TV stations? It's not sanctioned, but they do it anyway. The protester leaders want the rest of the GDR to see tens of thousands of people protesting peacefully in Leipzig, then hopefully, other cities will follow."

"If you'd been caught...." Josh trailed off.

"I know," Rachel said. "I had some help at the checkpoint. One of the officers told me to hurry and not come back, and he said that my name was on a detain list. The phone rang in the guard's booth just as I left, it was as though someone had found out I was crossing, but they were too late to stop me."

"That makes sense, they were shouting at you to stop when you crossed, and the Americans all had their guns drawn," Juliette said. "I think the best thing would be for you to head back to London."

Rachel nodded. "I've got some amazing photos, and I think Jones is gonna be super impressed."

"What about your films?"

"Good point. I'll develop them now and send any good ones back to London. I need to get some away in case I was followed.

According to Leo, Stasi spies are operating in West Berlin too. Then I need to sleep for a few hours."

Juliette took her arm. "I'll come with you while Josh edits the footage into something we can use. You can fill me in on the details that I will need for my "exclusive" report." She drew air commas, with a huge grin on her face.

•••

Juliette ordered room service breakfast while Rachel shut herself in the bathroom and developed the films using her portable darkroom. Half an hour later, she'd selected what she thought were the best photos from the rolls of film taken at Leipzig and hung them to dry on the travel clothesline she'd strung up across the bathroom.

Juliette poured her a coffee, and Rachel relayed the last two days' events, confiding in Juliette about Leo.

"You sound like you like him."

"I do, but it's impossible," Rachel sighed. "He can't leave, and now I can't go back."

"You definitely can't go back," Juliette agreed. "The minute you enter the GDR, you will be arrested as a spy."

"There must be something that we can do to help. The East German people are ready for change, for a dialogue with the ruling party, at the very least."

"If you can get your images published, that will help draw attention to what is happening. Hey, why don't you write a piece on your weekend in the GDR?"

"I'm not a writer, Juliette."

"Yes, but I am. I could help you."

"I wouldn't want to put anyone in danger."

"We could be careful. It could be your impressions more than anything. About the mood of the people."

"That sounds like a tomorrow job," Rachel said. "Let's see if the photos are dry enough to send, then I have to sleep. This is when I need the Dixel picture transmitter. You can load in the negatives, and it sends everything quickly."

"Why don't you have one?"

"They're new and something like £40,000 each, so the paper only has one and Gilbert, the weasel, has it, wherever he is with Daniel. A rookie like me has to use the old-school methods."

Rachel pulled a silver briefcase from beneath her bed. She placed it carefully on the desk and opened it to reveal a portable photo transmitter the size of a small typewriter. She plugged the power cord into a socket on the wall and unplugged her hotel room phone, replacing it with a second cable from the transmitter. Rachel switched the machine on and fed the first photo into the machine, selecting the black-and-white option. With a loud squeak, the rollers pulled the picture in and rolled it around the drum, which rotated quickly, scanning the photo and sending it across the telephone line to London. The entire process took around eight minutes for the individual image.

Juliette sat with Rachel for another hour, prodding her awake each time a new photo needed sending.

Jones had called after she transmitted her last photo and plugged her phone back in, ecstatic at what she'd achieved. "Why didn't you tell me you were going to Leipzig?" he boomed.

"It was a last-minute thing, and there was no time."

"I think you should come home today, Rachel," Jones said.

"But…"

"Just until things die down, and then you can go back. I'll get Felicity to book you on a flight later this afternoon."

Rachel joined Juliette for a coffee in the hotel bar mid-afternoon while she waited for a taxi to the airport, having had a few hours of much-needed sleep.

"I wish I wasn't going back to London. It feels like I should be here where things are happening. Were you able to make something out of the footage?" she said.

Josh nodded. "Several reports actually."

"We're crossing live to the station in Australia for a slot on the morning news in a few hours," Juliette said.

"The authorities in the GDR are going to be furious that footage of another, even larger demonstration has leaked," Rachel said.

"All the more reason for you to go back to London." Josh took a gulp of coffee. "You don't want anyone linking you with it. The Stasi has a long reach."

CHAPTER 35

London, England
October 18, 1989

Rachel returned from lunch to find a small box sitting in the centre of her workstation. The newspaper office had a large number of empty desks, with many of the foreign section journalists abroad and others having a long lunch. She looked over to Jones's office, but he too was absent; clearly it was a slow news day.

"A courier delivered it," Felicity said from the next desk.

Rachel picked up the package and turned it over in her hands before a smile tugged at the corners of her mouth. Lettering on each side of the box spelled out the word, 'Hans'. She tore off the tape, opened the lid, and lifted out a china cup wrapped in plastic.

"No way," she whispered, setting it aside and pulling a single sheet of paper from the box.

"What does it say?" Felicity leaned over her shoulder to read.

'Hope you find some use for this.'

"What does that mean?" Felicity asked.

"Nothing, it's just a gift from an admirer," Rachel said, slipping the cup back into the box and reaching for her phone to call the flat. Juliette answered on the third ring.

"Leo has somehow gotten hold of a cup with Braun's fingerprints on it," she said in a low voice.

"What?" Juliette said.

"It just arrived by courier."

"Wow, you must have made an impression. I'm sure getting hold of that wasn't without some risk."

"He said he knew people who worked in the kitchen at the Stasi HQ, but I didn't expect they'd actually be able to do this."

"You want to give it to Monty, don't you?"

"He's the only person we know who could get William Brown's fingerprints from his classified file. They must have them on record. Imagine if we could compare them and they were a match."

"It's a long shot, Rach," Juliette said.

"I know that, but I have to try."

Rachel spent the rest of the afternoon working on a photo essay depicting the restrictions affecting life in the GDR. Juliette had helped her to write the accompanying article which she hoped Jones would agree to publish. She was about to call it a day when Jones burst onto the floor and turned up the radio on Felicity's desk.

'Following weeks of mounting pressure, GDR leader Eric Honecker has resigned, and whether this will appease a population demanding change remains to be seen. His replacement, Egon Krenz, is a long-serving Politburo member, and it is unclear whether he can deliver the sweeping changes demanded by the people of the GDR.'

Jones switched the radio off.

"Photo archive, Rachel. I want pictures of Honecker and Krenz, now."

•••

Rachel received a call at work from Juliette.

"I thought you'd like to know Monty has news about the fingerprints on the cup," she said. "I'm meeting up with him when he finishes work."

Rachel was the first to arrive at the Coal Hole and was still shaking the rain from her hair when Juliette breezed through the pub's entrance, battling an umbrella that the wind had turned inside out.

"I think the only place for that is the rubbish bin," she said.

Monty rushed through the door a few minutes later and joined them at the long, gleaming wooden bar.

"Sorry I'm late. The tube was packed."

"What would you like to drink?" Rachel asked, pulling her purse from her bag.

"Gin and tonic, please."

Rachel ordered their drinks while Juliette and Monty found an empty table by the window.

"So, do you have news?" Rachel said after she'd deposited their drinks on the table and sat down beside Juliette.

Monty smiled. "I pulled in some favours, and had the fingerprints on the mug you gave me compared to those held in the classified World War Two archives."

"And..." Rachel prompted.

"They match."

Rachel gasped. "William Brown is still alive and living as Wilhelm Braun in East Germany. My grandmother was right."

"It would appear so," Monty said. "And what's more, there's a huge file on him, but I can't get you access because it's classified. From what I can tell, his disappearance was investigated at the time because he had been accused of passing secrets to the Russians and your grandmother thought he'd had your grandfather murdered. She was connected, it seems, and her accusation went right to the top at Bletchley and at the Foreign Office."

"That all fits with the story she told me. How do we get him?"

"With difficulty. As you'd expect, the powers that be are a little preoccupied with everything happening behind the Iron Curtain. There are rumours that something big is about to happen in Hungary."

"Hungary?" Rachel's eyes lit up.

Monty clamped his lips together. "I've said too much already. I did get you this, though. It's from 1940 – he'd look different now." He slid a black and white photograph across the table of a tall, well-built man dressed in a smart double-breasted pin-striped suit.

Rachel picked up the photo and studied it. "If we were to locate William Brown, could he be arrested and brought back here to be tried for his crimes?"

"In theory, but I'm not sure how you'd get him out of East Germany without causing a political incident." Monty looked at his watch. "Anyway, I must go," he said, draining his drink.

Rachel was thoughtful as she watched Monty melt into the crowd outside the pub. "I need to get a message to Leo."

"Have you heard from him?"

Rachel nodded. "Only the cup."

"You really like him, don't you?"

"Yeah, I do," Rachel said. "There's something about him. I've never felt like this about anyone. I hope it's not just the star-crossed lovers thing. I mean, I don't think it is."

Juliette smiled. "Rachel, you're way too practical to get caught up falling in love with someone just because you can't have them."

"I guess. He creeps into my thoughts when I least expect it and I often find myself wondering what he's doing and wishing I could just talk to him."

"Oh, you've got it bad."

Rachel gave her a rueful smile. "The worst thing is that I don't know if he is safe. If the Stasi have finally caught up with him, he could be imprisoned and I'd never know."

"Rach, I don't know what to say, if you love him, it complicates things."

Rachel thought about Juliette's words on her way back to the flat. It was much easier to ascribe what she felt for Leo to passion, attraction, not love. Passion was a physical thing that would eventually burn out, whereas love... Rachel shook her head. Her experience of love was heartbreak, although if she conjured Daniel to mind, what she'd felt with him seemed insignificant to how she felt about Leo. Entirely how and when that had happened, she wasn't sure. This situation with Leo was impossible. Perhaps that's what had heightened things so quickly. She gave a bitter laugh. Maybe she was susceptible to the star-crossed lovers thing after all.

The weekend was uneventful. Juliette and Josh were away again, this time covering the San Francisco earthquake. Rachel spent Sunday in Hyde Park photographing autumn leaves and trying a new camera lens.

She mulled over what to do about William Brown. Sure, she could expose him as Leo had suggested, but what good would that really do? He was unattainable as far as seeing justice served was concerned, and there was the real risk that he'd simply disappear again. No, it had been more than forty years, there really was no need to rush this. Rachel decided that doing nothing for the moment was the best option.

On Monday afternoon, she returned to her desk when a commotion occurred in Jones's office.

"Hungary has declared itself a republic and announced the end of Communist rule," he shouted. "Daniel, Stan, Gilbert, Heathrow now. I want you in Hungary ASAP."

Rachel jumped up. "Can I go too?"

Jones looked across at her. "No, I want you and Bernard on standby to go back to Berlin should there be developments. Fenella and Thompson; Prague. Things are happening, people, and the Iron Curtain is unravelling. I want the stories first! Got it?"

"Won't the Soviets retaliate? Look at how brutally they put down the 1956 uprising in Hungary," said an older reporter, who lit a cigarette and sat back in his chair.

"I'm not sure, with Gorbachev at the helm. Times are a-changing, and I think he's very aware of the fact," Jones said. "But regardless, there will surely be developments over the next few days and weeks. Go forth, people, bring me stories."

CHAPTER 36

West Berlin, FRG
November 1, 1989

J ones came shuffling out of his office and crossed the floor to the foreign desk with an unlit cigarette dangling from his lips.

"Bernard, Rachel, back to Berlin. There are rumours of another big protest in the next few days in the GDR. No one is to cross the border, but I want you guys on the ground in West Berlin close to the action."

"Finally," Rachel muttered. The previous ten days stuck in London had dragged, and she was itching to return to Berlin. She told herself that it had nothing to do with Leo, although if she was honest, she hadn't heard from him again and felt a little anxious. Perhaps being in West Berlin she could get a message to him through Pierre.

She gathered her things and turned to Jones's assistant, who was already on the telephone with the airlines.

"Go," she mouthed to Rachel. "Your ticket will be waiting for you at the check-in desk."

"Thanks," Rachel said, grabbing a scrap of paper and writing down the name of the hotel she'd stayed at with Juliette and Josh the last time they'd been in Berlin. She put it down in front of Felicity, who nodded before speaking into her handset.

"Yes, I'd like to book flights for today."

Rachel signed out as many bricks of film as Ernie would allow her, along with a portable darkroom and photo transmitter, and rushed back to her flat to pack a small wheeled suitcase. She left a note on Juliette's bed with her whereabouts, and within an hour, she was on the Piccadilly line to Heathrow.

•••

The rest of the week was spent chasing down unsubstantiated rumours and taking photos across the Wall from various vantage points in West Berlin to send back to the office alongside Bernard's articles. Rachel once again had a windowless bathroom which made an ideal photo lab, and set up her portable darkroom, developing her photos each day and undertaking the time-consuming job of transmitting the best ones to London. She selected the images she and Bernard agreed best supported his articles on the military build-up in the GDR. She chose a couple of others showing an increased police presence on the Eastern side at the central Berlin checkpoints. Checkpoint Charlie, in particular, appeared to have a heavier military presence, with armed soldiers performing manoeuvres and drills in the streets immediately surrounding the Wall. She settled into a cordial working relationship with Bernard. He had accorded her some grudging respect for her work covering the Leipzig protest, although he could still be a condescending oaf. But she had to admit that he did have a different perspective on world events, namely that change took time and patience. He continued to remind her that their jobs as journalists were to report the facts, not to influence the speed at which they happened.

•••

Rachel knew most of the journalists who assembled at the American bar near Potsdamer Platz. She and Shelley ordered drinks and snacks at the bar and squeezed onto one end of a large table. Bryan Adams crooned from the wall-mounted speakers.

"They've had it approved, I tell you," an American reporter insisted to his incredulous colleague.

"What's been approved, Sam?"

"There will be a protest in East Berlin tomorrow, and it's state sanctioned."

"We've heard rumours that something might be happening," Rachel said. "Who has organised it?"

"A group of actors and writers, apparently."

"I suspect the SED will be using that to root out the dissidents and use it for their political benefit," another reporter suggested.

"Quite possible. They're on the back foot," a woman further down the table added.

"Which means that there will be a show of force. We gotta pray it's not another Tiananmen Square."

"Maybe under Honecker, but Krenz is more liberal," another journalist argued.

"Is anyone going?" Rachel asked.

There were headshakes from all around the table. "No visas issued."

"That means they're concerned," Shelley said.

"This could be the beginning of the end of the GDR. East Germans are protesting in every city across the country," Rachel added.

"It won't happen in our lifetime," Bernard said.

•••

Rachel returned to her hotel a little worse for wear. She'd discovered too late that trying to match Shelley drink for drink had been a fool's errand. It took several goes to get the key into her lock, but once inside she collapsed on the bed and stared at the ceiling, which looked a little blurry, like an out-of-focus image.

She had just drifted off to sleep when the loud jangle of the telephone on her bedside table caused her eyes to fly open. Her mouth was dry, and she swallowed several times before answering with a husky hello.

"Rachel, hey," said a deep male voice in accented English. "It's Hans."

"Hans, how?" Rachel sat upright and then wished she hadn't. Her head swam.

"I heard you were back, and I wanted to say hi. Did you get my letters?"

"Only the cup."

"The postal system is a little unreliable."

"I wish I could see you," Rachel said.

"Me too. Was the gift helpful?"

"Yes, and it worked as planned."

"Make sure you're around tomorrow."

"Ah, sure."

A couple of beeps sounded on the line.

"We're not alone," Leo said. "Gotta go."

The line disconnected.

Rachel replaced the receiver in the cradle and lay back on the bed, a slow smile forming. So, Leo was still thinking about her too. The smile faded as quickly as it had started. It was hopeless. They couldn't even communicate without someone intercepting their letters and listening in on their phone calls. He was trapped in the GDR, on the other side of the Wall, unable to cross. She was falling into the trap of making their impossible situation into a romantic drama.

Instead, she switched on the journalistic part of her brain, replayed the conversation in her head, and wondered what he meant about making sure she was around tomorrow; it wasn't as though he could pop across to see her. No, that wasn't what he was telling her; he was telling her something was planned for the next day. The rally the American journalist had mentioned earlier in the evening, that had to be it.

CHAPTER 37

West Berlin, FRG
November 4, 1989

The telephone rang, dragging Rachel from a deep sleep.

"Hello," she answered. Her head thumped and her mouth felt as dry as a desert.

"Rachel, you've got to come to my room, the protest is live on TV, and it's huge."

Juliette had the television on in her hotel room when Rachel arrived. Her room was identical to Rachel's, with the same beige walls and carpet, a white-sheeted double bed and a small round table with a single chair, also beige. She had just sprawled beside Juliette on the end of the bed facing the TV when Josh joined them, balancing cups of coffee and a bag of pastries. He set them down on the little table and removed his jacket, draping it over the back of a chair.

"This is being shown live by East German television," Juliette said. "I'll translate."

"The largest protest against the ruling SED party to date is being held today in East Berlin," the newsreader announced, accompanied by video footage of a large crowd listening to an earnest short-haired young man speaking through a megaphone. "An estimated half a million people have gathered to protest and listen to speakers demanding democracy, the right to travel outside the GDR, and generally denouncing the Communist regime."

"Look, there's Alexanderplatz. It looks a little different than it did a month ago," Josh said, ripping open the bag of pastries. Rachel leaned across and grabbed one. Coffee and carbs would help to cure her hangover.

Alexanderplatz, where Rachel, Juliette and Josh had witnessed the GDR's fortieth-anniversary parades only a month earlier, was filled with an entirely different crowd. Gone were the flags and banners proclaiming the GDR's greatness. Gone was the show of military might, no marching band or parading soldiers. Instead, ordinary people filled the square; men and women, young and old, some holding banners, but all facing a wooden platform built onto the back of a truck at one side of the square.

Rachel was open-mouthed. "I don't believe what I'm seeing. Half a million people?"

"Look, isn't that Stefan Heym, the novelist?" Josh said, as an older man with messy white hair was helped up onto the podium. The crowd clapped, then fell silent as he started to speak through the microphone, his voice echoing throughout the plaza. Juliette translated as he spoke.

"It is as if someone has forced open a window on years of intellectual, economic, and political stagnation, years of sluggishness and stale air, of empty words and bureaucratic, ah... something I can't understand, ah, of an officialdom blind and deaf to the world."

There was rousing applause from the crowd each time he drew breath.

"Oh my God," Rachel breathed. "They will kill him."

"Who's this?" Josh asked as a new speaker; a good-looking young man, embraced Heym and took his place.

"Ooh, that's Jan Liefer, the actor," Juliette said. "Isn't he gorgeous?"

Next up was a member of the ruling SED party. Almost as one the crowd booed, nearly drowning out his rhetoric.

"Look, his hands are trembling." Josh pointed at the TV screen where the paper the man was holding with his speech shook. "They know this is the beginning of the end. These people are calling for a different kind of socialism, a democratic one, and you can't help but think that they will get it."

"But at what cost?" Juliette asked.

"Look at the Volkspolizei." Rachel pointed at the screen. "They look almost overwhelmed." Police in riot gear lined the square waiting to lay into the crowd with their batons as they'd done on previous occasions, but somehow this time the police looked more scared than the protesters who dominated by sheer force of numbers. "I can't believe it was only a month ago that we were there as a witness to a show of strength by the SED. So much seems to have suddenly changed."

"Getting that footage out of the peaceful protest at Leipzig will have given more people the courage to protest," Juliette said, squeezing Rachel's hand. "I wonder if Maria and Leo are there? I'm surprised Leo isn't one of the speakers," Juliette said.

"He might have been, although he could be lying low after the beating he received in Leipzig. The Stasi would like nothing more than to match him to the man named Hans who has caused so much trouble." Rachel's eyes scanned the crowd intently, hoping for a glimpse of the man who hadn't been far from her thoughts for the last month.

The camera panned across the crowd to a building overlooking the square.

"I wonder if he is there?" Rachel mused.

"Who? Leo?" Juliette asked.

"No, William Brown. A Stasi captain is sure to be in the shadows for something this big."

•••

Rachel spent the next few days out and about in West Berlin, photographing the increasing numbers of people congregating at various points along the Wall. The Alexanderplatz protest seemed to have galvanised the youth of West Berlin, and all along the Wall the sounds of pickaxes could be heard, chipping away at the structure. Rachel strolled along Ebertstrasse, bordering the Wall, when she came upon a group of young men welding axes, chisels and hammers. She raised her camera, adjusted the focus and captured the image. Even a few weeks earlier, such activity would not have been allowed.

As she watched, the group worked on the plaster joining the large concrete slabs. A shout went up when the mortar fell away, revealing a gap on either side of one large section of Wall.

A high-powered hose manned by East German border guards sprayed through the cracks, soaking the men. Rachel photographed their laughing faces as they shook the water from their hair and continued swinging the hammers undeterred. She continued walking and passed a café just as a cheer resounded, and several people rushed outside, gleeful expressions on their faces. Intrigued, she stopped and spoke to a man at an outside table.

"Do you speak English?"

"Yes."

"What's happened?"

"The entire East German cabinet has resigned," he said.

Rachel's eyes widened. "Just now?"

The man nodded. "The Easties' protests are working."

Rachel turned and ran for the bus to take her to the Press Point.

She bumped into Bernard as soon as she reached the office. The place was in an uproar discussing the resignation news, with copy being written and filed with news outlets worldwide.

"Have you seen what's happening at the Wall?" Rachel asked him.

Bernard shook his head.

"People are gathering, and some are even chipping away at it with axes and hammers."

Bernard shook his head. "That isn't going to end well."

"I'm not sure. The East German border guards responded with a high-powered hose in the section where I was photographing. The youth of West Berlin is as good as telling their East German counterparts that they're ready for this Wall to come down too."

"The reaction will be force, mark my words. You must be careful how close you get – a stray bullet over the Wall will do much more damage than a water cannon."

"Even you have to admit that events are unfolding at pace," Rachel said. "Now that the government has resigned, perhaps that will lead to democratic elections and the freedom to travel that many East Germans desire?"

Bernard shrugged. "Or perhaps the Politburo will install an even more hard-line government who won't be swayed by dissidents."

"Or just maybe a peaceful revolution is possible after all?" Rachel said.

CHAPTER 38

West Berlin, FRG
November 9, 1989

A television on a wall bracket in one corner at the Press Point was tuned into a GDR press conference at the end of the day. A few journalists, including Bernard, had turned their chairs towards the TV and were taking notes. On screen, Krenz's press officer and three white-shirted officials were seated at a long table on a platform at the front of the East German media room.

"Anything interesting?" Rachel whispered to Bernard, crouching beside his chair.

He shook his head. "Just more rhetoric. He's been droning on about ministerial and administrative reforms – they're desperate to appease the protesters, saying they will liberalise travel restrictions. Still, there will be so many caveats in the fine print that, in reality, not much will change."

"That's just going to inflame the situation."

"You and I know that, but these guys are clinging on to power."

Rachel peered at the East German official on the screen. "Who is he? Didn't he address the crowd at Alexanderplatz a few days ago?"

Bernard consulted his notes. "Gunter Schabowski; he's a minor official. Just a mouthpiece sent to read a statement. Hang on, turn that up."

One of the other reporters pointed a remote control at the TV, and the volume rose.

On-screen, Schabowski was looking confused and shuffling his papers.

"That Italian reporter just asked when the new law lifting the travel restrictions would take effect," Bernard whispered as Schabowski turned to the man seated beside him, who shrugged.

Schabowski consulted his papers once more.

Silence fell over the assembled journalists as everyone stopped what they were doing and stared at the television.

Schabowski spoke again.

"What did he say?" Rachel asked.

Bernard turned to her and opened then closed his mouth. Around them, conversation erupted.

"What is it?"

"He said, as far as he knew, it goes into effect immediately."

"What does that mean? Can people cross the border now?"

Bernard shrugged. "I don't know, but he may just have opened the border by mistake."

CHAPTER 39

West Berlin, FRG
November 9, 1989

Rachel grabbed the nearest telephone and called her hotel, asking to be put through to Juliette's room, but there was no answer. She tried Josh's room, but he wasn't there either.

Shelley dropped the handset of her phone into its cradle. "Apparently people are already gathering on the eastern side of Bornholmer crossing," she said.

Pulling her coat on, Rachel filled her pockets with film, threw the strap of her camera case across her body, and rushed out into the cool night. She waved down a taxi outside the building and was climbing in when a voice called for her to wait.

She turned to see Bernard lumbering down the stairs behind her. She scooted across on the back seat and left the door open for him. To her surprise, Shelley jumped into the front seat next to the driver.

"To the Bornholmer crossing," Bernard instructed the driver in German.

The traffic grew more congested the nearer they got to the border crossing. Cars were being parked haphazardly and people were climbing out and all walking in the same direction. Anticipation hung in the air, a mixture of excitement and apprehension.

"I don't think I can get you any closer," the driver said.

"That's okay, we'll walk from here," Shelley said, handing the driver some Deutschmarks and leaping out. Together, they joined the stream of people hurrying towards Bornholmerstrasse. The steel grey struts of the Bösebrücke bridge stretched above the railway tracks in front of them. Just past the centre of the span, the red and white striped barriers were down, and armed soldiers were hovering outside the customs buildings. Rachel raised her gaze to the watchtowers on either side of the bridge. Guards were visible, watching the growing crowd, rifles in their hands.

"Listen," Bernard said.

A cacophony of voices reached them.

"Look." Rachel pointed.

Across the way, they could see hundreds of East Germans moving towards the bridge.

"Oh my God," Shelley said. "They risk arrest and three years in a labour camp for even approaching the border."

"Do you think they will let them through?" Rachel said, raising her camera and taking several photos, first of the closed border crossing, then of the crowds of people visible beneath the dim yellow streetlights. Beyond them, East Berlin appeared to be in darkness, like a sinister black hole. Rachel looked around her at the lights, colour and openness of the West. At that moment, the contrast between the two parts of the city could not have been more apparent. The headlights of a long queue of cars approaching the bridge from the East illuminated even more people coming on foot.

"I don't know," Bernard said. "I sure hope so, or there will be a riot, and God only knows what will happen then."

"We have to do something," Shelley said. "We can't just wait here for the border guards to open fire on the crowds."

"If we get the reports to the TV and radio stations, more people in East Berlin will realise what is happening. This is an anomaly that we can help exploit. Look at the border guards; they don't know what to do," Rachel said.

Over at the glass-walled border command post, a guard was talking into a telephone and gesturing with his hands. Outside, the guards patrolling the barrier looked agitated and nervous, clutching their rifles.

"God, it's cold," Shelley moaned, stamping her feet and rubbing her gloved hands together. Condensation formed as she spoke.

"I'm going to see if that bar over there will let me use their phone," Rachel said.

Rachel jogged across the street and into the deserted bar. Their patrons were all on the footpath staring at the border crossing, waiting to see what was going to happen. The bar staff were watching a small TV behind the counter.

"Hi, do you speak English?" Rachel asked a young woman with spiky hair and dark eyeliner, wiping down the long counter.

"Yes, what can I get you?"

"I'm a reporter with *The London News*," Rachel said, showing her press credentials. "Can I please borrow your telephone? We need to get reports of what's happening onto your local TV and radio stations now. It looks like they could open the border."

"Come on. The office is this way."

"*Danke.*"

Rachel put a collect call through the London office and was transferred to Jones.

"What's happening there?" he asked. "Have they actually opened the border?"

"There are thousands of people massing on the East Berlin side at the Bornholmer crossing demanding to be let across," Rachel said. "It's basically a standoff at this point. The border guards don't seem to know what to do. It could go either way."

"Get me photos of whatever happens. Is Bernard with you?"

"Yes, but, Jones, we need to ensure that this is reported on all Berlin radio and TV stations. The people of the GDR need to know that this is happening right now."

There was a pause. "I'll make some calls and get someone down there with a TV camera," Jones said.

"And get a message to RiAS. The East Germans listen to them."

"Keep reporting in."

Rachel called her hotel again and left a message for Juliette.

"Hold on," the receptionist said. "There is a message here for you from your friend. About half an hour ago, she said they are going to Bornholmerstrasse."

Rachel thanked the bartender and rushed back outside to find that the crowds of people had doubled while she'd been on the telephone. She fought through the groups of people, getting as close to the bridge as she could. Shelley and Bernard were nowhere to be seen. But Juliette was standing on a low wall at the edge of the road leading to the bridge, speaking into the camera balanced on Josh's shoulder. French soldiers had gathered to one side, looking across the bridge with apprehension and anticipation, weapons ready.

Rachel crossed the road and joined Josh as Juliette wrapped up her piece. She jumped down off the wall and threw her arms around Rachel.

"I feel sick," she said. "This is just like Tiananmen Square. Too many people defying the Party – it can't end well."

"They let the Alexanderplatz protest go ahead a few days ago without violence. This could be the same. Did you hear about the news conference? People are allowed to travel with immediate effect," Rachel said.

"That was a cock-up," Josh said. "I don't think he was supposed to announce that. The border guards don't know what to do. If they were planning to open, they would have been told."

Rachel peered over the edge and down onto the train tracks below. The Wall stretched in each direction parallel with the rails, separating the lines. The ghost station of Bornholmer sat abandoned in the centre.

"Oh no, look," Josh said, shouldering his camera and directing it to the East. A line of vans were driving along the road towards the checkpoint. "Please don't let that be reinforcements."

A low chant rose from across the bridge, eerie and echoing at first in the cool night air, then gathering strength and volume as more voices joined in.

"What are they saying?"

"Open the gate."

The people in the crowd around them began to call out, individually at first but then in unison.

"What?" Rachel turned to Juliette, who had a massive smile on her face.

"They are saying, 'come over'."

All of a sudden, the chant morphed into a cheer from those gathered around the Western approach to the bridge as several pedestrians began walking across the bridge towards them. Josh shouldered his camera and started filming as the four men and two women reached them. As Rachel raised her camera, she realised she had recognised one of the men.

"Siegbert," she called and waved.

The man turned towards her voice.

"It's Rachel. We met in Leipzig," she called.

Siegbert pushed his glasses back up his nose and embraced her, lifting her off the ground. "It's happened," he cried. "We're free."

Rachel turned to Juliette. "Siegbert made the film that I smuggled back from Leipzig."

Juliette embraced Siegbert. "Can I interview you? A couple of words about how you feel right now. I work for an Australian television network."

Rachel stepped away and watched as the first cars, rusty little Trabants, began to cross the bridge, and the chanting on both sides became louder and louder.

"Something has to give," she murmured, turning back to where Juliette was wrapping up her interview. Siegbert had turned away and accepted a glass of champagne that had appeared from somewhere.

"Benefits of being in the French sector," Juliette laughed as a bottle was passed to her.

"Siegbert," Rachel called. "Have you seen Leo or Maria tonight?"

He shook his head. "No, but they are sure to be crossing somewhere."

"I hope they get across before the authorities shut this down."

"I don't think that's going to happen, Rach. Look." Josh's voice rose with excitement.

It was as though the border guards had given up. The chanting turned into a massive cheer as the red and white striped barrier was raised, and a surge of people burst through. Car horns began to toot, and the crowd opened, allowing a stream of boxy Trabants into West Berlin, exhaust fumes trailing in their wake.

"Are you getting this, Josh?" Juliette called.

"You betcha."

Rachel took shot after shot, stopping only to change film. People were hugging, crying, laughing, and kissing. Champagne and beer flowed freely from the nearby bars as a manic party atmosphere ensured. And people and cars just kept coming across.

"Come on," Juliette grabbed her arm. "Let's see if this is happening at any of the other five border crossing points in the city?"

Rachel prised Siegbert from the arms of a jubilant woman. "If you see Leo, tell him I've gone to Checkpoint Charlie."

He nodded.

Rachel, Juliette and Josh weaved through the jubilant crowd

and hurried several streets away from the border before spotting a taxi.

"Can you take us to Checkpoint Charlie?" Juliette asked.

"I'll get you as close as possible, but it's madness there."

The taxi driver wasn't wrong. Several blocks away from the Wall, the traffic ground to a stop and they alighted into what could only be described as the world's largest street party.

"This is crazy," Juliette shouted above the music, singing, car horns, and cheering as they fought their way through the throng towards Checkpoint Charlie.

"Look." They followed Josh's outstretched arm. People were beginning to climb onto the Wall, and those on top were leaning down to pull more and more people up to join them.

"That's really dangerous," Juliette said. "There's a shoot-on-sight order for anyone touching the Wall."

"I don't think that's going to happen tonight," Rachel said as they watched two East German border guards appear beside the civilians on top of the wall and exchange hugs and backslaps with the revellers. Bottles of beer were passed up and shared with the guards as the crowd on the ground cheered and Rachel raised her camera and captured the scene.

In front of the Wall, people were dancing and singing. Patrons spilled from the bars onto the pavement and across the road, drinks in hand, giving them to the newly arrived East Berliners.

When they finally reached Checkpoint Charlie, people lined the streets, clapping every new arrival on foot and thumping the roof of each Trabant that passed through. Rachel took photos of people leaning out of their car windows, waving, crying, embracing, and dancing. The euphoria was contagious.

On the East German side, the border guards appeared to have given up their posts, but Rachel couldn't see past the crowds of people. She turned to talk to Juliette and realised she'd lost her and Josh in the melee. She looked at her watch. It was 12:30 a.m., and she had to get some photos back to London. Jones would be apoplectic if he didn't get something for the morning edition.

She started walking toward her hotel and was surprised to see some East Germans heading back across the border. Puzzled, Rachel stopped a young couple laden with shopping bags containing Western goods.

"Excuse me, why are you going back?"

"We left our sleeping children in the care of our elderly neighbours," the woman said in broken English. "But bananas for breakfast. They have never eaten bananas, they're a luxury."

"And good coffee," the man said. "Besides, I must be back for work in the morning."

Rachel nodded as the reality of the situation dawned on her. Still pondering the implications of this, she pushed through the doors of her hotel. The reception desk was unattended, the staff out enjoying the street party. She crossed the foyer and headed for the lift.

"Rachel."

A shiver ran down her spine, and she spun around.

The man leaning against the wall by the door, was the one who had occupied her thoughts for days. He pushed off the wall and ran his hand through his hair, giving her a lazy grin.

"Leo." Rachel rushed towards him and threw herself into his arms. Leo rained kisses over her face and hugged her tight, lifting her off the ground and spinning her around.

"I didn't know how to find you tonight, and I hoped you'd get across before they shut this thing down," she said when her feet touched the ground again.

"I figured you'd be staying here," he said. "And would return at some point."

"This is unbelievable. I can't believe you're here." Rachel ran her hands over his cheeks and his hair.

Leo laughed. "Believe it, babe."

Leo kissed her again, slower and more tenderly this time. Rachel smiled at him when they broke apart.

"Is Maria here?"

He nodded. "I've just left her and Annette at their aunt's house and came here to find you. They say hello and will see you tomorrow."

"I'm delighted for them."

Leo nodded. "Me too."

"Leo, I need to develop my photos and send them back to London in time for the morning papers. Sorry, you can join the party if you like, and I'll find you later."

"I'll stay with you," he said. "There's nowhere else I'd rather be right now."

Rachel kissed him again. "I hoped you'd say that. Let's go."

She led him to her room and upended her camera bag on the bed.

"I have a dark room set up in the bathroom. Do you want to help?"

"Yeah."

Half an hour later, Rachel hung the last photos up on the clothesline in the bathroom. "These first ones are nearly dry," she said. "I'll finish them with the hairdryer and send them. Are you still okay? I'm sorry that I have to work."

Leo slipped his arms around her. "I'm great. I love being here with you and watching you work. I don't care what we do."

"Are you hungry?"

He nodded. "Now that you mention it, I am."

Rachel led him from the bathroom and handed him the room service menu. "Choose what you'd like, and I'll have it delivered, if there's anyone left in the hotel to make it. I'm suddenly starving, and I think I'll have a burger. These photos will take a while to send."

She plugged the photo scanner into the power and phone jack

sockets, and spread out across the bed what she considered the best eight images capturing what had transpired in Berlin that evening.

"These are amazing," Leo said, slipping his arms around her waist and leaning his chin on her shoulder. "They tell a story."

Rachel nodded. "That's the idea."

She fed the first print into the transmitter. Leo watched, intrigued, as the rollers pulled in the photo. "How does it work?"

"It transmits the image across the phone lines. It will start printing on a photo printer in my boss's office in London in a few minutes."

An hour later, Rachel fed the last photo into the machine. She plugged the phone back into the wall socket and called Jones.

"Brilliant, Rachel," he said. "Front cover being laid out as we speak. Now get out there and get me more."

Leo was sound asleep in the armchair by the window. Rachel wrote a note explaining she would be back soon and draped a spare blanket over his sleeping form. Leo stirred and opened one eye, then the other, and a grin spread across his face.

"I thought it was a dream."

Rachel shook her head. "It's happened, I promise. Do you want to stay sleeping, or would you like to join the party now that I'm done sending these? There's a good bar nearby, and I'd like to get some more photos."

Leo leapt to his feet. "Lead the way."

"This is crazy," he said a few minutes later, snagging her hand as they weaved their way through the crowds of jubilant people. "Every Berliner must have descended onto these streets tonight."

The pub was packed, but they managed to squeeze their way to the bar, where Rachel ordered and paid for their drinks. Beer for Leo, and Selz or sparkling wine for herself.

"I'm sorry I don't have any Deutschmarks, only these, which are useless here," Leo said, pulling some East German marks from his pocket.

"It's on me," Rachel said. "Come on."

They pushed through the crowd until they found a small table by the front window that was being vacated. There was only one chair, so Leo sat and pulled Rachel onto his lap. Around them, the party continued. Pop music blasted from the bar's speaker system, and people sang along to the Scorpions' 'Winds of Change'.

"I still can't believe you're here," she said. "I didn't think I'd ever see you again."

"The thought of seeing you again has kept me going these last few weeks," Leo said. "I knew that no matter what happened, I had to see you. I've never felt this kind of instant connection with someone before."

Rachel gazed into his eyes and stroked his cheek with her hand. "And I haven't been able to stop thinking about you, but I didn't dare believe this would happen."

"I've skipped all my classes since Leipzig and thrown myself into the protest movement. You gave me the final push and incentive to break down these barriers. We've been working hard, rallying people, and putting pressure on the Party. I've narrowly avoided being arrested many times, and I've been sleeping on a different couch every night."

"The pressure worked."

"Tonight was a mistake," Leo said. "They didn't mean to open the border fully."

"That's what concerns me," Rachel said. "What will the response be in the cold light of day?"

Leo shook his head. "We've come this far. There's no going back now."

"When I was walking back to the hotel tonight, some people were returning to East Berlin. I asked a couple, and they said they were returning to their children and their jobs. It was like they'd visited but couldn't stay."

Leo nodded. "There will be lots of people like that, but the main thing is that they have that choice. They can come over and visit, shop, party, whatever, if they want to, not because someone tells them otherwise."

Rachel nodded and sipped her drink before kissing him again. The music changed, and Bowie boomed from the speakers. Leo drained his beer and eased Rachel upright. "Come on, dance with me."

They joined hundreds of others dancing outside the bar on the road and danced until Rachel could see that Leo was flagging.

"Are you staying in West Berlin tonight? Do you want to come back to the hotel with me?"

"Of course," he said, stifling a yawn.

"You must be exhausted."

"Yeah, but I don't plan on sleeping tonight," Leo said, grabbing her hand, intertwining his fingers with hers, and pulling her up against him. "There are other things I'd much rather be doing."

Rachel raised an eyebrow. "You're very bold."

"They say fortune favours the bold."

"I think it's the brave, but okay." Rachel laughed.

They fought their way through the partying crowds back to the hotel. Rachel stopped every few metres to take another photo of a reunion of old friends, new friendships being made, and people dancing, singing and celebrating. At one point, she turned the camera on Leo and captured the joyful expression on his face. She held the camera at arm's length and photographed the two of them, grinning, with revellers on the Wall behind them. As they made their way along the Wall, weaving through the partiers, a whoosh of flame rose into the sky.

"Look." Rachel followed Leo's outstretched hand. A fire eater stood on top of the Wall surrounded by people, blowing flames into the night sky, like a fiery dragon celebrating a long-awaited victory. Rachel captured his image.

They finally returned to the hotel and took the lift to her fourth-floor room. Once inside, their smiles slipped as they regarded one another. Leo lifted Rachel's camera over her head and set it down on the desk. He cupped her cheeks with his hands and kissed her gently. Rachel sighed and leaned into him as their kiss deepened. Leo slid his hands down her back and under her bottom, lifting her so she could wrap her legs around his waist. Still kissing, he walked them to the bed, where they tumbled laughing. Leo rolled off her, propped himself on his elbow, and unbuttoned her top. He leaned down and kissed the swell of her breast above her bra, moving lower to her stomach, before sitting up and lifting his t-shirt over his head. Rachel pulled him back down and ran her hands over his shoulders and muscular arms.

"Are we doing this?" Leo asked.

"We are."

CHAPTER 40

West Berlin, FRG
November 10, 1989

Rachel woke wrapped in Leo's arms. He was already awake, lying on one side studying her.

"*Guten morgen, Schatz.*"

"Hi." Rachel gave him a shy smile as their previous night's activities flooded back.

"You look very peaceful when you sleep."

"I hope I didn't snore or anything."

"I got used to it after the first hour."

Rachel's eyes widened in horror before she realised he was teasing her. "That's not fair."

There was a loud knock at her door. "Rach, open up."

"Shit, that's Juliette," Rachel said, sitting up and hunting for her discarded clothes.

"Hang on," she called.

Leo leaned back against the headboard, with the sheets covering him from the waist down, and watched Rachel dress. "Don't put too much on, it's just coming off again," he said.

Rachel blushed as she buttoned her jeans and unlocked the door.

Juliette rushed into the room and stopped dead.

"Oh," she said. "Oh, Hans, I mean, Leo."

She turned her back to him and pulled a surprised face at Rachel.

"Hi, Juliette," Leo said, grinning.

"I, ah… will come back later," she said.

"What's happening out there?" Rachel asked.

"Well, lots of East Germans are still crossing over. People are chipping away the wall with whatever they can get their hands on, and a whole section has been pulled down. The party shows no sign of slowing down."

"What has the reaction been from the GDR?"

"There hasn't been anything official that I've seen," Juliette said. "Krenz has been strangely silent. The biggest concern is the Russian reaction to the border's opening, as Gorbachev has yet to make a statement."

"What about the border guards?"

"Many of them are just standing on top of the Wall watching the party, looking stunned."

There was movement in the doorway, and Josh rushed into the room.

"There you are. I've just heard a rumour that the GDR Minister of Defence, Heinz Keßler, has declared a state of emergency and has the National People's Army troops on standby, including an elite Stasi-led motorised formation." He paused, looking from Rachel to Leo.

"Ah, I've missed something here."

"I'll fill you in later," Juliette said, spinning him around and pushing him out the door. "We're heading back to Potsdamer to get some more footage. We've just come from the Brandenburg Gate, it's a bunfight trying to get space to film, there are so many

TV stations set up trying to use the iconic backdrop for their reports. CBS's Dan Rather turned up in a cherry-picker and scooped everyone."

"See you later." Rachel shut the door behind them and turned to Leo.

"I need to go, also," she said. "Jones will want more photos, and I'd better talk to Bernard before he comes barging in here too." She chewed her bottom lip and looked at Leo. "Sorry, rain check?"

He grinned and reached for her, kissing the tip of her nose and then her lips. "Of course. Anyway, I need to go back and collect some of my things."

"You will come back, though?"

Leo nodded. "Try and keep me away. I need a change of clothes and some of my stuff."

Rachel ordered an extensive room-service breakfast which was delivered while they showered.

Leo's eyes widened at the spread. "Just as well; I seem to have built up an appetite."

While he ate, a plan formed in Rachel's mind. "Can I come with you?"

"I'll only be a few hours."

"I know, but every Western journalist will take photos from this side of the Wall, and I want to get some from the other."

Leo looked concerned. "Don't take this the wrong way, but I don't think it's safe for you."

Rachel bristled. "Why?"

"As Josh said, there's a high chance that the Soviets will decide to send reinforcements to defend the border."

"I think they're too late to do that. Besides, I could be in and out quickly at the first sign of any trouble. And you're going back; you could get trapped, and we'd be back to where we started.

"That's not going to happen, Rach."

"How do you know?"

"You're right, I don't," he conceded. "Let's go together and stick together, but no more than a couple of hours and at the first sign of trouble we cross straight back. I don't want to lose you, just when I've found you again."

Rachel kissed him. "I don't want to lose you either."

She packed her camera bag with extra film, slipping the photos taken by her grandfather in Paris into her jacket's inside pocket.

"I just need to make a quick phone call before we go," she said.

•••

The day had dawned clear and sunny. Rachel and Leo walked hand in hand along to Checkpoint Charlie. Someone had laid wooden planks across a section of no man's land, and people were streaming across. West Berliners still lined the streets, clapping the continual stream of Trabants driving through the border. The party atmosphere from the night before still hung in the air.

The sound of axes and hammers hitting stone reverberated through the streets as people chipped away at the Wall, executing Reagan's plea to tear it down. Every so often a cheer went up as a large portion of the structure broke off and fell, and souvenir hunters rushed in to grab a piece.

There was little resistance from the East German border guards. They passed a group of youths rocking a large Wall section back and forth, loosening its foundations. They continued their efforts until the whole section toppled over. The crowd peered through at the border guards, who hastily retreated.

American soldiers were still on patrol at Checkpoint Charlie, checking the passports of arrivals to West Berlin and waving through those going in the opposite direction. The barriers on both sides were up, and the Eastern side's checkpoint was strangely silent and abandoned. Rachel took many photos of the cars streaming across, the grinning Americans and the ghost-like East German border post.

"Rachel."

Rachel turned in the direction of the person calling her name. Daniel hurried towards her, followed by Gilbert, with his camera swinging on a strap around his neck. Daniel's dark hair hadn't seen a comb that morning and his clothes were crumpled. He flashed his trademark charming, dimpled grin. Rachel groaned.

"Isn't this wild?" Daniel said as he caught up to them. He put his hand on Rachel's arm and leaned forward as if he was going to kiss her, when he noticed her hand in Leo's. He took a hasty step back and frowned.

"I know it's unbelievable," Rachel said. "Dan, this is Leo. Daniel works for the same newspaper as me."

Daniel gave Leo a wary nod.

"I didn't realise Jones sent you over, too," Rachel said.

"He didn't," Daniel said. "We were in Prague, just arrived this morning."

"In the wrong bloody city," Gilbert grumbled, running a hand through his long, wispy fair hair. His slightly hunched, dishevelled appearance always reminded Rachel of a weasel. Given how he'd poached her job with Daniel, she felt it even more justified to use the description.

"Can't always be in the right place at the right time," Rachel said.

"I heard about Leipzig, Rach," Daniel said. "That was reckless."

Rachel shrugged.

"So, where are you going?" Daniel asked, glancing at the joined hands again. Rachel could tell that wasn't the question he wanted to ask.

"Leo needs to pick up some things from his flat, and I want to get some photos from the other side," Rachel said.

The furrow in Daniel's brow deepened. "You mean you're an East Berliner?"

Leo nodded.

"Rach, you shouldn't go there today," Daniel said.

"Why not?"

"They could reseal the border anytime, and you don't want to be on that side if they do."

"Look around you, Daniel. They're not resealing the border. The people are pulling the Wall down with their bare hands. This is the peaceful revolution that everyone hoped for."

Around them, the celebrations were unrelenting as people and cars continued to pour across from East Berlin. A group of teenagers sat on a flat-topped section of the Wall, a foot on either side, clapping and cheering each new arrival. Further along a cluster of East German border guards stood in a row, watching the festivities but neither stopping them nor joining in.

Daniel shook his head. "The SED and the Soviets will not stand for this. My sources tell me that 30,000 elite troops are gathering on the city's outskirts, ready to take it back."

Leo shook his head. "Won't happen."

"That's naïve," Daniel said.

"Were you at Leipzig or Alexanderplatz?" Leo asked. "The people want this, and the SED is powerless to stop it."

"If one Soviet state falls, they all could. No matter how progressive Gorbachev is, he won't want to see his empire crumble any further."

"Bye, Daniel. Gilbert." Rachel started to turn away.

"Rach, don't do this. It's not safe. Just because you've picked up some guy in all the excitement doesn't mean he can protect you over there."

"You don't know what you're talking about." Rachel felt anger at his insinuation. She and Daniel glared at one another while Gilbert smirked.

"I'll come with you," Daniel said.

"No."

"You can't stop us," Gilbert said, sounding like a petulant teenager.

"I can't stop you from going, but you're not coming with us. Come on, Leo." Rachel tugged at his hand, and together they passed through the open barrier at the checkpoint. Rachel glanced over her shoulder to see Daniel gesticulating at Gilbert before the flood of people walking in the opposite direction obscured them from view. They hurried past the mostly abandoned East German border guard post, where a few guards milled around, looking uncertain.

"I sense there is some history there," Leo said. "Do I want to know?"

Rachel shook her head.

"My flat is several blocks this way," Leo said, leading Rachel down a side street. "Keep your wits about you. As much as I hate to admit it, that guy was right. This is far from over. At the first sign of trouble, we leave."

Rachel nodded. "Can we go via Pierre's office?"

"Sure."

Several blocks into the city, they spied Pierre standing outside with a group of television cameramen.

"*Bonjour*, Rachel, Leo," he called as they approached, kissing Rachel on each cheek and enveloping Leo in a back-slapping hug. "Who would have thought the Wall would come down just like that?"

"I know, it's crazy," Rachel said. "What's the reaction been like on this side?"

"We've heard rumours that the Stasi are destroying documents," he said. "There is a group of people gathering to try and stop them. Anyway, after you called earlier, I asked our scouts, and there has also been a sighting of your man, Braun, entering a Stasi building near here about an hour ago."

Rachel glanced at Leo, who started shaking his head. "No, Rachel."

"Yes, Leo," she said, grabbing his hands. "This could be my only chance to confront him."

"I don't think that's wise," Leo said.

"It's worth a try."

"I think they've got more to worry about than one journalist right now," Pierre said.

"Leo, you go get your things and meet me back here in an hour," Rachel said.

"No way. You're not going anywhere near the Stasi without me."

"This is not your fight, Leo, but it could be my only chance to confront him."

"I'm coming with you," he said, turning her to face him. "We are not debating this."

Rachel rolled her eyes.

Pierre signalled to his colleagues, and together they rounded the corner. "Are you two coming?" he called.

The ugly, square concrete structure in the next block looked sufficiently forbidding to be the home of the secret police. Rachel felt a shiver run through Leo's hand, which clutched hers. She glanced at him, but his face held an expression of firm resolve.

The main doors to the building were wide open, and there was no guard.

"That's unusual," Pierre said. "Hundreds of people work here around the clock. Are you sure you want to do this?"

Rachel nodded.

"I will stay with the camera crew and raise the alarm if you're not back in half an hour."

Rachel turned to Leo. "I wish you would stay here with Pierre."

Leo shook his head. "That's not happening."

They cautiously advanced towards the building and watched as uniformed officials loaded boxes into waiting cars and vans, which drove away, only to be replaced by more vehicles.

"They're relocating."

Rachel and Leo climbed the stairs and entered the foyer of the austere building. The lobby was unadorned, containing a large reception desk to the immediate left and an enormous concrete staircase in the centre. A large East German flag covered one wall, and the vast space felt cold and impersonal. Rachel gripped Leo's hand tighter as they approached the desk where two armed officers were stationed.

"I'd like to see Hauptmann Braun," Rachel said in English. Leo translated her request into German.

"He's my grandfather." Rachel added, feeling rather than seeing Leo glare at her as his grip tightened on her hand.

The soldier eyed her for a long moment.

"Your name?"

"Rachel Knight."

Leo gave a sharp intake of breath.

"Wait," the soldier replied in English, picking up a telephone. He spoke in German to the person on the other end.

Two officers in the black uniforms of the Stasi marched along the corridor from a back room towards them. Both carried semi-automatic rifles. Leo and Rachel exchanged a nervous glance. The soldier replaced the handset and stood towering over Rachel, his expression stern. Rachel could hear her heartbeat accelerating and bit her lower lip to stop from betraying her fear.

"He will see you," the soldier said. "But you will leave your camera and your boyfriend."

The words caught in Rachel's throat, her mouth dry.

"No, he comes with me," Rachel said, suddenly terrified. She shouldn't have let Leo come with her. What if someone recognised him?

"It's that, or you can both leave."

"It's fine, Rachel, I'll wait here for you," Leo said, looking towards the two Stasi agents standing behind them. They pointed to a chair against the wall, and Leo crossed the floor and sat down.

Rachel lifted her camera bag over her head and sat it on the desk. She gave Leo a tentative smile, desperately hoping it wouldn't be the last time she saw him, and followed the officer up the stairs.

She was shaking uncontrollably by the time she was led into a large office on the first floor. A hefty man sat behind a desk on the far side of the room. She hoped this wasn't a trap. She had been so swayed by the opportunity to face the man she had been pursuing she hadn't stopped to consider all the repercussions.

"Come." The man at the desk didn't look up.

Rachel gulped and crossed the room, coming to a standstill in front of the desk. One armed officer remained at her side whilst the other took up a position in the office doorway, effectively blocking any escape route. The man put his pen down and looked up. He was wearing a flat peaked cap and a pressed black uniform with shiny buttons and insignia that designated him as a Stasi captain. A pistol resided in a holster at his hip. He pushed his chair back and stood.

Rachel took a deep breath and tilted her chin upwards to meet his gaze. It was him, the man from the photo that Monty had shown her. His face looked older than she'd anticipated, with thin, grey hair cut short, military style. His posture was that of a much younger man, straight-backed and upright. He was broad-shouldered and tall, well over six foot. The shortages and austerity that had plagued East Germany for many years hadn't affected Brown, who was portly, tending towards overweight. Built for comfort, not for speed, as Mae would have said. There were two small screens on his desk, and Rachel could see that one was focused on the reception desk in the lobby where she'd just been, but she couldn't see any sign of Leo. Fear gripped her, as she realised she'd just made a grave mistake.

MAE

1944

CHAPTER 41

London, England
November 25, 1944

I had just lit the fire to heat the cold flat and kicked off my shoes when the telephone rang. The kettle was starting to whistle on the stove in the tiny kitchen where I'd set a pot ready to make tea to warm my insides. I'd spent several hours queueing for food, and my feet were killing me. The one-bedroom ground-floor flat in a terraced block in Victoria was small but comfortable, although I couldn't wait to move when Jack returned for good.

"Hello."

"Mae, you got my message."

"Yes, where are you?"

"King's Cross station. I will be home very soon, my darling…."

Static erupted on the line.

"Jack, Jack, I can't hear you."

"…I witnessed…in Paris. …is a sharing secrets with the Soviets…I have proof which I will deliver to Whitehall on my…".

His voice was gone again.

"Jack, I know too. I have much to tell you," I said, but a dial tone sounded. We'd been cut off. I replaced the receiver and felt a smile cross my face; Jack was back in England. I cradled my small, rounded belly.

"Daddy will be home soon," I whispered as my heart soared. I'd missed him very much. I couldn't wait for this damn war to be over so that we could start the rest of our lives together. I hoped he wouldn't have to go away again, at least not for too long. It seemed that we were pushing the Nazis back to Berlin on all fronts, so surely there would be peace soon.

The previous week, Mrs Winter had taken me aside and asked if there was anything that I wanted to tell her. I had tried to bluff it out, but she could tell that I was pregnant, and I'd been forced to give my notice, along with a stern reminder about the classified nature of my work at the Park, of which I was never to speak.

Leaving Liscombe Park and the girls was more difficult than I expected, but Mavis and Nancy had already been to London to visit me. It seemed like the bonds of friendship we'd formed wouldn't be easily broken.

An hour later, I put the kettle back on. Something must have held Jack up.

Two hours later, I was getting worried. Jack said he was on his way and something about going to Whitehall first.

Three hours later, there was a knock at the door.

I rushed to open it and found a police officer standing there holding his hat. "May I come in?"

"Jack?"

"Yes, ma'am, it's about your husband."

I gripped the doorframe as a wave of nausea hit me.

"This way," I managed to grind out, ushering him into the tiny front room and offering him a seat, which he declined.

"I'm sorry to inform you that your husband has been killed in an automobile accident tonight," the young policeman said. "He was struck by a car crossing Whitehall."

I dropped down onto one end of the sofa.

"No, you must have the wrong person," I said. "He was just on his way here."

There was another urgent knock at the front door.

"That'll be him now," I said, rushing from the room and wrenching open the door.

A dishevelled Charles stood on the doorstep, his face drained of colour. "Mae," he began.

"Oh no, it's true?" I said as the world faded to black.

I came to on the sofa in the front room. I sat up to find Charles murmuring with my physician, Doctor Andrews, a usually cheerful white-haired man, on the far side of the room.

"Ah, here she is," Doctor Andrews said in gentle tones, approaching me. "Mae, you've had an awful shock. How are you feeling?" He reached for my wrist and felt for my pulse.

I looked past him to Charles, who had helped himself to a glass of scotch.

"Is it true, Charles?"

He nodded. "I'm sorry, Mae."

"What happened?"

"A motorcar hit him. He died at the scene, Mae."

I closed my eyes as the world swayed again. "Jack was on his way here. I haven't seen him since August."

"Take it easy," Doctor Andrews said. "You need to think about the baby."

"What about the driver?"

Charles looked down at his feet before replying. "He drove away."

"You mean it wasn't an accident because of the blackout? He was hit deliberately, and the driver drove off?"

Charles shrugged. "It would seem so."

"Can I see him?"

"Yes," Charles said. "In the morning."

•••

Mavis and Nancy were waiting outside the flat when we returned from the morgue the following day. I was clutching Jack's broken camera, and Charles carried the canvas kit bag that Jack had over his shoulder at the time of the accident. It had a large, dried blood stain on one end. His camera bag was missing.

"Oh, Mae, I'm dreadfully sorry," Mavis said, taking me in her arms. Nancy put her arms around us both as Charles unlocked the door.

I mumbled my thanks before we made our way inside. Nancy took Jack's bag and sat it on the floor at our bedroom door.

"Shall I make a cup of tea?" Mavis suggested. "And sandwiches?"

"Tea would be good, but I'm not hungry," I said.

"You need to eat," Mavis said, resting her hand on my shoulder. "Even if you don't feel like it, your baby does."

I sighed. "I don't know if I can keep anything down. I can only see Jack's lifeless body lying on that cold slab." I stifled a sob. "It was just awful. It didn't even look like him. He had so much energy and vitality, but that inert... Oh God, I have to let Joe and his parents know."

"Won't the army or foreign office do that?"

"I don't know."

"Who did he work for?"

"That's an excellent question," I said. "I'm not entirely sure, but Charles will know."

Charles shook his head and left the room. I heard him talking to Mavis moments later.

Nancy's eyes were wide as she sat down beside me. "Does that mean he was..."

"With military intelligence?" I finished for her. "Honestly, I don't know, it might have been the SOE or something like that."

The flap on the mailbox rattled, and I heard the post land with a thud on the mat. Nancy jumped up and wandered into the hall to retrieve it as Mavis returned with a tray of tea and sandwiches.

Nancy handed the post to me. The writing on a large brown envelope caught my attention. It was from Jack, and the address was scribbled as if written in haste, and postmarked yesterday. I frowned.

"Excuse me for a moment," I said, hurrying into my bedroom and closing the door behind me. I eased the envelope flap open as I sank onto the edge of our bed, my thoughts churning.

I eased out three photos, some negatives, and a one-page handwritten note. I unfolded the paper.

My darling Mae

Should anything happen to me, I need you to keep these safe and, when you can, deliver them to the highest authority you can manage – Churchill himself, if need be.

I don't want to frighten you, but a spy network is operating deep within the British establishment, and I'm this close to exposing it. One man in the photos is Yuri Montan, a known Soviet agent, and of course, we both know who the other man is. I'm sorry, Mae, I wish this wasn't true.

Don't trust anyone.

Hopefully, you won't receive this, as I will already be home with you and our baby.

All my love, always.

Jack

I spread the photographs out on the bedspread. They had been taken at dusk and were of two men meeting and exchanging something. I studied the images. The first man's face wasn't visible in any pictures, but the second man's was. I didn't recognise him. This must be – I checked Jack's letter – Yuri Montan. He looked frightened. I turned my attention to the other man. There was something very familiar about him.

My mind went to William. I never had the chance to tell Jack when he was back for the night in August what had happened with William or about the subsequent arrest warrant and his disappearance. Now it seems we were both trying to expose the same person. Jack was right about this being deep within the British establishment. I'd been there when William met with Churchill himself.

The bedroom door gave a loud creak, startling me, and I glanced up to find Charles leaning against the frame.

"Everything alright, Mae?"

"It's just a letter that Jack sent before…" I choked on a sob as I stuffed the photos, negatives, and letter back into the envelope and tucked it under the pillow. I couldn't deal with them right now, not when my head was reeling.

Charles reached for my hand. "Come, Mavis has prepared lunch. And I must go, but I will be back later."

I returned to the living room, forcing myself to eat the sandwich Mavis had fixed.

"Let's go for a walk," Nancy suggested after she'd cleared away the dishes. "Some fresh air will do you good."

I shrugged.

We left the flat a short while later and walked towards the entrance to Hyde Park at the end of the road. Winter was fast approaching, and I shivered as I pulled my coat over my protruding belly. I hiccupped a sob. Jack would never get to hold our beloved baby. Mavis hooked her arm through mine, and we strolled along the paths that bisected the park, dappled sunlight filtering through the trees and leaves crunching beneath our feet.

Reality seemed suspended as though my mind was protecting me from the harsh reality of my loss. On any other day, I could be strolling through the park with my girlfriends on our way somewhere for tea and gossip. But not today.

We left the park and retraced our steps reaching the corner of my street when an explosion ripped through the air, causing the ground to shake. I looked skyward, expecting to see a German plane, but the sky was clear.

Nancy, Mavis and I clutched one another and watched in horror as flames and smoke poured from the front window of my flat.

•••

There was a knock at the door of the hotel where we'd spent the night, and I opened it to find Charles standing there holding his hat.

"Mae, how are you holding up?" he said.

I stood aside to let him enter. "As well as can be expected," I said, resting my hand on my belly and feeling the baby flutter. "When can I go back to the flat?"

Charles shook his head. "It's been destroyed, if not by the fire, then by the water used to put it out."

"But what about our things? Did the fire brigade say what caused the gas to explode like that?"

Charles shook his head and shuffled his feet.

"What's going on?" Nancy demanded. "What are you not saying?"

"Our intelligence tells us that the same person who killed Jack has just tried to kill Mae," Charles said. "The gas leak wasn't an accident."

Nancy's hands flew to her cover her mouth as she stifled a little shriek.

"Why?" I asked.

"Jack told you something or gave you something that someone doesn't want anyone else to know about," Charles said.

I nodded. "It was some photographs and negatives."

"And where are they now?"

"They were in the flat."

"These people don't know that," Charles said. "Your life is still in danger, and we need to get you as far away from here as possible."

"Charles, it was William that Jack was about to expose."

Charles gave me an odd look. "William?"

"William Brown. He worked with me at Bletchley, and Jack knew him too. I think they'd worked at the Foreign Office together."

Charles nodded and looked thoughtful. "How much do you know about what Jack's role was?"

I shook my head. "Not a lot. I know he was more than just a war photographer, but he never said what it was that he did."

"Good, he was protecting you." Charles turned to Nancy. "Don't you have to be back at Bletchley?"

Nancy nodded. "But I don't want to leave Mae."

"It's fine, Nancy," I said. "You've been such a darling, but I'll stay with Charles while we sort things out."

Nancy gathered her things. "Are you sure?" she said, folding me into a hug. "They can do without me for a few days."

"You go. I'll see you at the funeral."

Nancy pulled on her coat and gloves. She stood in front of the mirror, settling her hat on her head. "Bye then, darling. I will see you soon."

"What happens now?" I asked Charles after the hotel room door had closed behind her.

"Mae, I can get you on a hospital ship that will eventually land in New Zealand, but you must go today. Go to Jack's family in New Zealand and have your baby. You will be safe there. I can't protect you here."

I cradled my belly. "But they are on the other side of the world, and it's such a long way to go."

"Isn't that where you and Jack planned to go after the war?"

"Yes, but that was with Jack. I don't know his family."

"But they will want to know you and the baby; you are the last link to their son."

I sighed. "Does it have to be today? There is something I must do first."

Charles looked at his watch. "We must go now if you are to depart."

I hesitated.

"You can write to your friends from New Zealand once you are settled. The fewer people who know of your whereabouts just now, the better. By the time you get there, we will have found the person responsible for Jack's death, and you will be safe."

"But…"

"Come on, my dear girl, you need to think of the babe. Let's get you away to the train and safely on that ship."

RACHEL

1989

CHAPTER 42

East Berlin, GDR
November 10, 1989

"**M**y camera," Rachel began, her eyes darting around the large spartan office.

"Will be returned to you once we've had our little discussion." Forty years in Germany hadn't dampened William Brown's public-school accent. He waved his hand towards a chair in front of the desk. "Have a seat."

Rachel glanced at the soldier beside her before perching on the front edge of the hard-backed chair he'd indicated. She slipped her hand into her pocket to start recording their conversation on the tiny tape recorder that Josh had given her. She couldn't believe she'd been allowed to see Brown without being searched. Perhaps he didn't intend for her to leave. She gulped at the thought.

William Brown folded his large frame into a more comfortable-looking leather chair behind the desk. His demeanour was that of a kindly uncle rather than the ruthless Stasi officer she'd been led to believe him to be.

"Leave us," he instructed both soldiers, who vacated the room, closing the door behind them. Rachel looked over her shoulder to see that they remained outside through the glass panel in the door. Rachel gulped and returned her attention to the man in front of her.

"You wanted to see me, although I don't believe I have a granddaughter or any grandchildren." William steepled his fingers and leaned backwards, and the expression in his eyes hardened. "So, who are you?"

"I'm the granddaughter of a man you murdered."

"You might have to narrow that down." Perhaps 'kindly uncle' was a stretch.

Rachel swallowed hard. "My grandparents are Jack and Mae Knight."

Rachel watched as a fleeting expression of shock crossed William's face before he hid it.

"So, you knew them."

"I was very fond of your grandmother," he said.

"But not fond enough to spare her husband."

"Miss Knight..." he began.

"Rachel Talbot."

"Miss Talbot, I'm not sure why you think I had anything to do with your grandfather's death."

With shaking hands, Rachel extracted from her jacket pocket the three photos Jack had taken in Paris.

"I believe this is you," she said, leaning forward and placing the photos on the desk facing Brown. "You found out that Jack had taken these, evidence of you sharing secrets with the Soviets, and you had him killed before he could submit the photos to the authorities."

A knock on the door interrupted them.

"Come."

A red-faced soldier rushed in, lugging a large bag. He spoke in rapid German. Rachel caught Brown's concerned expression as he sent the man away with instructions that she didn't understand. The door closed again, and Brown eyed her with a steely gaze.

Rachel felt a trickle of sweat run between her shoulder blades. She was anxious about what was happening to Leo but didn't want to give Brown any ammunition to use against her, by asking.

Brown's attention returned to the photos, and he nodded. "This explains so much. I could never understand why the intelligence service was after me for murder, as I hadn't killed anyone."

"But my grandmother identified you."

"Mae was mistaken."

"She said there was evidence that you were stealing decrypts from Bletchley Park."

"I was framed. Someone with links into Bletchley made sure it looked like I was responsible for the thefts."

"But didn't my grandmother catch you?"

"Well, yes, but I only stole those to show Churchill the information we COULD share with our Soviet allies, and it was a one-time thing."

"Why did you defect?"

"I didn't, not in an ideological sense anyway. In the chaos that was post-war Europe, I reinvented myself. If I'd stayed in England, I would have been hung as a traitor for a murder that I didn't commit. Someone either wanted me dead, or I was a convenient patsy. I never discovered who set me up, but I know one thing. I did not murder Jack. Your grandmother was my friend, and I wouldn't do that to her."

"So, you're telling me that you didn't run down Jack when he was on his way to the Foreign Office with evidence that would prove the leak from Bletchley Park was you?"

"No." Brown's voice was firm. "How is Mae? Is she...?"

"She's well. She's lived in New Zealand since the war."

"I'm not surprised, given your accent."

"Someone blew up Mae's flat the day after Jack was killed. She was pregnant with my mother, and someone, she believed you, was trying to kill her too. She escaped on the next hospital ship to New Zealand."

Brown gave a bitter laugh, picked up one of the photos, and examined it closely in the light streaming in the windows. "Well, it wasn't me, and I always wondered who'd killed Jack. Now it makes perfect sense." He set the photo down again.

"I don't understand," Rachel said.

"You haven't done your research properly. Not good for a journalist, jumping to conclusions." Brown's voice had taken on a mocking tone.

"I never said I was a ..." Rachel began.

"You've let emotion cloud your judgement. Two things. Look long and hard at that photo. Do you think that is me? That person is short and slight. I have always been large, big-boned and tall. Find old photos of me, and you will see. Secondly, I wasn't in London when Jack died. After Sept 1944, I left England, never to return. How could I when I was accused first of treason and later murder?"

"So, who killed my grandfather then?"

"Work out who the man in the photo is, and you have your killer. I will give you a clue. It is closer to home than you think." Brown stacked the photos and handed them back to Rachel. "Now, because I was once very fond of your grandmother, I will let you and your boyfriend go. Do not try to find me again, or I won't be so accommodating."

CHAPTER 43

East Berlin, GDR
November 10, 1989

Brown stood and ushered Rachel to the door. The corridor was filled with uniformed police and clerical staff rushing along, some carrying large boxes, others lugging rubbish sacks.

"Return her belongings and let them both go," Brown instructed in English to the two guards before repeating the instruction in German.

Rachel turned back to Brown. "If what you've told me is true, then I'm sorry for what you've endured."

Brown gave her the ghost of a smile. "Don't feel sorry for me. I did what I had to do to survive. Now go before I change my mind."

Rachel was marched along the corridor towards the main staircase. She glanced through the open doors of the offices along the passage and saw staff tearing files apart with their hands and stuffing the shredded papers into large bags.

Leo was still seated under the watchful eyes of the two Stasi officers when Rachel descended the staircase to the reception area. They didn't stop him when he leapt to his feet and rushed across the foyer to join her. He rested his hand on the small of her back and propelled her towards the reception desk, where she was handed her camera bag. Rachel slipped the photos into a side pocket and threw the strap over her head and across her body as they hurried through the front entrance. Leo grabbed her hand, and they raced down the front steps.

"Are you okay?" he asked. "I was climbing the walls to get to you, but they drew their guns on me."

"I'm fine," Rachel said. "I was anxious about what was happening to you. I'm sorry, Leo, I should never have put you in that situation. I wasn't thinking."

They rounded the corner and stopped. Rachel's heart was thumping so hard that it almost hurt. She leaned against the wall of a building and sucked in a deep breath. Leo reached up and tucked a strain of hair behind her ear. "You are passionate about finding the truth. It's one of the things I love about you. I chose to go with you, whatever could have happened was on me."

"But…"

Leo placed his fingers on her lips. "Nothing happened, I'm all good. Now tell me, did you see him? What did he say?"

"I think I managed to record the conversation. He said we were free to go, but we should get out of here."

"Agreed, we should get back across the border now," Leo said, breaking into a jog. "There was a huge amount of activity going on in there. They're up to something, and it can't be good."

"What about your belongings?"

"They can wait for another day. I'll collect my Deutschmark welcome gift this time when we cross and buy a change of clothes."

Pierre was relieved to see them.

"I got to see him, but we must get back into West Berlin. I promise I will fill you in," Rachel said. "Oh, and your source is correct. They're shredding documents."

Pierre nodded. "Go. I will watch your backs."

Rachel and Leo covered the 900 metres in less than five minutes and found to their relief that the border was still open. Leo lined up to have his passport stamped at Checkpoint Charlie and was handed 100 Deutschmarks, along with a cheery 'welcome to the West.'

•••

Rachel and Leo arrived, exhausted, at the hotel, to find Juliette and Josh waiting in the bar.

"Thank God," Juliette said throwing her arms around Rachel. "I was beginning to worry."

"What's happening on the other side?" Josh asked.

Rachel and Leo sat down at the table.

"I saw William Brown, and I talked to him."

"No way." Juliette was astonished. "What did he say?"

"Hang on," Josh said, peering at Leo before signalling to the waitress. "I sense we need drinks."

"I think I managed to record our conversation," Rachel said. "They didn't search me. Can you believe it? They just took my camera and then returned it to me and basically said, on your way. Although, they held Leo as insurance that I wouldn't do anything."

"Mate, no wonder you look a little pale, are you okay?" Josh said.

"The Stasi are shredding documents," Leo said. "They are panicking, and the last thing on their mind is someone like me."

"They're shredding documents?" Juliette repeated.

Rachel nodded. "I saw several offices where staff were ripping files apart and filling rubbish bags with torn-up papers, and that was just on one floor. Anyway, listen to this." Rachel pulled the tiny recorder from her pocket and rewound the cassette.

The waitress arrived at the table, balancing a tray of drinks, and

Rachel waited until she'd left before pressing play on the device.

They sat and listened to her recording of the meeting.

"I hate to say it, but he sounds genuine," Juliette said when it had finished.

"What did he mean about working out who the man in the photos is if it isn't him?" Leo said.

Rachel produced her grandfather's photos and laid them on the table. She studied them with fresh eyes and gasped.

"What is it?"

"He was right. I'm stupid. I didn't even do the basic research to corroborate my grandmother's assumptions."

"What do you mean?"

"There is no way this man is William Brown. William Brown is at least six foot two, has broad shoulders and carries quite a lot of weight. Whereas, this man," Rachel tapped the photo closest to her, "is shorter than me and slight. Look at him compared to the height of that doorway or the car in the photo. This is not William Brown. Mae, in her grief, jumped to the wrong conclusion."

"Then who is it?" Juliette asked.

"I haven't a clue, but Brown seemed to think he knew and suggested the answer was close to home."

"Well, I think we should share this tape with Monty and see if he has any ideas," Juliette said.

"I agree, and I have some other photos that I'd like to compare this to, but they are back in London." Rachel turned to Leo. "I don't know your plans, but would you like to fly to London with me for the weekend?"

"I'd love to, but wouldn't I need a visa to enter the UK?"

Juliette nodded. "Yeah, you would and given everything that has happened these last few days, that's not going to be quick."

A grin spread across Rachel's face. "I think I may have a way of speeding up the process."

•••

"You know, I thought I'd feel different having confronted William Brown," Rachel said later that evening as she lay in Leo's arms. "But I don't."

"It's because you still don't have the answers you seek," Leo said, running his fingers up and down her arm. "But you have an idea, don't you?"

Rachel rolled over to face him. "That's very perceptive of you."

Leo leaned over and kissed her. "I'm very observant, and you chew your lip like this when you are mulling something over, and you've been doing that a lot since we got back to the hotel."

Rachel's smile was short-lived. "Yes, I have an idea, but I don't like where it might lead."

"Ah, sometimes you must face your demons to get to the truth."

Rachel nodded.

"I can't believe that you convinced your boss to fast-track a visa for me."

"You will have to give him an exclusive interview. Jones never does anything for free," Rachel reminded him.

"That's okay, I can do that, but the thing is until I go back to my flat, I don't have access to any more money. I wonder how that's all going to work now. Will our currency convert to Deutschmarks?"

"I don't know, but don't worry about it, this won't be an expensive weekend, and besides, the paper is paying for your flight."

Leo give her a quick kiss. "Thank you. You know, it's hard to comprehend that the Wall is gone," he said. "I mean, even if I don't believe my own eyes, all those photos you took this afternoon prove it to be true, and all the stories that your colleagues have been gathering, but it's hard to grasp. It's been there my whole life. Everything has changed so suddenly. Everything we've been fighting for has just happened. It almost seems too good to be true."

"I think Maria was feeling the same when we saw her and Annette tonight," Rachel said. "Will her boyfriend join her, do you think?"

"Yeah, I hope so, although he doesn't want to leave his job until he has another one."

"You're going to have to give yourselves time to adjust. Do you know what you're going to do?"

"Now that I don't have to fight for the right to travel to the West? Honestly, I don't know. Before, I would have said I'd stay in East Berlin, finish my degree and support reunification efforts. I mean, stitching together the two Germanies is going to be a huge logistical nightmare. Each country has its own flag, anthem, education, healthcare system and armed forces. I've always thought that if this happened, we can't all just leave, but now, especially since I've met you, I'm not sure. I mean, I don't want to be an engineer. That path was chosen for me. I didn't choose it."

"You would have chosen to study law, right?"

"Mmm...."

"Yeah, they would never have allowed someone like you to study law," Rachel said. "That would give you more ammunition to challenge the state."

"Exactly."

"Well, I don't think you have to decide tonight," Rachel said. "Let me confirm our flights and then I'm sure we can think of something to occupy us until morning."

CHAPTER 44

London, England
November 11, 1989

L eo couldn't stop smiling the whole next day.

"Was that your first flight?" Rachel said after they'd caught the tube from Heathrow to her flat in Earl's Court.

"Yeah," Leo said. "First, but definitely not last. I'm sorry I'm ignoring you, but I feel like my head is on a swivel. There's much to take in, and I don't want to miss anything."

"That's absolutely fine," Rachel laughed. "I don't feel ignored. We'll drop my things off, and I'll take you on a whirlwind tour of London."

Rachel inserted her key in the front door and entered the flat. With Juliette still in Germany, it was just their other two flatmates at home, but neither appeared to be in.

They continued up the stairs to Rachel's bedroom.

"Wow, this is a lovely room," Leo said, taking in the space. The half-drawn dusky pink blind matched the large rose pattern in the double bed's duvet. The walls were covered in framed photos of moody landscapes, and a free-standing rack in one corner was hung with Rachel's clothes, neatly colour coordinated.

She dumped her suitcase at the end of the bed and turned to him. "I just want to say this once." A guarded expression crossed Leo's face. Rachel reached for his hand. "I know you're worried about money, but this weekend is on me, and anything you want to do or try, you just have to tell me."

Leo nodded. "I will pay you back."

Rachel slipped her arms around his waist. "I don't have much, but what's mine is yours."

Leo leaned down to kiss her. "How did I get so lucky finding you?"

"I think I was the lucky one." She kissed him back.

"Right, shall we go?" Rachel checked her watch. "We have three hours before we're due to meet Monty."

"Before we do, let's look at those other photos you mentioned and compare them to your grandfather's ones," Leo said.

Rachel hesitated.

"Come on," Leo coaxed. "You've got to face this sooner or later."

Rachel disengaged from his arms and crossed the room to the small desk beneath the window. She opened a drawer, pulled out a cardboard folder, placed it on the bed, and retrieved her grandfather's photos from her camera bag. Taking a deep breath, she spread all of the pictures across the duvet.

Leo slipped his arms around her waist from behind and held her as she studied them.

Eventually, she turned her head to look at him, her eyes filled with tears.

"It's the same guy," Leo whispered her thoughts aloud.

"My grandmother will be devastated," Rachel said.

"If she's anything like you, she will survive this."

•••

Rachel took Leo into the centre of London, first to Buckingham Palace, then down the Mall through Admiralty Arch to Trafalgar Square, before walking along Whitehall to Westminster Abbey and the Houses of Parliament. They strolled along the Embankment, stopping for lunch at a favourite Italian restaurant of Rachel's.

"Thank you for showing me around," Leo said after they'd ordered.

"My pleasure." Rachel reached across the table for his hand. "I love this city, and besides, it took my mind off what I'm going to say to Monty."

Monty was already waiting at the Coal Hole on the Strand, seated at a table by the window, dressed the most casually that Rachel had ever seen him, in jeans and a jumper. They ordered drinks and joined him. Rachel introduced Leo, who excused himself to use the bathroom.

"You brought home a souvenir?" Monty teased. "Most people are bringing back a piece of the Wall, not a real live East German."

"Very funny."

"Juliette tells me you managed to track down William Brown."

"Yeah, I also managed to record my conversation with him. Would you like to listen?"

"Smart man."

Rachel frowned. "What do you mean?"

"If he's innocent, as he claims, then by letting you record the conversation, he will know that it will get back to the establishment here."

"Ah," Rachel said as Leo slipped into the seat beside her. "That makes sense. They took my camera and held Leo at gunpoint but never searched me."

Monty nodded. "That's what I would do if I wanted my version of events recorded. Let's listen."

Rachel played the tape of her conversation with William Brown on her mini cassette player.

When it finished, she handed him a copy of the tape that Josh had made. Monty took a sip of his drink before speaking. "He certainly sounds convincing, but have you double-checked your sources as he suggested?"

"Yeah, and I'm ashamed to admit, he was right," Rachel said, her voice catching. Beneath the table, Leo squeezed her hand.

Monty frowned as Rachel pulled out her envelope of photos. She spread Jack's pictures on the table along with two more that she'd taken copies of when she was in Oamaru. Realisation crossed Monty's face.

"It's the same man, and you know who he is," he said.

Rachel let out a shaky breath. "His name is Charles Montague, and he is my grandmother's uncle."

Monty sat back. "Sir Charles Montague the war hero?" Disbelief hung in the air.

Rachel nodded.

"You're telling me that a decorated veteran passed secrets to the Soviets throughout the war?"

"Maybe not throughout the war, but definitely at the end and perhaps long after," Rachel said. "If you think about it, he had access to Bletchley Park, he could easily have framed Brown. Jack would have recognised him in Paris. He says as much in his letter to Mae, except she misinterpreted who he meant."

"Did she or was she protecting her uncle?"

"How dare you?"

"I'm just saying that before jumping to more conclusions, you must look at this from all angles." Monty raised his hands as if to appease her.

Rachel visibly struggled to bring her emotions in check. "What will you do with this information?" she asked after a long pause.

"I will share it with my bosses, but honestly, with everything that's happening in Europe right now," he nodded at Leo, "they will probably refuse to do anything with it."

"Perhaps the papers will be interested in the fact the British secret service is refusing to investigate a Soviet double agent," Rachel said.

Monty shook his head. "Don't threaten that, Rachel. You know as well as anyone that this has the potential to be very damaging at a time when international relations are on a knife edge."

Rachel's head dropped, and she let out a heavy sigh. "What do I do then? What do I tell my grandmother? I can't let her go on believing that an innocent man was responsible for Jack's death."

"I wouldn't call Braun innocent," Leo spoke up for the first time.

"Leo is right, he mightn't be guilty of Jack's death, but he is surely culpable in many others," Monty said.

"So, Charles Montague just gets away with it?"

"For now." Monty rose and slipped the tape into his pocket. "I'll be in touch."

Rachel slumped in her chair after Monty had departed. "I don't know why I'm surprised. Trust the British establishment to protect their own."

"That's probably a little unfair," Leo said.

"Yeah, I know, but I'm not feeling very charitable right now."

"What happened to this Charles Montague? Is he dead?"

"I don't think so. Mae lost touch with him years ago. He wasn't that much older than her which would put him in his late seventies," Rachel said, a smile spreading across her face. She jumped up. "Come on. I've got an idea."

CHAPTER 45

London, England
November 12, 1989

The large white stucco house in Putney was set back from the road behind a tall hedge. Rachel and Leo pushed open the wooden front gate and entered a neat, formal garden of old-fashioned rose bushes and box hedges. They followed the path to a front door set between two sizeable double bay windows.

"Searching your newspaper's records to find his address was a good idea," Leo said.

"It wasn't until Monty called him by his full title that I realised who he was," Rachel said. "I didn't know that I was related to Sir Charles Montague, but I recalled that someone did a piece on some of the older veterans a year or so back, and he was mentioned."

"I enjoyed seeing where you worked, too," Leo said with a grin as footsteps sounded from behind the door. "That library archive is unreal."

The door was opened by a woman in a floral dress topped with a white apron. She smiled at the visitors. "Hello, can I help you?"

"Hello, I'm Rachel Talbot from *The London News*, and this is my colleague, Leo Schmidt. We haven't got an appointment, but we were hoping to speak with Sir Charles."

"Wait here, and I'll see if he's free."

The door closed.

"Well, it wasn't a no," Rachel said before it opened again.

"This way."

They followed the woman into a large entrance hall with a mosaic-tiled floor. The air was heavy with the scent of flowers from an overflowing vase on a side table, and a wide staircase with a polished wooden banister rose to the next floor. The housekeeper ushered them into the first room on the left, a library lined with floor-to-ceiling shelves filled with books. A small fire burned in the grate at one end of the room, and an elderly man stood by an armchair waiting to greet them.

Rachel recognised the slim figure, albeit slightly stooped with age, from her grandmother's photos, and approached with her hand outstretched. "I'm Rachel, and this is Leo. Thank you for seeing us at short notice, Sir Charles."

Charles shook her hand with a firm grip. A shock of thick silvery white hair framed his lined face.

"My bridge game has been cancelled this afternoon, so I happened to be free. I spoke with one of your reporters a while back. Please have a seat." He indicated a sofa of deep green velvet opposite the armchair. "Tea?"

"No, thank you. We won't take up too much of your time," Rachel said, perching on the sofa's edge. Leo sat beside her.

"So, what would you like to know?" Sir Charles said.

"I believe we have people in common," Rachel said. "My grandmother is Mae Knight, née Webster."

Sir Charles paled and clutched the armrest of his chair. He stared at Rachel, gasping for air. An awkward silence followed.

"You would have known my grandfather, Jack," Rachel said.

Sir Charles recovered some of his composure. "You look like

Mae, although your hair is different," he said, his voice cracking.

"And Jack?"

"I only knew him briefly before his untimely death."

"Which you had something to do with."

"I beg your pardon?"

Rachel opened her bag and retrieved Jack's Paris photos. She handed them to Sir Charles. "I believe the man in each of these photos is you, passing information to a Soviet spy called Yuri Montan."

"How…" Sir Charles spluttered before tearing the photos in half and half again.

"There are many more copies than you can ever destroy," Rachel said. "You see, Jack posted the negatives to New Zealand before he was killed, as he guessed his life was in danger."

"What do you want from me?" Charles whispered.

"I suppose I want to know why," Rachel said. "I need to explain to Mae why Jack had to die."

Rachel watched myriad emotions cross the old man's face, before he nodded to himself and took a deep breath.

"I tried to make him understand, but he wouldn't listen," Sir Charles began. "I saw the large amounts of signals intelligence passing through Bletchley, and I knew from discussions with colleagues in Whitehall that we were not sharing this information with our allies. I saw intelligence that contained such precise detail on both the Luftwaffe and Wehrmacht that we were building up a clear picture of the land and air capabilities of the Germans and, indeed, some idea of their battle plans. It was morally unjustifiable to me to keep this information to ourselves. I knew that information would be of the greatest use to the Soviets in their struggle against the might of the German forces, especially such details as the strength and location of enemy units. That kind of intelligence would give our allies enough advanced information to plan their counter-defences appropriately. If the Nazis were to overrun the Soviets, which they nearly did, they could have redeployed their forces to Italy and refocused their efforts on Britain, and the war would have been lost. I couldn't allow that to happen."

"But you could have exposed the Bletchley secret."

"I understood that Churchill didn't trust the channels he had available to pass the information to the Soviets, and I debated that with him on several occasions, stubborn man. But I had a KGB contact whom I trusted, and I thought that passing the information directly to him would carry the greatest assurance of reaching the correct people without compromising the source of the intelligence."

"And that's what you were doing when Jack saw you in Paris?"

Sir Charles nodded. "My actions directly contributed to the success of the Soviet's Operation Bagration. I passed crucial intelligence; why do you think they were prepared for the German tanks?"

"How did you get the decrypts out of Bletchley Park?"

Charles was silent for a moment. "I suppose it doesn't matter, she's dead now. A dear friend who shared my beliefs worked in Hut 3. Her name was Margaret, and Mae was billeted with her."

"You betrayed your own country."

"I never considered myself a traitor," Sir Charles said, straightening his shoulders. "I still don't. I thought of myself as a patriot in the struggle against the Nazis, and I felt a deep disgust towards fascism, and I only did what I did to strengthen the Allied cause."

"But why did Jack have to die?"

Sir Charles closed his eyes, and when he opened them again, Rachel could see that he was far away. "He confronted me in the bar of Hotel Scribe in Paris the evening I'd been in contact with Montan. He wanted to believe that he'd misinterpreted what he'd seen. But I couldn't give him that reassurance. I followed him back to London, thinking I could use Mae to help make him understand. I watched him make a phone call, then post something at the station, but when I saw that he was headed to the Foreign Office rather than going home, I knew I had to act."

"So, you ran him down and stole his bag."

"I didn't mean for him to die. I just had to get the photos."

"Then why blow up their flat the following day?"

"Once I started, I had to see it through. When Mae told me that Jack had sent her some photos of a man she assumed was William Brown, passing secrets to a Soviet agent, I couldn't risk her studying the photos more closely and realising it was me. I needed her to be frightened enough to leave the country."

"But you didn't realise that Jack had posted two letters, one to Mae in London and one to New Zealand."

"I thought he only posted the envelope to Mae, which was destroyed in the fire," Charles said. "Why has she never used them against me?"

Rachel shook her head. "Because she thought it was William Brown, and he disappeared at the end of the war. I suppose after a while she just wanted to get on with her life. Nothing was going to bring Jack back."

"What are you going to do?" Sir Charles asked.

"My contact at MI6 tells me that the authorities will do nothing with this information, especially now with how things are in Europe. Mae, on the other hand...."

"Does she know?"

"Not yet, but she deserves to know."

Charles bowed his head. "Please go now."

Neither Rachel nor Leo spoke as they rose, leaving the old man to his memories and his guilt.

The housekeeper was hovering in the hallway.

"He might need a cup of tea," Rachel said. "Or something stronger."

The housekeeper frowned and opened the door for them. Three

men in suits stood on the porch, one with his hand raised to knock. Rachel's mouth dropped open in surprise. The youngest of the three was Monty. Behind them, four uniformed police officers waited. Through the front gate, Rachel saw that the street outside the house was filled with cars.

"I should have known that you wouldn't leave this alone," Monty said.

"You left me with no choice. I had to know," Rachel said. "What is this? What are you doing here?"

"You were right. This couldn't be allowed to stand."

The crack of a gunshot sounded from within the house. Leo pulled Rachel into his arms and tried to bundle her outside.

"Get down," he shouted, easing them both into a low crouch on the porch.

Police officers rushed along the path towards the house.

The shattering of china resonated from inside the house, followed by an anguished scream. The officers pushed past Rachel and Leo, weapons drawn, shouting, "Police, put down your weapon."

The library door opened, and Sir Charles's housekeeper stepped out, ashen-faced. "He's dead."

CHAPTER 46

East Berlin, GDR
January 10, 1990

Rachel sat at the small table in Leo's tiny flat, rereading the essay she'd finally finished writing. A vase filled with winter lilies scented the room and took up most of the space on the table. With access to Western goods, Rachel had helped Leo redecorate his flat. The walls had been painted a fresh white and now displayed many of Rachel's best photographs in black frames. New curtains hung in the window, the sofa had a bright colourful new cover, and Rachel had replaced nearly all the kitchen crockery and utensils.

In the end, the decision to leave London and move to Berlin was an easy one. She and Leo assumed their futures were together without discussing it. Each was willing to do whatever was needed to be with the other, but when it came down to it, Rachel figured that she could do her job from anywhere, whereas Leo needed to be in Germany to follow his dreams of becoming a lawyer. Deep down, she also knew that he wanted to be part of whatever would come next for his country, and she loved him even more for that. Now that they were no longer doomed lovers, unable to be together, they'd taken the time to get to know each other and their feelings for one another had only deepened.

She looked up as a key turned in the lock, and Leo entered carrying a paper bag which he deposited on the kitchen bench.

"Hello, you," he said, leaning down to kiss her. "How was your day?"

"Good, I had lunch with Maria and Annette. Annette is doing much better at school now, and Maria has a job at a hair salon near their aunt's place."

"Fantastic."

"And I spoke to Pierre. He's just discovered that the Stasi had twenty-five file boxes of information on him. They'd been monitoring his every move."

"I'm not surprised."

Rachel rose and wound her arms around his neck. "How was your day?"

"Good, I can cross-credit several papers, which means I won't be starting my law degree from scratch."

"Leo, that's great. We should celebrate," Rachel said.

"My thoughts exactly," Leo said, leaning over the bench and producing a bottle of wine from the shopping bag.

"I think my article is ready, too," Rachel said, sitting down again and picking up the pages she'd proofread.

Leo placed two wine glasses on the table and uncorked the wine.

"Is that what you've been working on?"

She nodded. "When Jones gave me the assistant foreign correspondent job, he said I could work on some of my pieces as well as working with Bernard on his. There is so much going on in this part of the world, that there is plenty of work for us both. But since this is my first solo project, it has to be good."

"Has Juliette read it?"

"Yeah, and she thinks it's ready to submit."

"What are you waiting for?"

"I'm scared, I guess. You know how much I wanted to write a piece about Charles and the hypocrisy of the British establishment. But I don't think Jones would publish that given the ongoing investigation. Somehow, Charles's death has been kept out of the papers. Mark my words. This will be quietly dropped."

"What have you written instead, and when can I read it?" Leo said.

"Well, I've shelved the Charles exposé for the time being and instead written a piece celebrating the life and achievements of Jack Knight – the little-known Kiwi War Photographer. I've hinted at his military intelligence work and that he uncovered a Soviet spy network, but nothing that will upset the paper's legal team."

"Come here." Leo pulled her up out of her chair and kissed her. "I'm so proud of you."

"You may not be when you hear my next project."

Leo looked wary.

"I've been looking into the Stasi. After speaking with some of the group of pro-democracy protestors who stormed the secret police precinct over recent days, I'm hearing stories of thousands of bags of shredded documents being recovered. One group still found junior officers shredding, pulping and burning documents, just like I saw when we were at Brown's headquarters the day after the Wall fell. The Stasi are desperately trying to destroy four decades of surveillance records that show it was spying on its own citizens. The German people deserve to know that."

"You're wrong. I'm still proud," Leo said, tucking a stray strand of hair behind her ear. "But just be careful, the Stasi still have influence and a long reach. I crossed quite a few of them over the years and they wouldn't hesitate to use you to get back at me."

"I'm sure you did," Rachel said. "But I'm not going to let fear get in the way of the truth."

MAE
1990

CHAPTER 47

Oamaru, New Zealand
February 12, 1990

I pulled on my gumboots and tucked my slacks into them, before closing the cottage door. I would never tire of the view from my front door across the farmland and down to the coast. Sheep frolicked in the lush green paddocks irrigated by the nearby Waitaki River. The long row of poplar trees provided a much-needed windbreak that sheltered my ever-expanding garden, formal with roses and shrubs at the front, and cottagey with an enormous vegetable patch at the rear. Hens pecked in the dirt around an old wooden hen house to one side of the cottage, and my faithful black cat, Whiskey, wound around my ankles.

So much had happened in the last couple of months. Rachel's call when it came in November hadn't been entirely unexpected. I figured that after the speed of East Germany's collapse, she would be in that part of the city searching for William. I hadn't realised the danger I had put her in by telling her my story. I closed my eyes and leaned against the porch railing for a moment. I would never have forgiven myself if something had happened to her. But it hadn't. It turned out she had inherited some of my resourcefulness along with her grandfather's bravery.

The revelation that William wasn't responsible for Jack's death took my breath away. But I still couldn't comprehend that Charles was the guilty one. I was pleased that Rachel had insisted that her mother was with me when she phoned with the news. After assuring Rachel that I wouldn't keel over from the shock of her exposé, Alice and I dug out my old photos, including my copies of Jack's Paris photos, and compared them with the couple I had of Charles. How I had never seen the resemblance before, I would never know. I'd spent forty-odd years raging at the wrong man. How could Charles have done that to Jack? To me? To our baby? I now understood why Charles had lost touch with me. I could only begin to imagine his guilt. His deception had kept me away from my homeland for more than forty years.

I had to decide whether I would make a long overdue journey back to England. By publishing her article, and the subsequent interest from television documentary makers, Rachel had ensured that Jack's life would finally be celebrated, and the world would learn about the intelligent, brave and artistic man I loved. The British establishment seemed determined to hide the embarrassment of Charles's hitherto unknown deception under the carpet, and ignore the fact that another Soviet spy had been operating at high levels within the British intelligence community. I for one wanted to see Charles brought to justice, but of course, that would never happen now. He ruined my life and could have destroyed thousands more if the Enigma secret had been exposed.

I wasn't sure how I felt about William. Sad, indeed, that he'd been forced to flee. But I'm not sure I would have chosen his path. He was a survivor; I'll give him that.

I wasn't afraid of flying. I'd flown to Australia several times over the years. But I hadn't returned to London in forty-four years. I had left the city, a widowed, pregnant and fearful twenty-two-year-old, and I would return as a sixty-six-year-old woman. Part of me wanted to spend some time in the country of my birth and reacquaint myself with my roots. Another part of me wanted to remain here, hiding in the safe haven I'd created. I straightened my shoulders; I was stronger than that. Charles could no longer hurt me, and the house I'd rebuilt on the site of Granny's home would still be there. I hadn't been able to bring myself to sell it. The agent sent me photos once a year. It was an embassy residence and had been for many years now. It was probably time to decide what to do with it. As for Granny's country pile, I'd got rid of that years ago when the farm needed investment.

I hooked the egg basket over my arm and stepped off the porch, heading to the hen house to collect the eggs. Yes, I would go. Time to face the past.

CHAPTER 48

London, England
March 20, 1990

Rachel was waiting for me in the arrivals hall at Heathrow Airport, at the front of an enormous gathering of people, all greeting their friends and loved ones as they emerged through the arriving passenger doors. Being surrounded by so many emotional people was a little overwhelming, especially as I was exhausted after the long flight, but I was grateful to see her beautiful, smiling face.

"You're here," she exclaimed, enveloping me in a bouncy, excited hug. "I can't wait to show you everything."

"I will need a cup of tea and a good sleep first."

"That can be easily arranged," she said. "But first, there is someone I want you to meet. Grandma, this is Leo."

The slim young man with scruffy blond hair standing at her side gave me a shy smile. "I am delighted to meet you, Mrs Knight. Rachel has told me much about you."

"Likewise, Leo," I said, clasping his hand before pulling him into a hug. "You have been through so much."

He smiled and slipped an arm around Rachel's waist. "I'd do it all again if it meant meeting your granddaughter."

The look they exchanged melted my heart and took me back forty-five years to another young man who had looked at me with a similar intense, intimate gaze.

"Leo is flying back to Berlin shortly, but he wanted to meet you first," Rachel explained.

I busied myself with my bags while they said goodbye in the way only young lovers do, as though no one else exists for a precious moment or two.

We took a taxi back to Rachel's old flat, where she settled me in a tiny bedroom on the first floor.

"Gemma has only been here five minutes, and she's already off travelling for two months, but she said the room is yours for as long as you want it," she explained.

"What about you, dear?"

"Juliette is away and I'm staying in her room for a few days."

"Good, I've arranged to see my dear friend Nancy and I would love for you to meet her."

"I'd love that too, Grandma."

The following day, refreshed after a long sleep, we caught the train to Evesham. The centre of the village was dominated by a grey brick Norman church surrounded by moss-covered gravestones. Rachel took my arm as we followed the path around the church to where my parents and grandparents were buried.

"This is beautiful," she said. "I'm really sorry I haven't made this trip to pay my respects before now."

I patted her hand. "It wasn't the right time, and now it is."

We stood in front of my parents' grave. "My mother was much fun and very beautiful, and she died far too young."

"The Honourable Mary Webster," Rachel read. "Honourable?"

"I was an Honourable, too," I said. "It was quite the thing back in the day."

We stepped sideways, and I felt my eyes mist. "And Granny. Oh, what a wonderful woman. Formidable, but very kind."

"Lord and Lady Webster," Rachel read aloud. "Lady? Does that mean…"

I shook my head. "No, not a hereditary title."

We took one more sidestep. A simple gravestone marked Jack's final resting place.

"Lt Jack Knight, NZDF. *I hope to stay unemployed as a war photographer til the end of my life.*' Did Jack say that?" Rachel asked.

I shook my head, unable to form words past the lump in my throat. "That's Robert Capa, but very appropriate," I said finally.

We stood there clinging to one another as dappled sunshine filtered through the trees. I arranged the large bouquet I was carrying into the stone vases embedded at the base of each gravestone, finishing with the largest display for my Jack.

"I'm finally here, my love." I rested my hand on the ground before standing and slipping my arm around Rachel's waist and smiling through my tears. "Jack, this is your granddaughter who you would be delighted to know is continuing your legacy."

AUTHOR'S NOTE

The War Photographers is a work of fiction, but it's grounded in actual historical events. World War II was monumental in shaping Europe for the remainder of the twentieth century. In Britain in the early 1940s many women were drafted into the armed services and into jobs previously held by the men who were away fighting, triggering massive social change in the post-war years.

The clandestine work carried out at Bletchley Park has long fascinated me, along with the fact that knowledge of the achievements of the individuals who worked there was almost lost to time.

Much has been written about Bletchley Park in recent years, and I am indebted to McKay Sinclair whose books *The Secret Life of Bletchley Park* and *The Secret Lives of Codebreakers* capture so much about the men and women who worked there. The Bletchley Park Podcast is a fascinating and invaluable source of information, particularly their oral histories. The rescuing of Bletchley Park in the 1970s and the establishment of the Bletchley Park Trust has ensured that this historic site, and the knowledge of what was achieved there, has been saved for future generations.

On my several visits to the Park over the last few years I have gained such an appreciation for the tireless work carried out there during the war. The Bletchley Park Trust has done, and continues to do a fantastic job of restoring the property and making it available as a museum and educational resource. The garages behind the eclectic mansion house with their old vehicles and an uncomfortable looking dispatch rider motorcycle are not to be missed. Bletchley Park, only thirty minutes by train from Euston, is well worth a visit next time you're in London.

Several of the many anecdotes recalled by veterans have made it into my story. For example, Commander Travis who led the Bletchley operation from 1942 until the end of the war, was affectionately known as Jumbo due to his size and did indeed write using brown ink jokingly referred to by those at the Park as the director's blood! Rationing in England meant that there were great shortages of all manner of things, not just food, so the weekly opening of the NAAFI (Navy, Army, Air Force canteen) was always greeted enthusiastically as I have depicted, and there were indeed a number of top rate musicians and actors working at the Park, who would put on concerts and shows for the Park's "inmates."

The character of Mae is a drawn from the smart young debutantes from "good" families who were sent to Bletchley early in the war for their language skills and supposed discretion. They worked in largely clerical roles supporting a growing contingent of male academics brought to the Park from Oxford and Cambridge Universities for their mathematical and linguistic skills, although there were a number of intelligent and talented women recruited who also became codebreakers. Later, a large number of young women in uniform, Wrens (Women's Royal Naval Service) and WAAF (Women's Auxiliary Air Force) would work at the Park, many operating the machines designed by Alan Turing and Tommy Flowers to speed up the code-breaking process. These machines were the precursors to the modern-day computer. By

1945, nearly 9,000 people worked shifts turning Bletchley into a 24-hour operation. How the secret was kept defies belief in our social media/immediate information age. In fact, the men and women who worked at the Park took their signing of the Official Secrets Act so seriously that many never told their parents, spouses or children what they did during the war, many even taking the secret to their graves.

The Normandy beach landings did happen on June 6th, 1944 and those in the know at Bletchley were on a full lockdown to ensure the information couldn't leak. Officials at Bletchley were always on the lookout for spies. The fear was initially that a German bomb could destroy the whole operation, but towards the end of the war, concern turned to the tenuous alliance that Britain had formed with its allies, particularly the Soviets. Churchill, presciently, didn't trust the Anglo-Soviet pact to last post-war and was reluctant to share the extent of Britain's code-breaking success.

Jack, Mae, Rachel and Leo are all figments of my imagination, but the bravery of the real-life war photographers is often overlooked. The award-winning photojournalist Robert Capa was with the expeditionary force when it landed at Normandy, but in a true story that I've also attributed to Jack's images of the invasion, sadly nearly all of Capa's photographs from the landings were destroyed due to an error by a lab technician.

The London Transport Museum's exhibit, London at War, provides a fascinating glimpse into life in the capital during both World Wars, when the underground was used by hundreds to shelter from the Blitz. The bravery and tenacity of the British people who lived through the Blitz and the Little Blitz, that I've depicted here, is inspiring. The spirit of Keep Calm and Carry On must have been sorely tested at times, especially as the war dragged on.

The Churchill War Rooms is one of my favourite London museums, capturing life in Churchill's bunker beneath the

Treasury buildings. I have walked in Mae's footsteps through the corridors a number of times and on each occasion discover something new.

Gordon Welchman and F. Winterbottom's books about their time at Bletchley Park, though controversial at the time of publication, allowed more people to come forward to share their stories and through this the unrecognised genius of Alan Turing and his role in modern-day computing was finally revealed. His posthumous pardon in 2013 and his recent appearance on the British fifty-pound note attest to this.

The town of Oamaru that Mae arrived at in early 1945 would have been very different to the cosmopolitan, war-torn London she'd left. The journey itself would have been arduous and she would have found Oamaru to be a sleepy backwater. My father shared his recollections of life in rural New Zealand after the war and his years living on a poultry farm north of Oamaru, a lifestyle not dissimilar to the one Mae would have lived.

1989 was a year of change in the world; a major earthquake in San Francisco, the violent putdown of protests in China's Tiananmen Square, and the unravelling of the Iron Curtain in Eastern Europe, which culminated in the fall of the Berlin Wall.

The internet made my research into the changing political and social climate of Berlin in 1989 a little easier, with access to video and newspaper articles from the time along with many contemporary accounts. My visit to the Checkpoint Charlie Museum was invaluable, as was walking around the double-brick route that marks the position of the Wall in a unified Berlin today. Not much of the Wall remains, only a few sections which serve as a reminder of those dark days. The longest stretch of the Wall, the East Side Gallery, has been turned into a giant artists' canvas.

The Press Point next to Checkpoint Charlie was in fact the location of a room for members of the Western media, so it made sense for Bernard and Rachel to base themselves there during their visits to Berlin.

There are numerous stories of escape attempts, some successful, others not, during the years that the Wall dominated Berlin, and many sad stories of families divided. The bravery of the leaders of the East German protest movement cannot be underestimated. In a society where the Stasi spied on its own citizens and strictly controlled all aspects of life, the risks associated with defying the Party were huge. The character of Leo is my attempt to represent these courageous individuals.

Siegbert and Aram were in fact the two men who daringly filmed from among the "pigeon crap" in the bell tower of a church in Leipzig during the October protests, and an equally brave Western journalist smuggled the footage in his underwear across the border to be released on Western television. I have taken literary licence and attributed this brave act to Rachel. And as coincidence would have it, Siegbert was one of the first East Germans across the Bornholmer Bridge on November 9th, 1989.

Rachel was a young woman operating in the male-dominated world of the press in the 1980s. Photojournalists in particular were a macho breed, as I have shown here, but talented women such as Maria Fleet, Jane Evans and New Zealander Margaret Moth helped to shatter the glass ceiling. Rachel's drive, determination and desire to be where history was being made, enabled her to be one such woman.

ACKNOWLEDGEMENT

A heartfelt thank you to my editor Gary Smailes for his encouragement and improvements to the manuscript and to my copy editor Julia Gibbs for her attention to detail and helpful advice.

I'm grateful for the guidance of Karen McKenzie from Lighthouse PR and Christine Borra from Your Books. The amazing cover is by Amanda Sutcliffe.

Thanks to my father Jack, and to Katrin and Murray who generously shared their memories with me. Dad spent a number of years living on a North Otago poultry farm, a lifestyle similar to the one Mae would have led when she arrived in New Zealand at the end of World War II. Katrin, who grew up with the Wall, kindly shared her memories of the day it fell, and Murray, a fellow Kiwi serendipitously just happened to be in West Berlin on the weekend of November 9th, 1989. There is no better historical resource for a writer than those who have witnessed events as they unfold.

My advance reader team, Sarah, Kathy, Craig and Jude have once again been hugely supportive with their advance reads and comments. I continue to be thankful to my Readers Group including Shannon, Melanie, Judy, Eveie, Roger, Milena, Eileen, Jackie, Carol, Suzanne, Karen and Graham whose continued support I appreciate beyond words.

Thank you to my writer friends for their unwavering encouragement, particularly Gillian and Tresna, who know what it's like to put a new book out into the world.

This novel couldn't have been written without the support of my family. My sons Jude, Zak and Scott, once again travelled with me while I was researching and have been "dragged" around many of the locations depicted in this book. And to my husband Craig, always my first reader, sounding board and fellow history lover, I couldn't do it all without you.

And finally, a big thank-you to my readers.

If you would like further information about me or my books you can check out my website (www.slbeaumont.com) or join my Reader's Group to be kept up to date about up-coming book launches, exclusive giveaways and competitions and receive a FREE copy of *The Reluctant Witness* novella.